FALSE DAWN

Brian Rider

MINERVA PRESS

LONDON

MONTREUX   LOS ANGELES   SYDNEY

FALSE DAWN
Copyright © Brian Rider 1997

ISBN 1 86106 706 2

First Published 1997 by
MINERVA PRESS
195 Knightsbridge
London SW7 1RE

Printed in Great Britain for Minerva Press

FALSE DAWN

By the Same Author:

Snatched

Golden Inca

Dangerous Plateau

*

The author is donating fifty per cent of all royalties from the sale of this book to tiger conservation.

If a species becomes extinct its world will never come into being again. It will vanish forever like an exploding star, and for this we hold direct responsibility.

David Day (1981)

Dedication

This book is dedicated to the memory of Kenneth Anderson and Jim Corbett, two great stalwarts of the Indian jungle. Their heroic tales of the past enriched my boyhood.

Also included here are all the unsung heroes and heroines, involved in the often dangerous task of conserving the noble tiger, in far-flung parts of the globe.

Because of the efforts of people like these, I was prompted to write this book.

Long live the tiger.

Acknowledgements

I am indebted to the following individuals and organisations who helped in the research towards the preparation of this book by supplying me with factual evidence.

Peter Jackson, MA Chairman IUCN/SSC, Bougy, Switzerland, Cat Specialist Group
Dr Terry Moore, The Cat Survival Trust, Welwyn, Hertfordshire
Sue Fisher of Tusk Force, London
Robin Hanbury-Tenison, writer and explorer
Celia Nicholls, zoologist, Care For The Wild, Sussex
Steve Trent of the Environmental Investigation Agency, London
Mr P Muller, The International Tiger Studbook, Leipzig, Germany
Steve Samson, Paradise Wildlife Park, Broxbourne, Hertfordshire. Also Global Wildlife Trust
The Tiger Trust, Bury St Edmunds
Virginia McKenna and Will Travers of Born Free, Dorking, Surrey
John Aspinall of The Howletts and Port Lympne Foundation
Tiger Showdown
The World Wildlife Fund
Arin Ghosh of Project Tiger, India
The Exxon Corporation, Esso Petroleum Co.
Kim Simmons, Linton Zoological Gardens
Woburn Abbey Wildlife Park
Nigel Whittle of Lifeforce
London Zoo, Regents Park, London

About the Author

Brian Rider is a podiatrist (foot surgeon), married, with two children and two step-children. He lives and practises in Hertfordshire. A seasoned traveller, who would find it harder to tell you where he hasn't been, both he and his wife love to explore the remoter areas of the world.

As an international lecturer he has worked in many countries, including the United States, both in his own field of surgery and in research. He is an accomplished broadcaster with TV and radio experience over the last eighteen years. Brian has already written a medical book and many magazine articles. He has written three adventure thriller novels:- *Snatched, Golden Inca* and *Dangerous Plateau.*

His many interests include drama, theatre, all forms of sport and a lively interest in history.

Contents

Chapter One

Trapped

The awesome silence of the jungle night was shattered by the roar of a tiger, half-crazed with pain and fear. In desperation, the maddened beast, in a futile effort to evade the iron trap that encircled the outer side of his forepaw, twisted and plunged. All to no avail. The rusty iron trap was anchored to a thick tree stump which yielded not one inch. His eyes wide with terror, the tiger's mouth curled into a snarl of defiance, the moonlight flashing on his teeth and reflecting the yellow of his uncomprehending fearful eyes.

Desperately, his gaze stabbed into the blackness of the surrounding jungle, vainly searching for some form of escape. His only answer, the chatter of a langur monkey, obviously disturbed by his anguished snarling and roaring, seemed to mock him in his hopeless predicament. The fearsome trap, cunningly placed by poachers, had all but cut through the lateral part of his forepaw. The poor animal's instinctive efforts to free himself had only increased the pain and torn a larger gash in the tissue.

The tiger slowly sank down on his belly, licking at the bloodied and trapped paw. The relief was minimal. An inquisitive jackal entered the moonlit clearing, but was careful to keep his distance, slowly circling the captive animal, sniffing the air suspiciously. After a last inspection he scampered off into the thick bush. Once more the tiger was alone with his terror.

In a renewed effort of energy, born of desperation, he struggled to his three sound feet. Instinctively, he knew that he must break free of this captive trap or he would surely die. Fully ten feet over his curves, and weighing nigh on five hundred and fifty pounds, the magnificent beast pulled backwards with all his considerable power.

The pain was almost unbearable as the tissue of the iron-encircled paw tore still further. Blood drenched the earth round the mangled paw, staining the soft green moss red. Almost exhausted by his efforts to free himself, the large tiger slowly sank down and recommenced licking in a futile effort to numb the pain. Several times during the long night the poor beast slowly rose and renewed his efforts to break free, twisting, turning, bucking and tearing at the trap with his good forepaw and teeth.

Dawn found him in a poor way, with much energy expended and considerable blood loss. Much of the blood from his wound had transferred itself to his magnificently striped coat. Even in his agony, this habitually clean animal attempted to clean the congealed blood with his tongue.

Mist began to rise from the jungle floor, moisture dripping from the bracken fronds. The tiger, by now almost gasping from thirst through dehydration, licked with his long tongue at the surrounding vegetation. His eyes probed the clearing and beyond for some inspiration to escape his fate. Lantana scrub and 'wait-a-bit' thorn, bracken and elephant grass met his gaze. Vines encircled some of the larger trees, and he could hear troops of langurs high in the treetops chattering excitedly at the arrival of a new dawn.

The first rays of the sun lanced through the lower branches, flooding the clearing. Early warmth settled on the distraught animal, restoring a little energy to his aching and weary frame. Why had this happened to him? The confused beast had no knowledge. Why did this iron thing hold him captive? Then, quite suddenly, he understood. His keen ears picked up the sound of humans, still some way off but approaching towards him through the jungle. He could hear the twigs and rotten branches cracking under their feet, marking their progress as they came ever nearer. Now he understood. Man had done this to him. Why? He had never done anything to them!

Instinctively, he gave a low snarl of defiance. They were coming for him. To kill him.

He could hear their voices now. They couldn't be more than a hundred metres from him. Excited chatter.

In desperation born from renewed danger, the tiger tore at the trap with all his remaining strength, pulling himself backwards from the captive iron. Quite suddenly, with a great gush of blood, he tore free, but, alas, the outer half of his forepaw remained in the vile contraption. For a moment he stood rooted in a pool of blood almost unable to believe that he was free.

With a sudden grim realisation, which momentarily dulled the pain, he was aware that the voices were almost upon him. Limping and crawling, dragging his injured paw, he slunk off as quickly as his wounded frame would take him. If he could only reach the low-lying lantana and elephant grass, he knew safety, at least temporarily, was within his grasp.

Literally, as his tail disappeared from view into the tall waving grass, the two men burst into the clearing.

Luckily for the tiger, his departure had gone unnoticed. Unable, through weakness, to go any farther, the animal sank down gratefully in the long grass, panting from his efforts and desperate for water, sleep and rest.

From his vantage point he lay quietly watching the arrival of two natives, dressed in *lungis*, a type of wrap-around skirt, one red, one white. Both had tattered white vests, and, whilst one was bareheaded, the other had a dirty white rag head-dress hanging down on one side. The tiger was more concerned with the ancient blunderbusses both men carried at the ready. His panting ceased and he lay still, terribly weakened, but ready. If they came after him here, he would attack. He waited and watched. If necessary the magnificent animal would still sell his life dearly.

The men advanced, seeing the trap surrounded by blood – the outer part of the tiger's forepaw, still intact, remained there.

One of the men, the one with the white headcloth, rushed up to the trap and jabbered excitedly in Hindi. He pointed out the gruesome spectacle of the bloodied remains. The tiger tensed. Now they had picked up on the trail of blood, which would lead them right to him. Slowly, ancient guns at the ready, they began to advance towards the elephant grass concealing him. Slowly, he edged backwards further into the dense cover.

The men stopped at the edge, uncertain as to their next move, still excitedly chattering away in Hindi. "No way am I going in there after a wounded tiger, my brother," exclaimed the one with the dirty head-dress.

"Think of the rupees, my brother, we will get for the dead tiger. You know well what we have been promised," replied the other.

"Some good that will do us if the tiger kills us. What good are rupees then, I say?"

The braver of the two took a pace forward, parting the tall grass at the edge of the clearing with the rifle barrel.

The tiger gathered his remaining strength for a last, desperate, rearguard defiance. He let out a low snarl and prepared himself for the final attack. The leading man leapt backwards as if hit by an electric shock, almost colliding with his brother in his efforts to escape. The second man fired wildly into the grass, buckshot randomly parting the tall, swaying fronds, then turned and ran, screaming. The man without the head-dress stayed just long enough to hear a second snarl from the tiger, then turned tail and ran.

The injured tiger withdrew further into the cover of the low lantana and 'wait-a-bit' thorn. Here he would be safe from pursuit, at least for the time being.

He was still alive... just!

New York

Carla Wayne pushed her way through the large swing door of *Liberty* magazine's front entrance. She crossed the foyer to the lifts and pushed the button designating her floor. Entering the lift, she offered a cursory hi to the two occupants departing – a reporter and photographer from another department, whom she knew on acquaintance value only. *Liberty* was a huge concern with a truly international flavour. At twenty-eight, Carla counted herself lucky to be with them, having been appointed from a much smaller magazine six months earlier. Reaching her office, she crossed to her desk, kicked off her high-heeled shoes and put her stockinged feet up on the desk. Placing her hands behind her head, she stretched back in her swivel chair contentedly. Stretching her long elegant neck backwards, she rotated her head, spraying a cascade of shoulder-length silver blonde hair around her. She was five foot six and perfectly proportioned, and her firm breasts pushed provocatively against the grey designer two-piece suit she wore. Her pretty little nose and vivid blue eyes screwed up in horror at the sight of her in-tray, on which her gaze finally homed in. Right on the top was a scrawled memorandum. All it said was simply *See me. Edwin Strobe.*

Picking the note up, she turned it over. The word *immediately* was printed in large capitals on the back. 'My God, what have I done now?' was Carla's first thought.

Edwin Strobe was the president of *Liberty* Publishing. He spent most of his time apparently in his penthouse suite at the pinnacle of the building. For any employee, let alone a junior editor, to be summoned to his presence was almost unknown.

Carla rubbed her strong young chin thoughtfully and toyed with the clasp on her gold necklace with her other hand. She knew some of the staff resented her appointment. It was even rumoured that she had achieved the position because of her looks and shapely legs. It was indeed true that Vice-President Joe Murphy, who had engaged her, was known to be 'one for the girls'.

In the six months she had been with the magazine, she could count the times on one hand, that she had even come into contact with him. Once he had made a suggestive remark, which she had easily side-stepped, but that was all. Her thoughts were interrupted by the arrival in the office of her secretary, Anne Schultz, a petite brunette of about her own age. She had an engaging smile which showed a perfect set of teeth. Both women exchanged greetings and Anne began to take the covers off the computers ready for the day's chores.

"Do you know anything about this, Anne?" enquired Carla, waving the memo in one hand.

"Indeed I do," exclaimed Anne, enthusiastically. "The great man himself looked in here, just after you went home last night. I told him you wouldn't be back until this morning... he seemed a bit peeved. Said first thing in the morning then, and left that note in your in-tray and went without so much as a goodbye to me."

"Well, I guess there's only one way to find out what I've done wrong," said Carla, greatly puzzled. "I'll go beard the lion in his den."

Carla left the office for the lift, to Anne's amused chuckling. "Mr Strobe is a bit like a lion with that mane of hair, I suppose," she said, almost to herself.

Carla's office was on the tenth floor, but the lift had to climb through another nineteen to reach the summit of power. She studied her reflection in the lift mirror, swept a wisp of blonde hair into place and smoothed down an imaginary crease in her grey skirt.

The lift door slowly opened to reveal a large outer office. Three secretaries were busy behind desks.

Carla swallowed hard and stepped up to the first.

"Miss Carla Wayne to see Mr Strobe," she announced.

The grey-haired shrew-like woman looked distastefully over her pince-nez at the young woman before her.

"Do you have an appointment?" she enquired brusquely.

"Yes, Mr Strobe has requested my presence," exclaimed Carla somewhat formally, taken aback by the woman's manner.

Without replying, the woman picked up one of four different coloured telephones on the large desktop and a female voice answered. The woman glared at Carla once more over her glasses and spoke into the mouthpiece.

"A ... Miss Wayne to see Mr Strobe," she said in a superior voice.

"Good. Send her through. Mr Strobe will see her now," Carla heard the more pleasant voice reply before the phone was replaced.

"Go on in then. What are you waiting for?" said the grey-haired shrew irritably.

One of the other women in the outer office looked up from her VDU and gave a sympathetic smile. Carla returned it as she passed towards the inner office.

"What side of the bed did she get out of this morning?" said Carla softly, jerking a thumb over her shoulder towards the shrew.

"I don't know, but one thing's for sure – it was her own," she said in a conspiratorial half-whisper. Both women laughed, and Carla went through to the inner office, closing the door behind her. It was smaller and led to a glass-panelled door beyond. Boldly, in gold lettering, it stated MR EDWIN STROBE – PRESIDENT.

In front of it sat a pleasant-looking woman of middle age, attractively and fashionably dressed in designer clothes. She smiled warmly in welcome at Carla, and stood up and offered her hand.

"I'm Gillian Parish," she stated. "Mr Strobe's private secretary. Won't you take a seat? Mr Strobe won't keep you long. I know he's expecting you. He's on the phone at the moment, so I can't interrupt him."

Carla smiled and sat down on a comfortable velvet divan.

"Can I send for a coffee for you?" Mrs Parish enquired.

"That's very kind, but no thanks. Do you have any idea what Mr Strobe wants me for?" enquired Carla hopefully.

"I'm afraid not, my dear. Mr Strobe never discusses anything to do with staff members with me."

The minutes ticked by in small talk – the weather, politics, holidays. It was fully twenty minutes before a green light appeared on a console on Mrs Parish's desk.

"Ah, good. He's free at last," beamed the secretary. "I'll ring through and tell him you're here." She picked up the phone and a conversation ensued.

"You can go in now, Miss Wayne," she said, with a smile, indicating the gold-lettered door.

Carla rose to her feet, crossed the room and slowly entered. As she closed the door, she realised she was in an ornately furnished office – large and spacious with several rare and exotic plants displayed on marble stands. Her high heels sank into a densely piled carpet of a rich red. Matching armchairs complemented the floor covering. At the far end of the room, seated behind a heavy mahogany desk, was a huge broad-shouldered man. He was studying papers in front of him on the desktop. All Carla could see of his face was a mane of iron-grey hair covering an outsize head.

She stood, somewhat uncertain about whether to approach the desk or not. Without looking up from his papers, he exclaimed in a deep voice, "Well? Are you going to stand there all day, girl?"

Carla coughed, embarrassed. "Take a seat. I'll be with you in a minute," he grunted, impatiently indicating a leather-bound chair facing his desk.

Carla quietly sat and crossed her legs, anger beginning to rise in her. If they were going to sack her, everyone didn't have to be so damn rude. Seconds ticked by. She could feel her annoyance getting the better of her and was about to remonstrate with him when, quite suddenly, he pushed the papers aside and looked long and hard at her. Carla thought she had never seen a stronger countenance. A square jaw and heavy bushy eyebrows dominated the face. She judged him to be in his middle fifties, but, with the strong bold lines of his face, he could have been almost anything. The mouth was firm and positive. Strangely, the whole effect was countered by a dimple between mouth and chin. He placed both large hands on the desk in front of him and looked right through her.

"Now, Miss Wayne, I expect you wonder why I've sent for you," he began, in a softer tone than before. Strobe picked up the file on his desk and tapped it with the index finger of his other hand. "This is you, young lady," he exclaimed. "Your past and present record. I make it a point to familiarise myself with all the details of my editors."

There was a long pregnant pause. Carla waited for him to continue. He didn't. Those grey eyes bored into her enquiringly. What did he expect her to say, for heaven's sake?

"I hope it's all good," she blurted out, mainly to break the uncomfortable silence.

"Not bad. Not bad, at all. You write well, young lady."

"Thank you, Mr Strobe."

"However," he began again.

'Ah, here it comes,' thought Carla. 'Now for the worst.'

"However," he repeated, "if you don't mind my criticism, your writing lacks something – something vital."

Carla looked alarmed. "What do I lack?" she asked, hesitantly.

"This, my dear," Strobe exclaimed, placing his right hand over his heart. "Feeling! That's what makes a good journalist great!" Leaning forward across his desk, he said sympathetically, seeing the dismay on her face, "You are very young and the feeling will come with experience perhaps, but looking at your record, I see that you come up short on the fieldwork side. I intend to rectify that, with your permission."

"Or without it, I expect, Mr Strobe," replied Carla, with a wry smile.

"Ah, good. I see you have a sense of humour, Miss Wayne. That's always a good place to start from." He rose, walked round the desk and placed a fatherly hand on her shoulder. "Now listen. You are an intelligent woman. Rumours have been leaked to me that you obtained your seniority here through your appearance." Carla tried to cut in with a protest. "No, young lady, I know that's not true. You deserved your appointment on merit, but how would you like the chance to prove it to everyone here at *Liberty*?"

"How would I do that?" put in Carla.

"Quite simple, really. Undertake the assignment in this portfolio," Strobe exclaimed, picking up a red file on his desk.

Carla reached across and proceeded to open it eagerly.

"No, not now. You will need to study the details well, at a later date," he said, putting a restraining hand on hers. "In the front you will find the name of a man, Mr Nikhil Swarmy, with an address in Delhi. You can study the file on the flight there."

Carla's face expressed puzzlement. Strobe went on, "Do you have any commitments? You're not married or living with anybody or anything like that, are you?" It was Strobe's turn to look anxious.

"No, nothing like that, but I have commitments with my work here, and—"

Strobe cut in quickly. "No matter, Miss Wayne. Your assistant editor Gary Tucker will take over whilst you're in India. Oh, you do *like* travel, I take it?" he added as an afterthought.

"Well, yes," Carla replied, "I—"

"Quite so, my dear, excellent. Have your secretary arrange your air tickets and visa requirements. Send her downtown to the Indian High Commission for the papers. You have some photographs available, I take it, and your passport is up to date? Yes?" Carla felt as if she was being blown over by a tornado. "You can do this job – I know you can."

Finally, Carla forced her way into the conversation.

"Am I allowed to ask what it is I'm *supposed* to be doing in India, sir?" she enquired somewhat sarcastically, with the accent on the supposed.

"Certainly, my dear. Tiger poaching is the name of the game. I'm sending you to look into what is happening. What this magazine needs, and what the world needs, is a five thousand word or more article from you, to prod governments into acting to make the sale of potions and powders for aphrodisiacs and medicines totally illegal."

"But, surely," Carla replied, "nobody in this day and age believes ground-up bones of tigers enhance their sexual prowess – do they?"

"Not only that. The superstitious – and there are thousands of them – believe in cures for toothache, baldness, laziness, epilepsy – you name it – almost anything. The bones, skin, claws, eyeballs, whiskers, just about every bit of the poor beast's anatomy are used by the unscrupulous makers of these so-called medicines."

Carla reasoned, "But I thought it was mainly the Chinese doing this, and anyway, I read that Vietnam had signed an International Trade in Endangered Species Agreement to prevent this slaughter of tigers."

Strobe smiled. "You are well read, Miss Wayne. I congratulate you. However, it's only the tip of the iceberg. If the campaign is to be successful, pressure must be put on Laos and Cambodia for starters, Malaysia and Thailand must also act. It's so bad that live tiger cubs are being openly sold on their borders. You probably won't believe me when I tell you that these tiger products have even been sold in pharmacies in Great Britain."

"Can't the World Wildlife Fund do anything?" asked Carla.

"They are doing everything possible, as indeed are Project Tiger, but, if the campaign is to succeed, everybody – and that includes this international magazine – must act. And that is where you come in. The tiger needs you and you need the tiger!"

Carla's face expressed surprise. "Why me? Surely you have other people on the staff here far more knowledgeable and qualified than I?"

"You need a cause, my dear. A cause worth fighting for, to develop that one vital spark missing in your journalism. I'm handing you one, and I won't pretend it's going to be easy."

"Why India?" questioned Carla. "It wasn't one of the countries you mentioned."

"Remiss of me, wasn't it? Yes, as you will see in this file we have evidence that it's starting there too. Estimates indicate that just five hundred tigers are left in Vietnam, Laos and Cambodia, and something between five hundred and a thousand in Burma, Thailand and Malaysia. Now they are beginning to decimate the Bengal tigers of India."

"Surely Project Tiger has safe areas – game reserves and the like, patrolled by forest officers to protect the animals?"

"Indeed they do, Miss Wayne, and it may surprise you to know that these greedy killers have become so bold as to even shoot it out with the officers in some of the game parks. However, all of this is documented in your file, and, when you arrive in Delhi, Swarmy will tell you much, much more. Now, do I take it you accept the assignment? However, I must warn you, the mission could be dangerous!"

"You mean there are people who will try and stop me digging around?"

"Aptly put, my dear. That is exactly what I do mean. Keep a low profile until you are ready to go to press with your findings."

Carla slowly rose to her feet and reached for the red portfolio.

"I'll have Anne Schultz make the necessary arrangements for the visa, air tickets and accommodation in Delhi. I'll leave just as soon as the paperwork can be completed."

Strobe enthusiastically pumped her hand.

"Good girl, I knew you'd do it. Look – I can give you one month out there, to deliver the goods. *Liberty* needs an article from you, to make the world aware that if something isn't done – and quickly – the tiger will be wiped off the face of the earth in five years from now."

"I'll give it my best shot, sir," replied Carla, turning to leave.

"I know you will. Good luck, and don't forget – one month. Fax your article through directly to me on this number," he said, producing a silver card with embossed black numerals.

Carla left the president's office with the red file tucked under her arm. She had no illusions that her mission was going to be easy. She searched her mind for a reason for Strobe selecting her for the task. It was a project obviously very dear to his heart, so he must have confidence in her anyway. She gritted her teeth and glared at the old shrew on the way through the outer office and left for her own floor via the lift.

She'd show them at *Liberty* what she was made of. Here was a story if ever there was one.

'Just a pretty face, eh. Well, we'll see about that!' she found herself saying aloud to the empty lift.

Chapter Two

Assignment

During the flight on board the Air India 747 flight to Delhi, Carla carefully went through the file with which Edwin Strobe had entrusted her. It would appear that Mr Nikhil Swarmy, her contact in India, was well informed. Facts and figures of tiger disappearances were recorded throughout India, and other countries too. Before finally closing the file, she noted his last comments:

> Names I can give to *Liberty* magazine, but I prefer not to list the offenders here. Rather I will give them to your reporter should you choose to send one. I still have some regard for my own life and will not be much use to the tiger species dead.

Carla placed the portfolio carefully in her hand luggage at her feet and sat back thoughtfully. Edwin Strobe had intimated that there would be danger, and, from Swarmy's last comment, she felt the reality of the warning sinking in. Maybe she shouldn't have agreed so readily, but, then again, why not? Hadn't she something to prove? If people doubted her ability, Strobe had offered her the chance to prove herself. Life had never been easy for Carla.

Ever since she could remember, she had always wanted to write. Losing her father at the age of five, in a road accident, hadn't helped her ambition. Carla's mother had never really recovered from the shock and had withdrawn further and further into herself. Consequently, at an early age Carla had quickly learned to depend on her own ability to survive. Fortunately, she had a grandmother who idolised her and encouraged her every effort, both at school and in life generally.

Even as a child, she was vivacious and pretty. Teachers noticed her and took an avid interest in her career. She found it easy to mix with her peers, soon becoming popular and making many friends. High school followed with great success, finally leading on to university at LSU. Carla's first position, at the age of twenty-one, was with a small Louisiana newspaper as a junior reporter. After a year there, she had obtained a position with a much larger paper in Atlanta, Georgia. Although comfortably placed in a secure reporter's job, she realised the big money lay in New York, and had successfully applied for a post with the *Tribune* there. This was where Joe Murphy, Vice-President of *Liberty,* had first approached her and invited her to apply for a feature editor's job with his 'outfit', as he so colloquially put it.

No doubt, reasoned Carla, this was responsible for some of the resentment surrounding her at *Liberty*. In spite of her general popularity, Carla had been too preoccupied with her career to lay down any lasting relationships or roots. There had always been another challenge to interest her another 'windmill to tilt at' as her grandmother put it so aptly. Like most young women, she was interested in the other sex, but, although there had been numerous suitors, she hadn't met one with whom she wanted to settle down, on a lifelong basis. Maybe she was too choosy, she told herself. Carla really had no idea what she expected or wanted from a partner anyway. She dozed off, and dreamt that she was being pursued by a knife-wielding dark-skinned fellow in a dhoti and turban.

Waking with a start, she was relieved to find out where she was, and that the seat belt sign had come on. Buckling up, she brought her seat into the upright position, and replaced the tray table in front of her. 'Oh well,' she thought, 'in a few minutes the plane would be landing in Delhi.' A booking had been made for her there at the Surya Hotel. It would be at least 10 p.m. by the time she cleared customs and arrived at the hotel. Time enough to contact Mr Swarmy first thing after breakfast.

India

The wounded tiger lay weak from loss of blood, concealed in the lantana behind the tall elephant grass. Most of the following day had been spent licking his badly torn paw, which had now congealed and stopped bleeding. Dame Fortune smiled on him when, at about 10 p.m., torrential rain began and continued throughout the night.

It was almost the last great rain of the monsoon season. Water ran everywhere, off the trees and into the gullies. The tiger crawled out from the shelter of the lantana and thorn. Stealthily emerging from the elephant grass, he sniffed the air for danger. All was tranquil; there was only the swishing roar of the deluge.

Flopping down by a gully brimful with water, he drank to quench his burning thirst. Water had never tasted so good.

For the next two or three days the tiger remained in the area. Water was still plentiful in the hollowed-out roots of trees and cavities in the forest floor. Some strength was returning, but, by this time, hunger pains were an added discomfort. He knew that he must push his damaged body to hunt for food or he would not survive.

At sunset on the third night, he ventured forth, limping painfully on three legs, unable to put any weight on the now festering paw. Progress was undeniably slow and his night's hunt fruitless. At dawn he came across a waterhole in the forest. Several sambar deer were busily engaged in drinking. The tiger selected his prey. The one on the perimeter nearest to him was a young buck. Edging forth on his belly, he slowly approached until ready to make his final charge. As is customary with tigers, he forewarned his prey with a low growl before launching himself at the buck in an ungainly three-legged charge. Even without the growled warning, the sambar would have had no problem evading the crippled tiger. Fleet of foot, it made good its escape, together with the rest of the herd.

Dejectedly, he lay down on the soft earth, the need for food of paramount importance. By midday the sun was scorching down on his weary frame, and he dragged himself into the middle of the waterhole. Contrary to many people's belief, the tiger is the only one of the big cats with a liking for submerging himself in water. Even in his poor state, the bathing refreshed him. He was offered another bonus when he located a large bullfrog on a water lily. Normally, he would not have looked twice at it but, in his famished and ravenous state, he wolfed it down before it had a chance to vanish under the weeds. The taste was unusual and bitter, but it did something to nourish him and appease his hunger. He looked all around for another, but only the weeds and the dark flat surface of the water met his scrutiny.

Nightfall again found him resting in the tall grass licking his badly swollen paw.

Bangalore, India

Matthew Barlow, known to his friends as Matt, and to everybody else as 'Tiger' Barlow, rested in a cane-backed chair on his balcony. It was just before sunset, the time he liked best. Born of English parents, he had been born in India, and had lived there all his life.

From his vantage point he could look right down on to his tea plantation, which he had inherited from his father. Cast by the slowly sinking sun, shadows were lengthening across the plantation. Barlow meticulously filled his pipe, lit it and drew contentedly on the stem. Tall at six feet two, he swung his long legs up on to the balcony rail and surveyed the tranquil scene in the valley.

The native workers had all returned to their huts. A good hour earlier the scene would have been one of happy singing and lively activity. Now the only sign of life was a solitary waterbuck over on the far edge of the forest.

Barlow was a contented man, who didn't ask for much in life. Now at the age of forty-four, he had never married, although everyone, even his native employees, knew about his mistress, the beautiful Rachana Dev, who lived in downtown Bangalore.

'The sahib is like the tigers he loves: he mates not only with one,' they would say. These comments were derived from the habits of the tiger species, where the tiger stays with the tigress for a lengthy coupling process, and then moves on, having left her with cubs to bring up. The cubs, in turn, will stay with the mother for a year or two and then, having been taught how to hunt, each goes its own way.

Barlow was ruggedly handsome and deeply tanned from long exposure to the sun. In the last two years his dark hair had silvered at the temples, lending him a distinguished look. The mouth and chin were strong and determined, but his most striking feature was his grey-green eyes, which seemed to dance with humour and vitality, accentuating the laughter lines at the corners.

In repose, pressed up against his cane chair, was a magnificent full-grown tigress. Barlow had found her in the jungle as a six week old half-starved cub, her mother dead nearby, the victim of senseless safari vandals. These mindless morons, who drive the forest tracks in a jeep at night, shoot wildly at the eyes of anything reflected by their lights, totally unaware of the disgraceful suffering and carnage left in their wake, and caring even less.

Jana, as he had named the rescued cub, was now an adult tigress of three years. She followed Barlow everywhere round the plantation, even to the extent of perching on the passenger seat of his utility estate truck.

Of late, there had been problems. Barlow had ignored three letters from the authorities to hand over Jana to a zoo or safari park. They pointed out that it was against the law to keep a potentially dangerous animal as a pet. Even the self-assured and independent Barlow realised that the matter would come to a head soon. Silas Craig, who ran a nearby plantation, and been at odds with him for years, had been making waves, constantly complaining to the police about the presence of the tigress on the neighbouring estate. Probably the only reason the authorities hadn't acted before now against Barlow was his greatly appreciated help over the years.

Like his father, James Barlow, before him, he was at home in the jungle. What he didn't know about the flora and fauna there probably wasn't worth knowing. On more than one occasion he had acted for the commissioner and forest officers in hunting down the panthers and tigers that had unfortunately turned into man-eaters. Matt Barlow knew that somebody needed to protect the reputation of the jungle animals, and if the odd bad one had to go, so be it. After all, he reasoned, there were bad doctors, bent lawyers, bogus priests, so why not the occasional bad tiger.

He ruefully reflected that it was man who forced even the bad tigers to be man-eaters. Almost always in these cases, it was because man had damaged them in some way. No longer could they hunt and catch their normal prey, so the only course open to them to survive was to kill humans – the weakest and easiest to catch of species.

Barlow concluded this train of thought by deciding that it was a pity innocent native villagers had to pay with their lives for the sins of the butchers who had forced the tiger into this course in the first place. Still, luckily, he ruminated, there hadn't been a man-eater in this region for three years now. He remembered well the last one, as he fingered subconsciously the scar on his right shoulder through the thin khaki cotton shirt. That had been too close for comfort! Even then, Barlow held no grudge against the tiger concerned, the man-eater from Andhra. His only sorrow was that it had cost so many lives before his final confrontation with the 'Bad One', as his trusty guide would insist on calling it.

Zabu had been with him on all such perilous tasks. Of indiscriminate age, and all skin and bone, the little native tracker worshipped 'Barlow Sahib', and was never happier than when on a trail with him. The last one had been a cattle-killing panther, six months earlier.

Barlow smiled at the mere thought of Zabu with his wide toothy grin and ragged dress. Once he had given Zabu some old clothes of his own, and the shirt had nearly come down to the little man's knees. He knew, however, that no better tracker existed than the little 'untouchable'.

Suddenly his thoughts were interrupted by Jana stirring and pricking up her ears. He heard it too, the far-off drone of a jeep approaching. Scanning the valley in the gathering dusk, he made out the glow of the sidelights. Standing against the balcony rail, he watched the vehicle wind its way up towards them.

Five minutes later it came to a stop at the foot of the steps. Barlow's father had built the house on raised stone pillars as a protection against snakes.

Rachana Dev, a beautiful Eurasian, gracefully stepped down from the jeep and ascended to the veranda. Barlow swept her into his arms and embraced her. Dark-skinned with finely chiselled features, her lithe body responded warmly to his welcome. She wore a clinging red silk sarong with very little underneath. Barlow's hands slid down over her curvaceous yet slender hips, ascertaining the fact. Her dark, flashing eyes were warm, vibrant and exciting.

"I was just thinking about you," said Barlow, standing back and looking at her appreciatively.

"Liar!" she laughed.

Jana rubbed her head against Rachana's thigh. Stroking the silken, striped head lovingly, Rachana exclaimed, "I don't know whether it's you or her I come all this way to see."

Barlow smiled. Rachana was a rare thing in India: an emancipated woman. Maybe that was what had attracted him to her in the first place – that insular brand of independence and capability she outwardly exuded. Like him, she valued the ability to come and go as she pleased. True, she hadn't any financial worries and could indulge her whims.

The daughter of a rich industrialist, Rachana had made her own way in life, and now ran a thriving travel agency in downtown Bangalore. An unhappy arranged marriage had ended in divorce two years earlier, the end result being that her parents had disowned her completely. At thirty, she was, as she put it, her own person. This, thought Barlow, summed her up to perfection. Both shared an intimacy which made no demands on the other. At times, even their love-making was violent and passionate, not, in fact, unlike the tiger species.

Once, two months earlier, in a weak moment, Barlow had asked her to marry him. Rachana, for once in her life, had looked at him with serious dark eyes, and, after a long pause contemplating the offer, had finally replied, "No Matt, I don't think so. It's not that I'm not in love with you, but what we have is too precious to lose. I prefer to keep things the way they are between us." Accepting this, Barlow hadn't raised the issue again.

Some hours later, both lay back naked on Barlow's king-sized bed. His one luxury, he called it. Outside on the veranda Jana the tigress lay, curled up, sleeping. Only the sound of crickets chirping in the hot, dark night pervaded the room. Rachana rolled on to her stomach and teased the hair on Barlow's chest, lovingly. Their passionate love-making over, they were just content to be together.

Rachana looked serious for a moment. Brushing dark, silken hair from one eye, she spoke slowly, sadness in her voice. "I saw Silas Craig in town today, Matt. Coming out of the commissioner's office. No doubt complaining about Jana, again."

"We don't know that, Rachana," snapped Barlow defensively.

"Oh come on, Matt. We know Craig. He won't rest until he completes what he set out to do – make you get rid of Jana."

"Well he's damn well not going to. Jana belongs here and she's not doing anybody any harm." His jaw set stubbornly in defiance.

"What are you going to do? You've ignored three letters from the authorities about it already."

Barlow stared straight up at the ceiling fan, which was quietly turning in whisper mode, and made no reply.

Rachana continued, "Look Matt, I love Jana too, but you can't ignore the authorities for ever. Sooner or later they will serve you with an order and you will have to comply... or..." Her voice trailed off.

"Or they'll come and take her by force. Is that what you're saying?" snapped Barlow, irritably.

"Or worse," whispered Rachana, looking away so that she wouldn't see his face.

"They wouldn't do that – they need me."

Rachana turned towards him and caressed his face lightly with her long elegant fingers. "Don't count too heavily on that, Matt."

"Maybe... we'll talk about it in the morning," murmured Barlow, placing a protective arm round her slender waist.

Locked in one another's arms, they were soon both soundlessly asleep.

*

The wounded tiger dragged himself ever onward in his futile search for food, taking shelter, whenever danger in the shape of humans presented itself, in the tall elephant grass or in the dense outcrops of lantana scrub. Several times he painfully stalked sambar and waterbuck, having meticulously used all the jungle craft of his species, but he was continually thwarted by a lack of pace in his final charge. Once he had surprised a troop of long-tailed langur monkeys on the ground, but again was doomed to disappointment when they scampered into the trees. From the high treetops their excited chatter seemed to mock his lame efforts.

The days since his encounter with the iron trap had taken a serious toll on the tiger's health. His formerly magnificent, muscular and sinewy body was already emaciated from lack of food, his belly distended. It was fully a week now since he had last eaten, and that had been only the mere morsel of the bullfrog.

Nearly exhausted from starvation and malnutrition, the tiger dragged himself painfully along on three legs. Finally, he sought refuge in a dried-up nullah or watercourse. Here he collapsed and lay panting. Instinctively, he knew that if he failed to find food this evening his life would be terminated.

High above the nullah wheeled a black kite, one of India's scavengers. Soon it was joined by another and another. One became so bold as to settle on the rim of the nullah and fix its beady eyes on him. By tomorrow morning he knew they would be picking his bones, until the jackals took over and drove them off. The tiger had seen it all before.

Suddenly, he became aware of human voices approaching. Almost too exhausted to move, he crouched even lower on the dried-up river bed. Perhaps they wouldn't see him and would pass by. The kite on the rim of the nullah vacated its perch and ascended skywards. A moment later two natives, men in white *lungis*, appeared, one carrying a stick, the other smoking a hookah or waterpipe.

The tiger crouched back on his haunches, self-preservation still paramount in his mind. One man, the one with the stick, shouted at him, and advanced down the nullah, brandishing the stick wildly, to drive him off.

Chapter Three
Grim Discoveries

Carla Wayne rose early to get her first look at Delhi before breakfast. What she saw was quite a shock for her urban American eyes.

There were teeming masses of people: women in colourful saris, braided hair and tikas, red or blue spots on their foreheads; men in dhotis, some with turbans of different types, some even wore European-style jeans with T-shirts. A few more elegant ones, on their way to work, were dressed in long white smocks over white trousers. All was hustle and bustle: lorries, ancient buses, cars, rickshaws, auto-rickshaws, bicycles, oxcarts, handcarts and market stalls. Scruffy-looking shops lined the pavements whilst in the road, camel carts, fully-laden, were propelled by their drovers. Even an elephant trundled by, his mahout perched on his neck with a heavy load of wood behind.

Carla found herself constantly besieged by hawkers, eagerly displaying their wares. She did her best to ignore them, but they were very persistent, as were the numerous beggars. The plight of some of these she found quite distressing, and after twenty minutes of walking round, she was pleased to return to the inviting peace and sanctuary of the Surya Hotel.

After a light breakfast of orange juice, toast and coffee, Carla decided it was time to make the acquaintance of Mr Nikhil Swarmy. From her hotel room she telephoned the number given on the file. Swarmy himself answered. Yes, he would be delighted to give her an audience. How would twelve noon suit her? Then he would escort her to lunch.

Carla readily agreed to go to his residence at the appointed time. After replacing the telephone, she decided to shop for some lighter clothing. With this Indian heat, she was going to need more flimsy garments. The girl at the desk recommended a suitable store, and telephoned for a taxi to take her there. The staff at the store were very friendly and helpful, so by the time Carla was ready to leave she had increased her wardrobe by two silk dresses in red and green, two white cotton blouses and a full cotton skirt.

It was still too early to go on to Mr Swarmy's, so she took a taxi to the Red Fort and used up an hour and a half there, exploring. Yet another hawker attached himself to her, appointing himself her guide. It was useless to protest; he just carried on talking anyway.

"The fort was made of red sandstone, and the moat round it was once occupied by crocodiles for protection," he informed Carla. She wondered whether it was to keep in the inmates or invaders out!

Once the residence of the Moghul emperors, it measured two and a half kilometres all round. The entire fort was surrounded by a colourful scene. A giant funfair with roundabouts and ferris wheels, and a busy shopping area bordered it. Beyond, the golden dome of a Sikh temple could be seen. Outside the main Lahore gate was a snake charmer, playing his pipe, whilst a cobra rose and weaved from a basket.

Inside the walls of the fort, a grey ox, harnessed to a mower, and driven by two natives, cut the lawns. Also in the interior were Indian military buildings with soldiers drilling. She saw the Hall of Royal Audience, which was magnificently inlaid with malachite, jade and other semi-precious stones. There too was the harem.

To Carla's surprise, there were recumbent forms sleeping under every shred of shade on the grass and under the neem trees. She found herself admiring the dress of the women. Saris of brilliant assorted colours, both plain and patterned, covered one shoulder, whilst the other exposed a silken blouse or T-shirt. All had lustrous black hair, plaited, swept up in a bun or gathered back in a pony tail. Most of the women had gold earrings, whilst some had gold studs in their noses. All wore sandals. Some sported headscarves worn in such a way that one side hung to the waist. A few of the women wore loose baggy silk trousers covered by a coloured tunic or sari.

Finally she left the fort, easily acquiring a taxi once outside. Hurriedly paying off her guide, who was still telling her that the Red Fort was built in 1648, she clambered into the seclusion of the car's interior. More hawkers persistently tapped on the car windows, holding up their wares for her inspection.

Carla gave the driver, a turbaned Punjabi Sikh, Mr Nikhil Swarmy's address, and sat back enjoying the temporary peace. The car moved off, in and out of swarming masses of pedestrians, following an ancient lorry belching clouds of black smoke. On the back it said boldly in black paint Horn Please and every other vehicle complied in a cacophony of endless sound.

Past the fort walls, on to Rajput Avenue and down to India Gate, a memorial to the soldiers of World War One. Behind them was the governor's palace, which the driver proudly informed her had three hundred and seventy rooms.

This was New Delhi – full of elegant and colonial architecture. They drove along the Rajpath past three more imperial buildings sitting on Raisina Hill. On past the Secretariat Buildings and Connaught Place to Jan Path, the radial road. Finally, the taxi, one of the numerous Ambassador cars common to India, came to a halt.

"This is the place, memsahib," said the driver, grinning from ear to ear. Carla paid him the requisite fare in rupees and the vehicle pulled away, leaving her standing at the kerb.

She checked the address. In front of her were apartments in a salubrious area, set back from the road. She wound her way up a spiral path, surrounded by numerous flower beds and brightly coloured shrubs. She went in through the main entrance, checked the numbering system on the index panel in the lobby and proceeded to the first floor.

A long corridor lay before her. Every twenty or so yards was a numbered door. Ultimately, she arrived at twenty-two. A brass plate on the door read *Nikhil Swarmy*. The door was ajar, and no sound issued from within. She rang the bell and waited – nothing! Again she pushed the white button, longer this time, but only silence greeted her.

Pushing the door open further, she peered round it.

"Mr Swarmy, are you there?" she called loudly. Her voice seemed to echo back to her.

Carla checked her watch. It was already 12:05. Surely he was expecting her. 'Maybe he's just slipped out for a few minutes and left the door open for me', she thought. She slowly entered, a little uncertainly, and called again. Silence reigned.

Carla found herself in a tidily furnished room, not overly elaborate or ornate but tasteful. A door beyond it was open, so she crossed the room and went through. A tidy kitchenette revealed itself, everything fitted and in its place. The Formica tops were all scrubbed down and smelt of pine. At the end of the kitchen was another door, closed this time.

Carla knocked boldly, but only a hollow unlived-in sound echoed back at her. Turning the door handle, she found that it opened easily. The sight that met her eyes shocked her to the core. The room was in turmoil. It was a study or office. Cabinets had been turned over and drawers lay upturned, their contents scattered everywhere. A broken chair lay on its side. The desk, a heavy mahogany one, was littered with papers, but worse was to come.

Carla peered over the top of the desk. Lying face down on the floor, was a man in a rapidly enlarging pool of blood, staining the deep-pile grey carpet in an ever-increasing circle.

Without thinking, Carla rushed round the desk and picked up the man's arm, feeling for a pulse. The arm was still warm, but no pulse was present. Coolly, she withdrew her compact from her handbag and held the small mirror in the lid over his nose and mouth. After several seconds she withdrew and examined it. Clear as a bell. If this was Mr Swarmy, then he was very dead. Carla, still kneeling beside the body, considered her next move, then the blood in her veins froze. She heard a distinct noise from the room beyond. Her mouth went dry and her skin ice-cold.

*

In a luxurious apartment on Delhi's south side, three men sat round a polished table. Two of them were Indians, the other Chinese. It was the latter who addressed the other two.

Feu Chon Soo was a wrinkled, little man of some sixty years. His expensive suit hung on his gaunt, emaciated frame. A small pencil-slim moustache above a thin, cruel mouth, turned down at the edges, gave him a melancholy appearance. His scalp clearly showed through thin black strands of hair, whilst his eyes darted furtively around him.

"Are the carcasses ready for transport to my factory in Jaipur, Mr Tata?"

"Of course. Did I not promise this?" replied Ravi Tata, an elegantly attired Indian of high caste, who was inspecting his nails, a superior expression on his countenance. Possessed of good looks, but with cold unfeeling eyes, he was tall for an Indian and quite light-skinned. Turning his attention to the second Indian, he enquired, "How many tigers have we for Mr Feu Chon Soo that are ready for collection, Venkat?" The man addressed – Venkat Singh – a huge and muscular Sikh, dark of face and manner, dressed in European garb, screwed his huge fist into a ball, twisted it in the palm of his other hand and glared at the Chinaman.

"Five dead tigers for which I have paid the tribesmen 2,800 American dollars, or equivalent in rupees, for each carcass."

Feu Chon Soo bit his thin bottom lip before speaking. His shifty eyes suddenly alighted on Venkat Singh's dark ones.

"Not nearly enough tigers, and you pay men too much," he remonstrated.

Venkat's huge bulk looked as if it would explode. His expanding chest and biceps put a strain on his smart city suit. Reaching across the table, he seized the little Chinese by his lapels and dragged him forward, out of his chair, waving a fist under his nose.

"Why you snivelling toad of a welcher! I'll smash—"

Ravi Tata placed a restraining hand on Venkat's arm, and exclaimed in a soothing voice, "Now, now, Venkat. I'm sure Mr Feu Chon Soo is going to pay us what he owes."

Reluctantly, the huge Sikh released his grip on the Chinaman, who virtually fell back into his seat.

Ravi Tata continued, "Now, Mr Soo, as Venkat has told you, we pay the tribesmen, and you pay us three times as much. By my reckoning, that's $8,400 per carcass – agreed?"

Feu Chon Soo looked aghast.

"That is preposterous, gentlemen. You need not pay illiterate tribesmen so much. If you pay them half that, it will be plenty. Then I need not pay you more than three thousand or possibly four, if I am very generous."

Venkat leapt to his feet. "Let me silence the yellow dog, Mr Tata."

Ravi Tata smiled, but no warmth reached his eyes, only his mouth creased.

"Sit down, Venkat!" he commanded. "I will explain to Mr Soo exactly the position, so that he may understand, completely!"

Tata turned, his attention and gaze on Soo. "Now, as to your complaint about the number of tiger carcasses. This business is in its infancy in India, compared to Indochina, Burma and Thailand. We have to take risks. The tribesmen we use have to be armed. That all costs money, Mr Soo."

Feu Chon Soo made as if to cut in. Ravi Tata held up a restraining hand.

"Do not take us for fools. We are well aware what you make from each tiger's carcass. You see, we have done our homework on you. Your canning factory in Jaipur is a front."

Surprise, for once, showed on the Chinaman's face. Again, he made as if to interrupt.

"No, listen!" commanded Tata. "In that factory you use every part of the tiger, even his whiskers. In fact, Mr Soo, you sell him by the ounce, in little jars in all kind of medicines and aphrodisiacs, even if none of them do work. A tiger, my Oriental friend, can weigh up to five hundred pounds." Pausing, he watched Soo's face, letting his information sink in, then added, "Just think of how many ounces that constitutes, and what do you charge for the ounce?"

Soo tried to look enigmatic. "Very little. We try to offer the customer a bargain, Mr Tata."

Tata and Venkat both roared with laughter.

"Come now, do you take us for fools, Mr Soo? We have confirmation that some of these products can fetch as much as $500 per ounce in certain markets. We calculate that one tiger can make you megabucks, as the Americans would say."

Feu Chon Soo shifted uncomfortably in his chair and fingered his collar nervously.

"Well, perhaps I was a little hasty, gentlemen."

"I'll say you were," snapped Venkat, leaning forward menacingly.

"Very well, then," Soo reluctantly agreed. "I will pay you what you ask, but I will need many more tigers to make it worth my while."

Ravi Tata straightened and smoothed down his silk tie. Looking hard at Soo, he exclaimed in a slow, deliberate tone, "We can be very difficult should anyone decide to double-cross us. Do I make myself clear?"

Soo coughed with embarrassment. "Quite so, gentlemen. There would be no question of that." An evil smile on his broad face, Venkat cut in, "I'm glad you choose to see reason, Mr Soo."

Tata interrupted his assistant's veiled warning. "Oh, and there's one other thing, Mr Soo. We have been experiencing some problems with a certain Nosy Parker – a conservationist, by the name of Nikhil Swarmy."

Soo, for once, swung his furtive gaze back to Tata. "And just how does this affect me?"

"We are in this together, so it is also your responsibility. However, apart from sharing the cost – for his disposal which, I add, will have taken place by now, you need not concern yourself."

Feu Chon Soo appeared about to have a fit. His thin cheeks puffed up in alarm.

"I, I don't want anything to do with murder. I c, can't afford to become involved."

"You will not be called upon to do anything other than pay your dues, Mr Soo," snarled Venkat. "Of course, failure to do this, well..." He left the sentence unfinished.

Soo's face showed that he had understood the threat. "Well, certainly, gentlemen. If you have removed the risk, and you can confirm I will not be involved, then I think we can come to an agreement over this matter. Now I will leave everything to you and go about my business. Deliver the carcasses to me tomorrow morning and I will have your money ready for you."

"Plus $1,000, as your share of the operation we have just mentioned. We want it in cash, remember. There must be no records of any transaction."

Soo opened his mouth to protest, took one look at Venkat's menacing countenance and decided against any form of argument. "Very well, gentlemen. You shall have it. Until 9 a.m. tomorrow then."

Ravi Tata nodded. Soo picked up his briefcase and left. After his departure, the two Indians looked at one another and smiled.

"That was a great idea of yours, Mr Tata, to resurrect the cult of the Thuggee. This way, no blame can fall upon us for the assassination of Swarmy."

"Quite so, Venkat. It will be the Sons of Kali the blame will be attributed to."

"Even if they did become extinct almost a century ago!"

Ravi Tata smiled, exposing pearly white teeth. "Even so-called extinct volcanoes have been known to erupt after centuries lying dormant."

The room echoed back the two men's laughter from its richly panelled walls.

*

Early the following morning, Rachana Dev left Matt Barlow's bungalow to make an early start at her office.

Jana, the tigress, trotted along at her side until she reached the jeep. Once inside the vehicle, Rachana wound down the window. Jana placed her huge front paws on the sill and peered in. Rachana reached out circling the tigress's neck with her arm and was, in turn, nuzzled by the big cat. Barlow stood on the veranda, laughing at Jana's display of affection which was usually reserved for him alone.

"You've made a friend for life there," he called.

Rachana smiled and patted Jana's head. The tigress went back down on all fours, and as the jeep drove away she trotted some distance behind. Barlow gave a cheery wave and went back into the bungalow. For some while, Rachana watched Jana following the jeep in her rear-view mirror. She wasn't unnecessarily worried as the tigress usually turned back pretty soon. On the winding road across the plantation, she was soon lost to view.

At the estate border, Rachana swung the jeep out on to the road. It ran right round the perimeter of Silas Craig's land. She had gone no more than a mile when she found the road blocked by a bulldozer. A car was pulled up abreast of it, and the two drivers were obviously conversing. The car driver was lolling against the bonnet.

As she braked to a stop, Rachana saw that it was Silas Craig and his foreman George Brook. Both men looked up and Craig ambled towards her vehicle. He was a large, heavily-built man, running to fat. The beginning of a paunch protruded over the belt holding up his khaki shorts. A leering grin appeared on his bulbous, flaccid face, in deep shadow underneath a white pith helmet. Rachana thought he cut an absurd figure with his long turned-over woollen socks and heavy walking boots.

Walking up to the jeep window, he placed a fat hand on the sill.

"Well, what have we here, George?" he called back to the man sitting in the bulldozer. "Bless my soul, if it isn't Barlow's whore."

Rachana bit her lip angrily, her elegant fingers taking a firmer grip on the steering wheel, causing the knuckles to whiten.

"Will you please move your vehicle, Mr Craig?" she exclaimed icily.

Craig grinned and insolently mimicked her remark. "Or you will run and tell lover-boy Barlow, will you?" he leered in at the window.

"I have nothing to say to you other than to request politely that you move over your vehicle, so that I may pass."

Craig laughed. "I will move over when I'm damn well ready, not before. Anyway, you ought to be more friendly to your superiors."

"You, Mr Craig, are nobody's superior," she hotly retorted.

"Get out of that vehicle you whore. I'll show you who's master here."

Rachana picked up a spanner lying on the passenger seat and brought it down on Craig's podgy hand, still resting on the sill. He let out a howl of rage.

"Now you're for it, you coloured slut."

Wrenching the door open, he seized her by the arm and pulled her sprawling on to the dirt road, while the spanner, flying from her grasp, landed several feet away. Moving quickly for a man of such bulk, Craig was on her, pinning her arms down. Rachana let fly with her feet, fighting for her life, but Craig's massive bulk prevented her from getting to her feet.

"Get over here, George," he called over his shoulder. "Hold the bitch down whilst I teach her a lesson she'll remember."

Climbing down from the bulldozer, George Brook eagerly joined the mêlée. Desperately, Rachana struggled to get free of the vile pair.

"Hold her, George, while I whip her good. Turn her over. She won't forget this in a hurry," exclaimed Craig, loosening his belt and withdrawing it from his shorts. Grasping the buckle, he gave the thick leather strap a practice swing.

"You dare, you swine!" screamed Rachana, almost hysterical. "I'll have the law on you."

"That's funny, that is," roared Craig. "You have the law on us! You, a half-caste and us English aristocrats." He looked at George Brook. "Okay George, you hold her down whilst I teach her some manners – afterwards we'll take her back to the barn and have some fun with her, in private like. Teach that high-falutin' Barlow who's top man round here – knock up his woman!"

Craig raised the buckled belt. It never descended. A blood-curdling roar stopped both men in their tracks. Standing high above them, on the grass bank at the road's edge, was Jana, her teeth drawn back in a terrifying snarl of aggression. Brook released his hold on Rachana, who scrambled to her feet like lightning. She rushed up the bank towards Jana. The tigress nuzzled into her, all aggression gone.

Rachana glared down at the two men standing below them on the road, uncertain of their next move.

"Not so brave now, are we, gentlemen?" retorted Rachana icily. "Give me one good reason why I shouldn't set Jana on you, you filth! Now, get back to your vehicles before I do just that!" She felt herself shaking, from both fear and anger, but fought to avoid showing it.

The two men slowly backed away towards their vehicles as Rachana kept one arm round Jana's neck. Neither dared take his eyes from the tigress, who watched them with large, baleful eyes.

"Come on, Jana, into the jeep, girl," exclaimed Rachana. "Let's get back to your master."

Obediently, on reaching the jeep, the huge tigress bounded in. Rachana scrambled down the bank and leapt in after her. Craig and Brook stood, cowed, by their vehicle.

Rachana gunned the engine to life, and swung the vehicle round in a tight circle before heading back in the direction of Barlow's plantation.

Craig shook his fist at the retreating jeep and turned to Brook.

"Let's go and prepare a reception for Barlow, shall we?"

"Why?" said Brook, a heavily built man of limited intellect.

"Because if I know Barlow, he'll be coming to see us pretty damn soon..."

Chapter Four

Retaliation

The foolish village native scampered full tilt down the sloping side of the nullah, brandishing his stick and shouting loudly.

The weakened tiger snarled in an attempt to frighten the man off. Still he came on, brave to the point of stupidity. The tiger backed away, still snarling in defiance, finally turning to break away up the dry river bed. The native, following at a run, soon began to overhaul the retreating limping animal. With a great yell, he brought the stick crashing down on the tiger's rear end.

It proved to be his last action. With a roar, the tiger turned and pounced, ripping out the foolhardy fellow's throat, with one mighty snap of his powerful jaws. The impetus of the tiger's spring made him land squarely on top of the native.

His compatriot, still rooted to the rim of the nullah, let out a fearful scream and ran off, at full speed, for the nearby village. The ravenous tiger, bewildered by events, licked at the salty blood flowing from the native's jugular.

The taste was strange to his senses, but here was food, a chance to live. With his last remaining strength, he dragged the man's body along the rocky bed of the nullah, finally coming to an area, round a bend, where the terrain levelled out somewhat. With difficulty, he dragged his burden over the rim. Another thirty yards and he concealed it in thick jungle vegetation.

Here he lay down and gorged himself on his first meal for a week. The following night he returned to the hidden remains and finished what he had started.

Two days later, a search party from the village found what was left: a pair of sandals, some torn clothing and a few bones. Thus the man-eater of Nagarjunasagar was created – a tiger forced to kill humans in order to remain alive, due to the greed and stupidity of mankind.

Now that the tiger had experienced the ease of killing the frail humans, his terribly restricting injury could be borne. A week later, a second kill from a neighbouring village followed. A native woman, washing clothes in a stream, was taken. There then followed a steady flow of killings as the tiger moved south towards Bangalore.

By now, the paw had healed, although he still walked lame. His strength had returned, but still he couldn't catch sambar and gazelle. However, it no longer mattered. Now there was easier game to keep his hunger appeased.

*

The unexpected sound from the room beyond set Carla's nerve ends jangling. She slowly rose from her kneeling position beside the body and backed away, towards the door of her entry. Her gaze swept the room for some form of weapon with which to defend herself, alighting finally on the broken chair leg. Grasping it tightly in her right hand, she crouched down behind a large filing cabinet.

Seconds that seemed like minutes ticked by. Carla was unsure of her next move. If she risked a run for it, back through the apartment and down the stairs, the assassin could very well catch her before she reached the comparative safety of the road. Even then, she reasoned, there wouldn't be anyone around to help her.

Then, after what seemed eternity, she heard the unmistakable sound of a window being slid up, or could it be down? She had no means of knowing.

With bated breath, still clutching the chair leg, she waited. A shuffling noise filtered through to her. From it, she deduced that the assailant was probably climbing out of a rear window. This was borne out by the sliding sound being repeated. He, or she, was closing the window behind them.

Silence now reigned. Carla knew instantly that she had two options. Stand and do nothing – otherwise playing safe – or creep through and try to obtain a view of the intruder as he made his escape. She decided on the latter course. If it worked, perhaps she would be able to identify the murderer to the police. Creeping forward gingerly, and taking a firmer hold on the chair leg, she approached the connecting door.

Slowly and deliberately, Carla turned the handle and then threw open the door violently. What met her eyes was an almost empty, though ransacked bedroom. The window was still slightly open, and the net curtain gently swayed in the breeze.

She rushed to the window, pulled the curtain aside and peered out. There, in the act of climbing over a high fence that bordered a small flower garden, was the assailant, a dark-skinned Indian, large and swarthy, a curly black beard running right up to meet his grey turban at the sides. The man, with one leg either side of the wooden fence, suddenly looked up. Their eyes met for an instant only, but Carla would never forget that face, with the jagged scar running down the left side.

A moment later, and he had dropped down on to the road and was lost to her field of vision. What if he should come back round and enter the front, thought Carla – now that he knew it was only a woman who had disturbed him? She slammed the window shut and bolted it, then raced through the apartment to turn the key and throw the bolt on the front door. Next she rushed for the telephone. Agonising seconds ticked by before it was answered. The operator had trouble understanding her, but finally she managed to effect a connection to the police. The whole time she was occupied on the telephone, Carla's eyes never left the locked door. At last a voice arrived on the other end speaking excellent English.

'Thank God', thought Carla. Hurriedly, she explained the situation and gave the address.

"Stay locked in where you are and don't admit anyone until I knock and push my card under the door. I am Inspector Ramon Srinath and I will be with you just as soon as I can."

Carla, still gripping the wooden chair leg for protection, went back through the apartment, and stood looking down at the body. It suddenly occurred to her that she didn't even know how Swarmy – if this indeed was him – had been murdered. She was tempted to turn the body over on to its back, but realised that she had better not touch anything. She went back and checked that the door was still firmly locked, then went to the back and checked the window once more. Fifteen agonisingly slow minutes crawled by, in which time Carla began to wonder whether she had done the right thing in calling the police. Everyone said the authorities in India were corrupt. What if they arrested her for the murder? Only now did these thoughts strike her.

Her wildly racing mind was brought back to earth by a loud *rat-tat-tapping* on the door. She nearly jumped out of her skin, but, recovering, rushed to the door. She was about to turn the key and draw back the bolt when she remembered to wait for the card. A moment later the white diagonal edge appeared under the door. Carla bent and eased it through. Reading it, she confirmed the contents and opened the door. A handsome young Indian, dressed in a smart light-weight, dark-green suit, stood there. Behind him were two uniformed and armed constables, dressed in khaki. One carried a large case.

"Miss Wayne, I presume? I am Inspector Ramon Srinath of Homicide." Before she could answer, he went on anxiously, "You haven't touched anything have you?" Carla looked taken aback; she was still quite white and shocked.

"Well, yes, I expect so, Inspector, I mean things like the door handle, the telephone, the window – and this," she said offering him the chair leg.

"Anything else?"

"I don't think so, I can't really remember."

"Right," he replied, matter-of-factly. "Where is the body?"

Carla took them through to the inner room to disclose the grisly sight.

Srinath bent down and turned the body over. A curved and ornately handled knife was still protruding from the victim's chest. Whilst the inspector examined the corpse the two constables kept suspicious beady eyes on Carla. Finally Srinath stood up and barked orders to the two underlings in an authoritative tone.

"Then," he continued, "take Miss Wayne's and the victim's prints too."

One of the constables opened the case, taking out bottles, potions and equipment. Meticulously, the two men went to work.

"Now, Miss Wayne," said Srinath in a kinder tone, "let us go through to the other room and talk, shall we?" Seated opposite, both scrutinised the other. Carla concluded that he was probably no more than five or six years older than herself. Srinath's brown eyes were shrewd, although not without warmth. Placing his fingertips together, he appeared deep in thought. When he finally addressed her, it was in a more sympathetic tone.

"Now, Miss Wayne, suppose you tell me what you were doing here at Mr Swarmy's apartment."

Still trying to keep calm, but not yet over the shock, Carla outlined her mission and the appointment she had come to keep with the deceased.

"That's if the murdered man *is* Mr Swarmy," she added.

"Oh, I see, so you have never met him before?"

"No. Today was to be our first meeting."

"And the last, Miss Wayne. I'm sorry to say the deceased is indeed Mr Swarmy."

"But why would anyone want to murder him?"

"I think you probably know the answer to that one yourself." He studied her face for a reaction.

"You mean this file?" said Carla, producing the red portfolio.

Ramon Srinath reached eagerly for it, and leafed thoughtfully through the pages. After two or three minutes, he handed it back.

"Nothing much in there that he hadn't already acquainted us with. It's names we need, Miss Wayne, and I gather that was what Swarmy was going to pass on to you today."

"Yes, he said it was too dangerous to put into print."

"That I can believe," muttered Srinath, with a wry smile. "Well, he won't be passing anything on now."

After a further thoughtful pause he questioned Carla again. "Might I ask what you were going to do with this information?"

"Research it and prepare an article for *Liberty* magazine."

Srinath looked puzzled. "An article? On what, might I ask?"

"Tiger poaching for the purpose of making so-called aphrodisiacs and bogus medicines."

"And this, er, *Liberty* magazine are your employers, yes?"

"Correct."

"Do you think it would do any good to help stop the poaching?"

"If I could have obtained the names from Mr Swarmy – maybe I could have done something."

"So what will you do now, Miss Wayne?"

"Scratch around and about a bit. See if I can turn something up to give me a lead."

Srinath smiled indulgently. "Don't you think we have already tried?"

Carla looked embarrassed. "I didn't mean to suggest—"

"Quite!" he cut in. "No doubt you have to justify your mission here."

It was Carla's turn to be aggressive.

"I don't have to justify anything. I've been given a month in India to do a job, and I damn well aim to do it!"

"You will be meddling on very dangerous ground, Miss Wayne. Your own life will be in danger, for I must warn you that these people stop at nothing. Are you still going to go on?"

"Yes. I have to try."

"Commendable! Now tell me everything once more. Right from the time you arrived, until now."

Carla patiently related every little detail, right down to the man whose face she had seen from the window.

"Would you recognise him if you ever saw him again?"

"Would I!" she replied enthusiastically. "I'll never forget that face as long as I live."

"That might not be very long, Miss Wayne, if you persist with your enquiries. Don't forget that the man will also have had a good look at you too."

Carla shuddered involuntarily.

"I'll have to ask you to accompany us to the police station. We shall require a statement and I want you to look through some photographs. There's just a chance you might recognise someone in our rogues' gallery."

"Certainly, Inspector."

They were interrupted by one of the constables at that point.

"I'm ready now, sir, to take the lady's fingerprints."

Carla rose and followed the constable back into the other room. Inspector Srinath followed in their wake. Whilst she was fingerprinted he continued to talk.

"It might surprise you to know that I have a lot of sympathy with Swarmy's cause." Carla looked up expectantly. He went on, "You see, Mr Swarmy had given me more or less the same details as in your file, but, like you, no names. I was hoping he might have said something to you before he died."

"I told you, Inspector, he was dead when I got here."

"Ah, mmm. Quite so."

Everyone fell into a pregnant silence whilst the routine fingerprinting was accomplished. Inspector Srinath seemed to be battling with himself over something, searching his conscience.

"Look, Miss Wayne, maybe I shouldn't do this, but I'd like to help you. Swarmy did have two close friends, men interested in conservation, like himself. A Sonjay Patel in Jaipur and a tea planter in Bangalore, Matthew Barlow. I've never met them, mind, but it's possible that Swarmy confided in them. Worth your following up I'd say, wouldn't you?" he enquired hopefully.

Carla's journalistic mind was at work.

"Could I ask why you haven't followed up these leads, Inspector? I would have thought that—"

Srinath raised his hand to stop her and then beckoned Carla to follow him into the other room, out of earshot of the two constables. He smiled.

"You are a very shrewd woman. Yes, indeed I would be following up those leads, but my superior has banned me from anything to do with Swarmy's conservation bunkum, as he called it. Yes, I can investigate the murder, but that's all."

"But surely the two are linked?" put in Carla.

"I feel so too, but I am powerless to proceed on that course, unless I want to lose my job. Do you understand? I have already given you more than I should."

"I realise that, but—"

Srinath raised his hand to stop Carla in mid-sentence.

"Say no more. I will give you the addresses of the two men down at the station. I can do no more. The rest will be up to you. There is one thing though..."

"What is that?" questioned Carla.

"I would get out of Delhi as soon as you can."

"Why?" It was a foolish question, and yet Carla felt she must ask it.

"The murderer has had a good look at you, Miss Wayne, and I can assure you that even in a city where a million people a year are pouring in – since the trouble in Kashmir – you won't be hard to find."

"Surely in a city I should be safer?"

48

"Attractive, blonde young American ladies can hardly be inconspicuous here, I'm afraid," he retorted.

*

Matt Barlow was just climbing into the driving seat of his utility truck when he saw the dust raised by Rachana's jeep in the distance. 'Guess she must have forgotten something,' he reflected. Leaning against the vehicle, he waited patiently.

"She's in one hell of a hurry," he said aloud.

Clouds of dust trailed behind the oncoming jeep. Finally, it came skidding to a halt beside the utility. Rachana, followed by the bounding form of Jana, piled out.

One look at Rachana told Barlow that something was very wrong. Her hair was dishevelled and her dress torn and dusty. Throwing herself into Barlow's arms, she sobbed bitterly, her whole frame shaking.

"Whatever's the matter?" exclaimed an alarmed Barlow.

It took some time to tell him, but between sobs the story gradually unfolded. Jana sat patiently, watching, her head on one side. Barlow could feel the anger welling up inside him.

"This time that swine Craig has gone too far," he snapped.

Gradually, Rachana calmed down and the shaking stopped. Barlow brushed away the tears on her cheeks, very gently, with the backs of his fingers. "You're safe now," he consoled her.

"I, I wouldn't have been if it hadn't been for Jana," she exclaimed, turning with grateful eyes to look at the tigress. Jana obediently trotted over almost on cue and nuzzled them both.

"Will you ring the police Matt, or do you want me to?" said Rachana, calm once more.

"Fat lot they will do other than speak to the swine. No. I'm going to pay Silas Craig a visit and right now!"

"No, Matt! Don't!" exclaimed Rachana. "He'll have men waiting there for you. I don't want you hurt! Leave it to the police."

Barlow took her arm.

"Go inside and pour yourself a drink. Jana will look after you."

"Wh, what are you going to do?"

For answer, Barlow reached into the back of the utility and emerged with a Winchester 405 rifle, which he promptly proceeded to load with shells from a box taken from the glove compartment.

"No Matt!" exclaimed an agitated Rachana. "You'll be one against several. He's bound to be waiting for you."

"Well, he won't have long to wait then, will he?" snapped Barlow, then, feeling apologetic about being so curt with her, he added, "Look, Rachana, you know as well as I do that he's got the police here in his pocket."

"All the more reason to do nothing or he'll have the law on you for assault," argued Rachana.

"Now, love, no more arguments. Go inside with Jana and leave Craig to me."

She realised it was useless to argue with Matt in this mood. Head down, she slowly ascended the bungalow steps to the veranda.

Jana looked at Barlow expectantly.

"Go with her, Jana, and guard!" he exclaimed, waving a hand towards the bungalow.

Obediently the tigress bounded after Rachana. Barlow climbed into the utility and gunned the engine into life.

Five minutes later he brought the vehicle to a stop outside a small lodge on the perimeter of his plantation. With the engine still running, he called out in a loud voice, "Zabu!"

Seconds later, as if by magic, a shiny black face with a smile that exposed all his teeth peered round the door. A moment later and the thin bony frame, wearing a white dhoti, followed.

"What is it, Barlow Sahib?"

"Get that old shotgun of yours. We are going to pay Silas Craig a visit. I'll explain on the way there."

"Ah, Craig is bad man indeed, sahib." Within a minute, the smiling countenance of Zabu reappeared, clutching his very old and battered twelve bore. He clambered up beside Barlow, who let in the clutch and started off immediately. Rapidly, he brought Zabu up to date on the recent happenings.

"Is it not true, Barlow Sahib, that Craig will be a visit expecting from us?"

Even at a time like this, Barlow never ceased to be amused at the little 'untouchable's' turn of phrase.

"Quite so, Zabu, so listen whilst I outline the plan of campaign."

After he had been told what was expected of him the toothy grin re-emerged. There were so many creases in his face that Barlow thought it sometimes resembled a bag of spanners.

Some way from the Craig plantation Barlow halted the utility and backed it off the dusty track into thick undergrowth. The sun was already well up, and the metal of the gun barrel quite hot as he extracted it and checked the magazine. Next he took a coil of crow scarers out of the back of the truck and slipped them round his neck, leaving his hands free.

Zabu looked expectantly at him. Barlow took off his watch and gave it to the little tracker. He pointed to the large hand, explaining that it would be on the eleven by the time they were in position. With obvious pride, Zabu strapped it on to his own skinny wrist. Barlow made a mental note to reward the little man's unquestioning loyalty with a watch of his own next Christmas.

Slowly, making use of every shred of cover, the two men edged painfully closer to the outskirts of Craig's plantation. Lying in the long grass, within touching distance of the fence, Barlow picked up Zabu's bony wrist and showed him that the watch was indicating 11 a.m. He explained where the hands would be at 11:30.

"When that happens, Zabu, you set off these crow scarers at five second intervals." The little native nodded in assent. Barlow went on explaining his plan. "Meanwhile, I shall circle the area and come up on them from the back."

"It is true what men say in the village, Barlow Sahib you are half tiger."

Barlow chuckled for he knew Zabu was referring to the tiger's habit of attacking from the rear.

"Unlike the tiger, Zabu, I shall not be giving warning. You will!"

"How is that, Barlow Sahib?"

"When your crow scarers go off, that will be the diversion, the signal for me to go in. Then when the last cracker has gone off, head for the 'ute' and bring her round to Craig's south gate. Understand?"

The little man grinned from ear to ear.

"Me very good driver, sahib. Best in all India."

Barlow, without more ado, set off crawling on his belly, rifle held horizontal in both hands. The going was slow. Where possible, Barlow used the colour line, blending in with his surroundings. Years of jungle craft stood him in good stead, but he was only too aware that he needed to be behind the white domed house by the time the fire crackers began.

Having given his watch to Zabu, it was necessary for him to guess the time. Looking up at the sun climbing towards its zenith, he knew it was going to be close. At last he reached the white picket fence at the rear of the house. Worming his way forward, he peered through the narrow slits. Piled against them were some petrol cans and wine bottles.

A sudden idea came to him for an unexpected bonus. He edged along until the high pile of cans shielded him from view from the house. The cans, as he had guessed, were empty. Quickly he shook several, transferring all the dregs into one petrol can. A dozen provided about a couple of inches of gas.

Tearing off his shirt, he tore it into strips, then, pouring the petrol into a wine bottle, which half filled it, he stuffed strips of the shirt into the neck, leaving approximately a six inch fuse outside. Having done this, he gave the bottle a good shake, which had the effect of soaking the submerged section of the shirt with the inflammable liquid. No sooner had Barlow completed this than all hell broke out on the facing side of the house.

Zabu had done his work well. The crow scarers were going off like rifle fire every five seconds. Now was his chance. Grabbing the bottle in one hand, Winchester in the other, he climbed the fence, and sprinted for the rear of the house. Once there, he flattened himself against the wall to regain his breath. Bedlam was occurring in the front of the house. He could even hear Silas Craig's voice bellowing orders to his men.

Barlow edged round to the side of the building, still keeping close to the wall. The fire crackers were still exploding at regular intervals, but he realised that Zabu's supply would soon run out.

To his right, about thirty metres from the house, was a pile of wooden tea chests. The crow scarers ceased. Then he heard the unmistakable sound of Zabu's twelve bore being fired twice. From his jeans he took a box of matches and lit the fuse to the bottle, waited for it to burn furiously, then, drawing back his arm, hurled it straight at the tea chests.

Whooomph! The whole lot went up in a sheet of flame, as the bottle burst right in the middle. Barlow, without waiting for the result, sprinted back round the house and came up the other side. Men were yelling everywhere, converging on the blaze.

"Get buckets and hoses," roared the voice of Craig, heading for the inferno.

Barlow counted off a minute, then, with rifle at the ready, advanced boldly out front of the house. Everyone was too busy to notice him as he managed to advance upon them.

It was Craig who wheeled and saw him first.

"Get him!" he roared.

Two men made as if to jump forward, but the menace of Barlow's rifle muzzle directed at them caused them to reconsider. After all, it wasn't their affair. Discretion was definitely the better part of valour.

"Brook – you get him!" screamed Craig to his foreman.

Brook, however, visibly paled and moved not one inch. Barlow eyed both men coldly.

"Nobody takes advantage of any friend of mine. You thought to whip a woman, did you, Craig?"

"N, no," stammered Craig, all his bombast gone like a deflated balloon. "It was Brook who wanted to whip her. He said she was only a half-caste. It was his idea."

"You liar!" screamed Brook. 'You were going to whip her and worse, if that tiger hadn't arrived and—"

"Stopped the two of you cowardly swines," cut in Barlow. "Well, gentlemen, now's the time for you to pay the piper."

Indicating with the rifle the native employees, he said, "You lot, line up over there by the fire. I've no quarrel with you."

Obediently, the natives filed into a line and stood watching, wide-eyed.

"Now, Craig, take off your belt," ordered Barlow.

"N, no! I won't!"

Barlow fired the Winchester. A spurt of dust kicked up at Craig's right foot, barely five centimetres from his toes.

"The next one's got your toes on it. Move!"

Without more ado, hardly able to unbuckle his belt for shaking, Craig complied.

"Stand up against that gate post and remove your shirt, Brook."

The foreman hesitated only for a moment, then, taking a lingering look at the Winchester, did as he had been bidden.

At the post, he whined, "I told you, Mr Craig, Barlow would come after us."

"Now, Craig," ordered Barlow. "Lay into him with that whip until I tell you to stop."

The relief on Craig's face was evident for all to see. Barlow had believed him, after all, when he had blamed Brook. With the foreman still loudly protesting his innocence, Craig waded in with the leather belt. Great welts appeared on Brook's back. Each stroke was interspersed by his screams. After fully a minute, Barlow said curtly, "Enough!"

Craig hit the foreman once more. Brook sagged against the post, his back bleeding.

"Now, Brook, I expect you would like to get your own back," said Barlow in an amused voice.

Slowly, George Brook turned, fixing his gaze on Silas Craig.

"You bet I would," he snarled through gritted teeth.

"Be my guest, then," exclaimed Barlow. Then to Craig he snapped, "Off with your shirt, and take his place on that gate post."

"You wouldn't dare have me whipped on my own plantation, you swine, Barlow. I'll have the law on you for violence."

A second shot from the Winchester tore into the ground a couple of centimetres from Craig's toes.

"If you want to keep your toes, I suggest you move."

Craig, shaking with fear, slowly removed his shirt and moved reluctantly to the post. Brook snatched the belt from his employer and grasped the buckle maliciously.

"Y, you wouldn't dare, Brook – I'll sack you. You'd never get a job anywh... ahh!"

The statement was cut short by a scream as Brook waded in with uncontrolled venom. Again and again the belt found vicious contact with Craig's bare back.

Barlow let the flogging go on for fully two minutes, until both men fell exhausted on to the dusty yard, Craig still moaning with pain.

Barlow wheeled around on his heel and headed for the utility, which had just arrived at the south gate. None of the natives made any move to molest or interfere with his exit.

Chapter Five

A Warning

Within sight of Jaipur's Amber Fort, probably the most famous of all the Rajput palaces, was Feu Chon Soo's canning factory, the waters of Lake Moata lying between the two buildings. A sign on the front of the dingy building, belied its true purpose. Patel's Canned Foods it read. Above and beyond the lake the awesome Jaigarh Fort dominated the skyline, some eleven kilometres on the Delhi road from Jaipur.

The inside of the factory building was no more imposing than the front. Several lines of makeshift wooden benches were manned by poorly dressed natives. The workmen, or women in some cases, operated archaic grinders and mixers, cutters, pounders and labelling devices. At the end of the assembly line – if such it could be called – two native women filled one ounce jars with various compounds of powders, creams and liquids. The full jars were then moved on a manually operated conveyor belt through a hatchway into another room. Here they were given their final treatment, polished and labelled with an assortment of glossy descriptive instructions. Potions for all kinds of ailments, in fact, so-called panaceas. Feu Chon Soo knew full well that none of them worked, but he cared even less.

There was big money to be made from the sale of tiger parts in whichever shape or form he cared to present. Why, in some markets, he could obtain $800 an ounce for the aphrodisiacs. Feu smiled to himself. He had been impotent for years, but as long as superstitious people believed in the potions he would continue to laugh all the way to the bank.

A native brought news that a truck had just arrived at the back entrance. Feu went through to inspect it. A lorry load of cow bones. Ground down, they would make the tiger parts stretch further and double the profit. Who would know the difference? Rapidly, Feu gave orders for the lorry to be unloaded. This done, he went to his office to study his profit balance columns. As yet his operation in India was only just beginning, but he had confidence that it would soon match his very worthwhile project in Laos.

'Time enough, then, to consider updating this ancient factory. Why pay out more than you have to?' he asked himself, stroking his pencil-slim waxed moustache. 'The labour was cheap here. Long may it continue.'

Feu Chon Soo might not have felt quite so complacent and contented had he been party to a conversation between Ravi Tata and his henchman Venkat Singh. Tata was speaking softly.

"We have made a good start, Venkat. When the police check out the knife used to kill Swarmy, they will see it is of the type used by the Thuggees. Soon they will know the cult of Kali, the goddess of Destruction, is reborn. Now you and I will travel to Ranthambhore."

Venkat Singh screwed up his face in puzzlement.

"I don't understand, Mr Tata."

"Oh, you will, Venkat, my friend, you will. There in the forest at Ranthambhore we shall stage an impressive festival, in honour of Kali."

"How will that benefit us?"

Tata gave a knowing smile and touched his nose with his index finger.

"Our little ceremony will be organised to impress the native people. After what they witness, we shall be able to get them to do anything."

"You mean kill more tigers for Feu Chon Soo?"

"At the start, yes. Once you and I have learnt all about Soo's organisation, the cult of Kali will make a take-over bid. One that Soo will not be able to refuse."

Both men laughed, Venkat at last comprehending the full meaning.

"Why have only a piece of the pie when we can have it all?" exclaimed Venkat.

Tata began again.

"Now Venkat, I want you to get hold of that fakir from Rajasthan. Offer him 5,000 rupees for his services. We shall need him for one night only."

"You mean Anil Dehra, that rogue of a magician? What do we want with him?"

"Rogue yes, magician yes, but of the Indian fakir illusionists there is none better for our purpose."

The slow-thinking Venkat struggled with this for a while, then his face began to lighten, as realisation suddenly dawned.

"I see. You want him to create illusions for us at the festival, yes?"

"At last, Venkat. You see!"

"We could stage the festival at one of the deserted old forts of the Rajputs, in Ranthambhore itself."

"My very thought, Venkat. Now, one more thing. That mistress of yours."

"You mean Rania?"

"Yes, if that is indeed her name. The one you told me was becoming tiresome."

"So she is. I wish to be rid of her."

"So you shall, my friend. If she is expendable, she will serve our cause well."

"How is that, Mr Tata?"

"I will explain, when the time comes."

*

The tiger had just made his eighteenth kill, a woodcutter venturing into the forest for firewood. On this occasion, the luckless native had omitted to put the usual face mask on the back of his head, a custom used by all forest dwellers to prevent tiger attacks.

Usually, it confused the animal, as the tiger always attacks from the rear. A simple remedy, but nevertheless one that usually worked. For this poor fellow there was no second chance. His only consolation was that it was instantaneous.

The tiger, now fully recovered in everything but his lameness, was possessed of all his old strength and power. To that he had now added the diabolical cunning of the true man-eater. Covering literally miles of territory, he was striking at regular intervals. Once he had even become so bold as to take a native from one of the straw and mud huts on the edge of a village. Having made his kill, the unfortunate victim would be carried off to a place of concealment and there disembowelled and half devoured. The tiger would then either lie up, over the kill, or remain somewhere in the vicinity before completing his consumption of the corpse the following evening.

It was almost unknown for him to return on the third night. This tiger still had a long way to go to match the incredible score of human kills attributed to the notorious Champawat tigress, which had accounted for no fewer than four hundred and thirty-six people. It was way back in 1907, when Jim Corbett finally ended her reign of terror. On examination after death, she was found to have a broken canine, which was almost certainly the reason she had embarked on such a deadly course years before.

Only in the marshy sunderbans is the incidence of man-eaters high. Many reasons for this have been given, none truly holding water. Some say it is the brackish salty water of the marshlands that induces the practice. Others profess a hereditary tendency. Here tigers have even been known to swim out and take fishermen from their little boats, and there are frequent attacks on honey and wood collectors too.

However, no normal tiger attacks man. His is a shy, insular and majestic nature and, on the whole, the tiger goes out of his way to avoid humans.

This tiger, like so many before him, had been forced to adopt a course totally alien to him. If he was to survive, then he must learn to be an expert. Sadly for the folk of the forests, he was a quick learner.

*

Carla Wayne was relieved to be back in her air-conditioned hotel room after spending the entire afternoon studying pictures of criminals at the police station. After making and signing a complete statement, Inspector Srinath had allowed her to leave. First Carla had been forced to agree to advise the police of her every move whilst in India.

Was it possible they thought she had murdered Swarmy, or was it just routine procedure, she asked herself. Stripping off her clothes, she lay relaxing in a tepid bath, for the heat outside and in the police station had been stifling all afternoon.

Tomorrow she would leave for Jaipur where she hoped to contact Sonjay Patel, the conservationist friend of the murdered man. Inspector Srinath had intimated that it would be safer for her to leave that evening. Resting her head back on the edge of the bath, she reflected on the day's events. Hard to imagine a worse start. Carla was tempted to fax *Liberty* magazine's Edwin Strobe and request a recall. After all, they couldn't really couldn't expect her to put her own life in danger.

Almost as soon as the thought dawned on her she dismissed it. No way would she go back to New York a quitter, with her tail between her legs. If she stayed with the project maybe she could pull off a scoop, and perhaps Srinath was over-accentuating the danger.

In her mind's eye she saw Swarmy's dead face, with the knife projecting from his chest, and shuddered as she realised nobody had exaggerated the perils involved. Once out of the bath, she towelled herself dry, vigorously, and slipped on a pale blue silk caftan. Whilst tying the belt loosely about her slender waist, she heard a slight sound at the bedroom door. Looking up she was in time to see a small buff envelope being slipped underneath the door.

Not unduly alarmed, thinking it was probably a message from the hotel, she ambled over and picked it up. Tearing it open, she found a small piece of white paper inside. As she unfolded it the words, printed in capitals, hit her like a sledgehammer.

> CARLA WAYNE GET OUT OF INDIA OR INCUR THE VENGEANCE OF THE SONS OF KALI. THIS IS THE ONLY WARNING YOU WILL RECEIVE. IGNORE IT AT YOUR PERIL

The hand holding the note was shaking. What should she do now? Whoever they were knew who she was, and where she was. How could they possibly be so well informed? One thing for sure, she must leave Delhi at once – this evening – for Jaipur. Srinath had been right, after all. Carla supposed she should telephone him and acquaint him with this latest development. Making up her mind, she picked up the handpiece and requested an outside line. When the station – after what seemed an age – answered, they informed her that Inspector Srinath had gone off duty, and, no, they couldn't possibly disclose his home number.

"Strictly against regulations, memsahib," said the officious voice at the other end.

"In that case then," Carla exclaimed, "please give him a message when he comes in tomorrow. Tell him I have received a threatening note from somebody calling themselves the Sons of Kali and I am leaving Delhi tonight.'

"Where can he reach you, memsahib?"

"I'll ring when I get there tomorrow morning, probably Jaipur."

Carla heard the phone go click at the other end, so she replaced the receiver.

"Damn!" she exclaimed in exasperation. "Officials!"

Taking off the silk caftan, she rapidly dressed in more suitable garb for a journey, then scurried round the room hurriedly packing. This completed, she checked out with the cashier at the desk downstairs, and had the bellboy order her a car. She didn't have long to wait. Remembering the advice given to her by the hotel she negotiated a price with the driver, a Sikh, for the journey to Jaipur.

"It will take us until the early hours of tomorrow morning, memsahib," he informed her.

"Then I guess we had better get started," she replied.

He proved to be quite correct in his assessment. The journey by road from Delhi to Jaipur, although only about two hundred and eighty kilometres, took an age. It was still daylight when they left the Surya Hotel but it seemed to Carla to take an eternity to even clear Delhi.

The area was made up of eight cities, in fact, and there were traffic jams with hooters blaring noisily everywhere. Even after they cleared the urban zone it proved to be slow going, with an endless stream of lorries ahead of them.

Darkness soon overtook daylight, and twice they were held up in long traffic jams. Approximately every five kilometres, an overturned or broken-down lorry littered the verges. It was single track, both ways, sometimes the tarmac turning to dust and shale. Twice Carla thought her end had come as her driver overtook lorries with headlights coming straight at them. More by luck and divine providence than skill, they squeezed through.

Feeling drowsy, she dozed off, only to be jolted awake as the car bounced out of a pothole. She was disturbed to notice that the driver was watching her overtly in his mirror, and realised that her skirt had ridden up whilst she had been dozing. Quickly she smoothed it down and took up a more elegant posture. The Sikh driver spoke very little, Carla finding it question and answer in her efforts to converse with him.

She was relieved when the outskirts of Jaipur appeared. It was 2:30 a.m., but by the time they reached the centre of the city there seemed to be just as many people about as there would have been all day.

Everything seemed to be hustle and bustle. Barrows, ox-carts and pedestrians were everywhere. On her right she saw the famous Palace of the Winds, from where the ladies of the harem used to look out in the days of the great Moghuls.

Purposely, she hadn't left a forwarding address at the Surya. No sense in making it easy for anybody to follow her. In any case she hadn't a clue where she would stay in Jaipur.

She asked the driver to recommend a nice clean hotel. In a non-committal grunt, he mumbled some names. The only one she registered was The Holiday Inn, so she requested to be taken there. By the time she had paid the driver off, booked in and arrived in her room, it was fully 3 a.m.

She waited another ten minutes before her case was brought up, but decided not to unpack until the morning. A quick shower improved her spirits and, realising she was very tired, Carla towelled off and scrambled naked between the sheets.

It was already 9:30 when she awoke to find the sun streaming in through a crack in the curtains. She rummaged in her case for a dressing-gown, looked at the room service menu and phoned down an order. Whilst waiting for it to be delivered, she drew the curtains and took stock of the view. 'Interesting,' she decided, 'without being exciting.'

After breakfast Carla felt ready for anything. Systematically she unpacked and hung up her clothes, using the plentiful supply of hangers provided. She allowed herself the luxury of a relaxing warm bath before meticulously attending to her hair and make-up. Now she felt human again and could face the world with all its tribulations. No time like the present to get down to business.

Inspector Srinath had given her the name and address of Sonjay Patel, the conservationist friend of Swarmy, but she hadn't managed to extract a telephone number. With a call to telephone enquiries, this proved easier than she had expected. Carla made the call, listening to the ringing tone with her fingers crossed. It was answered by a female voice, who confirmed that Mr Patel was in, and yes, he would speak to her.

After a delay, he came on the line. Carla was amazed that he seemed to know all about her, until he explained that Inspector Srinath had telephoned him last night, saying that she would be coming to see him.

"You understand, young lady, that I wouldn't want you to be seen coming here, in view of what Srinath has informed me has happened to my friend, Nikhil Swarmy."

"Yes, I do understand."

"However, I would wish to help you, so perhaps we could meet somewhere."

"Where do you suggest?" enquired Carla.

"I think somewhere very public, where we can meet, apparently by accident. Let me see. Yes – I have it – the Shila Devi Temple at the Amber Fort. You will find it tucked behind the stairs, almost out of sight of the outer courtyard. You can ride up to the fort on an elephant, as it is a steep climb up from the car park. Shall we say, 3 p.m. in the temple?"

"How will I know you, Mr Patel?"

"Good question, my dear. I know, I will wear a white speckled orchid in my lapel, to make it easier for you."

"That's fine then," agreed Carla. "I shall look forward to meeting you there at three. Goodbye for now."

"Goodbye, and enjoy the elephant ride."

*

Carla arrived by taxi, half an hour early for her appointment. As she emerged from the taxi she saw several elephants, howdahs in place on their backs, being fed armfuls of sugar cane. A small gaggle of tourists were taking their turn at the loading bay. Carla joined the queue and didn't have long to wait. She climbed the stairway to the platform. Here all she had to do was literally climb aboard when her elephant was brought round.

The howdah had two bench-seats either side, so she found herself back to back with a pleasant English couple. The huge animal lumbered off, his mahout seated on his neck. She looked with horror at the instrument in the native's hand, a kind of hooked skewer, and hoped he wouldn't use it on the poor elephant. A colourful array of flowers and stars had either been tattooed or painted on the animal's face and trunk. A tapestry carpet covered his forehead. All the way up to the fort they were subjected to hawkers and photographers selling their wares. Even here they couldn't escape. The ride up gave a breathtaking view of the Moata Sagar below, and the Amber Fort above.

At the top, the passengers disembarked and were immediately besieged by photographers, trying to sell photographs they had taken earlier.

Carla marvelled that they could have developed them so quickly, as none were of the Polaroid variety. She bought one of herself mainly to get rid of the persistent hawker. It was of little use – two more took his place and walked with her, past the Victory Gate.

Producing her ticket she entered, pleased to leave them behind. Her watch showed a quarter of an hour still to spare so she used the time exploring the fort. The Jaleb Chowk was filled with souvenir shops when she returned to the outer courtyard. Quickly she bought a few postcards and then, noting that it was now 3 o'clock, located the Shila Devi Temple, behind the stairs.

There were a few tourists around, but she saw him immediately, finding the white orchid buttonhole on the lapel of his light cotton suit. He was a distinguished-looking man with white hair and steel-rimmed spectacles. Carla judged him to be around sixty or thereabouts.

He approached, as if by accident. Not apparently seeing her, he bumped her shoulder, knocking the postcards she had bought on to the floor.

"Pardon me, madam. Allow me," he exclaimed, stooping to retrieve them for her. As he handed them back, he said, "Alas, you will find them quite useless. More often than not the stamps are removed and they never get sent. It is better to send letters."

"I will remember that," said Carla, with an engaging smile. Then in a softer voice, "Mr Sonjay Patel, I presume?"

"At your service, madam," he said with a smile. "Allow me to guide you round the fort. It is a magnificent example of Moghul architecture."

As they ambled round he informed her that the temple was dedicated to Kali, Goddess of War, and he pointed out a sixteenth-century Bengali image.

Carla caught her breath and whispered, "Did you say Kali?"

Noting her dismay, Patel exclaimed, "Why, yes. That appears to bother you, young lady."

"Well, you see, last night I had a warning note whilst in Delhi, from the Sons of Kali – warning me to leave India."

Patel looked at her, disbelief on his face. Carla produced the note from her handbag. He read it and, obviously disturbed, handed it back to her.

When he didn't comment, Carla enquired, "Who are the Sons of Kali?"

"If you had asked that question at the turn of the last century anyone in India could have given you the answer."

"How do you mean?"

"Well, should I say, they are supposed to be an extinct cult of assassins, known as Thuggees – worshippers of Kali, the Goddess of Destruction. No one has heard anything of them for decades."

"Now it appears they have been resurrected and are after me," whispered an alarmed Carla.

Patel took her by the arm and led her out into the open to a quiet spot overlooking the waters of the lake.

"My dear, you are obviously getting in over your depth. Is it worth the risk? Somebody has already murdered my friend, Swarmy, to prevent him talking to you. Wouldn't it be safer for you to return to America, whilst there is still time?"

"You mean I could be next?"

"That is exactly what I do mean, or if I help you it could be me," he said meaningfully.

"But, surely, whoever they are, you don't want them to get away with murdering your friend – do you?"

Patel looked to right and left, then ran his fingers round his collar nervously before speaking softly.

"I am not a young man any more. Yes, I am a conservationist like Nikhil, but I do not have, how do you Americans say, the fire in my belly today that I had ten years ago."

"But did not Mr Swarmy tell you some of the facts he had found out? After all, you had been friends for years."

"Ah, I see Inspector Srinath has been speaking out of turn. Can I say Nikhil Swarmy was a bold man – far bolder than I. He had been conducting a crusade to save the tiger for years."

"Surely then we shouldn't let his efforts go to pot?" urged Carla.

"You don't understand, my dear. There is big money involved here and you are dealing with unscrupulous people who will stop at nothing... even killing."

"Look, Mr Patel, can't you tell me anything that will help me to start my investigation here in India?"

Patel looked worried, and fingered his collar nervously. He then withdrew a silk handkerchief and patted at his forehead, still looking all around him.

"I feel I shouldn't have come here today. I was wrong to encourage you, young lady."

Carla decided a firmer line was going to be necessary, as obviously coaxing was not going to work.

"Look, all I need is a name of someone, or a place to start my investigations. If anyone is watching us, then they have already seen us, so you might as well tell me what you know... then I will promise not to bother you again."

"You must think I am a very timid man, Miss Wayne, but I can assure you it was not always so."

Carla switched on her most bewitching look and grasped his arm imploringly.

"Please, Mr Patel. Help me. Help your friend Nikhil Swarmy who died for what he believed in."

Patel, with another look to left and right, seemed to come to a decision.

"I will tell you what I know, but you must promise not to mention me in any article that you write. Do I have your word?"

"You have it."

"Very well then. You must understand all of what I am going to tell you is second-hand from Nikhil Swarmy. I cannot vouch for its accuracy or authenticity."

"Go on. Please go on, Mr Patel."

"Nikhil said that the tiger carcasses are being shipped out from here in Jaipur. According to him, there is a factory called 'Patel's Canned Foods'. No connection to me, you understand, for Patel in India is like your equivalent of Smith. It is run by a Chinese, Feu Chon Soo by name. Apparently the factory is only a front for its true purpose. In fact, I remember it from the old days. Been there for years and perfectly reputable. This man Soo took it over within the last two years, I think."

Carla waited for him to continue but, when he gave no sign of doing so, chipped in with, "Do you know the people supplying him? I mean, the poachers or the people organising the natives to do it?"

"I regret not, my dear. Nikhil, however, did. He was going to tell me on his next visit here. Now we shall never know, will we?" he added sadly.

Probe as hard as she could, it was plain that Carla would extract nothing more from Sonjay Patel concerning the matter. Either he really didn't know any more details, or he was just too frightened to say anything further. He showed her round the remainder of the Amber Fort, concentrating on its Moghul history rather than material useful to Carla's investigations.

Finally, as they were about to depart, he took her hand in his.

"Try Matthew Barlow in Bangalore. If anyone in India can help you, he can. Here – I'll give you his address."

Chapter Six

Ranthambhore

It was almost midnight, but an orange glow lightened the sky over one of Ranthambhore's many ancient ruined Moghul forts. The enveloping darkness behind screened from view the rugged hills of one of India's most beautiful parks. Below the fort, the waters of the lake reflected scores of burning torches held aloft by a large multitude of natives. From their throats, in unison, came one repeated chant – "KALI, KALI, KALI". All were dressed from head to foot in long black hoods and cloaks. In the centre, behind a stone wall which served as an altar, were three figures. Between them and the darkly clad multitude of natives a bonfire crackled and hissed.

Two of the three men, dressed in white, were hooded, the other had a mass of wildly bedraggled grey hair, which seemed to meet up with an equally wild and unkempt beard. In fact, it was only his fervently dark and staring eyes that seemed to break up the abundant flow of grey hair about his face.

The taller and larger of the pale, hooded figures turned to the other.

"We are ready, Mr Tata."

Ravi Tata, the other, turned to the wildly gesticulating apparition with the flowing mane.

"Proceed, Anil Dehra, and make it impressive."

Across the lake a herd of samba pricked their ears at the unaccustomed sounds.

Venkat Singh whispered to Ravi Tata. "We must not tarry here, my master. It will go badly for us if we are discovered desecrating a national park."

"You worry too much Venkat. The park is one hundred and fifty square miles in all. The chance of us being discovered before we have concluded our business is almost non-existent."

Their conversation was interrupted by a blinding blue flash, followed by green, red and purple ones as Anil Dehra, his beard and hair flying in the wind, threw handfuls of assorted powders into the blaze. The eyes of the multitude were now riveted upon him. He began to chant in an eerie, high-pitched cackle.

"I am the instrument of Kali, also known as Devi, Durga, Parvati and Sati. The most powerful consort of Siva, and the most powerful of all goddesses. The gods Siva, Brahma and Vishnu have decreed that Kali, the Goddess of Destruction, must be appeased. Her lord and master, Siva, the Lord of the Dance, so decrees it."

With this, Dehra threw another handful of powder into the flames. Tongues of assorted colours climbed into the darkened heavens. The darkly hooded assembled natives gasped. Suddenly, the fakir produced a coil of rope which he flung skywards. Before the eyes of the audience it turned into a rigid pole. The fakir, incredibly spry for his advanced years, began to scale the pole with alacrity.

"I must talk with Kali," he intoned. At the height of some fifteen feet, he totally disappeared from sight in a cloud of blue smoke. Again, the watching crowd gasped and waited in expectation.

Suddenly he reappeared sliding down the pole. Then came Anil Dehra's greatest trick. The erstwhile rope, or pole, turned into a writhing cobra in his hands which he held aloft to the audience before placing it in a wicker basket and replacing the lid.

Raising his hands palms out to the multitude, once more he began a long incantation, which, although nobody understood, seemed to have an amazing effect on the watchers. Whilst this was going on, Venkat Singh disappeared within the confines of the ruined fort. The massed crowd pushed expectantly forward, some craning their necks to see over the heads of others.

"Bring the maid forward," commanded the fakir.

Venkat Singh emerged, pushing a young woman before him. Dressed in a long flowing purple robe, she looked dazed and bewildered. Her long dark hair had been carefully braided. Venkat prodded the girl forward until she was confronted by the wild-eyed fakir.

"Drink this girl," ordered Dehra, producing a glass of green coloured liquid.

The girl looked wildly about her and then at Venkat and shook her head, recoiling from the long-haired apparition before her.

Venkat took her by the arm, and whispered, "It is good, Rania, and it will refresh you for the marriage ceremony," he lied. Mollified, she took the cup and drank very slowly, the three men patiently waiting. Dehra then took her hand and led her to the wall, which was to serve as an altar.

First he backed her against the wall then, standing back, transfixed her with his wild dark eyes. He began, again, to intone and moan in a low voice that the watchers could not discern. Producing a crystal eye pendant hanging from a chain, he started to swing and wave it before her. The girl's eyes followed its erratic course.

Gradually the motion became more stable and the crystal swung back and forth before her. Soon its mesmeric effect had imposed its control over Rania. Her head swayed back and forth – unseeing – her eyes glazed.

"Kali is your mistress," Dehra urged, in a soft voice.

"Kali is my mistress," she repeated.

"And you must do as she wills you, is that not so?"

"It is so," repeated the hypnotised Rania.

"Today you are to wed your mistress in blood. She demands it."

The girl swayed and looked as if she were about to fall, then steadied again, leaning against the wall.

Venkat stepped forward and produced two poles which he handed to Dehra. The fakir drove each into the ground about five feet apart. This done, he scooped up the purple-robed girl and placed her horizontally, so that one pole rested under her head, the other at her heels.

Standing back, he held his hands aloft to the watching throng. A low expectant murmuring answered him. Next he removed the pole at the heel end of the recumbent form. The girl remained static and horizontal. Another gasp from the crowd. Dehra walked twice round the still suspended Rania and then, with a flourish, removed the second pole supporting her head.

She remained there, seemingly floating in space. The audience went strangely quiet.

"Who would question the will of Kali?" roared Dehra. Only silence greeted the question.

Next Venkat Singh produced an ornately curved handled dagger, which he handed to the fakir, who held it up for all to see. The tip of the dagger he inserted between the girl's breasts and under the top edge of the robe. Then, with one deft movement, he cut transversely through the ties holding the garment together. It fell to the earth, leaving the girl suspended in space and totally naked.

Again there was a concerted gasp from the whole assembly. Once more, placing his arms under her naked and slender body, Dehra scooped up the girl effortlessly and placed her on the altar wall, now covered with a bright red cloth. For a moment he stood back surveying the onlookers, then turned back to the comatose girl.

"Now you will show your love for your mistress, the Goddess Kali," he commanded.

"What must I do?" she replied in a monotone.

"Do? Why surely you know. You must take this dagger and make a cut from your breastbone down to your pubic region. Make the cut only as deep as the skin for your mistress Kali has other need of you."

With this, Dehra handed the girl the curved dagger. Without any pause, she inserted the point just below her throat and commenced to make one firm cut down the entire length of her torso. Immediately, a thin stream of blood followed the knife edge. In the process of this act the girl showed not one tremor and, on completion, handed the blood-stained dagger back to the fakir.

"Very well maid, you have proved your love for Kali, but further proof is necessary if she is to reward you with eternal life. So that you may re-enter this world reincarnated as a princess, you will now do as I say."

"Yes master."

Again there was the expectant hush.

"Rise to your feet."

Rania slowly moved to a vertical position, blood running freely down her naked torso.

"Go into the fort with the white-robed figure to your left. He will convey you to a suitable position for your future royal incarnation."

Obediently, Rania walked towards Venkat, leaving a trail of blood in her wake. Taking her by the hand, he led her away, both disappearing from view within the fort's confines.

Anil Dehra turned again to the assembled masses and raised his hands to silence the chatter that had broken out. There was instant silence. He began to address them.

"You gathered here tonight have witnessed the power of Kali. Doubt it not, or you too shall die. I, the mouthpiece of Kali, have the power to order the deaths of each and every one of you, should she so order me. Should you doubt this, you are about to witness the supreme power of Kali, she of many arms. Any one of which can reach out for any one of you," he added menacingly.

Suddenly he was aware of natives in the crowd shouting and pointing past and above him. Dehra did not turn – he had no need because he knew the cause of their excitement.

High above him, in a ruined tower of the ancient fort, stood the naked and bloody figure of Rania. Venkat remained out of sight, having prodded her forward to the very edge of the parapet. She looked down without fear, for she felt none, and her eyes were still glazed.

"Behold ye peoples of Kali," chanted Dehra, once more raising both arms to the multitude. "The handmaiden of Kali stands before you. See how she offers the blood of life to her mistress. Now she will make the supreme sacrifice."

He turned his back on the crowd, put his arms down to his sides and looked up at Rania in the tower, calling to her in a loud voice that seemed to echo and bounce back from the very walls of the ancient fortress.

"Look down on your mistress, the Goddess Kali. See how she combines benevolence with ferocity and destruction. Soon you will leap into her arms and be born again."

An expectant eerie silence fell on the gathering.

Dehra continued, "I shall count to three. On three I shall snap my fingers and you will leap from the parapet. Do you hear me, maid?"

"Yes, master, I hear you."

"Then prepare to meet your mistress. One... two... three!" Dehra loudly snapped his fingers.

Rania threw herself upwards and outwards, her near-comatose form turning in the night air, the bloodied form casting a ghastly reflection in the glow of the bonfire and torches. It spiralled downwards to hit the earth with a sickeningly dull thud.

Ravi Tata whispered to Venkat, who had appeared again at his side, "I think we can say you are rid of your nagging mistress, Venkat."

Venkat's unseen smile, under his white hood, confirmed the statement.

Two or three natives made as if to dash forward to inspect the fallen body.

Dehra stopped them in mid-stride.

"Back, dogs – or you will suffer a like fate! The Goddess Kali is hungry for blood this night."

As if electrified, the whites of their eyes rolling in fear, they backed away.

The fakir began again, "Behind me are two men in white. They are the servants of Kali. Soon they will remove their hoods and you will feast your eyes upon them. Whatever they instruct you to do you will do, without question, or the Goddess Kali will surely destroy you in a ball of fire."

The crowd cowered before him.

"The power of Kali is far-reaching. Do not think you are safe from her in your villages and homes. She will reach through the very walls with her fingers of fire." With this, he indicated to Ravi Tata and Venkat Singh to remove their white hoods.

Slowly and dramatically they proceeded to expose their faces.

"Look on these men well. If they tell you to kill men you will do so without question. If they tell you to kill tigers you will do that too and the goddess, your mistress, will be well pleased." Dehra stepped boldly towards the pressed mass of natives. "Now all remove your hoods so that Kali will recognise you the better."

Reluctantly, shuffling their feet uncomfortably and eyeing one another expectantly, the entire assembly complied. Dehra looked long and hard at the throng, his hair flying wildly in the night wind.

"Kali now knows all of you!" One or two showed the whites of their eyes in abject terror. Picking on the two most affected, Dehra roared, "Now you two – go to the body of the maid and carry her to the flames. There she will be consumed by the fires of Kali."

For an instant one of the natives looked as if he would protest, but one more look at the terrifying countenance of Dehra convinced him of the error of his ways. The two carried the body of the girl, Rania, and cast it into the flames. Dehra again raised both hands.

"Now begone from this place until you are called again by either myself, or these two servants of Kali."

There was a mad scuffle as everyone tried to vacate the area, some bumping into each other in their haste to escape. Soon Dehra was left alone with Ravi Tata and Venkat Singh, both in the process of removing their white cloaks.

"You did well, fakir," snapped Venkat.

"Indeed so," confirmed Tata, producing a wad of notes and offering them to Dehra.

To his amazement the illusionist, for such he was, pushed Tata's hand aside.

"Do you take me for a fool, gentlemen? What you offer here is a pittance."

Venkat Singh took a menacing step forward. "Why you shyster! You agreed the price!"

Dehra moved not one step backward, but thrust his own wild and hairy face into Venkat's.

"That was before I knew what was planned here and just how much money is involved."

Before Venkat could respond, Ravi Tata stepped in.

"Now, Anil, there is no need for us to haggle. I can promise you a fat bonus as you have done so well. You don't understand the position."

Dehra cut in.

"No, gentlemen, it is you who do not understand. Because of what I accomplished here in Ranthambhore tonight, these natives will carry out your every wish." He waited while that sank in, then continued, "In fact, you will tell them to kill tigers, for which you will be paid a handsome price. Do you think I am not aware that aphrodisiacs and so-called medicines can fetch five hundred dollars – or more – for as little as one ounce. Superstitions, gentlemen, but the fools will pay. I know... and you offer me this paltry sum!"

Venkat raised a mighty fist, but Ravi Tata placed a restraining hand on his arm, then addressed himself to Dehra.

"So what is it that you want from us, Anil?"

"Come now, Mr Tata. You have seen how I accomplished control over this gathering tonight. I want a third-share partnership in the venture."

Venkat Singh looked as if he were about to explode.

"I'll give you a partnership in hell!" he belligerently threatened.

Dehra showed not a vestige of fear, but continued calmly, "Be warned, gentlemen, I can turn people against you just as easily as I have them eating out of your hands now."

Suddenly Ravi Tata began to laugh and to Venkat's surprise capitulated, saying, "Very true, Anil. But let us not be enemies. I see that I have totally underestimated your worth to us. We will be very happy to have you as our partner."

Venkat Singh scowled and shook his head in disbelief.

"Come on, Venkat. Shake hands with the man," commanded Tata in an authoritative voice.

Sullenly Venkat stuck out a reluctant hand. Dehra smiled and took it.

"You will not be sorry, gentlemen. Together we shall make a lot of money out of tiger products."

Somewhere, below the fort and across the lake, a solitary tiger roared his defiance – almost on cue – as if he had been witness to these very words.

Chapter Seven

One Good Turn

Matt Barlow had a visitor. Across from him in his lounge was seated the police commissioner. An unusually chubby, rotund face was broken up by lively and intelligent eyes. When agitated, the DC would twiddle the ends of his grey walrus-like moustache or stroke his small pointed beard. Dressed in khaki shorts and tunic, he wore the insignia of rank on his shoulder epaulettes. Looking much older than his years, a mere forty-five, he answered to the name of Kepel Rao.

The two men had been on good terms for many years, but Barlow was uncomfortably aware of the purpose of this visit. Rao took a long pull on his pipe, followed by closer acquaintance with the brandy provided by Barlow.

"This is good cognac, Matt."

"Come now, Kepel. You didn't motor all the way out here to compliment me on my alcoholic preferences." The DC looked edgy.

"No, you're right. I didn't. There are three very urgent matters."

"Only three?' quipped Barlow, sarcastically. "Well I suppose that will do for starters."

Rao shuffled his feet uncomfortably, not sure where to begin. Then, after a moment's hesitation, he ploughed on.

"I gather you've been causing a rumpus over at Craig's. He's been in and filed a complaint against you for grievous bodily harm and to damage of his property."

"Has he now? Well, after what he tried to do to a friend of mine I reckon he got off lightly."

"You mean Rachana Dev?"

"Of course I do. And you should have received a statement from her – I know she made one at your office."

"Well, er... yes, she did, but you understand it cannot be taken very seriously, as she is not of a high enough caste."

Matt Barlow nearly choked on his cognac.

"God! You people make me sick with your so-called caste system. Does she not have the same rights as anyone else? Legally, I understand the caste system is finished. Try telling that to you Indians! Hell man! If you can't take Rachana's word, I'll give you a statement."

"Unfortunately, you were not present at the so-called incident. Mr Craig, like yourself, is a respected planter and Miss Dev is—"

"Is a woman in India and half-caste at that," snapped Barlow, finishing the sentence for him.

"There is no need to take that attitude, Matt. I want to help if I can."

"Sounds like it!" exclaimed Barlow, taking a large gulp of his brandy.

"Apart from the physical injuries to Mr Craig, it appears you blew up some valuable property with a petrol bomb."

"If you call a few empty wooden tea chests valuable then yes, I did. Total cost would be a pittance."

"He says there were over a hundred stacked there."

"Did he now. Then I expect he's right."

"You are not being very helpful Matt. Look, I know you and Craig have had this feud going for years. It would take a lot of pressure off my department if you cooled it."

"It's not me that's pressing charges. I've exacted my own brand of punishment on Craig and Brook."

"Yes, that's another thing. The foreman over there, Brook, he's disappeared completely."

"I'm not surprised, after what Craig tried to pin on him."

"What do you mean?"

Barlow related his version of the incident from start to finish. After the narrative was completed Rao said, "It might have helped if you had told me all this in the first place, Matt."

"Where do we go from here then?"

The DC looked thoughtful.

"Well, you have satisfied Miss Dev's honour, and luckily no real harm was done to her."

"Only thanks to Jana," exclaimed Barlow, patting the tigress' head as she lay curled up at his feet.

"Be that as it may, Matt, I think if you make good his tea chests, I can smooth things out this time."

"Very well, I'll send a cheque over by one of my men tomorrow, enough to cover the wholesale price of replacement but I warn you, Kepel, that's as far as I am going."

"An apology wouldn't come amiss."

"The hell I will. You tell Craig when he sends a written apology to Rachana, I just might think about it," snapped Barlow, glowering at the DC.

"I doubt he'll do that, Matt."

"Then he will need to wait a long time for an apology from me! Tell him not to hold his breath. You said three things had brought you here. What are the other two?"

"One of them you already know about. My department has sent you three letters on the subject – which I hasten to add, you've ignored!"

"You mean Jana?"

"Yes Matt, I mean the tigress."

"Good God, man, you can see she's harmless enough. Ask any of the natives on the plantation, they'll tell you."

"Watching her there, curled up at your feet, I find myself almost believing you."

"Then why don't you?"

"Because, Matt, she's a wild animal and cannot roam free unless she is within the confines of a national park or zoo."

"It would be totally cruel to pen her in. To survive in a national park she would have had to learn to hunt for her own game. Jana never has."

"A zoo, perhaps?" put in Rao hopefully.

"No way, Kepel."

"Good gracious, Matt, you are the most unreasonable man I know. You don't make my job any easier."

"Sorry about that!" said Barlow, his voice heavy with sarcasm.

Rao stroked his beard and fiddled with his moustache, deep in thought.

"I'll strike a bargain with you, Matt."

"Let's hear it."

"Well, I said three things, which now brings me to the third. The department needs your help again."

"What is it this time?"

"A tiger – man-eater – already chalked up twenty-eight killings and averaging one every week. Unusual pattern. Most tigers, as you well know, keep to a territorial zone, although that can be over a huge area."

"And this fellow doesn't?" put in Barlow.

"No. Started well south of Hyderabad, thought to have come off the Nagarjunasagar reserve originally – hence the forestry department have chosen to call him the 'Nagarjunasagar man-eater'."

"Where was his last kill?"

"Just north of Chik Ballapur. Took a lineman working on the railway there – carried him off still screaming, eye witnesses said. Little village called Megapur, about a week ago."

"Have the forestry people sent anyone out to get him?"

"Well, er... yes, they did actually." Rao looked decidedly uncomfortable.

"What happened, Kepel?' asked Barlow, the suspicious expression on his face doing nothing to ease the DC's discomfiture.

"Well, they sent out an army chap, crack shot I'm told. Sat up in a *machan*[1], close to the remains of the kill, waiting for the tiger to return the next night."

"And?" put in Barlow impatiently.

"Well, the tiger came back all right. Only it wasn't the remains he came for. The hunted became the hunter. He took the man and made off with him."

"Thought you said the man was holed up in a *machan*, up a tree?" questioned Barlow.

"So he was, but apparently it wasn't much more than a sapling. Don't ask me how, but somehow the tiger got wind of the man's presence, and—"

"And rushed the tree, knocking the fellow clean out of it," put in Barlow.

"How in blazes did you know that, Matt?"

Barlow, ignoring the question, went on.

"When will the forestry people ever learn? A man-eating tiger becomes diabolically cunning. He has to, if he is going to survive.

---

[1] *Machan* – a hastily built platform set up in a tree, for a hunter to lay up in wait for his prey.

To catch him, you have to think like him, and even then he can sometimes out-fox you. It's plain this poor devil was cannon-fodder."

"But he was a crack shot, Matt. Even won army competitions, apparently."

"Means nothing. That tiger would have sussed him out and known he was in that tree even before he suspected the animal was there."

The DC shuffled his feet, an embarrassed look on his face.

"Look, Matt, I won't beat about the bush. The forestry people have asked for you. Get Tiger Barlow, he's half tiger and thinks like one, were their exact words. He can do the job!"

Barlow looked angry.

"One minute you want to lock up Jana and take her away. Then in the next breath you want me to risk my neck going after a man-eater too tough for the forestry authorities! You really have got a nerve, Kepel."

"I did, er... speak about a deal."

"Yes, you did. What is it? Out with it, man!"

"Simple really. You go out against the man-eater and succeed and you can keep Jana here provided you cage her."

"No deal!" snapped Barlow. "Jana stays free!"

"Just a minute. I didn't mean you had to put her in the cage – only that you had to build one for her."

"What are you getting at Kepel, you artful old devil?"

"Just this. If any top brass come snooping around to check, I tip you off and you put Jana in the cage for their visit, otherwise keep her where you like."

"Done!" said Barlow, his face beaming. "You're not a bad scout after all."

"So how do you want to go about it – the man-eater, I mean?" enquired Rao.

"Well, if he's running true to form... Let's see, you said the last kill was about a week ago?"

"Correct."

"Megapur is about ninety kilometres away from here. A week's passed so the trail will be cold now," assessed Barlow. "Nothing for it but to wait for the next kill. From what you say, the tiger is moving south, so we can assume the next one is going to be even nearer to Bangalore."

"I can get you a full report from the forestry people setting out the locations of the attacks, if that will help."

"Yes, I'll need that as soon as possible. Sometimes a territorial tiger attacks in a huge roundabout circle, which brings him back to his starting point. With local knowledge, and a calculated guess, you can figure out his future movements. However, I don't think it's going to help with this tiger... sounds as if he's a one-off. Are there any descriptions, physical oddities, anything that may help?"

"Yes," replied Rao. "Big fellow, apparently estimated about five hundred and fifty pounds in weight. Runs lame on right front leg. Pug marks severely distorted on right front."

"I knew it! Every time we find a man-eater it's physical damage that turned him into one. The poor devil has no choice. I'll lay a pound to a rupee that some swine has wounded him so that he can no longer catch his natural prey," said Barlow, ruefully.

"That's as may be, but he has to be stopped. Twenty-eight people have suffered because of him."

"No, Kepel. I disagree. The real blame lies with the humans who won't leave the tigers alone in the first place. If you went out and met a normal tiger in the jungle, he'd give you a wide berth and make off."

Rao smiled. "You and your tigers, Matt. Maybe they are right. Perhaps you are half tiger."

"Grrr..." snarled Barlow, making his fists into claws and emitting an imitation snarl that awoke Jana. She looked up at him, putting her head on his knee.

"She understands you," laughed Rao. "Blessed if I do. All I can say is, don't waste too much sympathy on that man-eater, when you go after him."

Barlow, for once, looked deadly serious.

"In the jungle, Kepel, it's you or him. He knows it. I know it. That's all that matters."

The DC got up to leave, offering his hand.

"Well, good luck. I'll have the details you want faxed over to you this afternoon. Will that do?"

"That will be just fine," replied Barlow, escorting him to the door, Jana in his wake.

As Kepel Rao walked to his Land-Rover he gave an involuntary shudder. He asked himself how a man like Barlow could bring himself to go out after a man-eating tiger. Rao was no coward, but there wasn't a chance in hell of his even attempting to take such a risk.

He looked back and waved to Barlow standing on his veranda, the tigress by his side. 'What makes such a man tick?' he enquired of himself, shaking his head in quiet disbelief.

*

The next morning in Jaipur Carla Wayne was reading the *Hindustan Times,* a paper published in English. A small column on the front page nearly jumped out and hit her. Eminent Conservationist Murdered At Home were the headlines in bold black type.

Carla, seated on the edge of a lounge chair in the hotel, nearly fell off in her shock. In trepidation she read on. The article was short and had obviously been rushed to press to meet the paper's deadline.

> Mr Sonjay Patel, eminent and widely acclaimed conservationist, was found by his housekeeper yesterday evening, brutally murdered. Police are concerned that the knife used was reputed to be of the type employed by the worshippers of Kali. The cult was thought to have been extinct since the early years of this century. A spokesman for the police stated last night that it was too early to jump to any conclusions.
>
> 'Obviously we shall be making extensive enquiries,' he said.

The article went on to give details of Mr Patel's past history and achievements. Carla read on in shock and found that her hands were shaking when she replaced the newspaper on the coffee table.

"My God," she exclaimed, half under her breath. "I'm responsible for the poor man's death. They must have followed me to the Amber Fort yesterday and seen me talking to him." The impact of this conclusion hit her hard. "If they were watching me then, no doubt they are watching me now!"

Alarmed, she looked to left and right across the lounge, examining its occupants. It was 10 a.m. and several people were around. Most, she decided, were tourists, either couples or pairs. One man – an Indian – however, attracted her attention.

He was a swarthy-looking character, well-dressed in a well-cut linen suit. He certainly looked innocent enough, standing at the foot of the huge spiral staircase, reading a newspaper.

Carla decided that if anyone was spying on her, then this probably was the culprit. 'Only one way to find out,' she reflected. Leave the hotel and walk round for a bit see if this character followed.

She rose as nonchalantly as she could and briskly walked to the main foyer, leaving the hotel by the main entrance. Out of the corner of her eye, she tried to observe the man. As far as she could ascertain, he made no move to follow and appeared uninterested in her.

Maybe she had been wrong and he was just another guest from the hotel. Carla walked to the end of the building, then stood, trying to give the appearance of watching the hustle and bustle of the passers-by and general street scene. As far as she could make out, he hadn't emerged from the hotel.

She moved off, circumnavigating the hotel, keeping a wary eye on everything and everybody. As she worked her way towards Jaipur's main street hawkers descended on her, plying their wares.

Normally she would have taken them in her stride, but anything now that distracted her attention had to be bad news. She tried to ignore them, then, with horror, realised that one of them could just as easily be the murderer.

Trying to fight down the feeling of panic, she strode purposefully onward. Even more hawkers tugged at her arm, waving objects before her.

"You buy, memsahib... Very good quality... Yes?" whilst another propositioned with, "Special price, for beautiful ladee... velly cheep."

Carla pushed on through them and entered a small café. At least there, for a few minutes, she could escape, although hopeful faces on the pavement still watched her through the establishment's large windows. She ordered a coffee and took her time drinking it. To her relief, the hawkers gave up their scrutiny and moved off in search of other victims.

Silently, sipping her coffee, she took stock of the situation. Two men had already died, brutally murdered. Might they not have been still alive had it not been for her visit to India? It was plain that anybody helping her would be in like danger. Was she to be the next victim? Wouldn't it make sense to comply with the wishes of these Sons of Kali, whoever they were, and leave India? Then again, if she did that, they had won, and two good men would have died for nothing.

Carla resolved to stay and investigate further, but knew she would have to be extremely careful. She was aware that she needed to contact this man Barlow, in Bangalore, but it would have to wait until she could throw the assassins off the scent.

Suddenly, through the window, passing by on the pavement, she saw the swarthy Indian from the hotel. So he was following her, after all. Carla smiled to herself. Well, for the next two days she would lead him a merry dance! Time to be a normal tourist now!

She settled the tab and went back to the hotel. Picking up her camera, she returned to the streets of Jaipur. After photographing several local scenes, she set off on the Pink City Walk, taking a multitude of shots along the way. The stroll took her past all the best aspects of the walled city. It included the shopping bazaars and the city palace. Although the entire walk occupied slightly more than an hour, Carla filled up the rest of the time shopping until lunch, at which time she found a small restaurant for a light snack and a further coffee.

In the afternoon, she walked up to Kishanpol Bazaar and turned right into the Tripolia Bazaar. She saw the Nawab-Ki-Haveli, a merchant house and one of the finest in the city. At this point she caught another glimpse of the swarthy-looking Indian. He ducked into a doorway, but not quickly enough that Carla didn't notice. So he was staying with her and watching her every move. She smiled to herself. He wouldn't learn much today!

Past the merchant's house and a little further on to the left was a white tower. Here Carla stopped to take more photographs and caught another glimpse of the man.

This time he appeared to be buying something at one of the numerous stalls. Hurrying off, she found two gateways, both leading into the palace complex. The main gate, the Tripoloc Gate, was opened only for special ceremonies, so she entered by the smaller one. Proceeding onwards through the palace area, she left by the gate to the Siredeori Bazaar.

There, she turned right and found herself back at the Howa Mahal, or Palace of the Winds. After a further stop for more pictures, she went straight over at the crossroads and strolled down through the Johari Bazaar. It had a very broad street, but even this was jam-packed with people. Most of the shops here specialised in jewellery, and Carla found herself almost distracted in her resolve.

At the end of the street was the Sangarieri Gate, which led back through the city walls. Here she filled in some time in the museum before hiring a rickshaw to return to the hotel. She spent an uneventful evening in her room, and the following day – although frustrated by the loss of time – visited the zoo and bird garden in the morning and in the afternoon the Jantar Mantar, an astronomical observatory built in the eighteenth century.

During the day she had several sightings of the swarthy Indian, and thought that either he was getting careless or she was becoming more observant. In any event Carla decided he wouldn't have much to report. To all intents and purposes, she was an ordinary tourist.

The next morning she made a big show of ordering a taxi at the hotel main desk and having them book her into the Sheraton in Agra. This time Carla wanted to make sure everyone knew just where she was going. She behaved like a typical American tourist, attracting as much attention as she could. Desperate to get on with her investigation into the factory at Jaipur, she knew that the best way to allay suspicion was to vacate the city.

She dared not contact the man Barlow in Bangalore, much as she needed his help. The last thing she wanted on her hands was another death. Carry on like a tourist in Agra, she reasoned, for as long as it took, then *when* she had shaken off the shadow, get back to Jaipur once more.

*

Two days later Ravi Tata answered his telephone in Delhi. The voice at the other end began.

"Look, Mr Tata, are you sure about this American woman? I've followed her for the last four days, since she was seen talking to Patel."

"And?" put in Ravi Tata, impatiently.

"She just behaves like a normal tourist. Takes pictures of all the usual things. You know, palaces, monuments, bazaars – just about everything."

"Anything else?"

"Goes shopping like other tourists."

"Has she been in contact with anybody?"

"No. Nobody. Stays in her room at night."

"How about the phone? Has she made any calls?"

"No, not one."

"How can you be so sure?"

The voice at the other end of the line laughed.

"I bribed the telephonist at the hotel, so I would be informed if she did make any calls."

"Okay. Stay with it and we will see. If she starts nosing around, we will have to eliminate her."

"Yes, sir."

Ravi Tata slammed the phone down and turned to his mistress Deepta Sharma, stretched out on the ivory satin counterpane beside him.

"Now, where were we, Deepta?" he said, softly stroking her smooth and shapely naked thigh.

Chapter Eight
Alone in the Jungle

New York

In his penthouse suite office at *Liberty* magazine, Edwin Strobe stretched his bulky frame, seated in the swivel chair behind his leather-bound mahogany desk, fixing his piercing gaze on the other occupant of the room, Steve Berkeman, an ex-marine and now a private investigator.

"We go back a long way, Steve," he began.

Berkeman knew Strobe alluded to their days together in the marine commandos. He had been a young lieutenant and Strobe his commandant.

"Quite a lot of water gone under the bridge since those days, sir," Berkeman said, with a smile. "I must say I was surprised to get your call. How can I help?"

Edwin Strobe looked thoughtful.

"Do you know anything about India, Steve?"

"Can't say geography was my strongest subject," said Berkeman, a smile dimpling his chin and the corners of his mouth attractively. A man of average height, but powerfully built, he ran his fingers through wavy dark hair, and studied Strobe with intense dark brown eyes that made him look younger than his thirty-eight years. "Why?"

"I have a job for you if you want it," said Strobe, matter-of-factly.

"Well, I can't say work is exactly bursting at the seams at the moment. I could sure use some right now, sir."

"Very well. I'll fill you in with the details and you can decide whether you want it. It could be dangerous," Strobe added.

Berkeman's brown eyes lit up.

"We never exactly ran away from it in the old days, did we?"

"No, we didn't," replied Strobe, looking into an unseen and distant past somewhere in his nostalgic memories. He continued slowly. "A week ago I sent a young woman journalist – promising girl – Carla Wayne, to India, to investigate the tiger poaching thing. Nothing has been heard from her since."

"I wouldn't have thought that particularly remarkable in a country like India," put in Berkeman.

"Nor would I, but if you would let me finish," said Strobe pointedly.

"Sorry, I did rather butt in."

"Well, not only has nothing been heard from Miss Wayne, but her contact in Delhi was murdered the day after she arrived."

"Could have been a coincidence," said Berkeman, helpfully.

"Yes, but a couple of days later his best friend, another conservationist, was murdered in Jaipur."

"Sounds highly suspicious," agreed Berkeman.

"You haven't heard all of it, yet," exclaimed Strobe.

"Go on."

"It appears that both men were murdered using the same method. Stabbed with a particular knife – one used long ago by the Sons of Kali, a group of Thuggees."

"I've read about them, but surely they disappeared ages ago? They were the assassins of India, weren't they?"

"Correct, but apparently they seem to have been resurrected, by something or somebody."

"And you think your Miss Wayne must have found out something?"

"Yes, I have been in touch with the police there, and it appears that she discovered the body of the first victim, Nikhil Swarmy. She went to keep an appointment and found the body at his apartment."

Berkeman leaned forward, his interest showing.

"And nothing has been heard of her since?"

"Well, it appears she rang the police station at Delhi, to speak to an Inspector Srinath there, and left a message for him because he was not there."

"What was the message?"

"My, my, you are impatient, Steve. Kindly allow me to finish. It seems that she was going on to Jaipur, as she had received a threatening note from the Sons of Kali. We don't know if she ever reached Jaipur. Nothing has been heard of her since."

"Do we know what was in the note?"

"Apparently it ordered her to leave India, or else."

"But, for some reason, she decided to stay on and investigate. Wouldn't you have expected her to return to New York under the circumstances, sir?"

"Normally, yes, Steve. But I suspect I'm to blame for her staying on in India."

"How's that?"

"Well, I criticised her for lack of heart in her writing. Told her to go out and give me an article with feeling – something dynamic on tiger poaching. From what I know of the young lady in question, I think she is probably trying to do just that."

"But wouldn't she have tried to contact you?"

"I asked myself that. Then I thought what I would do under the circumstances, had I been in her place myself."

"And?"

"The least people who knew what I was up to the better. In India the very walls have eyes and ears. I think she'll lie low, then continue to probe."

"Then she could be in real danger," put in Berkeman. "It sounds as if these so-called Sons of Kali are the very people responsible for the tiger poaching."

"Exactly!" agreed Strobe. "So, therefore, Miss Wayne is in obvious danger and I want you to go out to India and find her. Persuade her to return to New York. I had no right to endanger her life."

Berkeman looked apprehensive.

"You realise that she may have already been killed herself? If she was getting too close to the truth for comfort, for some people."

"The thought had struck me, Steve, but I would prefer not to think about it. When can you leave?"

"Just as soon as you can arrange a visa for me, sir. My passport is valid."

"Good man! Be here tomorrow morning, packed, ready to go. I'll have all the paperwork attended to for you, and ready for immediate departure. Photography will do the necessary mug-shots before you leave, and you can sign the papers. We'll have someone run them post-haste down to the Indian Embassy."

The two men shook hands, and, as Berkeman reached the door, Strobe said, "Bring her out safely, Steve."

"If she's still alive sir, I will."

*

Inspector Srinath poked through the ashes of the night before's bonfire at Ranthambhore. Two of his men looked for clues in and around the deserted and ruined Moghul fort.

That morning he had received an urgent call in Delhi, informing him of strange goings-on in Ranthambhore's National Park. With his subordinates he had left at once. Now, an hour before sunset, after a long drive from Delhi, he was following up the reports.

One of the young officers stepped smartly up to Srinath.

"There is much blood, Inspector. Both on the ground here and in the fort, on the steps. A trail right up to the tower, in fact." Turning, the young policeman waved an arm towards the tower behind them.

Before Srinath could answer both men were interrupted by a loud shout from the third member of their party, poking about in the bonfire ashes.

"Come and look at this, sir!"

Both men joined him with alacrity, impressed by the urgency in his voice. Standing up, he extracted something from the ashes and handed it to Srinath.

"Looks like a bone. Is it human, sir?"

"Yes, it's a femur."

The blank expression denoted the young officer's lack of comprehension.

Srinath added, "A human thigh bone."

Putting the bone to one side, he concluded with, "Continue to sieve right through those ashes – with a fine-tooth comb if you have to. Miss nothing!"

Leaving his subordinates to continue their macabre search, he passed through an old stone buttress into the ruined Moghul fort. Several weeds had grown up between the crumbling walls and flagstones. The whole place had a distinctly uncared-for look about it.

The young constable had been right though. A regular trail of blood led across the raised stone section to the foot of the old stone stairs. Following it, Srinath found it continued on up, right to the top. There was an even greater concentration of blood staining the stone floor of the tower landing and on the masonry of the palisade.

Whoever had stood here, or had been carried, was surely losing one hell of a lot of blood. 'Must have been badly wounded,' ruminated Srinath.

After poking around for a while in the tower, he descended to the base of the crumbling stairway and worked his way systematically through the old fortress. Nothing more was revealed until he was about to exit through a battered archway. A dark object almost hidden in the recessed portals, or, more aptly, portico, took his attention. Removing the bundle, for such it was, he slowly unfurled it.

A curved knife clattered to the stone flags, narrowly missing Srinath's feet. He stooped and gingerly picked it up, giving a low whistle of astonishment. It was another of the ornamental dagger-type knives, with a curved handle, used in the last two killings. There were bloodstains on the tip. Pointedly, he examined it, then switched his attention to the material it had been concealed in. To his surprise, the wrapper revealed itself to be a long purple robe.

Carefully, taking care not to touch the handle of the knife, he rewrapped it in the garment, and went out from the fortress to rejoin his men. Dusk was approaching fast, as is the way in India. The shadows thrown by the old sandstone walls had lengthened since his entry and were now reaching out forebodingly towards the pile of ashes which had once been a bonfire.

As he approached, his men were still poking around in the embers. Srinath was startled to see that a small pile of bones had been collected and stacked. One of the young officers walked to meet him, and indicated the gruesome findings.

"Obviously we have another murder on our hands, sir," he exclaimed, solemnly. Ramon Srinath grimaced and disturbed the pile of bones gently with his foot. Then, crouching down, he examined them. There was a motley assortment, the source of some being obvious, others not so easily identified.

Finally, he stood up slowly and spoke to the younger man.

"Right, Girota, get all this stuff into the bags. We'll get it to the forensic people and see if they can at least tell us whether the victim was male or female, and possibly the age. I guess that's the best we can hope for from this little lot."

Girota looked questioningly at his superior.

"Did you find something, sir?" he said, eyeing the bundle under Srinath's arm. The inspector explained, and when he had finished, Girota asked, "Any ideas on what happened here last night, sir?"

"Unfortunately, yes," muttered Srinath, toying with the tip of the approaching shadow with the tip of his shoe on the earth's dusty surface. Girota remained silent, expectantly waiting for him to continue.

"The Sons of Kali have been resurrected and I strongly suspect that a human sacrifice took place here last night and, unless I am very much mistaken, these are the same people who murdered the conservationists, Swarmy and Patel."

Girota let out a low whistle. Darkness was fast dropping. Srinath nodded towards the other officer, who was still poking around in the ashes.

"Get Kumar and finish packing these remains. I don't think we are going to find any more clues tonight. The sooner we get this stuff back to Delhi and analysed, the better." Girota turned to obey, then stopped and half-turned to his superior.

"By the way, sir, any news of that American woman yet?"

Srinath looked very grave.

"No, not since she left Delhi, but I have a strong feeling that we had better locate her before these Sons of Kali do, or..." he left the sentence unfinished.

In the gathering dusk, he could dimly make out a herd of sambar down on the plains on the other side of the lake. Any other time, he ruminated, they would have made a serene and beautiful tapestry in the encroaching dusk of Ranthambhore National Park.

*

Matt Barlow didn't have long to wait.

In fact the news came through the next morning. The forest officer telephoned him direct. Apparently, the Nagarjunasagar man-eater had struck again.

His twenty-ninth victim, this time taken only fifty kilometres north of Bangalore, in a densely forested area. A young woman collecting honey had been carried off, having gone into the forest from a nearby village, Velanga, situated on the railway line.

Barlow's first question seemed harsh, under the circumstances.

"Did you locate the remains of the woman, and can you persuade the relatives to agree to leave them there?"

"Yes, to the first. No, to the second," replied the officer. "They have already removed them for cremation, or what's left of them," he added ruefully.

"Damn!" snapped an exasperated Barlow, then expanded on his remarks. "Look, I don't mean it, like it sounds. But the only hope we have of the man-eater returning was to leave the remains untouched. Now I'll have to tether a goat on the spot where the remains were and sit up tonight, and hope. I can understand how the relatives feel. Naturally, they want what's left of the poor soul returned. If only they could be made to understand that we need the tiger to return if I'm to stop him killing more of them."

"Sorry, old chap," came back the reply over the line. "Did my best, but they wouldn't budge. How soon can you get here?"

Barlow consulted his watch.

"I'll be with you by lunchtime. In the meantime, purchase a goat, preferably a noisy one."

"No can do, old man. You will have to do that yourself when you arrive. Against the rules to get involved in transactions of that kind."

Barlow sighed in exasperation, and bit his lip to avoid losing his temper. After counting to ten he said sarcastically, "Perhaps when I get there, it will not be against the rules to show me the spot where the killing was made, and the area where the remains were found!"

"Oh no, we can certainly have a man show you that," said the forest officer, totally missing the sarcasm in Barlow's voice.

"See you round lunchtime then," snapped Barlow, slamming down the receiver irritably. Damned officials! They wanted your help, but ask them for any co-operation and you could forget it.

He sent for his plantation foreman, Surendra Naqshband, and informed him that he would need to take charge for two or three days, and then he telephoned Rachana at her office to explain the situation. As usual, she tried to talk him out of it, but wasn't surprised when she failed.

"Nothing else I can do then," she said ruefully, "other than to say, for God's sake be careful, Matt." After replacing the receiver, Rachana said half aloud, "And he wonders why I won't marry him!"

"What was that?" said her startled assistant, looking up from her paper work.

"Oh, nothing important," replied Rachana.

Barlow hurriedly packed, sticking to essentials, but systematically going through his check-list. For good measure, he added the Holland & Holland rifle to his trusted Winchester 405 and a box of shells. Somehow, deep inside him, he had a bad feeling about this one, and he couldn't figure out why.

After stowing everything away in the utility, he drove down to the edge of the plantation to pick up Zabu, having already sent down a message to the tracker to ready himself for the forthcoming task.

The little man was already standing outside his domain when Barlow drove up, a huge toothy grin on his creased face.

"We go after another bad one, sahib?" he questioned.

"That's about the size of it, Zabu. Are you sure you're not too old for this sort of thing?"

"Me, sahib? Too old? Never! Me younger than springtime," he replied, happily climbing into the truck with his meagre belongings.

The ride was a long, arduous and bumpy one. Indian roads, never good, were at their worst after the recent monsoon season, little more than a dust-track, complete with potholes and ridges. It was already past midday when they arrived at Velanga, and Barlow lost no time in seeking out the forest officer on the outskirts of the village.

After the introductions and a quick cup of stale, stewy coffee, the FO handed them over to a skinny native dressed in a white dhoti – a *poojaree* or jungle man – a type of aboriginal, by the name of Sayara. It appeared that he lived rough in the jungle, virtually in a hollow known as a 'gavvie' dug into a river bank. Most of the time he was employed in grazing cattle for a mere pittance in rupees and his allowance of rice. The FO explained that no one knew the jungle better and that Sayara would take them to both the place of the tiger's attack, and where the remains had been found. The wizened little man nodded his agreement, and indicated for Barlow and Zabu to follow him.

After taking their leave of the forest officer, a typical old colonial type, with mutton chop sideburns and a walrus moustache, the visitors were led away by Sayara. Once outside, Barlow questioned him about the possible purchase of a goat. A long discourse took place in Hindi, the only language in which the *poojaree* could converse. Finally, it appeared that he did know of someone who would sell such an animal to them.

It was agreed that first Sayara would show them where the woman had been attacked and where her remains had been found, then leave them whilst he attempted to purchase the goat.

Slowly, in the steamy midday heat, the trio set off, following the course of the railway line, which in many places was no more than single track. They passed right through Velanga Railway Station, if such it could be called. It was little more than a couple of wooden huts, one the station master's domain and the other serving as a signal box. The platform was a few planks at ground level and most of these were splintered and cracked. An ancient water tower, on stilts, and also made of wood, stood at the end.

Soon even this was left behind, and the scenery changed to wilderness on one side and high grassy banks on the other. Beyond this on both sides was dense jungle.

Barlow kept a wary eye to left and right, his Winchester at the ready. He knew it was most unlikely that any tiger would be even about, let alone attack them in the heat of the day, but, when confronted with a man-eater, always expect the unexpected; something he had learnt from his father many years earlier.

Once the orchid grass to his right moved, but it turned out to be nothing more ferocious than a heron, which, startled, took flight. Its presence indicated to Barlow, the possibility of water nearby.

Sayara confirmed his suspicions. Apart from his Winchester and the small pack of essentials carried by Zabu, the three men travelled lightly. Time enough, if he decided to sit up and wait for the man-eater, to send back to the village for the rest of his supplies in the utility.

It must have been about three miles out from the station when Sayara motioned for them to leave the railway line and climb the grassy slope bordering it into the jungle. Even at this bright time of day, the interior looked dark and forbidding. Sayara led the procession with Zabu in the middle and Barlow bringing up the rear, his rifle in readiness. Should the man-eater still be in the area, it was the last man in the column who would always be at greatest risk from attack from behind.

Some hundred metres in, Sayara halted, and gestured with his hand to an area of flattened grass.

"This is the place," he exclaimed softly, in his Hindi tongue.

Zabu at once stepped forward and dropped to his knees, examining the terrain methodically. Both Barlow and the *poojaree* watched his antics intently. For a long while, he analysed the area thoroughly before trusting himself to speak.

"The *poojaree* is right, Barlow Sahib. This is the place where the bad one struck. See here, to our right, where the tiger dragged the woman through the elephant grass." He pointed out small droplets of blood on the grass stems. "See here," he said, "where the woman's feet trailed on the ground."

Barlow peered closer. There was no doubt that the little tracker was a master of his craft. Even Sayara looked impressed.

Without waiting for Sayara to lead off, Zabu moved out, following a trail only he could read. Barlow and Sayara followed in his wake. After a hundred metres further, he stopped again to examine the forest floor. Here the earth was soft and marshy. He pointed out the clear pug marks of the tiger and bent to examine them more closely.

After a while he announced, "This tiger is a very big one, sahib. See here, where his right forepaw is badly damaged."

Barlow peered forward for a closer look. Zabu was right. Almost half of one paw was missing from the pug marks made in the soft earth.

Barlow nodded. "It's the man-eater of Nagarjunasagar all right." Then, turning to Sayara he enquired, "How far away from here to where the remains were found, Sayara?"

"Not far, master," came the answer in Hindi.

Already, however, Zabu was off again, following the trail left by the killer.

The going was slow, through fairly dense undergrowth. Barlow kept the Winchester at the ready. In all probability, the man-eater could be lying low anywhere round here, in this sort of terrain, waiting to return to the supposed remains that night.

More likely, Barlow surmised, given the incredible cunning of a man-eater, the tiger would have already seen that the remains had been removed and left the area himself, for pastures new.

A further four hundred metres on, and Zabu crouched down in a patch of orchid grass, backed by thorn bushes.

"This is the place where the kill was eaten, Barlow Sahib," he softly murmured, indicating the flattened vegetation and dried blood, abundantly in evidence.

Although there was no need, Sayara confirmed the fact, a grim expression on his wizened face.

"The woman's remains were removed this morning, master," came the Hindi statement.

Barlow, already a jump ahead, was examining the surrounding area and didn't like what he saw. No suitable place existed in which to build a machan near the spot, and there certainly wouldn't be time to build a hide before dusk.

Assessing the situation, he despatched Sayara to purchase a goat.

"Preferably one that is young and bleats a lot," he instructed the *poojaree* and gave the man what he considered to be an adequate supply of rupees for the purpose.

Zabu was also sent back to bring further supplies from the utility, which had been left at Velanga village, plus the spare Holland & Holland rifle – Barlow being ever mindful of a gun jamming.

He looked at his watch. Three p.m. already. The earliest he could expect the two men back with his requirements would be another two hours, so he made a further study of the terrain. Near the spot where the remains had been found was only grass and thorn bush. The nearest large trees were too far back, and, anyway, even if a machan could have been set up in them, his view of the area would be obscured by thick thorn bushes and lantana with its motley coloured flowers.

Another option, of course, would be to dig a deep pit nearby and, after descending into it, have Zabu cover it with vines and foliage. A risky thing this, but something he had done successfully once before. The greatest danger was that if your first shot missed, or only wounded the beast, you were likely to have five hundred pounds of muscle and sinew landing on top of you. Not a very attractive thought.

In any case, on this occasion Barlow dismissed the thought as unworkable. By the time Zabu and Sayara returned, there wouldn't be enough daylight left to dig the pit and allow the two of them to vacate the area before sunset.

Reluctantly, Barlow knew there was only one option left to him. Have Sayara tie the goat to a stake, where the remains had been, and try to conceal himself in the orchid grass, some twenty metres away. He was well aware of the dangers such a plan presented.

He would have to lie facing the goat, to get his first shot in, and was only too aware that, should the man-eater get wind of him, his back would be totally unprotected. If the tiger circumnavigated the goat and came in from the other direction, there would be no warning. He would have but a split second to turn and fire. Once again, the hunter could easily become the hunted. Barlow didn't relish becoming victim number thirty, but could see no alternative to the plan.

Time dragged by, although he busied himself meticulously searching the area in ever-widening circles. Try as he might, no better solution presented itself. If he was to get a clear shot at the man-eater, should it return, Barlow realised that he would have to lie low in the grass, hardly daring to breathe. He was relieved when Zabu returned with his supplies and the spare rifle, but, as time wore on, he became more anxious as there was still no sign of Sayara and the goat.

In fact, it was only an hour before sunset when the little man arrived, leading a small white goat. He complained that he had been forced to pay 20 rupees more than Barlow had given him for its purchase. Although Barlow in no way believed him, he produced the difference, to Sayara's obvious delight.

A wooden stake was driven in to the ground and the goat tethered to it, right over the spot where the woman's remains had been. Whether the goat sensed anything or not, there was no means of telling, but it soon began to bleat at regular intervals.

Barlow consulted his watch again. In forty minutes it would be dark.

"Okay you two, get going. I want you well out of here before dusk. You can return for me an hour after dawn tomorrow morning."

Zabu begged to be allowed to remain, but Barlow wouldn't hear of it. Sayara, on the other hand, was only too eager to depart.

Barlow watched them leave through the forest glade and soon the pair had disappeared from his sight.

Once on his own, Barlow selected his station in the orchid grass and moved his equipment alongside. Carefully clamping torches to the underside of each rifle barrel, he again checked the magazines and took off both safety catches for instant readiness. A vital split second in time saved could mean the difference between life and death.

Then he prepared his water flask so that he wouldn't have to make a sound foraging for it. Next he covered his exposed skin with mosquito repellent. It would be a long night, and he knew from experience the trouble these pests could cause.

By the time all the preparations were made, dusk had begun to descend on the forest. An eerie quiet prevailed, broken only by the occasional bleating of the goat.

A sudden noise above him and to his rear made Barlow start, but he relaxed when realisation hit him. It was a large number of flying foxes, or fruit bats, taking wing from the tall trees on their nightly excursion.

By the time full darkness was with him, Barlow had assumed the prone position in the grass, facing in the direction of the goat. Unable to see him, and thinking it had been left, the poor animal began to bleat loudly.

Although the night was black as only jungle nights can be, Barlow could see a myriad of stars above. Fireflies danced and hovered in and around the trees. Somewhere a night bird called. The high-pitched note of an owl joined in. The evening pressed on. There was nothing for Barlow to do now but wait.

Chapter Nine

Return to Jaipur

Carla Wayne continued to act like just another tourist at Agra. She spent fully two days exploring the Taj Mahal and the Red Fort. Although altogether an uninspiring city, she found some of the buildings, the latter amongst them, truly magnificent. The romantic story involving the Taj Mahal's history would have been enchanting, if Carla hadn't been aware of her own reason for being there.

Even there, she found her eyes darting to left and right looking for possible danger. More than once, she found herself staring at some individual or another, suspiciously. Nagging doubts began to assail her. Maybe she should have cut and run back to New York? After all, better a live coward than a dead heroine! On the third day at Agra she tried to put her fears behind her and booked a trip on the Yamuna river. Coming back up the river at sunset, she found herself marvelling at the view of the Taj Mahal once more, as it seemed to change colour in the fading light.

That evening, back in her hotel room, she took stock of the situation. As far as she could tell, she had shaken off her pursuers. Time was slipping away and she wouldn't accomplish anything here at Agra. One more day acting the tourist, and she would leave late tomorrow night by public transport for Jaipur.

The fourth day dragged by in excited anticipation. She spent the morning seeing the Ram Bagh Gardens, which had been laid out by the Emperor Babus, in the sixteenth century. Once magnificent, but now shamefully neglected and overgrown, even the pavilions were broken and in ruins.

The afternoon she spent in her room, trying to read, but found it hard to concentrate. After dinner, she packed and waited for the hours to pass. At 10 p.m. she vacated her room and settled her account at the front desk.

Outside the hotel, Carla hailed a taxi and requested that she be taken to the bus station. The taxi driver looked more than somewhat amazed at the request, but shrugged his shoulders resignedly and complied.

When Carla extricated herself from the taxi at the terminal, she understood why. She wondered whether she could bring herself to go through with her intention of taking a local bus back to Jaipur.

Never had she seen such an assortment of broken-down buses packed to the roof with teeming masses of humanity. Forced to overcome her instant reaction of panic and revulsion, she enquired which broken-down wreck was journeying to Jaipur. The answer was no more pleasing than the question. A shabby looking official in a dirty white tunic, over equally scruffy looking baggy trousers, pointed out the coach in question. Carla made her way towards it in trepidation.

To her Western eyes it seemed a physical impossibility to cram another body on to it, but her enquiry prompted the driver to hold his hand out for the stated amount of rupees. Carla obliged, and grinning faces inside held out hospitable hands to pull her on board. She found herself squeezed and squashed down the central aisle, through the mass of bodies, until, to her amazement, a seat was actually vacated for her.

"Sit here, pretty lady," exclaimed a plump middle-aged gentleman, offering her his seat. Carla thanked him and sat down gratefully. If she had believed the bus to be full, she was mistaken. When it pulled out of the yard, ten minutes later, on the road, there were nearly as many people hanging off the back and sides, not to mention the roof.

Seated next to her was a fat lady dressed in a floral sari, fast asleep and snoring contentedly.

Carla winced and settled down for a long uncomfortable ride. The unpleasant aroma of so many bodies in close proximity made her feel quite nauseous. From her handbag she extracted some Opium perfume and sprayed it liberally on herself. She hoped to goodness that the porter had put her case in the hold, but resignedly she told herself that there wasn't anything she could do about it now.

The journey through the night from Agra to Jaipur was a long one, and at times quite hazardous. The standard of road surface, driving and overcrowding, together with ill-maintained vehicles, did little to improve things.

Several times along the way, the bus stopped either to let passengers off or take more on. Either way, it seemed to make little difference to the numbers carried. Carla found herself getting hotter and stickier by the minute. She resisted the impulse to scratch, but the more she thought about it the more she wanted to.

After what seemed an interminable time, the bus finally arrived at Jaipur, just after daybreak, and, to Carla's relief, began to empty. She waited for almost everyone to leave. Even the fat lady seated next to her roughly pushed by, squeezing rolls of fat between Carla and the next seat in her endeavours to leave the vehicle.

Carla was last off. Even at this time of the day, all was bustle and activity. Stalls were being set up for the day's trading. Carts drawn by camels and oxen came and went with their respective loads, even the odd elephant packed high with material or wood. Outside the Palace of the Winds, she hailed one of the numerous rickshaws whilst in the process of retrieving her case which, to her relief, had made the trip after all.

The coach driver hovered at her elbow expecting his tip. Carla dug in her handbag and obliged. He departed back to his bus, very happy with his 50 rupee note. She looked all round whilst the rickshaw owner deposited her case inside the contraption. This time she was sure that no one had followed her.

"Where to, memsahib?" enquired the young lad, indicating for her to join her case, under the canopied chamber.

Without any hesitation, Carla replied, "I need an inexpensive quiet guest house to stay. Can you recommend somewhere please?"

"You no want nice hotel? Very good, hotels in Jaipur."

"No thanks, just a nice clean quiet guest house." The lad shrugged his shoulders.

"Very well, memsahib. I know just the place. You like."

With Carla and her luggage ensconced in the rear section, he pedalled enthusiastically away, in and out of the traffic with wild abandon. Twice, Carla noticed they passed the same place. She smiled to herself. Why shouldn't rickshaw drivers be like cabbies the world over?

Finally, he braked to a halt at the kerb, pitching Carla nearly out of her bench seat.

"This it, memsahib, very cheap, very nice."

After paying the lad off, she stood on the pavement, taking stock of the area. It certainly didn't look very salubrious. A tall, once whitewashed building with more flaked off than on. Grubby blinds were drawn at the windows. A sign at the door said 'Vacancies'.

'Oh well,' resolved Carla, 'it would be as good a place to hide as anywhere else.' No one would think of her staying here. She knocked boldly at the discoloured, paint-chipped, red door.

It was opened by an elderly man with pince-nez spectacles, and grey hair protruding over his collar. He eyed her suspiciously over the rims of his specs.

"What are you selling? We don't want it," he began gruffly.

Carla cut in. "No. I'm not selling anything. I want a room, that's all."

"I see," said the man. "How much you pay?"

Taken aback, Carla replied, "Well, I'll tell you that when I've seen the room."

"Very well, come this way, laydee."

She followed him up rickety bare board stairs and heard their footsteps echo throughout the house. He stopped at a door marked with a number nine, which had come unscrewed, turned turtle, thus making it a six.

Turning the handle, he exposed the room to her anxious gaze. It was bare in the extreme, but at least the bed appeared to have clean linen. Carla crossed the boarded floor and turned back the bed. To her amazement, the sheets were spotlessly white.

"How much?" she enquired.

"Three hundred rupees per day, bed only, no food – food extra."

"I'll give you 200," said Carla boldly.

"Done!" said the fellow, polishing his glasses with his well-worn shirt cuff.

"Is there anywhere I can have a shower, and clean up?"

"I show you, laydee. It will cost extra 50 rupees, you understand?"

"I'll give you 25."

"Done!" agreed the man, replacing his specs, and eyeing Carla approvingly.

*

Carla had a plan germinating in her mind. Keeping a low profile all day, she stayed in her room reading, apart from a brief journey out for lunch, to both relieve the boredom and refurbish the inner woman. On her way back, she purchased some wrapped sandwiches and a bottle of water. At 4 p.m. she dressed in a dark T-shirt and jeans, and made her way on to the streets of Jaipur.

It took several enquiries and much foot-slogging to reach the factory designated as Patel's Canned Foods. From the outside, it looked about as scruffy as the street in which it was located. Waste paper and litter, old plastic bottles and cardboard boxes were scattered against the plaster walls and in the gutter and on the pavement. The surrounding aroma was none too pleasant either, quite nauseous in fact.

Carla walked nonchalantly by the wide-open corrugated iron doors. There appeared to be very little activity going on inside. She could see only one man with his back to her, stacking boxes. She strolled by, and turned right at the end of the building, which faced on to another equally dingy side street. A light breeze blew dust in her face and paper wrappers fluttered by, one sticking to her jeans. Whilst stopping to remove it, she took stock of the points of entry on that side. Two small windows, curiously barred, and an old wooden door painted a bright yellow contrasted strangely with the dour surroundings. It was closed.

Carla knew she would have to decide whether to come back later and force an entry after the business was closed for the day, or risk getting in now and finding somewhere to hide. She decided on the latter course. If someone did detect her, she would have to bluff it out, and say she was looking for someone, giving a fictitious name.

Consulting her watch, she found that it was already 5:15 p.m. Carla had no means of knowing at what time the factory would close. It was even possible that there might be all-night work, but the risk, she decided, was worth taking.

Making her mind up quickly, she retraced her steps round to the front of the building. The corrugated iron doors were still open. A few people were moving about in the street, but none appeared to be taking any notice of her. She hesitated in front of the doors and tried to appear to tie her shoelace. Whilst doing so, she faced inwards, peering into the darkened interior under long lashes. No movement there now. Even the man who had been stacking seemed to have departed the scene. Taking her courage in both hands, or rather feet, she walked boldly in through the doors.

'Brilliant,' she thought. 'Not a soul in sight,' although a lot of noise of machinery and voices could be heard from somewhere deeper within the building.

Carla looked round for somewhere to hide. Then, to her horror, she heard people talking and obviously coming nearer.

There was no time to lose. Hastily, without waiting for a better option, she squeezed between the wall and some packing cases, squatting down to avoid detection. Two men stopped, one leaning on the other side of the packing cases. Carla could actually feel the movement with her knee pressed against one of them.

Holding her breath, she listened. To her amazement, the men were talking in English. How she wished she could get a glimpse of their faces.

"I still don't see why we need to let him have them, Mr Tata," said one, obviously complaining about something or other.

"Be patient, Venkat. When the time is right for us to take over the operation I will let you know."

"I do not trust the Chinese," went on the first speaker, still complaining.

"Nor do I, but for the time being I intend to go along with him."

"Why?"

"Leave the thinking part to me, Venkat. We need to know all about his contacts. The operation is not going to be any use to us with nowhere to dispose of and sell the products."

"It seems to me I could easily obtain that information for you, if you left me alone for a while with the Chinaman," exclaimed the first speaker pointedly.

This was followed by laughter from the other man.

"No need for violence at this stage. We'll just string Soo along, until we get what we want, then you can have him, and we'll ship the whole set-up down to Craig in the south. From there we can run the whole thing. Not just a bit of the pie, Venkat, but all of it. No one will suspect a respected tea planter of being in the tiger parts business."

Carla, hidden behind the cases, couldn't believe her luck. Dame Fortune had certainly smiled on her. She filed away in her mind the names she had overheard: Venkat, Tata, Soo and Craig, a tea planter in the south. In her excitement and awkwardly confined position, her left foot came in contact with one of the boxes. It didn't make an obvious noise, but it was enough to alert the two men hidden from her view.

"What was that?" said a voice she recognised as belonging to the second speaker, Tata.

"I don't know, but I'll find out," said the first voice.

Blood turned to ice water in Carla's veins and her mouth went dry.

Desperately, her eyes darted everywhere, searching for a further place of concealment. In a half crouch, she willed her body into a tight recess between the cases. Holding her breath, she forced her body to almost conform to the cardboard surface of the containers. The man investigating the disturbance was coming ever nearer.

"Can't see anything yet," he called back to the other.

"Make sure," came back the reply from the other side.

An instant idea came into Carla's frantic mind. With her fingernails she made a scratching sound on the cardboard, then stopped abruptly.

"It's all right," called the man, who seemed to be within inches of her hiding place. "It's only another damn' rat, the place is alive with 'em."

She heard him retreating to join his compatriot, and felt the relief almost flood through her.

A moment later, and the two had departed through the large corrugated iron doors, their voices growing ever fainter. Carla settled down for an extended wait. For a long time only the sound of machinery, from an inner chamber, reached her cramped position.

Somewhere a bell rang and continued to ring. She looked at her watch. Six p.m. Could this be the signal for the place to close for the night? Even whilst this thought was penetrating Carla's mind, she heard an inner door open. Laughter and a babble of mixed voices approached. She realised it was a general exodus of the native work staff, leaving for their homes. Some forty or fifty of them funnelled through the space and left by the outer door. Finally, she heard the doors being locked and padlocked from the outside.

Carla waited a good ten minutes. The only sound she heard in that time was the obvious scuffles of a real rat somewhere quite near. She shuddered at the thought, but it made her mind up to vacate her hiding place and explore the factory.

On emerging, she saw some fairly rusty looking and antiquated machinery, which appeared not to have been used for years. Over on the other side were coils of ropes and sackcloth in untidy piles. A good deal of rubbish and litter covered the concrete floor. There were some oil drums against one wall and on these were stacked hundreds of tin cans, all plain with no labels. Nothing else of interest was contained there.

She tiptoed over to the inner door through which the workforce had exited, and placed her ear against it. No sound emerged. Holding her breath, she slowly turned the handle. It was not locked. Quietly she opened it, just enough to slip her slender frame through and close it behind her. Only a little light filtered in, through a skylight and two high-up small windows. Dusk was fast approaching and soon this would be gone, when darkness enveloped everything.

Carla dared not turn on any lights for fear of detection from outside, but she produced from her jeans pocket a small flat torch which she had thoughtfully brought with her. Guarding the beam carefully, she began to explore. There were rows of wooden benches. On many of them were pieces of antiquated machinery, similar to those in the outer chamber – the one difference being that these were well-oiled and obviously still worked.

At one end of the room was a large desk, where she assumed the overseer or foreman presided. She tried the drawers in the desk, but, although not locked, none of them produced anything of significance or interest.

On the benches were some tins, all screwed down. Luckily a screwdriver lay handy on one bench so she appropriated it and prised open one of the tins. Inside was a powder, ivory in colour and ground very finely. She put it to her nose and sniffed. Not much smell, only a faint mustiness about it. She replaced the lid and stuffed the small tin in her pocket. The bulge in her jeans was very conspicuous, but there was nothing she could do about that. At the last bench, she made the most startling find yet, a box of labels.

Carla foraged through them. Most were in Chinese and other languages she couldn't understand, but right underneath were some in English. A low whistle escaped her lips.

From the first to the last, they all described products made from the tiger – medicines claiming cures for a multitude of maladies, ranging from bronchitis to impotence. Carefully, she selected one of each, in the beam of the torch, and pocketed these also. Another door at the end took her attention. This time she was not so lucky and found it locked.

'Oh well,' thought Carla. 'In for a cent in for a dollar.' She went back to the bench and borrowed the screwdriver she had used to prise open the tin earlier. Fortunately, the door lock was a flimsy affair and snapped at the first attempt with her appropriated tool. The door swung open to reveal a wooden staircase. Having broken the lock, the door proved impossible to close behind her. Carla went back into the room with the benches and, picking up an oil can, jammed the door shut from the stair's side.

Then she tiptoed up the stairs to a small landing. On the left was a door with a glass panel in its upper half. To the right was another door. This time, it was a heavy steel one. Carla shone the torch through the glass-panelled door. It revealed a small office. Filing cabinets, desk, typewriter, papers and books. Again the screwdriver worked, although it broke off at the shaft this time. The door was pushed open to reveal a genuine Persian carpet on the floor.

In fact, a quick torchlight examination revealed even the desk and swivel chair to be of good quality. To her amazement, the drawers of the desk were not locked, until she reached the bottom one, which denied her entry.

Impatiently, Carla inserted a steel ruler she found on the desk, between the drawer and the frame, but, to her annoyance, it bent too much to have the desired effect. In one of the other drawers, she found a stapler and tried the robust handle of that. It worked. The woodwork creaked, then split noisily.

Feverishly, Carla rummaged through the contents. Stacks of papers, letters and invoices. Every minute she spent in the building increased the chances of her being discovered. However, she had come this far so there was no choice but to sit down at the desk and systematically go through the papers. She found a file of plain paper and appropriated a sheet, plus a biro from the desk.

Slowly, and with difficulty, in the narrow beam of the torch, she recorded names and addresses. Some of the letters even discussed prices for tiger carcasses.

It took her a full hour to complete the task, and three sheets of foolscap paper, by which time the torch battery was becoming quite weak. She still needed to check the room opposite the office, and no doubt one of the keys she had found in the top drawer would open the steel door.

Standing outside, she fumbled with the heavy brass ring, trying to select the right one from a numerous assortment of sizes and types. The mixed feelings of apprehension, claustrophobia and imminent danger were beginning to weigh heavily on Carla. She could hear her own heavy breathing.

The sixth key she tried turned the heavy mortice lock with a sharp click. Slowly, she pushed it open, and shone the failing torch inside. Gasping, she recoiled in terror. There, in the poor light of the torch, was a tiger staring straight at her. An instant cold blast of air hit her full in the face. Carla focused on the deadly fangs exposed in the open jaws, and waited for her end.

She jerked and fell backwards on to the landing, shut her eyes and waited for the inevitable. Seconds ticked by. There was no movement from within. It was becoming colder on the landing. Realisation struck her. It was a refrigerated room. Therefore, nobody, not even a tiger, could survive and be alive in it.

Confidence restored, she climbed to her feet and shone what was left of the torch beam in through the doorway. The tiger she had seen was still there. It was, in fact, no more than a skin, with the head still on, facing her. Behind it were others. Carcasses hung from hooks suspended from the ceiling like in a butcher's shop. Carla had seen enough. Feeling sick, she backed out and closed and locked the door behind her.

Now she had the information, what was she to do with it? Well, the first thing was to get safely out of there!

*

Steve Berkeman, from the moment he arrived in Delhi, began to try and discover the whereabouts of Carla Wayne. He had been given the first address in Delhi by Edwin Strobe, and started there, at the Surya. Yes, they confirmed, a Miss Carla Wayne, an American lady, had stayed there but had checked out some days ago, leaving no forwarding address.

The clerk remembered her well though. Very pretty, fair-haired lady, he confirmed. Just as Berkeman was turning to go, the clerk said, "I do remember, she asked for an outside line, to the police, earlier in the evening, if that's any help, sahib."

Berkeman slipped the clerk a $5 note.

"Do you remember the date?"

"No, but I can look it up on the computer. It will give us the date she vacated her room."

"Good man," said Berkeman, enthusiastically.

A minute's worth of button pressing and scrutinising by the clerk produced the date.

"Can you get me a line to the Delhi police?" prompted Berkeman, producing another $5 note, which the clerk hastily pocketed.

"Certainly, sahib."

Two minutes later, Berkeman found himself connected. Did they know anything about an American, a Miss Carla Wayne? he enquired. There was an immediate response, which surprised him.

"Yes, we wish to contact her ourselves, concerning a murder inquiry. Inspector Srinath is dealing with the case. I'll put you through."

A moment later, an enthusiastic Srinath came on the line.

"May I ask who you are?" he demanded.

Berkeman filled him in as to his identity and purpose for the call.

"Then I think you had better come in and we can compare notes," replied Srinath.

An hour later found the two men facing one another across a desk at Delhi's police station.

Srinath was speaking. He had already told Berkeman how he had come to meet Miss Wayne at the murdered Swarmy's apartment, and about the second murder, of a conservationist, Sonjay Patel.

"Of course, we don't know if Miss Wayne was in any way connected with this, but she was told to report in regularly, and we haven't heard anything further from her."

"Nothing at all?" put in Berkeman.

"Well, there was a call for me, saying she had received a threatening letter from the Sons of Kali, and was leaving Delhi immediately for Jaipur. The message went on to say she would contact me from there – only she never did."

"Do you think she is still alive?" Srinath looked pensive.

"I think, yes... but I also think she has been very frightened and has probably gone into hiding."

"What makes you come to that conclusion, Inspector?"

"Well, I think she knows about Patel's murder also. It's too much of a coincidence. We understand from our enquiries, Patel's housekeeper told us that he had an appointment to meet Miss Wayne at the Amber Fort, in Jaipur. A day later, he was dead."

"Might I ask who are these Sons of Kali you spoke about?"

"You may, Mr Berkeman. And if you had asked me one week ago, I would have told you that they had ceased to exist a century or so ago. It would now appear they have been resurrected by someone or something."

"Could it just be a bluff, do you think? I mean, a warning to frighten people off, including Miss Wayne?"

"I thought so too... until what happened the other night at Ranthambhore." Srinath went on to tell Berkeman of the events and discoveries there. At the conclusion of which the American said, "Well, I'd be best occupied, I guess, in trying to pick up Miss Wayne's trail in Jaipur, since that's the last place we know she was heading for."

Srinath looked firmly at him.

"I hope, Mr Berkeman, that you will keep me informed of anything you discover in Jaipur, regarding Miss Wayne's whereabouts. She was told to keep me posted and we view that very seriously, the fact that she has not done so."

"If she's still alive and I find her, I will certainly let you know, Inspector."

"Do that, Mr Berkeman."

Chapter Ten

Jungle Confrontation

Matt Barlow's joints ached abominably, stiff from the cramped position he was forced to adopt in the midst of the orchid grass. Any attempt to raise himself above the level of the vegetation would certainly betray his presence. Inwardly, he cursed his own foolhardiness in having taken up such a position.

The night was blacker than the ace of spades. Even the white goat, which had quietened down to an occasional solitary bleat, could hardly be made out in the all-engulfing blackness. It was but a blurred shape.

If the man-eater turned up now, Barlow knew that he could be in deadly peril. It would be lunacy to shoot at random. He must have a clear sight of his target when and if the tiger appeared. In the torchlight, he would only have a moment to locate the killer in the gloom in his rifle sight. Then, Barlow knew, he must squeeze off one telling shot.

A miss and the man-eater would be upon him. Even with all his experience, Barlow felt an icy chill round his heart. He tried to reason down the momentary feeling of panic. Maybe the moon would soon come up, but, glancing upwards, he could see that even the majority of stars had been blanked out by dark fluffy clouds.

Down in the valley an elephant trumpeted and the sound of breaking bamboo carried up to him. In some way, it seemed to restore his confidence. Fireflies danced amongst the branches of a large tamarind tree to his right, and Barlow wished that the tree was nearer. It would have made an excellent site for a machan to be erected, giving him some measure of safety.

A long way off, he heard the sound of a barking deer, and a nightjar, much nearer, joined in the nightly jungle chorus. Then, for a long time, all fell quiet again. Somewhere behind him, he heard a slithering sound in the grass and hoped it was nothing more venomous than a python looking for rodents. After a while, even that desisted.

Maybe it was all in vain. Maybe the tiger wouldn't come now that the body had been removed. Perhaps Rachana was right, and he should have stayed at home. Barlow became angry with his own doubts. Somebody had to keep up the good name of the tigers and dispose of the rotten apples in the barrel, which is how he saw the occasional man-eater.

The goat, bleating again, stirred him from his momentary musing. He could barely make out the blurred form in the all-enveloping darkness.

Then, quite suddenly, at about two o'clock in the morning, it began to happen! Down in the valley the alarm call of the sambar sounded. Some way off as yet, but, to Barlow's experienced ear, it was the clear sign that a tiger was on the move.

Steeling his nerves, he took a firmer grip on the Winchester. 'Of course', he told himself, 'it might not be the man-eater. Nothing to say it wasn't an ordinary tiger on his nightly hunt. Supposing he shot the wrong tiger? How could he ever be sure in this light – or lack of it?'

Forcing himself to keep calm, he awaited the next sign. He knew from long experience in the jungles of India that it would come from the langur, the long-tailed variety of monkey common to these parts.

Sure enough, he didn't have long to wait. A langur watchman set up his agitated warning that a tiger was coming. This alarm was picked up by another much nearer. There was no doubt about it, the tiger – man-eater or not – was approaching.

The hair at the back of Barlow's neck prickled in excited anticipation. Every nerve strained to fever pitch. He peered into the blackness, but could see only blurred shapes merging into an even more coal-black mass.

Yet another langur, within a stone's throw this time, took up the sentinel's role. Blast the night! The man-eater could be anywhere within thirty metres of him now and Barlow couldn't see a damn thing.

All went quiet again. Lying full length on the soft earth, he listened as he had never listened before. Not a sound! If the tiger was moving, why couldn't he hear him? Given the diabolical cunning of a man-eater, it was possible that the animal had already detected his presence. Barlow broke out in a cold sweat. Maybe the killer was already squirming its way towards him on its belly, never making a sound. He tried to console himself with the thought that an attacking tiger always gave a warning just before springing. Then, he recalled with horror, that most man-eaters were habitual cowards. Could it be that at this very moment the brute was preparing to launch itself at him from behind?

Ever so slowly he turned his head, but he couldn't see any better in that direction or any further than he could in front. He nearly jumped out of his skin when the goat, which had been quiet for some time, suddenly bleated. He could just make out the dim blurred shape of it, nervously shuffling around within the circle of its tethering rope.

Instinctively, he knew that the tiger was somewhere very near. His mouth felt dry. On a blind impulse he wanted to climb to his feet and yell a challenge. The tension of lying there, waiting, waiting and doing nothing was driving him nearly mad. 'Think like the tiger', he told himself. 'Be prepared, be cautious and be patient'.

The seconds ticked by, then turned into minutes. Still no attack on either the goat or himself. Barlow became aware that the tiger had sensed something was wrong, and it was probably circumnavigating the area now. Five minutes later, this deduction was proved correct when he heard a langur sentinel set up a din further behind his position.

As slowly and as quietly as he could, Barlow swivelled his prone body round to face the newly expected area of attack. He needn't have worried. Shortly afterwards he heard another langur much further away, then another. He felt both relief and annoyance as equal emotions. His jungle knowledge told him that he had indeed been right in assuming the tiger had suspected something and moved on. Barlow knew that it would still be madness to move from his position in the orchid grass before dawn, but he would have taken a bet that nothing else would happen that night. Even the goat appeared to have settled down and was no longer moving round restlessly.

Barlow risked a drink of water from his hip flask. The night was hot and humid and his throat dry. In spite of the anti-mosquito preparation he had rubbed on to all his exposed skin areas, one of the pests was buzzing round his head expectantly, looking for a meal.

Nothing to be done but put up with it. That the tiger would be hungry, having been done out of finishing the remains of the girl,

Barlow was sure. He half-blamed himself for what he knew would happen next. Somewhere, within the next day or two, the man-eater would kill again and the whole process would have to be repeated.

Maybe next time the relatives could be persuaded to leave the remains, although he doubted it very much. After all, he had to ask himself, how would he have felt if it was someone belonging to him? The answer was obvious. He wouldn't have allowed any of his relatives to be left out as bait for a man-eater either.

Then, he recalled with a cold feeling, he hadn't any relations. The only kin he had was Rachana, who wouldn't marry him, Jana the tigress – who the authorities wanted to take away – and his old friend and tracker, Zabu.

Since his father had died several years earlier Barlow had been a loner. At home on his tea plantation, and in the jungles. No wonder the natives believed him to be half tiger!

The night wore on. At one point the moon appeared. Barlow cursed his luck; if only it could have been a few hours earlier. He would have seen and got a clear shot at the killer.

The whole clearing took on a totally different aspect, basking in silvery moonlight, and a gentle cooling breeze gently wafted through the grass and trees. A jackal emerged from the bracken over to his left, sniffed around for a while and then disappeared into the lantana.

Eventually came the false dawn. The phenomenon that belonged to India. He had seen it so many times on escapades such as this one tonight. The night sky would lighten, then, just when you thought day was breaking, it got suddenly darker again.

Barlow knew that about an hour or so afterwards would come the real dawn. Patiently, he waited. There was just a slim chance that the tiger would return, but in his heart he knew it was but a forlorn hope, and so it proved.

The black of the night gave way to purple, then dark red, followed by orange. To the east, the rim of the sun began to appear in a semicircle above the distant hills. An hour later and its warmth was already on Barlow's back as it made its presence felt in the clearing. He breakfasted on some biscuits from his pack and a flask of hot coffee, now that he could actually sit up. The Winchester remained close to his right hand – just in case.

Two hours after sunrise Zabu and Sayara arrived, after trekking from the village of Velanga. Disappointment showed on their faces when they saw the goat happily chewing grass and no dead man-eater to gloat over.

Barlow told Zabu he was sure that the tiger had put in an appearance, but had kept a low profile, obviously suspecting a trap.

This was borne out by the little tracker, who studied the surrounding ground meticulously. Not fifteen yards from the rear of where Barlow had been lying, he found the tiger's pug marks.

"Look, Barlow Sahib," he cried excitedly, "It was the bad one." In a half-crouch on his haunches, the wizened little Zabu pointed out the telltale signs. "See, the right front paw is badly distorted."

Barlow felt a cold shudder go through him, as if someone were walking over his grave.

He realised with horror that his instinct had been right. The man-eater had detected his presence and had actually been crouching there, in the dark, watching him all the time. How long had he been there? Thank God the animal had been too cowardly to attack on this occasion. Five hundred pounds plus of bone, muscle and anger coming at him from that range, in the gloom wouldn't have given Barlow a chance to even raise his rifle, let alone get off a shot.

"Barlow nil – man-eater one," said Barlow ruefully.

Zabu and Sayara looked at him, incomprehension written on both their faces.

"Can you follow those tracks, Zabu? I'd like to finish the job before he kills again."

Zabu, in the process of studying the tiger's pug marks, looked up.

"It would be madness, sahib," put in Sayara before Zabu could respond.

Zabu glared at him coldly.

"It can be done, Barlow Sahib. Not easy, even for master tracker like me. The bad one has gone into deep jungle. If tiger stay in jungle, I can find; if hills beyond all rock, impossible."

Barlow nodded and silently weighed the possibilities. By now, the man-eater, having been cheated of his dinner, would be very hungry, but also, after being on the move all night, he would need to rest in the heat of the day.

Given the direction the pug marks showed, the animal was probably, by this time, in dense jungle. Beyond that, the hills, strewn with spear grass and boulders, would provide little sustenance to appease his hunger. Coming to a decision, Barlow addressed Sayara.

"If the tiger continues in that direction will he be near any villages?"

"Yes, sahib. He will pass Chellah, a small hamlet, a kilometre short of the hills."

"Then we won't waste time tracking him, Zabu," said Barlow, turning to the little tracker. "Given this brute's form, I think he'll go for a kill at Chellah tonight. How long will it take for us to reach it, Sayara?"

The little man screwed up his nose, a clear sign that he was thinking.

"The going will be hard, sahib. We will have to pass through very thick jungle. It will be very hot – and then there is the tiger. We could stumble upon him and be killed."

Barlow drew Zabu aside and whispered to him. "Somehow I don't think he's very keen to guide us." Zabu looked cynical.

"Offer him more money, Barlow Sahib. Tell him I will lead. He in middle – no danger – you will come last with gun. Only danger, yours."

Barlow put the idea to Sayara. Finally, after much haggling, a deal was struck.

Annoying though the waste of time was, first it was necessary to return to Velanga for supplies and to return the goat. Fresh water was a must for a day's trek in that heat and a supply of fruit, bread and biscuits would have to be purchased too.

By the time the three of them had returned to the site of last night's efforts, it was already nearly 10 a.m.

Already the sun was hot and they were relieved to reach the shadow of the bamboo and teak. The going was slow and arduous. Barlow began to wonder if Chellah could be reached before sunset.

Sayara called out repeated changes of direction, from his place of security in the centre of the column, to Zabu at its head.

Parakeets screamed noisily at the intruders from the tops of tall trees. Once a panther crossed their path, rapidly disappearing from view amongst bracken and fern, bordering the semblance of a track.

This was the jungle that Barlow had loved all his life. Here he could be at one with himself. Today, however, he must be ever-mindful of the possible presence of the man-eater. He knew it was a gamble to head for Chellah. True, the tiger could go off in any direction, but Barlow had tried to put himself in the man-eater's place.

Chellah seemed the most likely area to find the easiest of prey without risk. The hamlet would not be expecting him, so he would have the element of surprise on his side. He could make a kill and be away before any pursuit was possible.

The three men made a short stop for lunch under a giant banyan tree, its trunk almost as wide as a small house. Vines hung down from its massive branches.

In the afternoon it began to rain. A few big spots at first, then came the deluge. At first, the foliage kept the worst off them, but soon they became soaked with the water dropping off the trees. Centuries of peat and moss squelched noisily under their feet as they advanced. Progress became slower and it was already dusk when they emerged from the dense forest and arrived at Chellah.

It was clear that something was wrong – very wrong – for not a soul was in sight.

The little *poojaree*, Sayara, called loudly, but nobody emerged to greet the trio.

It was clear from noises within that the huts were occupied. Barlow hammered with the flat of his hand on a rickety wooden door. It was opened a chink only and a pair of dark brown eyes peered out at him.

It was plain that the occupant of the hut was terrified. Barlow explained who they were. The hut dweller, a thin emaciated little man, babbled in Hindi that they were too late. The man-eater, it appeared, had struck only ten minutes earlier, and carried off a young lad from the village.

Gradually, other inhabitants of the hamlet appeared on the street, drawing confidence from the sight of a white man with a rifle. Everyone was gabbling, trying to tell their own version of the tragedy. Given the fright they had received, Barlow found it quite understandable. Something like mass panic had occurred. Terrified, as one, the villagers had run and locked themselves into their frail huts.

Barlow raised his hand to stop the babble of voices. In the last few minutes dusk had transformed itself into night, as is the way in India. He turned to Zabu, speaking softly.

"The tiger is very hungry. He won't have gone far with his burden. It's my guess that he'll be eating for a long time tonight. Remember, he was cheated out of the remains from his last kill."

Zabu looked shocked.

"It is madness, Barlow Sahib. You cannot go after the bad one, into the jungle, in the dark."

"Agreed," replied Barlow, "But the moon might come up later, and, after the rain we've just had, it should be an easy thing for you to track him."

Sayara cut into the conversation.

"You are quite mad, master, to even think of tracking this tiger into the jungle, in the dark of night."

"Possibly so, Sayara, but if the moon comes up I intend to try. I've missed out on him once."

Zabu puffed up his scanty chest measurement to its full thirty inches.

"I shall be at your side, Barlow Sahib."

Sayara shook his head in disbelief.

"Never have I heard such foolishness! You will certainly end up dead."

"We do not expect you to risk your life, Sayara," said Barlow.

"It is as well, for I will not go," replied the little *poojaree* stubbornly.

'Nothing for it now', thought Barlow, 'but to wait and see whether the moon will put in an appearance during the coming night'. He was already very tired, having not slept for fully thirty-six hours, but knew that he might never have another chance as good as this one.

Zabu, seemingly reading his thoughts, said, "Get some sleep, Barlow Sahib. If the moon comes up I will waken you."

Barlow knew this reasoning made sense, and one of the villagers put a hut at his disposal. No sooner did he get his head down than he was gone. Used to catnapping, he could sleep anywhere. He was awakened by Zabu gently shaking his shoulder. Surely it was only a few minutes since he had drifted off.

"The moon is up, Barlow Sahib. Bright as day," he exclaimed, excitement in his voice.

Wide awake, Barlow pulled on his boots, a necessity in the jungle, made of sturdy leather to protect the wearer against possible venomous snakes.

Outside the hut, Barlow quickly threw off the effects of sleep. It was 11 p.m. Moonlight softly bathed the little village. Shafts of silver filtered through the surrounding trees and glinted on the leaves still moist, from the earlier rain.

In the soft earth Zabu had no problems picking up the tiger's spoor. Pug marks were clearly evident, and, as they progressed further, droplets of the victim's blood could be seen on bushes and bracken where the animal had forced his way through with his human burden.

Gripping the Winchester, Barlow kept close behind the little tracker. Every now and again, they would stop, stand and listen for fully a minute.

After approximately a kilometre of cautious steady progress, the trail brought them clear of the jungle. Ahead of them were the hills, barren and strewn with rocks interspersed with spear grass. The moon cast a silvery glow over everything from a cloudless sky, creating a false eerie illumination. Barlow was puzzled. Why had the man-eater broken cover, and why had he opted to drag his grisly cargo so far from where he had killed? Running between the hills and the jungle was a small nullah, or watercourse. Heavy puddles of water still hung about in the depressions from the day's rain, otherwise its pebbly bed was dry.

Zabu followed the tiger's trail quite easily along it for about two hundred metres. Neither man uttered a word for fear of alerting the killer. Both knew that he could be round any one of several bends in the dry wadi.

Zabu stopped and suddenly pointed to where one side of the bank had dropped away. He indicated pug marks in the soft earth. Here the tiger had clearly left the stream bed and dragged his kill up into the rocks.

Silently, they climbed the slippery banks. Once on the rim, both men stood and listened intently. A strange noise floated down to them from the rocks above. Then they heard the unmistakable sound of bones being crunched.

Barlow knew that the moment of reckoning had arrived. They had located their quarry. Silently he laid his index finger on Zabu's bony shoulder to attract his attention. When he had it, he indicated for the little tracker to change positions with him.

For the moment it appeared that the man-eater was too engrossed in his meal to be aware of their presence, or of any threat to him. Barlow knew this situation wouldn't last for long. For, although tigers have little or no sense of smell, there is nothing wrong with their hearing.

Taking stock of the terrain, Barlow saw now why the tiger had chosen it. Completely hidden from anyone from below, the animal was ensconced on a little rocky plateau. To even approach him, Barlow knew, he would have to scale some thirty metres of slippery rocks and grass, then risk an entry on to the tiger's horizontal nature-made platform, over a vertical rock formation. The much easier alternative was to go back into the wadi, move downstream and climb the rocks there. It would be much simpler then to descend on the tiger from above.

The risk here was not to oneself but Barlow knew that if he missed with his first shot, all the tiger would have to do would be to leap over the rocky parapet and escape downhill to the wadi, and thence into the jungle. Therefore, he decided on the former and more dangerous course of action. Indicating to Zabu to stay exactly where he was, he began to squirm forward on his belly, rifle held in front of him, upwards towards the parapet of rocks.

Zabu, watching him go, knew better than to argue. Silently he held his breath, crouched on the rim of the wadi.

Metre by metre, centimetre by centimetre, Barlow clawed his way upwards. Some five metres from the parapet's edge, he paused to listen. Suddenly, he became acutely aware that there was now no sound of cracking bones or of tearing flesh.

In fact, there was no sound at all. Barlow felt icily calm, at the realisation that the man-eater now knew of his presence. He knew as surely as if he could have seen the brute that its jaws would be drawn back over razor-sharp canines. The striped terror would be back on his haunches, ready to spring the instant he tried to navigate the rocks on to the plateau. If that happened, there wouldn't be a chance in hell to get in even a lucky shot before the tiger was upon him.

The seconds ticked by, seeming like minutes. Utter silence! Neither adversary moved or even breathed. Barlow abruptly decided on a bold plan. One thing was certain: although the tiger knew there was an intruder below him, he hadn't as yet seen what it was, any more than Barlow had seen him.

Once before it had worked with a man-eater!

Would it work now?

Barlow brought himself up into a position where he was kneeling on one leg with the other braced down the slope. He brought the rifle up in readiness. Then he threw back his head and gave an ear-splitting imitation roar of a tiger.

All hell broke loose immediately. A series of answering roars were hurled back at him from above, a blood-curdling noise rising to a crescendo. A moment later, the head and shoulders of the man-eater appeared over the parapet, blood dripping from his slavering jaws.

Barlow coolly took aim, but not a second too soon. Seeing that he only had a mere human to face, the man-eater came over the top, straight at him – five hundred plus pounds of furious anger crashing downhill. Barlow squeezed the trigger and felt the impact of the Winchester as the recoil bit into his shoulder. A second later he was sent flying, the Winchester spinning from his grasp, as the tiger cannoned into his left shoulder. Both man and beast tumbled down the slope separately.

Zabu, seeing what had happened, the rifle spinning from Barlow's hands, bravely drew the knife he always carried in his belt and rushed forward to Barlow's aid.

He need not have worried. By the time he had reached Barlow the tiger was in its last death throes, convulsing some ten metres away from where his master had come to rest.

Barlow scrambled to his feet, and rushed to reclaim his rifle which had fallen some distance away. By the time he had picked it up and levelled it at the man-eater, all movement had subsided. The tiger was quite dead. A closer examination showed that the bullet from the Winchester had entered through the mouth and gone clean through the top of the animal's head.

The man-eater of Nagarjunasagar was no more, but thirty people had been forced to die. An end, but for the greed of man, would never have been necessary if the tiger hand been left alone to hunt his normal prey in the first place.

A closer examination of the animal revealed the appalling injury to one of his front feet. The entire outer half was missing.

Zabu looked at him with something like hero worship, but, before the little man could say anything, Barlow said softly, "Well done, Zabu." Then, after a pause, he went on, "Go and fetch the people from the village. Tell them their villager has been avenged. The relatives will want to cremate what is left of the poor lad, up there in the rocks."

Zabu replied, "Yes, Barlow Sahib, but what about the tiger? Do you want me to skin him for you? Make very good trophy.'

Barlow snapped, and wished he hadn't. "No! When the villagers have seen the carcass, I want it burnt, so that nothing of it exists! Do you understand, Zabu?"

"It shall be as you wish, sahib," Zabu said, miserably. Barlow saw that it was plain the little tracker didn't understand.

"We don't want the tiger's carcass to reach the wrong hands," said Barlow, "and be sold for illegal medicines. It's better this way."

Chapter Eleven

Captured

Carla Wayne found that getting out of the factory was going to present a far greater problem than getting into it had been.

A closer inspection of all the ground floor windows showed them to be barred on her side. All exits at the same level were padlocked with heavy chains on the outer side, a fact she could verify by peering through the cracks of the badly fitting doors.

Carla forced back a feeling of panic. She would surely be found when the factory opened for business the next morning, unless she could think of something between then and now. Of course, she could hope to hide and evade discovery until all the workers were in and then slip out.

Grimly she realised that whoever was behind the murders of the two conservationists had a hand in the canning factory also. Therefore, if she should be caught with this evidence on her, her life wouldn't be worth a cent. No, somehow she must get out of there – and before morning. Carla remembered seeing a long wooden ladder, stacked lengthways along the wall in the room with the benches. Maybe it would reach up to the skylight.

An examination, even in this poor light, showed the ladder to be in pretty poor shape. Two or three rungs were missing and some of the others were cracked. The torch had failed completely now, and the only illumination was the moonlight filtering through the barred windows and down through the skylight. A quick calculation presented Carla with the question of whether the ladder would even reach. Only one way to find out. Try it!

She dragged the dusty old ladder out from the wall and cursed as a splinter of wood jabbed into her index finger. Luckily, the end was still exposed and she was able to extract it with the fingernails of her other hand.

The skylight was situated above a little square turret arrangement. If she could just get the top of the ladder to rest on that, maybe, just maybe, it would take her weight. This was one time when she was pleased she only weighed some one hundred and nineteen pounds.

It proved heavy work, manoeuvring the ladder into the necessary vertical position. Eventually, after several tries, she accomplished the task, but saw to her consternation that less than two centimetres overlapped the wooden base of the turret arrangement. Carla looked with apprehension at the state of the ladder, and at the height she would have to climb, some ten metres to the roof.

Even if the ladder held her and she could successfully negotiate the blank spaces between the rungs, would she be able to open the skylight? What if the ladder slipped off the turret? Carla shut her eyes and winced at the thought.

Gingerly, with trepidation, she began the climb. Every time she was forced to make the big stretch between rungs, she anxiously watched the ladder's grip on the turret above her. Trying to control her shaking limbs, after what seemed an eternity she reached the top.

Reaching above her, she pulled and twisted at the skylight's handle, trying not to look down at the factory floor, ten metres below her. She cursed again, under her breath. It was either locked or jammed solid. After several more attempts had failed, Carla realised that she would have to think of something else. With difficulty, she retraced her passage down the ladder, which, in the poor light, proved even more arduous. Back on the factory floor, she searched for a heavy object and eventually found a large wrench under a bench. Now she needed something to wrap around her hand and wrist. A further survey revealed a hessian sack, screwed up in one corner of the workshop. This would do for the purpose she had in mind.

She tucked the sack ends into her belted jeans, behind her, knowing that the climb would be hard enough, having to carry the wrench in one hand. That was an understatement! It took twice as long, in fact, before she was again back in position under the skylight.

First, pressing her body flat against the ladder, she tried hooking the wrench on to the handle of the glass frame. There was no response whatsoever. Carla prepared to play her last card.

She removed the sacking from her belt and wound it round her right hand and arm. The thought of what she was about to do terrified her, but the idea of being discovered here in the morning appealed even less. This way, there was a slight chance of escape.

Gripping the wrench strongly in the sack-protected hand, she brought it down level with her knee on the ladder. Then, looking down at the floor, she shut her eyes to protect them from falling glass. 'Now for it,' she thought. 'Let's hope the jolt doesn't dislodge the ladder's grip.'

Savagely, with all her strength, she brought the wrench up in an upper-cutting motion. There was a shattering sound as it came in contact with the glass. Fragments of glass showered down on her and continued on their way to trickle on to the floor far below.

Carla waited a few seconds, then, holding her head down as best she could, she shook her long blonde hair. More fragments descended to the ladder's base. Slowly, Carla looked up and saw with relief that most of the skylight had caved in. Some jagged edges of glass, however, remained all round the perimeter of the frame.

Carefully, using the wrench like a billiard cue, she systematically knocked them loose and sent them on their way to join their fellows. The next thing was to unravel the sacking from her wrist and arm and loop it over one side of the frame.

Already, Carla saw that she was bleeding from a cut on her left arm, but, as far as she could see in the moonlight, it was only superficial. The warm, balmy night air descending on to her, through the aperture, felt good and invigorating. Now came the most difficult part of the operation – climbing to the very pinnacle of the ladder, and pulling herself up through the turret on to the roof. Would the ladder stand the manoeuvre or would it slip away from its slim anchorage, and plunge her into space?

For fully two minutes, Carla pressed herself into the wooden ladder anxiously contemplating her final bid for freedom. After a desperate battle with her inner self, she knew that she had come this far and would have to try. Trying to dismiss the horrific thought that this could spell her end, she slowly edged up the last segments of the rungs.

Just as her fingers closed on one side of the frame, the downward pressure of even her slender weight, dislodged one side of the decrepit ladder. The other followed, an instant later, sending the thing crashing down to the floor.

Carla was left suspended, hanging for her life with one hand, legs flailing wildly in the air. Fear and desperation turned into a tremendous urge to survive. Her left hand sought the other side of the frame and somehow found it. With every last vestige of her strength, Carla pulled her face level with the top, and her knees made contact with the wooden sides of the supporting turret. She hung there for an instant, her legs taking some of the tremendous strain from her arms.

Slowly, by sheer determination born of necessity, she forced her shoulders above the rim of the skylight aperture. With one final massive push downwards, the top half of her body was clear. From this position, it was a relatively simple matter to squirm her way out on to the roof. For fully five minutes she lay flat on her stomach, taking long, deep breaths and shaking like a leaf. Then, as she began to recover her composure, Carla began to wonder if anyone had heard the commotion below. Both the splintering glass and falling ladder had, after all, made quite a din.

A cold realisation hit her. Even if no one came to investigate the noise, she wasn't out of the wood yet. True, she had escaped from the factory, but just how was she to get down from a roof some ten metres high? Looking round, she took stock of her surroundings. It was a completely flat, felt-covered roof, of rectangular shape. She tiptoed to one end. No chance there – not even a drainpipe. The other two sides revealed a like situation; in fact, one was worse, as it backed on to a higher building.

The fourth and last aspect proved more encouraging. Another single storey building adjoined the factory's structure. Its roof was some four metres below. By lowering herself over the edge feet first, Carla reasoned that she would only have to drop around two to two and a half metres. Luckily, she had trainers on, so it was feasible.

In fact, she was surprised by the ease with which she accomplished it.

Then it seemed as if Dame Fortune suddenly smiled on her. The new roof proved to have a steel ladder on its far end, going straight down to the ground. Carla lost no time in descending the black-painted fixture to the bottom. She found herself in a fenced yard. No lights shone from the windows of the building and it appeared deserted. The fence was only a low one and this she quite easily scaled.

Once on the other side she found, with relief, that she was in the same side street where she had entered the factory earlier that evening. A simple matter now, thought Carla, to return to her rented room.

Briskly, she set off in that direction. It was then that she had a premonition. All her life Carla had experienced these strange warnings when something was likely to go wrong. She felt it now, stronger than ever. Suddenly, she knew that she must conceal the evidence she had gleaned that evening – but where? If the Sons of Kali, whoever they were, found her with evidence, there was no way they were going to let her live. Her mind worked overtime. Already she had been told that the police were corrupt. For all she knew, these Sons of Kali had them in their pocket. Supposing, in her absence this evening, they had discovered where she was staying. No, surely that couldn't be possible. She was positive that she had shaken off her shadow. But what was it that everyone said – even the walls in India have eyes and ears!

Grave doubts began to assail her. Perhaps she should just cut her losses and head for the airport. Wire Edwin Strobe at *Liberty* to pick up the charges and fly home with what she had already. No! Just a minute! That wasn't possible. Jaipur had no international airport and it would be too risky to return to Delhi.

Surely she was panicking with no reason. Why not just return to her room for the night, then tomorrow book into an hotel, and fax this evidence to *Liberty* in New York? Again doubts assailed her. But where could she hide the evidence she had obtained?

Stepping hurriedly into a darkened doorway, she removed the tin of powdered bone from her jeans pocket and also the lists she had made and the assorted labels. An idea struck her. The labels all had adhesive backs. She parcelled up the small tin and the majority of labels inside the foolscap lists, with the plain side outwards. Then she used a couple of the labels to fasten the package. Next she searched the surrounding area with her eyes. A tree-lined area lay almost immediately opposite her, but, as in everywhere else in India, scores of recumbent sleeping forms occupied the grass underneath the trees. No chance there, she decided, not wishing to run the gauntlet of the sleeping natives.

She moved on.

When nearly back to her rented accommodation, the strange urge to hide her stolen evidence became overwhelming. A sudden idea struck her. Even at this late hour a little shabby shoe-menders' shop was still open. She went inside. A young man wearing a dirty white apron was knocking nails into the sole of a shoe on an old iron last. On seeing her, he came forward immediately to the counter at the front.

"I can be of service, yes, memsahib?" he politely enquired, his dark brown eyes lighting up at the view of an unexpected sale.

"Yes. I would like you to look after a package for me."

The young man's expression turned to one of surprise.

"I do not understand, memsahib."

Carla produced her makeshift small package.

"You see, it is only small, and I will collect it some time within the next two days."

He gazed at her with uncomprehending eyes before enquiring, "Why do you want to leave it here, memsahib?"

"It's a present and I don't want the person it's being given to—"

He interrupted with a smile. "Oh, I see, memsahib. Yes, I will keep it for you."

With her most engaging smile, Carla handed over a 500 rupee note. The young man grasped the money with alacrity and stuffed it into his shirt breast pocket under his apron. Then, with his other hand, he took the package and placed it on a shelf under the counter.

"Be sure, memsahib, I will guard it well."

Carla switched on another bewitching smile and replied, "When I do collect it, I shall give you another 500 rupees, if you have kept it safely."

"Very good, memsahib. I shall guard it like it was never guarded before, you can be sure."

With the young man obviously feeling as though it was his birthday, Carla left the little shop.

Five minutes later, she was admitted into her rented apartment at the front door by a new face, a shrivelled-up Chinese woman. The woman showed no emotion, didn't speak, but slammed the door shut and bolted it after letting her in. Then, turning her back, she walked off and disappeared down the corridor. Carla shrugged her shoulders and set off up the stairs to her room.

She put the key in the lock, turned it, and opened the door. The sight that met her eyes almost froze her to the spot.

Two dark-faced Indian men were already in the room. One of them sat on the bed facing the door, a pistol in his right hand pointed menacingly at Carla's head. The other occupant, she immediately recognised as her shadow of the past few days.

"Come in, Miss Wayne. Do join us, won't you?" the seated man with the gun said, in a voice heavy with mock politeness. Whilst Carla stood, undecided, the man who had been following her stepped forward and, grabbing her roughly by the arm, dragged her into the room. This accomplished, he savagely kicked the door shut.

The man seated on the bed was about forty, fairly muscular, and had a small black beard. A livid scar ran from the corner of his mouth to just under his left eye. He wore a sardonic smile, obviously enjoying Carla's discomfort.

"You have led us quite a dance, Miss Wayne," he stated matter-of-factly. Then, continuing, he said, "Where have you been tonight?"

"None of your business. What are you doing in my room? I'll call the police," snapped Carla, feigning a confidence she didn't feel.

"You, Miss Wayne, will call no one. You were warned by the Sons of Kali to vacate India and to return from whence you came. Why have you chosen to ignore this good advice?"

Carla continued with her bluff.

"I don't know what you are talking about! I have come to India to see the sights as a tourist. I don't know who you people think I am, but—"

A stinging slap across her face cut her short, delivered by the man who had shadowed her.

"You lie, American woman!" he snapped.

"Now, enough of that, Ranji. I'm sure Miss Wayne will tell us what we want to know without violence," the armed man said amicably, then switched his tone to one of menace: "Won't you, Miss Wayne?"

Carla tried to look impassive. Her cheek still stung from Ranji's open-handed slap.

"Search her, Ranji."

Carla backed towards the door defensively. Thank heavens she had unloaded the evidence of her night's work. She squirmed as

Ranji's thick podgy hands ran all over her body, lingering unnecessarily on her breasts through the thin cotton T-shirt.

"Turn out your pockets," he commanded.

The man on the bed jerked the gun, reinforcing Ranji's command. With nothing to do but comply, Carla obliged. All she carried was the now useless torch, some money, a credit card and a handkerchief. Both men looked disappointed at the revelation.

The man on the bed slowly got to his feet, walked over to her and, with a hand under her chin, forced her head painfully back against the door.

"You will regret not co-operating with us, young woman. We are now going to take you for a ride. Our Mr Tata will want to question you. If you want to continue breathing, I suggest you answer all his questions."

With her mouth clamped shut, and with the hand forcing her head back, Carla could offer no objection.

Chapter Twelve

A Lucky Break

Steve Berkeman, by systematically eliminating the Jaipur hotels, one by one, finally succeeded in tracing Carla Wayne as far as the Holiday Inn. He had no means of knowing that from there she had gone to Agra, and was now back in Jaipur once more.

At every turn, he had drawn a blank. All they could tell him at the Holiday Inn was that she had checked out late one evening and left no forwarding address. He had talked to taxi and bus drivers, but not one remembered anyone matching the photograph of Carla with which Edwin Strobe had supplied him.

To all intents and purposes, she had simply disappeared from the face of the earth. Nothing for it, thought Berkeman, but to fax Strobe, first thing tomorrow morning and inform him of his failure to come up with anything.

Then came one of those inexplicable twists of fate, which, looked at in retrospect, seemed to have a million to one odds of against.

It was late at night and Berkeman was returning in a taxi to his hotel. A stop at traffic lights found him idly studying faces on the pavements. His attention was drawn to an attractive blonde girl being half-dragged by two Indians on to the pavement from a doorway. The girl was struggling and obviously disturbed. He realised that the men were trying to manhandle the girl into a car parked at the kerb. She tried to cry out, but the burlier of the two men clamped a hand over her mouth.

Berkeman had seen enough. He called the cabbie to wait there and jumped from the back of the vehicle. By the time he had reached the trio, one of the men had opened the rear door of a large sedan. The woman was struggling violently, with a leg either side of the door frame, resisting all attempts to get her inside. Berkeman came up behind the burly Indian and tapped him on the shoulder. The fellow half-turned, still supporting the girl.

This wasn't a time for politeness. Before the Indian could take in the newcomer's identity, Berkeman crashed a well-timed right cross to the man's temple. A lesser man would have gone down, but this one only reeled against the car, yet was forced to release his captive.

Before he could recover, the ex-marine followed up with a swift kick to the man's groin. With a sound similar to that of a deflating balloon, the Indian sank to his knees, clutching at himself.

For an instant only, the woman stood rooted to the spot with surprise. Then she saw the other man drawing a pistol from his pocket as he attempted to climb out of the car's rear seat. She reacted instantly and slammed the vehicle's door, just as the fellow's gun hand was coming up to fire. He let out a howl of pain and the small automatic clattered into the gutter.

Like lightning, the blonde scooped it up and levelled it at its former owner, who, by this time, was moaning on the back seat. The burly Indian had lost all interest in events and was noisily spewing up on the pavement. The whole incident had taken only seconds.

"Quick, Miss! The taxi over there – run for it," urged her rescuer.

The girl needed no second bidding and sprinted for the taxi. Berkeman was only a few steps behind her. The cabbie had luckily responded and had the rear door open for them. Berkeman virtually bundled the girl inside and nearly landed on top of her in his haste to vacate the scene.

"Get going, driver!" he yelled, slamming the door violently. The old ambassador car roared off, the lights fortunately at green. The girl recovered her composure quickly and addressed the gentleman.

"I don't know who you are, Sir Galahad, but thanks a million, anyway."

"Glad to be of service, Lady in Distress, and all that. Let me introduce myself – Steve Berkeman's the name. Say, you sound American, Miss?"

"I am. Carla Wayne's my handle."

Berkeman looked as if he had seen a ghost.

Before he could recover from the shock Carla said, "Is something wrong?"

Berkeman gulped.

"Hell no. I can't believe my luck. I've been searching for you for the last week – and here you are, falling on me from heaven, so to speak. I was about to give up."

"More like hell," put in Carla emphatically. Then her expression changed to one of suspicion. "But I don't understand. Why would you be searching for me?" she said, waving the captured automatic about absent-mindedly.

"I think I'd better take care of this little piece," exclaimed Berkeman, gently relieving her of the gun. "Does the name Edwin Strobe mean anything to you?" he enquired.

"Yes, he's my boss at *Liberty*. Why?"

"Mr Strobe hired me to come out to India and find you. Said he would never have sent you, with these murderers about, had he known what was involved. I'm to escort you back to New York, ma'am, post-haste."

"Sorry, Mr Berkeman, but no dice. I've come this far, and I've got the evidence I need. I want to stay and see it through. Not that I'm not grateful to you for rescuing me from those two fiends."

Berkeman looked completely taken aback.

"You mean you are actually going to stay out here and complete your assignment?" he said incredulously.

"I guess so, Mr Berkeman."

He scratched his head in disbelief, then began.

"Surely you realise, ma'am, that but for my intervention, those two thugs would have taken you somewhere quiet and snuffed you out?"

"Please don't keep calling me ma'am, and yes I do realise that, Mr Berkeman. Look, you may not understand, but your opportune arrival was, I believe, fate. Now I just have to stay and see it through. By the way, my name is Carla."

Berkeman sat quietly in the back of the taxi, considering her point of view. Finally, he looked long and hard at her.

"Where will you go now? They will be bound to search for you."

Carla quietly considered the question before replying, "Look, Mr Berkeman, I couldn't leave India now even if I wanted to. My passport, clothes, money and credit cards were all left in that building. Somehow I don't think it would be very advisable for me to return and try to collect them. Do you?"

"I can't figure out why you were staying in such a dive," said Berkeman acidly.

"I stayed there because I guessed they would be looking in all the hotels for me, and probably covering the airports too."

A more sympathetic look appeared on his face.

"I'm sorry, Carla. I can see you didn't have much choice. So what are your plans now?"

"There's this guy in Bangalore I need to see. I guess it's not going to be any too healthy to stay in Jaipur for me anyway, so I'll leave first thing in the morning."

"Okay Carla. If you are staying in India, that means I'll tag along to help out. Mr Strobe would never forgive me if I didn't."

"You don't have to."

"I know I don't, but take it as read. Now, for the moment, I'd better take you back to my hotel for safe keeping." He glanced out of the taxi window. "We should be there in a few minutes, anyway. First thing you had better do when you get there is make a telephone call to cancel your credit cards. In the morning I suggest you report your passport as lost, or stolen, and contact the American Embassy for a temporary one. No doubt they can arrange for a money advance to tide you over. If you need clothes, I suggest you wait until we arrive in Bangalore rather than buying here and risking the shops."

"Good thinking," agreed Carla.

"When we get to the hotel, I think you had better fill me in with everything that has happened to you since arriving here."

An hour later, in Berkeman's hotel room, Carla had just finished bringing him up to date on her movements until their opportune meeting.

"Do you think we could risk going round in the morning to see if my things are still there?" she added.

"No way, Carla. They will expect that, and almost certainly be waiting for us. How about the police? You could always inform them. Perhaps they could visit the place and recover your stuff?"

"No. By now those ruffians will have appropriated it. Besides, everyone tells me the police are so corrupt here."

"So be it then," Berkeman replied. "Have you eaten?"

"Actually, I'm famished."

"Good. I'll send down to room service and order us a meal. Then I suggest you take the bed and I'll manage in the chair for one night. You look pretty done in."

Carla did not object.

*

The following morning, in the little shoe-makers' shop, where Carla had left the package for safe keeping, an argument was taking place. The young man's father had found the package, just as they were opening for the day's trading.

"What is this, my son?" he said, removing it from its hiding place and holding it aloft. His son looked embarrassed, but turned away and did not answer. The old man read the label and looked on his son with disgust.

"This is a potion made from the tiger. Do you not know, my son, this is an evil trade, second only to the supply of harmful drugs?"

The young man hastened to defend himself.

"It has nothing to do with me, Father. An American woman paid me money to leave it here."

"Who is this American woman?"

"I do not know. She will pay more money, when she calls here to collect it."

"It is not to my liking, my son. I do not like to see our Bengal tigers so used. Soon there will be no tigers left in the wilds of India."

"What then shall I do, Father?"

"Do! You will report the matter to the police, of course."

"But what of the money the woman has given me?"

"You will return it to her, when she calls to collect the package." The young man looked crestfallen. "Do you understand what I am saying to you?"

"Yes, Father. It shall be as you wish."

"It is for the best. Go and telephone the police, now."

The young man, head bowed, shuffled out to carry out his father's instructions.

*

Carla awoke that same morning with the sun streaming through the bedroom window. For a moment she had to recall where she was, and why she was lying fully clothed on top of the bed.

An instant later, memory came flooding back to her. She sat up and swung her legs over the side of the bed. Of Steve Berkeman there was no sign, but she spied a note on the coffee table and went over to read it.

> *Carla,*
> *Just nipped out for a stroll. Have ordered breakfast*
> *in the room for 9 a.m. Hope this is okay. I will be*
> *back in time for the meal. See you then.*
>
> *Steve*

The reality of her situation began to sink in. She must have been mad. She had spent a night in a strange hotel room, with a man she had only met an hour before, but then, he had risked his own life to save hers. In any case, what could she have done but trust him, under the circumstances? She had nowhere else to go.

In the event, he had acted the perfect gentleman, and even spent an uncomfortable night in a chair when he had obviously paid for a soft bed. Even now, he had been considerate in leaving her alone to bathe or whatever. Carla decided to make best use of the time and was thankful, for once, of the toiletries the hotel provided, even a hair-dryer.

By the time she had finished in the bathroom and once again dressed in the only clothes she had, she heard Steve re-enter the bedroom. He called out thoughtfully, "Okay it's only me."

After enjoying a hearty breakfast together, she requested an outside line and made the necessary calls to cancel her credit cards and request new ones. Then she telephoned the American Embassy in Delhi to put into motion her passport needs. The next call was to the American Express Office to obtain a monetary advance. Everything she had ordered, she asked to be sent direct to care of Bangalore main Post Office, as she had no fixed address in India.

Steve Berkeman raised an eyebrow when he heard this part of the telephone conversation.

"I can always pick it up from there when we go to see this Barlow chap in Bangalore."

"Is he expecting you then?" enquired Berkeman.

Carla laughed.

"No, as far as I know, he doesn't even have a notion that I exist."

"Maybe he will refuse to see you. After all you are something of a Jonah. The last two conservationists you had appointments to see met with sticky ends," he remarked ruefully.

"Well, I certainly couldn't blame him if he did," replied Carla. Rapidly, she changed the subject. "Look, do you mind lending me some money to pick up some clothes in the boutique downstairs? I saw one as we came in last night, and I've only got what I stand up in."

"Be my guest, Carla. I'll charge it to Edwin Strobe's bill," Berkeman joked. "Then I suggest we get moving, and out of Jaipur as soon as is humanly possible. I have already hired a self-drive vehicle to be delivered here at ten-thirty for us," he concluded.

"Gee, Mr Berkeman, what would I do without you?"

"I was beginning to wonder. However, you could start by calling me Steve," he laughed.

"Thanks Steve."

"Come on then, we should just have time to get you a few clothes for emergencies. You can always pick up some shopping in Bangalore."

Carla, still dressed in jeans and T-shirt, accompanied Berkeman downstairs.

*

At the little cobbler's shop the police had arrived, one nearing retirement, the other a young recruit. The older one was addressing the shopkeeper's son.

"You say an American woman left this package with you?"

"That is so, officer – a beautiful fair-haired lady. She was lovely," he said wistfully, gazing into space.

"Never mind that! Give the package to me at once, boy."

Reluctantly, he handed it over to the policeman, who commanded him to telephone them the moment the woman returned.

"She fits the description of a woman Inspector Ramon Srinath in Delhi is searching for. We will forward this package to him," he said, addressing the younger constable.

When their car had departed the kerbside, the cobbler father turned to his son.

"You see, my son, it is good to be honest."

"But, Father, I am 500 rupees the poorer." The old cobbler patted his son on the head.

"Riches are not always counted in rupees, my son."

As his father left for the living quarters, behind the tiny shop, the son muttered, 'No, I might have been lucky enough to have been given dollars next time. Now I have nothing, and will have to explain to the woman on her return.'

Some half an hour later a hire car, one of the numerous ambassadors, drew up at the kerb. The driver, a man, stayed in the car whilst the woman alighted and entered the shoemaker's shop. All this the young shopkeeper saw through his grimy window. It was the American woman of yesterday. He rushed into the back and hid, after calling for his father. When his father appeared down the rickety stairs, he whispered, "It is the American woman. Will you tell her please? I beseech you, Father."

For the second time the bell rang in the shop impatiently summoning service.

"No, my son, you must go forth and face the woman. It was your mistake to accept the package. Be sure to return this money to her."

The younger man reluctantly took the money from his father and advanced with some trepidation into the shop. It was the blonde American woman all right, only this time she was dressed in an Indian sari of striking royal blue, reaching down to her feet, with a gold sash over one shoulder.

He stammered an awe-struck greeting.

"G, G, Good m, morning, memsahib."

Again came that bewitching and engaging smile which made the young man's heart melt.

"Good morning. I left a package yesterday in your safe-keeping. Perhaps you—?"

Unable to stand the suspense any longer, he interrupted her, pushing the 500 rupee note towards her.

"My father, memsahib. He makes me give to police your package."

Carla's expression turned to one of dismay. The young man visibly shrank down inside his shirt collar.

"You mean the police already have it?" Carla said, consternation written all over her face.

"I am afraid that is the case, memsahib." He pushed the money into her hand and whispered, "Even now my father will be on the telephone. He will tell the police you are here now. Better you leave, fast, yes?"

Carla, numb with the news, closed her hand on the money and rushed out of the shop. Berkeman, in the car, had the door already open for her.

From the front bench in the little store, the young man spoke to an empty space, "Very sorry, memsahib, not my fault."

He watched through the window as the car sped away from the kerb, a hangdog expression on his young face.

Outside Jaipur Steve Berkeman brought the car to a halt, under a grove of neem trees. On the road a continuous stream of traffic continued to roar by. It had taken only seconds for Carla to acquaint him with what had transpired in the cobbler's shop.

He spread out on his lap a map of India. After studying it for fully five minutes in silence, as Carla stared numb and unseeing out of the window, he exclaimed, "Do you realise it's going to take us at least four to five days to reach Bangalore from here?"

"Surely we can reach the place quicker than that?" said Carla, coming alive once more after her disappointment of the lost package, evidence she had risked so much to obtain.

"No way," replied Berkeman, still studying the map. "Hang on, though, maybe if we could reach Bhopal by tonight we could dump the car and, providing they have an airport, get a plane to Bangalore."

"Bhopal! Isn't that the place where they had that terrible industrial disaster with chemical leakage some years ago?"

"Sure is, one and the same. It's probably our only chance though, going south, to speed things up."

"Then let's take it, Steve."

Folding the map, he smiled at her.

"That's my girl – Bhopal, here we come."

Chapter Thirteen

Elimination

The village, or more aptly the hamlet, of Chellah, was experiencing two emotions, with equal feelings of celebration and despair. On one hand the relatives of the lad whom the man-eater had carried off and almost totally eaten were huddled round a funeral pyre. Most of the men and all the women were sobbing and mournfully moaning, lamenting the demise of their loved one.

Barlow attended as a mark of respect and to pass on his condolences to the family. After a while, he began to feel an intruder in the family's grief, and went to the other end of the village where Zabu was supervising a bonfire of a different type.

On it was laid the dead man-eater. Flames were now licking round the carcass and reaching high above it. Round the bonfire danced and chanted the happy villagers.

As soon as Barlow was seen to be approaching from between the trees, a loud cheering broke out. He felt strangely disloyal at having left the other family to their grief, but knew that there was little he could do to ease their suffering. Simple folk, hard-working and poor, who had lost a young member of their family for no good reason. At least no good reason other than man's greed. For that is what had turned this tiger into a man-eater.

Barlow watched the flames gradually destroying the body of the tiger, and felt neither vengeance nor animosity. In the beast's eyes, eating prey was done in order to survive. Man had been the only prey left standing between him and death. Barlow bunched his fists in a tight ball. If only these damn poachers, and the purveyors of animal so-called medicines could be stopped!

He was suddenly aware of Zabu at his side. Although the little tracker had enjoyed basking in the adulation of the villagers for his part in the killing of the man-eater, Barlow sensed that he was still sorely troubled.

"Come on, Zabu. Out with it. What's upset you?"

Zabu shuffled his feet and looked downwards at his toes, wriggling in the soft earth.

"Why Barlow Sahib? If you did not want this tiger for a trophy, like other hunters, why did you not give it to the family whose son it killed?"

Barlow understood the little man's feelings and tried to think how he could best explain to him, but before he could begin Zabu continued, "The family could have sold the skin, Barlow Sahib. It would have helped in some way – to pay for the son, that the tiger killed." Barlow placed a hand on the little man's shoulder and slowly tried to explain.

"Exactly, Zabu. Well-meaning though the poor parents are, they would have sold the skin for a pittance. Somebody, the person or persons who bought it, would have sold it on. In the end the whole carcass would have ended up – skin, bones, whiskers, et cetera – in little pots – sold at exorbitant prices to the Chinese, Vietnamese or whoever. No! Better it ends this way! At least it's a dignified end for a once gallant animal."

Zabu made as if to protest, but Barlow raised a finger to his lips and went on.

"That tiger wasn't always a man-eater. Remember what a man-made trap did to his front paw, Zabu. The only prey left to the man-eater for survival was man. The only creature that couldn't run faster than a wounded tiger."

Zabu looked at his master in wonderment.

"Sometimes, Barlow Sahib, I think it is true what people say about you. Half tiger yourself."

Zabu walked away, shaking his head and still not comprehending Barlow's reasoning. Barlow watched him in the glow of the firelight. How could he ever make people understand in India, if even his own beloved little tracker couldn't grasp it? A man born and bred in the jungle!

With a long sigh, Barlow turned on his heel and made his way slowly back to the hut which had been put at his disposal. After a good sleep, he must get back to his plantation in Bangalore.

First, though, he withdrew some banknotes from the inner pocket of his shirt. It wouldn't compensate the family for the loss of their lad, but at least it would make up for not letting them have the dead tiger to sell on. Before he left Chellah, he would have Zabu give it to them.

*

Meanwhile three men were seated in Feu Chon Soo's Jaipur office. Ravi Tata was berating the Chinaman for the break-in, whilst the menacing figure of Venkat Singh expressed clear malice in his watchful scrutiny of the little oriental.

"How could you have been so careless not to have employed a night-watchman, Soo?"

Feu Chon Soo shifted uncomfortably in his chair, and felt glad of the desk between them. "It costs money to pay such people."

"Bah! You make me sick! Never have I met such a mean individual. A watchman would have cost you a mere pittance."

Soo gave an embarrassed cough and failed to meet either of the two Indians' eyes.

"The robbers appear to have failed anyway. All the tiger carcasses are intact and unharmed," he said defensively.

Venkat stood up, placed his large hands on the edge of the desk, the scar standing out vividly on his threatening countenance. He spoke pointedly and slowly.

"Neither Mr Tata nor myself believe the motive was robbery. We think the raid was to obtain evidence against you, Chinaman."

Soo made as if to speak, but the dark menacing face before him induced him to remain silent.

Venkat continued.

"In fact, due to our – *thoroughness*," he accentuated the word, "we are sure that your raider last night was the American woman journalist. In fact, we apprehended her for our own interrogation."

"Ah, so you have her?" said a relieved Feu Chon Soo. It was Venkat's turn to look embarrassed.

"Well er, no. Not exactly. We lost her again."

Soo jumped to his feet and pointed a bony finger at the burly Indian.

142

"What do you mean – you lost her?" He fired the question like a bullet from a gun.

Ravi Tata intervened. "Now, calm down, both of you, and let us ascertain what damage has been done to our Organisation."

"How did you lose her? I want to know," demanded Soo.

Venkat replied, "It was an interfering passer-by who grabbed her from our clutches."

"And you call *me* incompetent? Who was this passer-by?" shrilled Soo, in a high piping voice.

In a soft authoritative voice Ravi Tata answered.

"We do not, as yet, know. However, soon that will be rectified. Shall I say our enquiries will be extensive. I do not accept that the man arrived by luck. He is obviously connected in some way with the girl." Before Soo could comment, Tata swung into the attack. "Now, Soo, you say nothing was taken. Was anything disturbed?"

"Some locks were broken on my desk, some door locks also, and yes, a skylight."

"But you are sure that nothing was taken, Soo?" said Tata, leaning forward expectantly.

"I do not think so."

"Very well. Venkat and I will leave you now, and I would urge you to be more careful in future." With this, Ravi Tata rose from his chair and, followed by his henchman Singh, walked briskly out without waiting for a reply.

As they drove away from the factory in a richly upholstered black sedan, Venkat, who had fought to restrain himself, could hide his impatience no longer.

"I cannot believe, Mr Tata, that you are going to let that Chinaman get away with it."

Ravi Tata chuckled softly as if to himself.

"Curb your temper, Venkat. I do not intend to put up with Soo a moment longer. He has served his purpose. It is time now for us to take over the entire Organisation."

Venkat's evil grin of satisfaction twisted the scar at the corner of his cruel mouth. There was no need for him to speak, his expression betraying his delight.

Ravi Tata continued, "Listen well, Venkat. Tonight you will take two lorries and raid Soo's factory. You will remove all the tiger carcasses and all the records in his office. When this has been accomplished – and only then – burn the factory to the ground."

Venkat's ear-to-ear grin disappeared momentarily, to ask a question.

"What of Soo himself?"

Ravi Tata replied, "He has served his purpose. You will go to the address I will give you and eliminate him." Venkat rubbed his hands together.

"It will give me much pleasure to ring his scrawny neck."

"No, Venkat! You will effect his end in the traditional manner."

"And the merchandise, Mr Tata? Where shall we take that?"

"We will transfer the whole operation to Craig's place in the south at Bangalore."

"But it will take all of four, possibly five, days to drive that far south," protested Venkat.

"So?"

"I only thought—"

"Leave the thinking to me, Venkat, and we shall do very well."

"It shall be as you wish, Mr Tata."

*

It was midday and very hot and sultry when Carla Wayne and Steve Berkeman drew up outside Barlow's house, on his tea plantation at Bangalore.

They had been fortunate in picking up a domestic flight from Bhopal to Bangalore. At the arrival airport, Berkeman had suggested that they hire a self-drive car, as it would be harder to trace than a taxi.

"The fewer people that know we are here, the better for everyone," he had said.

The drive out to Barlow's plantation had taken a good hour from the airport. All seemed quiet in the house, although plenty of activity appeared to be happening in the fields where a workforce of natives were going about their business.

Carla was about to open the door of the vehicle when, to her astonishment and terror, a full-grown tigress came bounding down the veranda steps towards them. Rapidly, Carla slammed the door shut again and grabbed at Berkeman's arm.

"Keep calm," he said, with a conviction he didn't feel.

By this time the tigress had bounded over to the vehicle and was staring in at the two occupants through the front windows.

"Don't move and keep quite still," hissed Berkeman to Carla.

"I wasn't planning on getting out," said Carla, trying to lighten the moment.

The tigress, however, showed no animosity, but merely stood watching them, almost as if she were assessing them in some way. A minute passed, in which time she transferred her presence to the other side of the car, where she then began to inspect the driver, Berkeman, in like manner.

Carla and Steve had little option but to remain where they were, their eyes fixed on the tigress. For this reason, neither noticed an attractive dark girl, in a red dress, appear on the veranda. It was only when she loudly called, "Jana!" that they became aware of her presence. The tigress, however, instantly responded and trotted off like a domestic cat to join her.

"Okay!" the girl called out to them. "You can get out. Jana won't hurt you."

Somewhat cautiously, the two of them left the vehicle and approached the girl on the veranda. Deciding that discretion was the better part of valour, they stood at the foot of the wooden steps.

"Can I help?" the girl called to them, one hand resting lightly on the tigress's shoulders.

"We were looking for Mr Matthew Barlow," called out Carla.

"Then you have come to the right place, but I'm afraid he's not here at the moment," replied the girl, who Carla could now see was very beautiful and probably, she thought, Anglo-Indian.

"Can I help?"

"Do you know when he will be back?" enquired Carla.

The girl shrugged her shoulders.

"Who knows with Matt? Could be today. Could be tomorrow. Maybe next week."

"Er, are you Mrs Barlow?" asked Berkeman, a trifle uncertain as to the next step.

The girl smiled and replied in a voice which was almost music to Berkeman's ears, so clear of timbre was the tone.

"No, I'm just a friend of Matt's. I look after the place in his absence. Might I enquire your names?"

Carla introduced them both and explained the purpose of their visit. The girl listened intently and then invited them in.

"I am sure if Matt were here he would want to help you. He is bitterly opposed to the slaughter of tigers. Why don't you come in and have a drink and tell me a little more about it?"

Both Carla and Berkeman looked a trifle uncertain, keeping a wary eye on Jana, unsure of their next move. Again, the tinkling musical laughter came from the hostess.

"Oh, don't mind Jana. She's Matt's pet really. Quite harmless – providing you both behave yourselves," she added archly, stepping back and opening the door for them.

A little later over drinks, when both parties had sounded one another out, so to speak, Rachana decided it would do no harm to explain the reason for Matt's absence. Carla and Steve listened almost open-mouthed. When the narrative was complete, Berkeman questioned her.

"Forgive me if I misunderstand you, ma'am, but I thought you said this guy was into conservation. Now you say he went to shoot a tiger."

"Obviously I didn't explain very well then," said Rachana. "Sometimes he is called in to deal with a tiger that turns into a man-eater and terrorises the villagers. Matt himself would define that as dealing with the rotten apple in the barrel. Protecting the good name of tigers, he says."

"I think I can understand that," said Carla.

"Damned if I can," put in Berkeman, who seemed to be more interested in Rachana's shapely crossed legs.

Jana was rubbing her head affectionately on Carla's arm as it rested on the arm of the leather chair.

"She seems to have taken to you anyway, Miss Wayne," said Rachana with a smile. Then, making her mind up, she invited the pair to stay for lunch. "It's only a salad, but you're both very welcome."

"Well, if it's not going to put you to any bother Miss... er..." said Carla.

"Miss Dev – but call me Rachana, everyone else does. I'd be happy to have some company. It gets quite lonely here with Matt away."

Steve Berkeman chipped in.

"A man would have to be a fool to leave a woman like you alone."

Rachana smiled, but Carla gave him a glare of disapproval. "Matt Barlow sounds anything but a fool to me. In fact, a very brave man to face dangers he doesn't have to."

An interesting afternoon was spent by the three of them, exchanging stories. Carla couldn't help noticing Steve's blatant attempts to flatter and curry favour with Rachana at every opportunity. Strangely enough, it wasn't jealousy that Carla felt, only annoyance that he seemed to be taking advantage of the man Barlow's absence.

Rachana, however, seemed quite taken with him and was obviously enjoying the flattery. Jana, on the other hand, seemed to have taken a dislike to him and actually snarled at him once, whilst never leaving Carla's side.

At about 6 p.m. Carla stood up and exclaimed, "Well, it doesn't look as if Mr Barlow will be back today, so we had better leave and find an hotel in Bangalore for the night. You have been very kind to entertain us, but we mustn't put you to any further trouble."

"Not a bit of it," replied Rachana. "We can put you up here. There's plenty of room in this great house."

"Oh, we wouldn't dream of putting you to that trouble," said Carla.

"Why not?" exclaimed Berkeman. "If Rachana's offering, I think we should accept. I mean, whilst we are waiting for Barlow..." The sentence trailed off.

"That's settled then. I'll show you to your room," said Rachana, with a smile.

Carla noticed the singular use of the word room and interjected quickly.

"No, you don't understand, Rachana. Mr Berkeman and I are not married."

Rachana smiled.

"Neither are Matt and I."

Carla decided to be blunt. "I mean," she said emphatically, "we are not an item."

"Oh, I see. Never mind, we have plenty of rooms. Come this way."

Rachana, taking her by the arm, led her away, Jana following in their wake.

Steve Berkeman remained in the lounge, quietly sipping his gin and tonic, a happy smile on his face. Hell, man, he told himself, this Rachana dame was sure some dish!

*

Inspector Ramon Srinath, at his office desk in Delhi, was studying his case notes. Amongst them was the analysis report from the laboratory on the package forwarded to him from Jaipur. The result was just as he had expected. Tiger bone crushed to a powder, thirty per cent, with forty per cent ox bone, fifteen per cent nutmeg with a further fifteen of maize. Srinath knew the *modus operandi* of the tiger poaching gangs well enough. To make the tiger parts go further, they would add just about anything to add bulk. He studied the names and addresses on the paper the mixture was wrapped in, and the translations of the various labels.

Snorting with disgust, he replaced the items on his desk and pondered on the findings. Srinath was one of the very few Indians who seemed to care about the decimation of the tiger. Only the other day, he had met two doctors, intelligent men who should know better, who had openly promised to introduce him to some poachers.

"They will take you out with them, when they go hunting," the doctors had told him. Srinath couldn't believe his own ears, but he had readily accepted an invitation to go out next week with the poachers.

Maybe he could actually catch some of the devils red-handed. Okay so it wouldn't wipe out the illegal trade in tiger parts, but it would put a few of the offenders in jail for a while.

The worst aspect of it all was not the native poachers themselves – they were very poor and readily grabbed at the rich inducements – but the gangs behind them, who made the real money out of the rotten business.

If he could grab some of the poachers it was a start. Now he had names and addresses on the list, perhaps he could nab some of the backers as well.

With a wry smile, Srinath concluded that, from the description given him by the Jaipur police, it had to have been the American woman journalist who had left the package. For her to have done so, at a cobbler's shop, must have meant someone was following her, and she was worried about it falling into the wrong hands. One thing bothered him, however. Why had she not contacted him from Jaipur?

He scratched his head thoughtfully, trying to come up with a logical answer. One thing for sure, unless he found her quickly, her life wasn't worth a shirt button. Two conservationists had been murdered already, and in some way he was sure that the Ranthambhore sacrifice of the woman, by the Sons of Kali, was definitely connected.

Suddenly it came to him like a bolt from the blue. Two conservationists Swarmy and Patel, the ones murdered. He, Srinath, had told her of a third, who might help. A man in Bangalore. What was his name? Rummaging through his papers, he found it. Matthew Barlow, a tea planter. If the American woman hadn't already done so, surely contacting him would be her next move. Srinath picked up his internal phone.

"Book me on the next flight to Bangalore," he commanded. As he replaced the receiver, he reflected on the odd coincidence that one of the names on the list was also a tea planter in Bangalore, a Silas Craig. Scooping his papers into a neat pile, Srinath left his office.

Time to return home and pack an overnight bag.

*

In Jaipur, a factory was fiercely blazing. The flames, reaching high into the night sky, lit up the whole area for miles around.

A large multitude had gathered at a distance and were blocking the passage of would-be fire-fighters in their efforts. By this time, it was doubtful if their earlier presence would have made any difference to the outcome.

The whole building was beyond human help, the roof already having inwardly collapsed in a cascade of sparks. The sheer heat generated by the blaze forced the viewing multitude back, the flames crackling and roaring, devouring all before them.

On the other side of town, the more salubrious south side of Delhi, where Feu Chon Soo lived, a dark hooded figure crept along the wooden veranda of a luxury bungalow, an ornamental curved dagger clasped in a large hand. He paused at a slightly open window and listened. A low sound of snoring could be heard.

Under the hood, the man smiled to himself and eased the window up slowly and quietly. When the aperture was large enough, the dark figure slipped over the sill and into the room. Moving aside, so as not to be silhouetted by the moonlight streaming through the window, he pressed himself against the wall, waiting for his eyes to attune to the light – or lack of it – in the bedroom.

The snoring was louder now and came from a bed at the far side of the room. On tiptoe, the hooded form moved, silently for a man of such bulk, towards the bed. The light in the room was now good enough to discern the occupant of the bed – Feu Chon Soo.

The hooded figure raised the knife in his right hand, and with his left violently shook Soo by the shoulder. The Chinaman awoke with a scream of terror at the apparition above him and tried to rise. The massive left hand held him flat against the bed, in spite of all his efforts.

"Die, Chinaman, at the hands of the Sons of Kali," said the dark figure, plunging the knife downwards. The scream was cut short in Soo's throat, almost as the blade entered his heart.

Chapter Fourteen
Surprise Homecoming

Matt Barlow came home mid-morning the day after Carla's and Steve's arrival. Having first dropped off Zabu, he was surprised to see a vehicle drawn up outside his home. The last thing he felt like was visitors. Jana came bounding down the steps to meet him, the two of them indulging in a rough and tumble play fight, before being interrupted from the veranda.

"Come and meet your visitors, Matt," Rachana called to him.

Barlow collected his rifles from the utility and, followed by Jana, went into the house. Rachana made the necessary introductions and, whilst he was conversing with Carla, Steve Berkeman walked over to where Barlow had stacked the rifles. He scooped up the Winchester 405 and gave it a once-over.

"You don't mean to say, Barlow, that you go after a man-eating tiger with this museum piece? I'd rather you than me!"

If Berkeman had wanted to make an enemy, he couldn't have made a better start. Barlow's expression said it all.

"I don't recall asking your opinion, Berkeman."

"What the hell do you do if the damn' thing jams?" questioned the American, not in the least deterred.

"My worry – not yours," snapped Barlow.

The two women, sensing the tension, looked ill at ease.

"Well, did you get the brute?" queried Berkeman.

"Not that it's any concern of yours, but yes – and with the 405, as it happens."

Rachana stepped in and placed a hand on Barlow's arm.

"Now, now, Matt. I'm sure Steve didn't mean anything derogatory."

Before Barlow could reply, Berkeman began again.

"Well, I wouldn't want my life to depend on an old piece like that!" he said, replacing the rifle in its erstwhile position.

"Mine often has, and it has never let me down yet. It was a present from my father before he died."

"Yeah, it sure looks ancient enough."

Carla sat there inwardly seething. She needed this man's help and here was Berkeman alienating him by the second. Barlow, hands on hips, jaw tightly clenched, turned to face Berkeman.

"What the hell do you want here anyway?" Rachana jumped in to remonstrate with Barlow.

"Don't be so rude to our guests, Matt."

Carla leapt to her feet.

"It's not Mr Barlow who's the rude one here. I would like to apologise for this invasion of your privacy and the impertinence shown by my companion in your house." She turned sympathetic eyes on Barlow. "You have obviously been through a very harrowing and dangerous time, and could have done without returning to this." She glared venomously at Berkeman, who just grinned back at her.

"Well, if you're waiting for an apology, don't hold your breath," he said insolently.

"Say what you've come for and get out! I need some sleep," snapped Barlow.

"I'm only along for the ride, to protect her," exclaimed Berkeman, jerking a finger at Carla, then continued, "it's Carla who wants to talk with you. I don't need your help."

"Okay. She can stay. You can leave now, before I kick you out."

"Don't worry, I'm leaving." Turning to Carla, he said, "I'll be at the Colonial Hotel, downtown. Call me when you're ready to leave."

In a few short moments the tension in the room had risen to boiling point.

Rachana looked angrier than Barlow had ever seen her.

"Mr Berkeman has been quite charming since his arrival yesterday, Matt. I insist that you apologise to him."

"When I hear an apology from him, I might consider it," said Barlow calmly.

The American continued to give that infuriating smile.

"I'm sorry, Matt, but if I don't hear an apology from you to Mr Berkeman – our guest – I shall have no alternative but to return to my own flat."

"If that's how you feel about it, do so!" snapped Barlow.

"I'll give you a lift into town, Rachana," said Berkeman.

"At least there's one gentleman round here!" replied Rachana. "Perhaps you will wait whilst I gather a few things together."

"Be my pleasure," said Berkeman. Then, turning to Carla, he added, "Are you sure you don't want to come as well?"

Carla's answering expression was enough, without the words that followed it.

"I never want to see you again – ever!"

"Mr Strobe wouldn't like that now, would he?" said Berkeman, with a smirk. "I'll wait outside in the car for you, Rachana." Without more ado, he turned and walked out.

Rachana stormed about the place throwing articles of clothing and toiletry items into a bag. Finally, she faced Barlow.

"Well, haven't you anything you want to say?" she snapped.

"I guess it has all been said," remarked Barlow sadly.

Rachana turned on her heel and stormed out. If steam could have come out of her ears, it would have.

A few moments later they heard Berkeman's engine come to life and the vehicle drive away. Carla quietly moved over towards Barlow and placed her hand on his arm.

"I'm so sorry. If I hadn't come here to see you, none of this would have happened," she consoled him.

"None of it was your fault, Miss Wayne. It's been coming for a long while. You see, Rachana finds it hard to live with a man who puts his life on the line too often. She thinks I should be here with her, not hunting down man-eaters or rushing round after poaching gangs."

"I can understand that, but it wasn't your fault, Mr Barlow. You were tense and tired and it was wrong of Steve to goad you like that. I can't think why he did it. I've never seen him like that before. I'll tell you one thing for nothing though – that girl loves you, or she wouldn't have got all steamed up."

"That's as maybe, Miss Wayne. By the way, what did you want to ask me anyway?"

"Look, call me Carla, please. Miss Wayne sounds so formal. Yes, I want to talk to you about tiger poaching. I gather what you don't know about tigers isn't worth knowing. But if you don't mind my saying so, you look all in. Why don't you go and get some sleep? We can talk later. I don't mind waiting, really I don't."

"Okay then," replied a tired Barlow. "I really could use some sleep. I haven't had much chance for rest in the last few days."

*

It was several hours later when Barlow awoke and it was already dark. He showered and dressed and went downstairs. An aroma of hot spicy food greeted him. He found Carla busily engaged in the kitchen.

"I hope you don't mind my taking over your kitchen, but I felt the least I could do was prepare a meal for you when you eventually woke up."

"Ummm, smells delicious," remarked Barlow. Looking at his watch, he saw that he had been asleep for over eight hours. It was already 8 p.m. in the evening.

"You should have woken me."

"Why? You obviously needed the sleep, and I wasn't going anywhere. You're my only hope now, you see. Anyway, the meal is ready. Let's eat – then I can tell you all about it afterwards, if that's okay by you?"

"Fine, Carla. I'll open a bottle of wine. Red okay?"

"My favourite."

"Good. That's settled then."

Half an hour later, a satisfied Barlow pushed his empty plate away.

"That was great. Where did you learn to make curry like that?"

"Hobby of mine, actually," replied a delighted Carla.

"Now, what's all this business about tigers that attracts an American lady?"

Carla began right at the beginning, from where she had been given the assignment by Edwin Strobe, and related the happenings and events that had befallen her up to the present time. Barlow proved an avid and attentive listener, expressing concern and shock at the murders of two of his acquaintances, Swarmy and Patel.

"You hadn't heard?" she expressed surprise.

"This is India, Carla. It's a big country and communication is often wanting."

"Perhaps I shouldn't have come here, Matt," she said, using his given name for the first time. "I could be putting your life at risk also. Steve called me a Jonah."

"He seems to make a pastime of being rude to people."

"Well I shouldn't be hard on him. He did save my life in Jaipur."

"If you had told me that before, maybe I would even have apologised to him," said Barlow with a smile.

The evening passed pleasantly for them both, in spite of the anxiety and agitation in their minds, with regards to the morning's confrontation. They sat talking until late into the night. Carla, making notes, was both appalled and fascinated by the facts Barlow put before her, and by the stories he related. It was 2 a.m. by the time he rose and said, "Now I think it's you who need to sleep. In the morning I will have my foreman, Surendra Naqshband, drive you into town so that you can do some shopping and pick up your documents."

"That's very kind of you, but I don't want to put you to any bother on my account."

"No problem," replied Barlow, with a smile.

*

For a long time Carla lay awake, tossing over the day's events in her mind. Why had Steve Berkeman acted so badly, deliberately provoking Barlow into a tense exchange? For the life of her, she found it beyond her understanding. Up until then, he had been nothing but helpful, and had certainly saved her life with his timely rescue back in Jaipur. Although Carla knew the situation had not been of her making, she couldn't help but feel guilty about Rachana's walking out on Barlow. She sensed that he was too proud to let it show, but was obviously hurt by Rachana's hostile attitude towards him, failing to comprehend the reason for it. Still, she tried telling herself, it was not her affair, and there was little she could do about their feelings – or lack of them for one another.

Barlow had kindly agreed that she could fax a report from his plantation office in the morning to Edwin Strobe at *Liberty*.

"Better get down, in black and white, what you already have and get it off for starters," he had said.

Carla felt elated that he was so supportive of her mission in India, and keen to help in any way possible. It was plainly obvious, just talking to the man, that he had nothing but bitter hatred for the tiger poachers, and even more for the men behind them who organised the rotten trade.

Analysing her own emotions, she was amazed at how readily and naturally she had accepted a real live tigress moving freely round the house, and, at this very moment, sleeping on the floor outside her bedroom door. Barlow laughed, and said how odd it was for Jana to take to a newcomer so quickly, something she had never done before. Even stranger, when she recalled, the tigress's instant distrust of Steve Berkeman.

Sadly, however, Carla realised that she mustn't outstay her welcome. Once she had all the information Barlow could give her, it was only right that she should move out into an hotel.

Finally, she drifted off to sleep, feeling a sense of security she hadn't felt since arriving in India, cocooned in the knowledge of the sentinel outside her door.

*

Rachana Dev, however, tossed and turned feverishly, lying on top of her bed in the small apartment.

When she had walked out on Matt there had been a definite plan in her mind to force his hand into following her. Berkeman, who had been positively charming and flattering to her since his arrival with the Wayne girl, could be used, she thought, to make Matt jealous.

It hadn't worked, and she was thoroughly miserable. There was no air-conditioning in the tiny room, and even with the window wide open, the hot air of the Indian night, coupled with the mosquitoes, was almost unbearable.

If she hadn't been so stupid, she told herself, she could have been curled up in Matt's arms in his beautifully air-conditioned house. There was no way, though that she could bring herself to run back with her tail between her legs. Let Matt come to her! Then she remembered the blonde American girl, and pangs of jealousy hit her anew. Matt would be cooped up in that great big house with only the two of them there. And, she had to admit, the Wayne girl was very attractive.

What was it the natives said of Matt Barlow? Half tiger. She remembered the mating habits of tigers. The female would call up the male, who, after a lengthy wild lovemaking session, would leave her and move on to the next tigress. Twisting and turning, she cried into her pillow.

Steve Berkeman had taken her out to dinner at a smart restaurant earlier that evening, and had been very attentive. True, she had only accepted his dinner invitation knowing it would get back to Matt, and she hoped, force his hand. She should have known better. There wasn't anybody who could hold a candle to Matt Barlow for stubbornness.

The evening with Steve Berkeman had been disastrous anyway. His attentiveness had proved a trifle too embarrassing and, as the evening wore on, his advances grew more blatant. Although an attractive man, she had no interest in him other than to use him as a pawn in her game to bring Matt to heel.

By the time he had escorted her back to her flat, he was becoming something of a nuisance, and she had been forced to be quite blatantly rude to him to stop his advances. In fact, he had left in high dudgeon, obviously having expected more.

*

Steve Berkeman's plans, in fact, had gone horribly wrong. From the moment he arrived with Carla at Barlow's house, he had been totally captivated by the vision of Rachana, in a tight red sheath dress which showed every curve. Her movements were those of a graceful gazelle. With her dark flashing eyes and sultry aquiline features, she had totally bewitched him.

From that first glimpse of the beautiful Anglo-Indian, he could think of only one thing – to possess her. He had used Barlow's absence well, with flowery compliments and charm in abundance. The next step had been to pick a row with Barlow and make it look like the other man's fault.

The ancient gun had given him just the chance he needed to effect it. As an ex-marine himself, he was well aware of the esteem in which a man held his lifeline – his rifle.

Everything, in fact, had gone just as he had planned it. That was, until he had taken Rachana back to her apartment after dinner. Once she had accepted his invitation to a meal, he had expected the conquest would be easy.

How wrong he had been! She had even turned away when he had tried for a good night kiss. Grimly, he knew that he would have to seek a way back into Barlow's good books. Somehow, by hook or by crook, he knew that he wanted Rachana as he had never wanted any other woman in his life before.

*

Matt Barlow too lay awake for a long time, inwardly cursing that he had spent so long asleep during the day. He missed Rachana terribly, but there wasn't any way he would have backed down and telephoned her. Maybe he had been wrong to have taken umbrage at the self-assured American, Berkeman, but he had just experienced having his nerves stretched to their limits, and had only just begun to calm down when Berkeman had pushed him too far.

In his heart, he knew Rachana could be just as stubborn as himself, but he would have expected her support and not her animosity. After all, she had actually taken the American's side, and even gone off with him. Now it was Barlow's turn to suffer the pangs of jealousy, as he reflected on the earlier events.

Finally, he dropped off into a troubled sleep, and dreamed that he was walking a tightrope with an endless black abyss beneath him.

*

Inspector Ramon Srinath arrived the following day at Barlow's plantation house, driven out from downtown Bangalore by the district commissioner for the area, Kepel Rao.

This time, Matt Barlow was expecting them, as Rao had telephoned him first, suggesting that he kept Jana the tigress out of sight for the police inspector's visit. He met them on the veranda, and, after Rao had made the necessary introductions, Srinath said to Barlow, "I thought and hoped I might find an American woman, Carla Wayne, here with you."

Barlow calculated for a moment before replying. He had sent his foreman Surendra Naqshband with Carla into town earlier that morning. As yet, they hadn't returned.

Having decided it wouldn't hurt to say, he finally replied, "Yes, she arrived two days ago, and is staying for a while."

"Do you think I could have a word with her, sir?"

"You could, if she was here. Gone into town to do some shopping."

Srinath enquired when she was expected back.

"Could be any time, I guess," said Barlow. "She didn't say."

"She was supposed to keep me informed, of her movements in India. She has not done so."

"Well, you are welcome to wait if you like, Inspector."

"I might just do that, sir."

"Okay then. You had better come in and join me in a drink gentlemen, whilst you wait."

Srinath and Rao followed him in.

Chapter Fifteen

At Home in Bangalore

Carla Wayne's morning had gone very well indeed. Before leaving with Barlow's foreman for downtown Bangalore, she had compiled a report on developments so far and then faxed it from the plantation office to Edwin Strobe, in New York.

The good-natured Surendra, an efficient and amiable young man, dressed in a white three-quarter length tunic coat with underlying long matching trousers, happily drove her round all her ports of call.

She was surprised to find, with all the talk of Indian inefficiency, that the necessary documents and monetary advances were waiting for her collection at the main post office. All she had to do was sign for them before a smiling clerk handed everything over. She had then explained to the foreman that she would like to purchase some Western clothes.

To her surprise, he said he knew of just the place, and promptly drove her there. By now the novelty of dressing in a sari was wearing thin, and the only other things she had were the jeans and T-shirt that she had been wearing when Berkeman had rescued her, back in Jaipur.

The store, in fact, had just about everything. Carla was able to purchase some pretty cotton dresses, a lightweight two-piece safari suit, a couple of blouses and skirts and even a pair of fashionable high-heeled shoes for evening wear.

She completed her shopping spree with an assortment of underwear, both silk and cotton, together with a pack of stockings and some tights. Although it was too hot to wear these in the day in this climate, Carla well knew that air conditioning in some of the hotels could make things uncomfortably cool. In another store she bought a handbag and a few accessories. Her last trip to a pharmacy provided some more essential toiletries and some perfume.

She had kept on the new safari suit and had the store pack the sari with her new purchases. Surendra patiently waited whilst she made a quick trip to a ladies' hairdressers for a shampoo and set. By now, lunchtime had been reached. Carla felt as if the least she could do to reward the foreman for all his patience was to treat him to lunch, which they consumed in a small, but clean restaurant. On the way back to the plantation, they passed a shoe shop.

Carla looked at the sandals on her feet, and realised that they were totally out of place with her new safari suit, so another stop provided her with the answer – strong walking boots and socks.

"If you are going into the jungle, memsahib, your ankles should be protected against snakes." Something Carla hadn't even thought about, but she readily agreed.

Feeling satisfied with her morning's work and almost human again in her Western clothes, Surendra dropped her off at Matt Barlow's house and, with a smile, drove off.

She was surprised not to be greeted by Jana, who usually seemed to be roaming about the house somewhere or in the immediate vicinity.

As she was about to knock, Matt Barlow opened the door.

"You have some visitors waiting to see you, Carla – the police," he whispered, so as not to be heard by those in the room behind him.

"Oh, I, er." She was thrown immediately out of her newly acquired sense of well-being. Shocked, she followed Barlow back into the house.

She recognised Inspector Ramon Srinath at once, and expected the worst. The other man she had never seen before.

Barlow effected the introductions. Both men studied her with stern expressions. Srinath was the first to speak.

"Miss Wayne and I have already met, Mr Barlow," he said. Then, turning back to Carla, in an official voice, he continued, "You were told in my office in Delhi that you must keep me informed of all your movements in India. Why then have you not done so?"

Barlow intervened, seeing that Carla still looked pale and shocked at this turn of events.

"I think you should understand, Inspector, that Miss Wayne has been through a very harrowing time since her arrival in India. In fact, she was very nearly kidnapped."

Srinath turned his attention back to Matt Barlow.

"So you have already informed me, Mr Barlow, but I want to hear from Miss Wayne herself – if you don't mind."

Barlow's intervention had, at least, given Carla a precious few seconds to compose herself.

"I did try to telephone you before I left Delhi, Inspector."

"Ummm, I seem to recall that the message left intimated that you would be in touch when you arrived in Jaipur."

Not wishing to say that she had heard the police in India were corrupt and therefore had not complied, Carla wriggled with words.

"I had intended to telephone you, Inspector, honestly. However, after the second murder – that of Mr Sonjay Patel – I knew I was being followed, and decided to go into hiding, for my own safety."

Ramon Srinath's sharp eyes gave her a quizzical examination. He paused before replying at length.

"Miss Wayne, usually when someone uses the word 'honestly' I tend to disbelieve them. I would advise you to stop playing games with me. I already know quite a bit about this affair, you see."

"I don't know what you mean, Inspector Srinath. I haven't murdered anybody."

"I don't recall saying that you had."

He watched her, an amused expression on his face, while a pregnant pause hung in the air. When Carla failed to break it, Srinath began again.

"There is the matter of a package handed into a certain shoemaker's shop in Jaipur. The woman handing it in fits your description to a 'T'."

"Oh," was all an embarrassed Carla could utter.

"Oh, indeed, Miss Wayne. Do you want to tell me about it? Or do I have to take you back to Delhi for questioning?"

Carla decided to come clean.

"Yes, Inspector, it was me. I managed to obtain evidence against one of these poaching gangs, but then some sixth sense told me I was being followed, and I tried to hide it for safety."

"Ummm," mumbled Srinath. "I suggest you would have done better to trust me without going and committing burglary, for which I could very well arrest you now."

Carla reddened.

"What can I say, apart from I'm very sorry! I see that now!"

"Like many foreigners, you have no doubt been told that the police here are corrupt, yes?"

"Well, I er, yes."

"At last we have the truth. Luckily for you I am a lenient man. Now perhaps you will start at the beginning and bring me up to date on your movements until you arrived here with the American, Berkeman."

Carla heaved a sigh of relief that everything was now out in the open, and realised that she had been wrong not to involve Srinath in the first place. At length, she related her experiences, right up to the present. At the conclusion of the narrative Srinath leaned back in his chair.

"Well, you are a remarkably resourceful young lady. But, I would stress, that you are very fortunately placed to be still alive!"

Carla wriggled uncomfortably in her chair, not really sure of what to say next.

Kepel Rao, the DC, broke his silence, having been studying Carla's face throughout her narrative.

"Luckily your story tallies with what we already know, and ties in with what Mr Barlow has recently told us." He extracted a briar pipe from his pocket and a leather pouch, from which he methodically filled the former with tobacco. Before lighting it, he began talking again whilst settling comfortably in his armchair.

"Although the responsibility is now mine, for Inspector Srinath comes under my area jurisdiction, I intend to give him free rein in this matter." Slowly, he lit the pipe and exhaled a cloud of aromatic blue smoke skywards. "Now, Inspector Srinath, the floor is yours," he said, a genial smile on his plumpish face.

"Thank you, sir," replied Srinath, then quickly continued. "I intend, Miss Wayne, to take both you and Mr Barlow into my confidence – something, I hasten to add – I would have appreciated from you." He paused, to give Carla a look that had reprimand written all over it, then proceeded, "It will probably surprise you to know that the factory you broke into in Jaipur was completely gutted by fire the other night. At the same time its owner, Mr Feu Chon Soo, was brutally murdered at his home."

Carla edged forward on her chair.

"Do you have any idea who did it, Inspector? Did you find evidence of all the tiger carcasses?"

"Whoa! Hold on, young lady, and allow me to finish."

Barlow grinned as Carla theatrically placed an elegant hand over her mouth. Srinath continued.

"The murder was once again committed by the so-called Sons of Kali. Any evidence would have been totally destroyed by the fire."

Both Barlow and Carla looked shocked. It was Barlow who recovered first and broke the silence.

"Any idea who is behind these Sons of Kali, Inspector?"

"Not at this moment, Mr Barlow but, quite obviously, the two men who Miss Wayne overheard talking, when she broke into the factory, are behind it. Luckily, the list she prepared after committing her burglary has many names and addresses which will be very useful to us. All will be investigated fully."

"But how about the names I overheard, Inspector, whilst I hid behind the packing cases?" Carla exclaimed excitedly. "The two men who were talking called one another Venkat and Mr Tata."

Srinath smiled indulgently.

"Do you have any idea of the numbers of Venkats and Mr Tatas there are in a country which has a nine hundred million population?"

Carla's face fell.

Barlow cut in quickly.

"However, Inspector, how many Craigs can there be who are tea planters in the south? Besides the blighter next door!" he added venomously. When he had first heard the name, in Carla's statement earlier, it had been all he could do to remain seated.

Srinath gave that indulgent and irritating smile once more.

"It may surprise you to know there are even three of those in the south of India – and all tea planters!" he said, pre-empting Barlow's next question.

"A pound to a penny it's Silas Craig on the next plantation here," exclaimed Barlow excitedly.

"Maybe – maybe not," replied Srinath enigmatically. "The other two Craigs are down here too, one in Madras, the other at Mandya. It could just as easily be one of those."

"The one at Mandya is Silas Craig's brother. South-west of here, following the rail tracks," put in Kepel Rao helpfully.

Barlow was on the boil now. He jumped to his feet excitedly.

"So, let's raid Silas Craig's place for starters. If they have moved the whole operation there we can nab the lot before they have a chance to do more damage decimating the tigers."

"Hold your horses, Mr Barlow. We can't just charge in on suspicion."

"You mean there's nothing you can do to stop them?"

"I didn't say that now, did I?" protested Srinath. "Believe me, I'm just as appalled as you about what is going on in India now, with this open tiger poaching. I have requested the DC here to have all three Craig plantations watched. If I can get proof I'll get a warrant and act."

"Until then, they get away with it," remarked Barlow dryly.

"That's about the size of it, sir."

There followed an argument in which neither Barlow nor Carla could sway the two officials. It ended with Srinath saying, "It's useless you two getting so steamed up. Even if we raided Silas Craig's place now. and he turned out to be the Craig we are looking for, we wouldn't find anything there."

"How do you work that one out?' said Barlow hotly.

"Think about it, man. The fire in the Jaipur factory was started deliberately, so you can bet your rupees the merchandise was off-loaded first."

"So?" said Barlow.

"So, they would have to move carcasses, products, papers, et cetera down south by road. It would take four or even five days on these roads to get here."

"How about rail?" prompted Carla.

"Too risky by half. No, they would certainly use their own transport and come by road," answered Srinath.

A thoughtful silence followed before the Inspector rose and said to Kepel Rao, "I think we have accomplished here all that can be done for the present. Are you ready to leave, sir?"

The rotund figure of the DC slowly unwound itself from the chair and stood up. Both men offered their hands to Barlow and then to Carla in turn.

Barlow walked both men out to their parked vehicle. Just as Kepel Rao was about to climb into the driver's seat, he turned to Barlow.

"By the way, Matt, my assistant saw Rachana at one of the downtown restaurants last night – with an American gentleman," he said. "Very elegantly dressed, apparently."

The DC waited for a response but got none for Barlow clamped his teeth down on his tongue, offering no explanation or reply.

"None of my business, of course," said the DC with an embarrassed cough, and climbed behind the wheel. A moment later, the two officials drove off. Barlow, rooted to the spot, watched the vehicle disappear out of sight before turning and going in to rejoin Carla in the house.

She was waiting for him, an expectant expression on her face.

"That's that then, Matt. Looks like the authorities are not going to accomplish much, other than to keep watch. Do you think they told us everything, or are they holding something back?"

"Quite probably the latter," replied Barlow, "but the more important question is what are *we* going to do about the situation?"

Carla looked thoughtful, and then said softly, "I don't think it's right to put you to any more trouble on my behalf, Matt. Besides..." she said, a slightly embarrassed look on her face.

"Besides, what?" prompted Barlow.

"What I'm trying to say is it doesn't seem right for me to be staying here with you, when your, er, Rachana, has pulled out. I mean, I, er..."

"I should quit when you're ahead," said Barlow, with an attempt at humour he didn't feel. Rao's information had hurt him deeply, but he was determined not to show it. "Don't let that worry you. I hear Rachana has already been seen out with your erstwhile friend, Berkeman."

"Surely not?"

"Surely so, but let's change the subject, shall we. You are welcome to stay for as long as you wish, Carla. In fact, I may soon need your help."

"You know I will help in any way I can," replied a puzzled Carla.

"It could be dangerous!"

Carla's eyes flashed with excitement, half reading his thoughts.

"You are going to do some investigating on your own behalf, aren't you, Matt?"

"Somebody has to do something positive." Carla placed a hand on his arm.

"Count me in then."

"Do I take it you are staying?"

"Try and make me leave," she exclaimed, with a laugh.

"That's settled then. As Srinath pointed out, those lorries can't get here for another two, possibly three days. So I'll organise my foreman to have a man watching for them at all times."

"And when they come?"

"I wait until they are settled in and sure of themselves, and then go in."

"One thing wrong with that, Matt. Delete I, and amend to we."

Barlow began to argue, pointing out the obvious dangers, but quickly saw it was no use and fell silent. Carla was not to be dissuaded from something she obviously considered her fight.

Chapter Sixteen

On the Poachers' Trail

With time on their hands, Barlow decided it was a chance to relax, and that evening took Carla into Bangalore for a meal. Carla was delighted to have the opportunity to give her newly-acquired finery an outing, and spent quite a lot of time on her make-up to achieve the best possible results. Time and circumstances of late had given her little chance to dress in any form of smart attire.

Dressed in a midnight blue gown with dainty gold motifs that enhanced her blonde, recently coiffured hair to perfection, she sported her new high-heeled shoes to complete the ensemble. The admiring glances and the effect she caused in the restaurant were a just reward for her efforts.

Barlow glowingly complimented her and expressed himself a lucky man to be her escort.

With the possibility to relax for the first time since she had arrived in India, the whole evening proved a delightful experience. Matt Barlow was an excellent listener, as well as an entertaining raconteur. Something one didn't always find in a handsome man. It was only when they were driving home and he was unaware of her gaze that she was able to study his clean-cut profile, and realise how attractive he was.

'Cool it!' she told herself. 'He belongs to someone else. Stick to business!'

It was already 11.30 by the time they arrived back at the plantation. Jana, once again roaming free, gave them a warm welcome. After a further coffee, Carla thanked Matt for a lovely evening and gave him a brief kiss on the cheek before retiring.

Not quite able to understand her own feelings, she experienced disappointment when he made no effort to stop her exiting.

Later she told herself in bed, don't be silly, of course he's not interested in you; why should he be when he's got Rachana?

She awoke after a good night's sleep, with the sun streaming in at her bedroom window. After a refreshing shower, she dressed in the safari suit and went downstairs. The table was already laid for breakfast, but of Matt Barlow there was no sign.

She heard voices out on the veranda and a moment later Matt entered from that direction. After greeting her, he explained.

"That was Surendra. He has come to inform me that some of the natives have told him of a gang that are going tiger poaching, not fifty miles from here, tonight. I intend to leave later today to put a spoke in their wheel. Will you be all right here on your own? I'll leave Jana, of course, to protect you," he said, patting the ever-present tigress's head, as she pressed up against him.

"No way! I'm coming with you!"

Barlow looked at Carla in amazement.

"I don't think you understand. These people are dangerous, as is the jungle."

Carla stuck her chin out defiantly.

"So?"

Barlow still appeared stunned at her request to accompany him.

"You don't understand the jungle, Carla. It is necessary to move and think like an animal."

"Then you can teach me. I'm a quick learner."

"You are an American girl from a big city – it takes a lifetime to understand the jungle," Barlow argued.

Carla switched track, seeing that she wasn't going to break him down.

"Okay then, Matt. Now with all your knowledge of the jungle and of the poachers, have you managed to stop them in their evil trade of tiger parts?"

"No, only slowed them down a little sometimes and caused them more than a little inconvenience on occasion."

"Quite so," Carla replied.

Barlow, on the defensive, said, "I try a damn' sight harder than most, even breaking the law more than once."

"Of course you do, Matt. Don't you think I realise that? All I'm saying is, take me along with you. Maybe I can write it all up in *Liberty* magazine, and do the cause more good that way. I won't get under your feet, I promise." Carla looked at him demurely. From under her long lashes, she could see that he was weakening.

Finally, after a long pause, he replied, "Okay but it's against my better judgement, and you must do exactly as I say."

"Oh, I will, I will!" Carla enthused, stepping forward to give Barlow a huge hug.

"I warn you, a night in the jungle with mosquitoes, wild animals and poachers will probably make you wish you'd stayed at home."

Ignoring the warning, Carla said, "When do we leave?"

"Be ready just after lunch. I want to be in position by sunset. Wear something dark – trousers if you have them and strong boots. I'll pack everything else we are going to need. We will take Zabu, my tracker, with us."

Carla was so excited that she could hardly wait until lunchtime. Thank goodness she had purchased those boots.

*

Ravi Tata and Venkat Singh were already at Silas Craig's plantation house being entertained to dinner. Craig himself was seated at the head of a long highly polished table, which had just been cleared by two servant girls. An elderly native with greying hair brought in a port decanter and glasses, which he served at a snail's pace.

"Hurry along, man," snapped Craig.

The native became agitated and spilt the plum-red fluid on the polished table top in his efforts to hurry.

"Dolt! Imbecile!" boomed Craig. "You girl – clear it up at once!"

The younger of the two servant girls dashed forward with a cloth to comply. On completion of the task to his satisfaction, he roared, "Out, now! All of you and see that we are not disturbed!"

All three servants scurried away. Craig turned his attention to Ravi Tata. "And now to business, gentlemen. I have had the refrigeration unit installed. When can we expect the lorries to arrive?"

"The day after tomorrow, all being well," replied Tata.

"Good. We are in readiness here. Already I have despatched a gang of poachers tonight into the jungle some eighty kilometres from here."

"Are there tigers there then?" enquired Venkat Singh.

"I had received a report that three have been sighted in the vicinity – a female and two males. That being so, I have despatched and armed the men. If necessary they have been told to shoot any forest officers that try to interfere."

"It is safer to bribe the guards and rangers in this business," said Tata acidly.

"Dead men tell no tales," replied Craig.

"Is there anyone in this area who might give us trouble?" questioned Venkat.

Craig thought for a moment.

"Only one. A man called Matt Barlow – better known locally as Tiger Barlow, because of his affinity with tigers. Even keeps one of the brutes as a pet, would you believe. Runs the next tea plantation to mine."

"Why do you think he will trouble us?" enquired Ravi Tata.

Craig gave an evil smile.

"Because he's spent all his life here in India. Loves the place and the people. Even has a half-breed mistress."

"If he interferes, I will deal with him," exclaimed Venkat, a malicious smile on his dark face.

"Correction," said Tata. "The Sons of Kali will deal with him, when and if the time comes."

"Speaking of which, what of this new partner of ours, the fakir Anil Dehra? When does he arrive?" enquired Craig.

"With the lorries. He is managing their safe passage here," interjected Venkat.

"When he arrives, we will stage another show for the locals, like we did in Ranthambhore. It will be good to have them eating out of our hands and doing everything we tell them to do. Gullible fools!" remarked Ravi Tata.

*

Rachana was feeling very sorry for herself. Too proud to ring Matt and mend the situation, she had expected a call from him all day, to no avail.

It was the second evening since her walkout, and the only person to telephone her had been the persistent Steve Berkeman. Twice during the day, at her office, he had rung in an effort to persuade her to join him for dinner again that night.

As politely as she could, Rachana had turned him down. Already she was beginning to wonder why she had. Matt obviously had too many other things on his mind, in the shape of the blonde Western girl, to bother about apologising to her! In her anger, Rachana did something that would not normally have occurred to her. She poured herself a strong drink of brandy which, although it made her cough, was quickly despatched. Another glass of the amber liquid followed. Within half an hour, she had drunk a third. If the desired effect had been to cheer herself up or calm down, the opposite was achieved.

She would telephone Matt and tell him just what she thought of him! Picking up the handset, she dialled his number. From what seemed to her to be far away, she could hear the ringing tone. Impatiently she listened, waiting for Matt to answer. After two minutes she slammed the implement back on its hook. Obviously, he was either in bed with that Wayne girl or he had taken her into town for a night on the tiles.

By now, fired up with the brandy, Rachana said aloud, "Well! Two can play at that game!"

Reaching, once more, for the telephone, she dialled Berkeman's hotel and was quickly put through. When he came on the line Rachana said, "Can a girl change her mind and accept your dinner invitation?"

"This man would be delighted if she did," said Berkeman, in a husky voice.

"Okay I'll be ready in an hour, if you care to call for me."

"I'll be there, honey."

Rachana replaced the receiver and poured herself another brandy. In a little while she would take a shower and get ready.

Half an hour later saw her dressed in an off-the-shoulder red silk dress, split to mid thigh. In her high heels, she strutted up and down in front of a full-length mirror. She would show Matt Barlow not to play fast and loose with her! Someone was bound to see her at

Berkeman's hotel and she knew that it wouldn't be long before the news reached Matt. If this didn't bring him running, nothing would.

She sprayed Calvin Klein Eternity liberally, and spent longer than usual on her make-up. She was just finishing when the doorbell of her apartment rang. She waited until it was repeated, and slowly strolled over to answer the bell. Steve Berkeman, in a smart white linen suit, stood in the hallway, a red rose in his hand, which he graciously offered to her.

"To the fairest damsel in all India," he purred.

Taking the rose, she laid it beside the telephone.

"Thank you, Mr Berkeman," she said, in a formal voice.

"I'm ready to leave now."

"Good. I've got a taxi waiting outside,' replied Berkeman. He was so taken with her appearance, that he failed to notice Rachana was not walking a very straight line as they left her apartment. His eyes were too busily fastened on the silken glimpse of shapely thigh visible through the exposed slit in her skirt.

*

Matt Barlow and Carla had left for the jungle soon after lunch. Carefully packing the requirements for the trip, they had picked up Zabu as they left the plantation. An hour before sunset saw them leave the vehicle in a hidden grove in the bamboo fringe of the jungle.

Looking inwards, Carla thought, even with the sun still shining, the jungle's interior looked darkly forbidding. Barlow unloaded the necessities for the trip and checked everything methodically. Then he produced a glass jar containing a black substance. Zabu grinned at Carla's puzzled expression.

"Come and sit over here, Carla. I'm going to do your make-up for you."

"Whatever is it?" said Carla, looking in horror at the black paste in the now opened jar.

Barlow laughed.

"Don't worry. It won't hurt you. It's a mixture of insect repellent and camouflage."

"Looks revolting!" said Carla, peeping into the jar, and screwing up her nose distastefully.

"Not as bad as it looks. Come on, shut your eyes," coaxed Barlow.

Carla sat down and raised her arms in mock surrender.

"Do your worst."

Gently, Barlow worked the paste all over her face and neck and then switched his attention to arms and hands. Finally satisfied, he stood back to admire his handiwork.

"You'd pass for a real native now, Carla," he joked, and then began to work on his own face with the substance. Carla laughed.

"With your tan, Matt, you don't need it."

"Maybe not, but you would be surprised how white skin shows up at night out here, especially if the moon comes out later."

"I must say it doesn't smell as bad as I expected, anyway."

"You lubberly black girl now, memsahib," said Zabu, his white teeth flashing in a huge smile.

Barlow strapped on a backpack and picked up his trusty Winchester.

"Let's move out, Zabu," he ordered. Then, turning to Carla he said, "Stay between us at all times. Watch where you're treading, and look out particularly for broken pieces of dead wood. If you step on one, they make almost as much noise as a gunshot. Keep one eye on Zabu, and stop when he does. He will be looking for signs of the poaching gang, and also for any traps they will have set earlier today."

"How do you know that?" Carla found herself whispering, already feeling the excitement of the moment.

"Unfortunately, I've seen it all before."

"Do you think the poachers have arrived yet, and are already here somewhere?"

"Yes. That's why we must maintain silence and only speak if absolutely vital from now on."

Carla made a sign, with her index finger and thumb in a circle, to show she understood – something he had explained to her earlier in the day. Barlow smiled. The girl was a quick learner.

Progress was slow through mostly dense bamboo, then came an area of all-consuming lantana, with its motley assortment of coloured little flowers. Zabu stopped at intervals to inspect the ground and listen, a hand cupping his ear.

They emerged on to, what appeared to Carla, some sort of trail between giant muthee and jum-lum trees. Several vines and creepers hung from their upper branches reaching right down to the earth, to entwine together in the long grass reaching skywards to meet them. Then, it seemed as if out of nowhere, they entered a clearing, broken only by a few isolated tamarind trees. To the east of them was still dense jungle, but they had a clear view of the setting sun in the west. The sky was streaked with orange and red flames with a backcloth of vermilion and indigo.

Carla thought she had never seen anything so beautiful, and wished that she had thought to bring a camera. She was interrupted in her reverie by Matt's hand on her arm. Fingers to his lips, he pointed in towards the jungle once more, indicating for her to follow Zabu. The glorious sunset was left behind as, once more, the dark interior swallowed them. Suddenly, Zabu stopped dead and held up his hand. Then the little man darted to the right and eased his way on all fours through some tall elephant grass. Standing up, he indicated to Barlow behind Carla, something in the grass.

Gently, Matt eased his way past her to inspect the discovery. Carla peered over his shoulder as he bent down and was able to discern a heavy, rusty iron trap, which was partially concealed with dead leaves. Near it, in the soft earth, Zabu pointed out the pug marks of a tiger.

Barlow whispered to Carla.

"This is what the swine do. Anywhere they find the evidence of a tiger having passed by, they will set up one of these contraptions."

"So they have come this way recently then?" enquired Carla.

"Yes, you probably didn't realise it, but Zabu has been tracking the poachers ever since we entered the jungle."

Carla looked at the little tracker in a new light, respect in her eyes.

"He even knows how many of them there are," added Barlow.

"He does?" whispered Carla, incredulously.

"There are five," said Barlow, softly.

"But how do you know? He hasn't spoken?"

"By signals he has made to me, that you would never have noticed. Stay where you are," said Barlow, moving silently away, to re-emerge a moment later with a piece of broken wood. With this, he sprang the jaws of the rusty iron trap noisily. Carla winced at the sound, and at the thoughts it conveyed to her.

"If they're anywhere near enough, they will hear that, and, hopefully, come to see what they've caught."

For fully ten minutes, the three of them lay concealed in the elephant grass, but the only sounds were of birds roosting noisily in the trees in the approaching dusk, and the occasional barking sound of a deer some way off. Once they heard something approaching, but it turned out to be nothing more than a young waterbuck, which came close to blundering into them before scampering for cover.

From his pack, Barlow produced a small foldable hacksaw, which, once assembled, cut loose the chain holding the trap. This done, he shouldered the contraption and signalled for Zabu to move on.

The last of the daylight was fast departing now, and Carla marvelled at how the little tracker could see where to go, let alone track, but with nose glued to the ground and the undergrowth about him, he obviously did.

In the next hour, to Carla's increasing wonderment, Zabu located two more of the fiendish traps. How he could even follow a trail let alone find these things in the jungle gloom was quite beyond Carla's comprehension. Each trap was dealt with in the same way, and appropriated.

Having found a suitable hollow, and rotting jum-lum tree, Barlow was able to free himself of the encumbrance of them, concealing all three deep within its recesses, Zabu covering them further with dead leaves.

"That's three that they won't use any more," whispered Barlow.

Another hour saw the moon rise, sending its silver shafts of light down upon them, and making the jungle seem to Carla quite ethereal and beautiful.

In the earlier gloom, she had been finding it quite difficult to pick out Zabu. Now he was etched quite clearly as he moved stealthily forward. Another area of dense bamboo loomed up. Suddenly, Zabu raised his right hand and stopped. Even Carla, with her non-attuned ears, used to city life, heard it this time. A loud breaking and crashing of branches.

She looked expectantly back at Barlow.

"Elephant," he whispered, signalling for them both to get behind him. Placing his index finger in his mouth, he moistened it, then held it out above him.

"Damn!" he hissed. "The wind is taking our scent right to them. By the sound of it, there's quite a small herd in there."

"Will they attack us then?" whispered Carla tremulously.

"The sentinel will, if he scents us, or at least try to drive us off. Keep close. We will try to circle round them."

There was no time, however. The party had taken hardly a dozen steps when a large bull emerged from the bamboo, some fifty metres to their right. He tossed his trunk at the air, loudly trumpeting and bellowing his rage. Flapping his ears back and forth, he pawed the earth with his right front leg, raising a cloud of dust in the moonlight. Menace was written all over him. Zabu looked at his master apprehensively.

"This is bad one, sahib. He will charge."

Barlow silently slid off the safety catch on the 405. The last thing he wanted to do was shoot an elephant, but it began to look as if the decision would be taken away from him. This fellow was clearly a brave old bull, intent on driving off the intruders.

For a moment, the bull eyed them venomously and appeared to be making his mind up whether to charge. Quite suddenly, it happened. Something clicked in his mind, and he began to move forward slowly and ponderously at first, then quickening his gait, straight at them.

Carla, standing behind Barlow, wanted to turn and run, but felt her feet glued to the spot with terror. Feeling herself mesmerised, she watched Barlow facing the oncoming giant. Rock steady and square on, he quite slowly and deliberately raised the Winchester and sighted it.

Why didn't he shoot, for Christ's sake! The brute would trample them all to dust. It was literally hurtling towards them now. Carla could feel herself trembling. The very earth seemed to shake as the bull's huge feet drummed on the earth in its onward charge.

It was no more than fifteen metres from them now, emitting terrifying and intimidating sounds of wrath.

Suddenly, the staccato crack of Barlow's rifle rent the jungle night. The huge bull slithered to a halt in the dust, seemed to pause for an instant, uncertain whether to come on or not, then, losing his nerve, it turned and made off into the bamboo, which quickly swallowed him up.

Carla found herself shaking violently. Barlow, sensing her fright, put a consoling arm round her shoulders. "It's over now," he quietly reassured her, as they could hear the whole herd moving away through the bamboo, the sound of broken and snapping vegetation receding.

"I thought it was all up with us when you missed, Matt," said a breathless Carla.

Zabu grinned from ear to ear.

"Barlow Sahib, him no miss. He shoot to frighten elephant, not kill, missee."

Carla studied Matt's face and realised it was true.

"But what if he hadn't turned, Matt?"

"Then I guess it would have been necessary to stop him. You must remember, Carla, he had nothing against us and was only protecting his herd."

By the time the noise of the departing elephants had finally died down, Carla was beginning to regain her composure.

She was, once again, conscious of the other jungle sounds – the chirruping of crickets and the occasional night birds, including several nightjars, answering each other from various directions in the forest. Carla was intrigued and amazed by the numerous fireflies as they hovered and danced in the jungle night.

It was all a complete and utterly new world for her city dweller's eyes and she was totally enthralled. Even more so now that the moon was illuminating all these new wonders. Some of the vegetation took on a silvery hue, as shafts of moonlight beamed down through the great overhanging branches. Each little clearing in the forest seemed to highlight something different from the last.

Once, she watched, almost mesmerised, as a huge python slowly unwound itself from the lower branches of a giant banyan tree and slithered to the ground. Once there, it smoothly slid away under a dense area of lantana.

Progress was slow, with Zabu giving everything a detailed scrutiny before moving on to the next area.

Raising his right hand and listening, he came to a halt. Even Carla could hear it – the sound of some animal lapping at water.

"Waterhole to our right," whispered Barlow, again checking with his finger for the wind direction. Satisfied with his conclusions, he indicated for Carla to follow.

Carefully, they edged between a natural grove of bamboo, and circumnavigated a clump of wait-a-bit thorn to where, whilst still concealed behind a wild mango tree, they had a clear view of the waterhole.

A leopard was crouched there at the water's edge, drinking his fill. After observing him for fully five minutes, they saw the animal stealthily make off in the direction of the rocky hills. The trio silently made their way back into the jungle to resume their hunt for the poachers.

Chapter Seventeen
Mask of the Tiger

By the time Rachana had consumed two glasses of champagne with her dinner, on top of the brandies she had already drunk, she was feeling extremely high and in a particularly garrulous mood. Steve Berkeman put this down to his irresistible charm, and assumed that the path ahead would now be easy.

How wrong he was! Too late, he realised his mistake when he made a detrimental remark about Matt Barlow. Immediately, Rachana leapt in with, "I'll have you know Matt Barlow is the bravest and noblest man in the whole of India."

"He's nuts if you ask me," retorted Berkeman.

"Why do you say that?" snapped Rachana, her dark eyes blazing.

"If he had any sense, he would come running after you," said Berkeman, trying hard to get back into a position of esteem with her.

"Matt Barlow doesn't go running after anybody," she said defiantly.

Berkeman blew it completely then, coming in with, "Only after man-eating tigers with a museum piece of a gun."

"That's his choice."

"A stupid one, if you ask me."

"I don't recall asking your opinion, Mister Berkeman!" exclaimed Rachana, emphasising the mister.

"Well, I'm giving it anyway."

Rachana pushed back her chair and stood up, conscious of the other guests in the dining room staring at her.

"I think agreeing to have dinner with you was a mistake," she said, and began to feel giddy. The room began to swirl around. Faces seemed to be everywhere. She grabbed at the table for support and succeeded only in clutching the tablecloth. Her legs buckled and she crashed to the floor, bringing the contents of the table down on top of her. Berkeman leapt to his feet as several waiters and guests rushed to assist.

Placing some notes on the table, he scooped Rachana up in his arms. The manager hurried up to him, full of concern and very obsequious.

"Is everything all right, sir?" he enquired.

"Perfectly!" snapped Berkeman, pushing his way with his slender human burden towards the door. "The lady's not well. I'm taking her home. The money is on the table," he flung back over his shoulder.

Once outside, he had little trouble in securing a taxi – two cabs immediately drawing up at the kerb.

Selecting the first, he gave the driver Rachana's apartment address and carefully laid the still comatose form in the back, after which he climbed into the front seat alongside the driver.

The drive to the flat took only ten minutes, in which time he searched in Rachana's handbag for her key. On arrival, he paid the driver off and collected the unconscious girl from the back of the vehicle. A puzzled driver drove away, casting a backward glance.

With difficulty, Berkeman carried Rachana up to her apartment, and let them in with her key. After closing the door, he carried her through to the bedroom and laid her gently on the bed. He thought how beautiful she looked stretched out in repose on the cream satin coverlet. How easy it would be – and he wanted her so much. There was nobody to stop him doing anything he wanted with her now.

Gently turning Rachana over on to her stomach, he undid the hook at the top of her sheaf dress and began to ease the zip downwards. Then, amazed at his own feelings, he drew it up again, and turned her gently on to her back.

"Even I can't be that much of a louse," he mumbled, half aloud and half to himself. After checking that Rachana was breathing easily, he let himself out and left the building.

*

Over a drink, Ravi Tata was planning with Venkat Singh and Silas Craig the impressive show they would put on for the natives once the fakir arrived with the lorries from Jaipur.

"A sacrifice works wonders at putting the fear of Kali into the natives. It will be an easy matter to purchase a young Nepalese girl. There are many such in the brothels of Bombay," Venkat explained, in a matter of fact voice.

"Surely we can find such a girl here, without bothering with Bombay," put in Ravi Tata.

"I know of one who would suit us admirably and who needs to be taught a lesson, as it happens," exclaimed Silas Craig, an evil grin on his face.

"Can she be easily purchased from her parents, or masters, as the case may be?" enquired Ravi Tata.

Again, the cunning grin from Craig. "Oh, we wouldn't have to purchase this one."

"What do you mean, man?" snapped Venkat. "Are you saying she would come for nothing – willingly?"

"Certainly not. I did not say that she would come willingly. We would sort of borrow her," said Craig.

"You speak in riddles, man. Do you know of such a girl for our purpose?" questioned Ravi Tata.

"Indeed I do, and a very beautiful one too, who would make a supreme sacrifice and impress the natives greatly."

"Beautiful, you say?" said Venkat, butting in. "Then why have you not kept her for yourself, Craig?"

"More beautiful than any maid you have ever seen, Venkat. We have only to catch her and lock her up until we are ready to use her."

"But are you sure she will not be missed by someone?" enquired Tata.

"Yes. She will be missed greatly. That is the heart of my plan. She runs a travel agency in downtown Bangalore, and is the girlfriend of the man I told you about earlier – Barlow, the neighbouring tea planter," explained Craig.

A concerned Ravi Tata looked doubtful.

"You mean to kidnap this girl, Craig? Will this not create a great stir in Bangalore? We can do without awkward questions from the police."

"There will be none," replied Craig. "Why should there be? No one can connect her disappearing with us, can they?"

"What of the natives that witness the sacrifice, will they not talk?" said Venkat.

Ravi Tata came to a sudden decision.

"No! They will be far too frightened of Kali's vengeance, the fear of which Dehra the fakir will have instilled into them. The more I think about it, the more the idea appeals. The fact that the girl will be well known will instil a still greater fear of the Sons of Kali, into more people."

"More co-operation all round from everybody," said Craig, metaphorically rubber-stamping Tata's statement.

"One thing, though, bothers me, Craig. Are you sure you are not suggesting this girl just to get even with someone? This man, Barlow, you spoke of?"

"Well, I won't deny it has an added attraction for me," said Craig, smiling.

"Just so long as we all understand one another. I wouldn't want this Barlow fellow poking round here," exclaimed Tata.

Craig threw back his head and laughed.

"No danger of that. He has already been warned off since the last time he trespassed on my plantation."

"Good. Then we'll leave the details to you. See that the girl is ready for Dehra two nights from now, Craig. In the meantime, Venkat and I will organise the next festival of Kali."

Silas Craig watched Ravi Tata and Venkat leave, then added, half under his breath, "You will wish you had never tangled with me, Matthew Barlow. I might even tell them later where they can find themselves another tiger. For the moment, however, your half-breed woman will do for starters."

*

Back in the heart of the forest, Zabu had located the poachers. Carla was amazed to find that there were, in fact, five of them, just as the little man had predicted, and all of them armed. Zabu, Carla and Barlow were crouched down concealed by the undergrowth, and could clearly observe the gang, as they stood in a huddle talking and, judging by the aroma that wafted to the observers, smoking hash.

Barlow looked at his watch – 3 a.m. Moonlight still flooded the clearing. He removed his backpack and opened it, bringing out to Carla's amazement a realistic-looking collapsible face mask of a tiger.

"Stay here, and don't move, whatever you do. Just watch. These natives are very superstitious. I'm going to use that as our ace in the hole."

With that, he pulled on the mask over his head and said to Zabu, "Go quickly some hundred metres back into the jungle and wait. When you hear a tiger roar, repeat the sound from where you are."

Without questioning Barlow, Zabu silently slipped away. Barlow dug into his pack again, and this time produced a small tape recorder. He inserted a tape into it and said to Carla, "When you hear the fourth roar from a tiger, do not be afraid, but press 'play' and turn the volume to full."

Carla, bewildered, just nodded and Barlow stealthily crept away on all fours. Carla watched as five minutes elapsed on her watch. The poachers were still talking when all hell broke loose.

From beyond them, somewhere across the clearing in the thick undergrowth, the roar of a tiger shattered the jungle night. As one, they all grabbed their antiquated muzzle loaders and set off in the direction of the sound. It was doubtful if they had covered more than five metres when another answering roar from further to their rear threw them into immediate confusion. Bewildered, they split up – three going in the direction of the first and two reversing slowly, guns at the ready, to meet the newer challenge.

Then came an even more deafening roar on the right-hand side. Carla realised that Matt had moved round in a circle, to confuse the gang still further. Confused was the word for it. Almost immediately came the fourth, from Zabu's new position to the poachers' left. It was Carla's cue to press the button and turn up the volume. The result nearly made her jump out of her skin, so startling was the impact.

The tape was of two male tigers locked in mortal combat over a female. A terrifying snarling and growling rent the air and continued for some thirty seconds. All five poachers stood rooted to the spot, absolutely terror-stricken. Two more tiger calls came from Barlow's and Zabu's positions to create further panic in the poachers' ranks.

Then, as abruptly as it had begun, the sound of the battling tigers ceased and a great powerful voice on the tape followed it. Carla understood not a word, for the language was Hindi, but the fear on the men's faces showed that they most certainly did. At a later date, Matt Barlow translated it for her.

'Be still you fatherless vermin. I am the Lord Shiva, most powerful of all the gods. The tigers of this forest belong to me alone, yet you dare to invade my domain. You are worthless curs, insolent in the extreme, and as such you shall be punished. Throw down your feeble guns, lest I crush you where you stand.'

Here the voice paused for effect, whilst the poachers instantly complied, tossing their guns into a clattering heap in the clearing. The voice continued:

'Now walk away, and stand in a line, whilst I decide whether to spare your worthless souls or despatch you with a bolt of lightning.'

At this point, Carla had seen the men shake with veritable terror, one of them actually dropping to the earth in a dead faint.

The men, of course, at this time, were facing Carla's hidden position, from where the voice was being projected. Now, as the tape ran out, a new challenge confronted them from their rear.

Emitting another terrifying tiger roar, Barlow stood up in clear view of the gang, clad in his tiger mask and naked to the waist. Carla had to admit that he looked a frightening spectacle as he advanced on them. The men cringed back in terror, holding on to one another for support.

Boldly, Barlow strode forward until he reached the pile of guns. Picking them up, one at a time, by the barrel, he swung each in turn against the stump of a fallen banyan tree, breaking them off with a loud snap at the stocks and thus rendering them useless. Then he swung his gaze back on the poachers, who by this time were looking as if they were in a trance. Zabu and Carla kept well out of sight, with the former still giving the occasional roar. Carla found herself wondering how both men could emulate such a sound so perfectly.

Looking at each poacher in turn, Barlow hissed through the mask of terror.

"Go now, before I disembowel you, tearing out your filthy entrails, before eating you. Begone from the forest – never to return.

Should you ever trap or shoot a tiger again, be sure that I will find and eat you!"

The men shook with terror, the whites of their eyes rolled in fear.

"And take that trash with you," exclaimed Barlow, pointing an authoritative finger at the prone member of the gang. "You are indeed fortunate that I am not overly hungry today."

Two of the poachers scooped up their fallen colleague, and the frightened group departed with alacrity, casting more than one terrified glance over their shoulders at the apparition behind them. Barlow stood, arms folded, legs astride, eyeballing their every move. Carla, in the undergrowth, was forced to push further in, lest she was discovered by the retreating group.

Zabu, from somewhere deep within the dense foliage, gave another ear-splitting roar. The gang visibly accelerated their departure.

Barlow, Zabu and Carla remained in position for some ten minutes before the little tracker joined his master in the clearing. Seeing this, from her place of concealment, Carla warily came out and joined them.

"Phew! That was impressive, Matt! I was wondering what you would do when we caught up with them, outnumbered as we were."

Once back in the grove of bamboo, Barlow peeled off the tiger mask, and stowed away that and the tape recorder in the backpack. Whilst occupied with this, he asked Zabu to hide the broken guns left behind by the poachers. This the little tracker did by crawling underneath the jungle-choking lantana and covering them over with dead leaves. Ready to resume their progress, Barlow smiled at Carla, and put an arm round her shoulders.

"You did well, Carla."

"I did nothing – you did it all – you and Zabu."

"You kept your head and picked up your cue, and that was vital, if the plan was going to work for us."

"Tell me one thing, Matt. How did you know it would work?" questioned Carla.

"Superstition out here in India is the strongest weapon one has. It's frequently used for ill. Here we were able to use it for good. Those men will never return. No matter what pressures are used against them. Sadly, others will, and we must find a more permanent method of stopping them, if the tiger is to survive in the wild."

"But I don't understand, Matt. Are the natives all so naive? I mean, although your rubber tiger mask was impressive, surely they could see it was but one man in a mask – couldn't they?" asked an incredulous Carla.

Barlow gave an understanding smile.

"How do you think the Indian fakirs are so successful? Firstly, one must create the illusion. This Zabu and I did with the roaring, and you yourself supplied the tape. The rest was easy."

Zabu entered the conversation.

"Do not forget, memsahib, in India there are many gods and even more superstitions. Already there is belief of a man, half tiger, in this area."

Carla, understanding beginning to dawn on her face, smiled.

"So you two rascals have pulled this stunt before?"

Zabu gave his toothy grin, his face creasing like parchment.

"Many times memsahib. Always work good."

"But how do you both make those wonderful bloodcurdling roars?"

Zabu was about to demonstrate but Barlow, with a smile, said, "Some other time, Zabu. It's time we were getting back."

A different, if equally fascinating route to Carla was taken on the way back. After some time the moon faded away, and it seemed to her to be getting lighter. Barlow explained at length the phenomenon of the false dawn and that the proper arrival of the new day would not begin for at least another hour or so. He went on to stress to Carla that she should keep her eyes firmly on the ground in front of her, as poisonous snakes could sometimes be found on the jungle paths.

"In actual fact, Zabu would have already warned you first," Barlow added, when he noticed the alarm written all over her face.

If Carla thought the forest sounds of the night had been impressive, it was nothing to what she was to experience with the coming of the real dawn.

Several jungle cocks heralded the coming of the new day, intermingled with the high-pitched cries of peacocks. An incessant chatter of monkeys in the high treetops saluted the sunrise in their own fashion, interspersing the sound of parakeets and other birdlife and the occasional call of a deer.

Mist began to rise eerily from the jungle floor, rising to meet and mingle with the lower branches of giant trees. The bamboo and lantana seemed to alter shape in the strange light, as beams of early sunlight filtered through the branches of the taller trees. A gold bundoo winged a heavy passage between one boram tree to another. The earth smelt fresh and damp, and a small muntjac scurried across in front of them to disappear into thick undergrowth.

Finally, they rounded a grove of bamboo and there, to Carla's amazement, was Barlow's utility, where they had left it. The rose-pink shades of dawn were clearly evident on the distant hillside, the mists from the valley rising to meet them.

Barlow stood appreciating his India, as he defined it, and pointed out the Cauvery river in the far distance.

Finally, when everything and everybody was safely aboard the truck, he fired the engine and eased out the clutch. Slowly bumping over the rough ground, they were on their way back to Bangalore. Soon they would pick up a rough trail, and then eventually a road, not much smoother.

*

The terrified poachers reported back to an almost hysterical and angry Craig later that morning.

Without giving them a chance to defend or explain themselves, he lambasted them with verbal abuse, his face contorted and black with rage.

"You dogs dare to return here, without having shot, or trapped even one tiger, and then tell me that you have lost the guns I supplied you with! You never even went! I suspect you sold the muzzle loaders in the local market. Is it not so, you scum?"

The bravest of the quintet tried to face up to him.

"It is not so, sahib. We went into jungle. There to find tigers."

"And?" thundered Craig, pushing his bloated face into the native's.

"It was not our fault. You did not tell us the forest was possessed by a demon tiger, half man."

"What is this you are giving me?" demanded Craig.

"It is true, Craig Sahib," said a second man, in support of his brother.

"What rubbish is this?"

"Not rubbish. Many tigers all belong Lord Shiva. Tiger man he take guns and break them to leetle pieces," added a third poacher.

"And you expect me to believe this cock-and-bull story, you imbeciles! You have been tricked!" roared Craig.

"Him no trick. We luck not get eaten by tiger man. We no go back forest, ever," put in the fourth.

The fifth watched Craig's face, the whites of his eyes popping nervously. Craig turned away and, screwing his fist into a ball, he pounded it into the palm of his other hand.

"You dolts will work for no wages until you have worked off the price of the firearms. Do you understand?"

The five of them just stood rooted to their respective positions.

"Do you understand me, dogs?" Craig repeated.

A murmur of grudging assent greeted the question.

"Now get out, all of you, except Bora," snapped Craig, indicating the bolder of the five. "He can relay in slow detail everything that happened in the jungle last night."

Bora shuffled forward, as the other four made good their escape, relief on their faces.

"Now, Bora, let's hear it. Don't leave anything out," commanded Craig.

Chapter Eighteen

Abduction

Rachana awoke the next morning, fully dressed on her bed, with a king-sized headache and a dry throat.

"I swear I'll never drink again," she murmured, half aloud. Then, as realisation hit her, she clutched a hand to her mouth. How on earth had she got home and on the bed? The last thing she remembered was grabbing at the restaurant table as she felt her legs buckling. Before that, there had been a row with Berkeman, she could remember that. Who had brought her home? Was it he? Had anything happened? Had he taken advantage of her? No, surely he wouldn't have stooped that low – would he? Doubt and panic assailed her. After a refreshing shower and couple of aspirins, she was beginning to feel a little more like facing reality. Wrapping herself in a long white bath towel, she telephoned Berkeman's hotel and was put through to him in his room. She recognised the strong American accent immediately when he answered.

Before giving him a chance to speak, she blurted out, "Did you bring me home last night?"

"Somebody needed to," he replied.

"Look. Can you tell me what happened?" she enquired, uncertainty in her voice. "I mean—"

"I know what you mean, Rachana,' said Berkeman, acidly. "Did I take advantage of you, whilst you were out of this planet. Right?"

"Well, er, yes. Did you? You didn't – did you?" stammered Rachana.

A long pause ensued, before the American replied.

"No, to be honest. I saved you for your precious Barlow."

Relief flooded through Rachana's whole being. Finally, she managed to utter a reply.

"Thank you for that anyway." Then she managed to add, "Look, I'm sorry about last night. I shouldn't have led you on, then rowed with you. I must have quite spoilt your evening."

Berkeman's voice moderated in its sarcastic and acid tone.

"Well, no permanent harm done. How about we start again, honey? Dinner tonight?"

For answer, there came over the line a silvery chuckle. "Thanks but no thanks. I've learnt my lesson. Time to say sorry in other places, I think."

"Barlow, you mean?"

"Yes, Matt's a proud man, and I guess it's up to me. I walked out, after all."

Berkeman gulped.

"I hate losing you now that I've found you, but I guess it's always been the tiger man with you, Rachana."

Rachana, ignoring the last remark, countered with, "Anyway, Steve, thanks for what you didn't do last night. Goodbye now."

Berkeman heard the click of her phone at the other end and said to the lifeless hand-piece, "I wish the hell I hadn't been such a gentleman. Perhaps it's time to remember what I really came to India for, and help Carla Wayne some!"

*

Later that afternoon, Rachana drove over to Barlow's plantation. After parking her car she was greeted by Jana. Both showed delight at the sight of the other. After a period of nuzzling and stroking, Rachana looked up as the front door on the veranda swung open. To Rachana's dismay it was Carla Wayne, looking very beautiful and well groomed in a pale blue silk dress.

"Hi there! Nice to see you again," Carla called out.

"Hi," answered Rachana, in a more subdued tone. "Is Matt around?"

"No, I'm afraid you've missed him. He's out on the plantation with his foreman, making up for lost time, he said. I'm expecting him back for dinner tonight, though. Come in, won't you?"

Rachana hesitated.

"No. Not to bother. I'll call him on the phone after dinner tonight."

By this time Carla had descended the veranda steps to join Rachana and Jana.

"Please do come in. I mean, after all, it's you who belong here, not me. I'm only a guest."

Rachana looked uncertain, unable to decide on the best way to tackle the situation. Carla began again.

"Look, Rachana, this is obviously your place a lot more than it's mine. Why don't you ask me in?"

The latter remark seemed to break the ice and Rachana smiled. 'God, she's beautiful,' thought Carla. 'No wonder Steve Berkeman lost his head over her.'

"Let's go in together. All three of us, then," said Rachana, putting her arm round Jana, who was nuzzling her again.

Once inside, Carla laughed and said, "Shall I offer you a coffee or will you get me one?"

Rachana chuckled and replied, "Let's go into the kitchen and make one together. On a tea plantation, it should be tea, really."

"I guess it should, but I prefer coffee."

"So do I, but it seems disloyal to Matt really, so I usually drink tea."

After some small talk between the two girls, they finally sat down round the kitchen table.

Rachana seemed a little ill at ease, before she blurted out, "Has Matt mentioned me since I walked out the other night, Carla?"

"Well, no. But from what I've seen of Matt, he's the strong silent type. I'm sure it's not because he hasn't thought of you often enough."

"You think so?"

"I'm sure so."

"He hasn't tried to contact me."

Carla gave Rachana a censorious look.

"Have you tried to contact him?"

"Well, er, yes. I rang twice one evening, but there was no reply."

Without thinking about the answer, Carla replied, "Well, that's because we went into Bangalore for a meal one night, and the next night was spent catching poachers in the jungle. That's why I may look a bit jaded today. Caught up with some sleep this morning, when we got back. Not nearly enough, though. That's why Matt's out on the plantation now, making up for lost time."

Realising the effect her remarks were having on Rachana, judging by the girl's obvious facial expression of distress, Carla attempted to rescue the situation.

"Look, it's strictly business between Matt and I. He's giving me a lot of material for my magazine report. I've already faxed one lot back to New York. Last night will provide me with more."

"I see," said an anxious Rachana, but didn't sound convinced.

"Look – I mean, there's nothing between Matt and myself," said Carla, blushing.

"You mean you don't find him attractive?" queried Rachana.

The enthusiastic Carla blew it again.

"Oh, I do, I do! He's lovely. I mean, but—"

"But what?" said Rachana, her hackles rising.

"But he's not interested in me anyway. It's you he wants, Rachana."

Rachana thought for a moment before replying.

"You know they say Matt Barlow is half tiger, do you, Carla?"

"Surely it's only the illiterate natives who say such nonsense?"

"Nonsense, is it? Do you know anything about the mating habits of tigers, Carla?"

"Of course not. I'm an American, remember."

"Well, perhaps I should enlighten you. A male tiger mates with a female, but once she has her cubs he will usually move on to a new female. All she has to do is call and two males will emerge to fight over her."

"Really, I don't understand what you are implying, Rachana. I'm sure Matt is nothing like that."

Rachana, ignoring the remark, went on. "Some say the female removes her cubs for fear the male will become annoyed with them and eat them."

Carla, tired of being pushed on to the defensive, countered, "Is that why you are running away from Matt, because you can't face his way of life?"

"Is that what he has told you?"

"He has told me nothing. All of this seems to be in your mind, Rachana."

Suddenly Rachana broke down and began to sob bitterly. Between sobs, she gasped, "You are right, Carla. I love him too much. Every time he goes out on one of these missions of his after man-eaters, poachers or even rogue elephants, I die a little. It's breaking me up, you see. I'll never get used to it. He has asked me before to marry him, but I cannot bring myself to take the risk of losing him."

Carla put an arm round the distressed girl.

"We must accept people as they are. People will always do what they feel is right. Matt is no different to everyone else. His life just happens to be dangerous."

Through the tears, Rachana peered at her uncertainly.

"You seem to understand him better than I."

"It is not only danger that Matt loves. I saw it today in the jungle. It's life itself. It's India, its people, its animals. They are part of the man."

Rachana dried her tears with a silk handkerchief before confessing to Carla, "Last night I nearly made a fool of myself with your friend, Steve Berkeman, just to get at Matt. I couldn't go through with it, though." She went on at length, to explain what had happened.

At the end of the narrative, Carla chuckled.

"Serves Steve right. He deliberately picked that row with Matt. He was after you from the moment he saw you here."

"But I thought he was—"

"With me? Oh, no! Nothing like that. He was sent out here by my boss to get me out of India. Then, when I wouldn't leave, he decided to stay and help."

Seeing Rachana's puzzled expression, she added, "Then when he caught one glimpse of you, our Sir Galahad forgot all about me."

"Why would he want me when he could have you, Carla?"

Carla laughed.

"Who said he could have me? Don't you think I might have something to say about that?"

Both girls, seeing the funny side, relaxed and chuckled. Then, quite suddenly, Rachana caught Carla off guard with her next question, which came like a bolt from the blue.

"Well, if you don't fancy Steve, do you fancy Matt?"

Carla, quite taken aback by her directness, replied, "What a question to ask."

"Well, do you?"

Carla considered her next answer.

"Let me put it this way. If I didn't know that you and he were an item, and he happened to show some interest, other than professional, in me, then I guess the answer would have to be – yes."

Rachana nodded, a satisfied expression on her face.

"At least you're honest with me, Carla."

"I think somehow you would see through me if I wasn't quite candid."

"Well," said Rachana, "we both know where we are at."

"Sorry?" replied Carla. "You've got me there. The situation simply won't arise because you and Matt quite clearly belong together. I don't intend to interfere."

"Somehow, although I trust you, it may not be in your hands altogether." Rising, Rachana offered her hand. "I must go now. I'm getting behind in the office too."

"But I thought you were going to wait and see Matt when he returns?"

"No, I think not. Just tell him I came to apologise for the other evening. It was all my fault. The rest is up to him."

Without more ado, she was gone, closing the door behind her. Jana trotted over to the now closed door and put her head on one side, then looked back expectantly at Carla.

"I can't unravel that lady either, Jana," she said softly, walking over and rubbing the tigress behind her right ear.

*

That evening, Craig was explaining on the telephone to Ravi Tata in Delhi what had happened to his band of poachers.

"You imbecile, Craig!" screamed Tata, down the line. Craig held the receiver away from his ear.

Tata continued with the abuse. "Must I do everything myself? You told me these men were reliable and would bring back tiger carcasses, so what went wrong this time, Craig? Eh?"

Silas Craig gulped. Somehow this man always seemed to be able to intimidate him. Once more, he tried to explain.

Tata cut him short.

"You dolt! You are seriously expecting me to believe that a man who was half tiger and a whole herd of tigers drove them off! What nonsense is this?"

"It's the truth. I—"

Tata again cut short Craig's attempts to vindicate himself.

"There aren't enough tigers left in India to make up a herd!" he snapped.

"I only know what my men have told me," argued Craig.

"Then find more men, or send these back into the jungle."

"They will not go there again. Not even on pain of death, or whatever monetary reward we offer. I'm telling you, they are scared witless."

"Then I will bring down with me tribesmen from the north who will show your feeble southern natives how it should be done. The lorries should be with you by tomorrow night, or the next morning at the latest. I take it you can handle that, Craig, without fouling up again."

"It wasn't my fault this time," whined Craig.

"You engaged the men, therefore the buck stops with you!"

It was useless to argue, so Craig changed the subject.

"When are you and Venkat Singh going to arrive?"

"We shall fly down to Bangalore from here, just as soon as you inform me that the lorries have arrived, and everything is safely stored away in your new refrigeration unit." With a curt goodbye Tata slammed the phone down.

Silas Craig massaged his ear and replaced his receiver, only to pick it up again and dial a number. When it was answered, he said, "I have a job for you. Listen well."

*

Ramon Srinath was addressing Kepel Rao, the DC in his office.

"It looks like you are going to be stuck with me for a little longer, sir. My superiors have given me permission to remain down here for up to a week."

The DC eased his bulky frame, on an uncomfortably small chair, behind his office desk.

"Do you really think you can get enough evidence to stop these people, Inspector?" he remarked, running a hand through his thinning, silvery hair. Srinath ignored the question.

"I take it you have posted a man, sir, at each of the three sites, to watch for lorries entering?"

Kepel Rao paused before replying, and looked thoughtful.

"Yes, I've done that, but you realise I can't issue three separate search warrants, one for each plantation. My superiors would never countenance that."

"You don't have to. It will only be necessary for the one the lorries arrive at. Once we know that, we can safely forget the other two."

"I'm relieved to hear that, Inspector, because I'm very short of manpower. It's all right for you fellows in Delhi."

Srinath again ignored the remark and continued. "Sometimes I get the feeling I'm the only person in India interested in stopping the poachers and wiping out these dirty animal product racketeers. Do you realise, sir, it's the second biggest thing now to drug smuggling?"

"I wish you luck then, Inspector, but I'm sure you will understand when I say I have other fish to fry."

"Are you telling me you don't want to help crack these gangs, sir?"

"No. I'm just saying you're largely on your own. I'll give you what help I can, but just don't expect too much. If it came to a show of force against these people, I simply don't have the men."

Ramon Srinath couldn't help the disgust showing on his face. Kepel Rao noticed it and said, "I have to admit I can't see what real damage these people do, and it would be pretty low on my priority list."

Srinath hammered his fist down on the desk.

"What!" he almost screamed. "These people are going to make the Bengal tiger extinct in the wild, in India, within the next four or five years, and you can't see the harm! I don't believe it!"

"Come, come, Inspector Srinath. Keep your temper. I wouldn't want to have to pull rank on you."

Ramon Srinath clenched his nails into his palms, inwardly seething. With this attitude, what chance was there?

"Good evening, sir. I'll keep in touch," he forced himself to say before turning and leaving the office.

"Very intense young man," muttered Kepel Rao, reaching for his pipe. Oh well, in ten minutes it would be time to leave for home and a relaxing evening. Only a few more years before he retired from the service now.

Outside in the street, Ramon Srinath counted to ten, and pondered on what a young constable had told him whilst he had been waiting to be shown in to see the DC. Something about a rumour, circulating the native quarters, about a man, half tiger, who was terrorising the jungle with a herd of wild tigers at his command. It appeared that a poaching gang had returned from the forest that morning fearful for their very lives. A weird story, to be true, thought Srinath. Then, smiling to himself, he reflected what he could achieve with a brigade of such tiger men.

'Maybe that chap I saw out at that plantation yesterday morning could throw some light on the matter. He's into tigers, so Rao tells me anyway. Might be worth having another word with him. I can do with any information or help I can get.'

He set off briskly towards his hotel. A slim gleam of hope dawning somewhere at the back of his mind.

*

Matt Barlow came in late for dinner, having been busily engaged on the plantation all afternoon. Carla quickly filled him in about Rachana's visit and apology concerning her earlier behaviour. There was no doubt, judging by his expression, that he was pleased with the news.

"I'll give her a ring after dinner," was all he said to Carla.

"Good," replied Carla. "Because I've earned my keep and prepared dinner for you."

"There was really no need for you to feel you had to do that. I've been very glad of your company."

"It was nothing, and it amused me to do it. Why don't you get a nice refreshing shower, by which time we will be ready to eat."

"Sounds good. What would I do without you around here, Carla?" he remarked lightly, heading for the bathroom.

Carla watched the door close behind him, and said under her breath, 'Matt Barlow, I'm going to miss you one hell of a lot...'

*

Just after dusk, Rachana Dev left her office and drove across town to her apartment. Her mind was far away, at Matt's plantation house, as she put the key in the lock of her front door and entered. It wasn't until she had closed the door behind her and turned on the light that she realised she was not alone. Two men were already there, both coloured. One leant against the wall, arms folded across his chest, whilst the other had made himself at home on her divan.

She found herself staring straight down the barrel of a sawn-off shotgun. Rachana half froze with terror. Was it robbery, or, worse – rape! Her mind was working overtime. She tried to convert her fear to anger.

"What is the meaning of this? What are you men doing in my apartment?"

The older of the two men, the seated one with the gun, grinned back at her insolently.

"Your apartment, you say. Don't worry, you won't have need of it much longer, woman."

"What do you mean?" exclaimed a frightened Rachana.

"Oh, you're about to become a very important lady, I've been told. The star of the show, in fact. Isn't that so, Ashraf?"

"What riddles are you talking in?" snapped Rachana.

"You will find out in good time. Now get down on your knees."

"I will not!"

The man with the gun nodded to the other, who immediately came round behind her, forcing one of her arms up behind her back. She screamed with pain.

"My brother said, on your knees," spat out the man the seated one had called Ashraf.

Rachana felt herself forced forward and down, on to the red pile carpet.

"It will go better with you if you co-operate, bitch!" retorted the older man with the gun. "Find something in there to tie her with, Ashraf," he said, pointing to the bedroom.

As the younger man went to look, Rachana looked desperately about her, in two minds whether to jump up and try for the door.

"Don't even think about it, woman," snapped the gunman jerking the firearm purposefully. "This could scatter your beautiful body all round this room and that would be a pity, don't you think?"

"But what is it you want? I have no money in the apartment."

"Have you not? Well, as it happens, we have no need of money."
He broke off and called through the open bedroom door. "What's
keeping you, Ashraf? I haven't got all day."

The younger man emerged with a silk scarf and a satin half slip.

"Will these do, Bagh?"

"Fine. Tie her hands behind her back and gag her."

Rachana tried to resist, but saw that she had little choice and was
only going to get hurt more if she did. Quietly, she put her hands
behind her and felt the younger man tying her tightly at the wrists with
the scarf. He then proceeded to tear the satin slip into strips. In spite
of her protests, one piece was bunched up and rammed into her
mouth, whilst another longer bit was stretched over her lips and tied
behind her mouth.

"That's better. All trussed up like a chicken," said the gunman,
getting up from the sofa, and chucking her under the chin with the
sawn-off shotgun.

Ashraf reached forward over her shoulder and ran his bony hands
down inside her dress. Rachana, unable to do anything, tried to
squirm and roll away from him, but his hand cupped one of her
breasts violently and squeezed.

"A pretty one this, Bagh. Can't we stay and enjoy her? After all
she can't stop us."

"That's enough of that, young brother. We have a job to do and
the sooner she's delivered, the sooner we get paid."

Reluctantly, with a final squeeze, Ashraf released his hold and
stood up.

"Waste of a good woman, if you ask me."

"No one's asking you. Come on. Let's get going."

Rachana was pulled to her feet, then she was prodded towards the
door with the gun in her back, by Bagh the elder. Petulantly, Ashraf
followed.

Chapter Nineteen

Confusion

Matt Barlow and Carla Wayne worked their way through the superb three course meal prepared earlier by Carla. Pouring them both a liqueur, Barlow complimented her on her culinary skills.

"Just something I threw together," laughed Carla.

"I could get used to having you round the place," he quipped.

Carla blushed.

"Why don't you ring Rachana? She should have got back to her apartment by now."

"Good idea," said Barlow. Walking over to the telephone, he picked it up and dialled. Carla could hear the number ringing, but it remained unanswered.

Replacing the hand-piece, he exclaimed, "I'll try again later."

Carla remarked, "Strange though, because she intimated that she was going home, although she did say work was getting behind at the office."

Barlow nodded and tried again, dialling another number. All he got this time was an answerphone, telling him that the office would open again at nine a.m. tomorrow morning.

"She must be somewhere between the two then, on her way home," put in Carla, helpfully.

"I guess so," said Barlow, sitting down once more and sipping his Cointreau. "I'll try again later."

"Tell me some more about tigers, Matt," prompted Carla, drawing her chair nearer.

Matt needed no urging. It was his favourite subject.

"Basically the tiger has an inherent fear of mankind, but not this one," he interjected, patting Jana's head as she lay at his feet. "I guess I'm the only parent she's ever known."

Carla chuckled.

"She doesn't seem to be complaining anyway."

Barlow continued. "Over recent years, tiger populations in all the nine species, two of which are already extinct, have been severely decimated. It's not only poachers who are to blame though." He waited for the words to sink in before continuing. "Loss of habitat, through the cutting down of large areas of forest, is one important factor. The pushing through of new roads another. The population explosion in humans, particularly in India, has brought its own problems to the animals. Herds of spotted deer and sambar, the tigers' natural prey, have disappeared, due to poisoning and poachers, plus an invading civilisation."

"That's awful," interrupted Carla. "Surely no one poisons them?"

"Technically, you can't blame the natives. They are very poor, and are really only trying to protect their cattle and crops."

"But to poison animals – that's terrible," said Carla.

"Let me explain," remarked Matt, dryly. "More national parks have been created to conserve the tigers we still have—"

"But surely that's good news, isn't it?"

"It would be if more consultation took place of the natives living in those areas. Buffer zones are created round the parks, often with little regard for the people living there. They naturally resent this. When someone is so poor that he can hardly eke out an existence, you cannot expect him – or her for that matter – to be sympathetic. Organisations also mean well, although one or two are misguided and use all their money to provide more game wardens in the parks."

Carla looked confused.

"I would have thought that helped to protect the tigers?"

"It should – in theory. Unfortunately, the wardens are so poorly paid that, once in their posts, they are usually open to bribes from the poachers. When you think about it, who better to know where the tigers are for the gangs to go and kill?"

"I see what you mean," said Carla, thoughtfully, now with her notebook out. She questioned Barlow again. "You told me what makes a man-eater out of a tiger, but how does a cattle killer come about?"

"Hunger, due to loss of natural prey. Firstly, the natives either drive off the deer or poison them, and the only food left for the tiger is their cattle. They usually hit back by poisoning the kill, so that when the tiger returns the next night and eats it, he dies. Another awful method are home-made bombs, concealed inside the carcass. The tiger that dies is the lucky one. Many are thus maimed and turn into man-eaters." Scribbling away madly in her notebook, Carla shot another question at Barlow.

"How serious is the threat to the Bengal tiger, here in India?"

"Desperately so," exclaimed Barlow. "Unless we can stop the filthy tiger parts trade and wipe out the gangs, the days of the Bengal are numbered in the wild..."

His voice trailed off.

"How long, Matt?" she whispered.

"Four, five years at most," he replied sadly.

"Is there nothing the human race can do to help?"

"Oh yes. But one has to get past the apathy of mankind. When the tiger is no more, people will say how terrible – how could we let it happen?"

"But you are doing so much yourself, Matt!" she said, passionately.

"Sadly a drop in the ocean. Every man, woman and child who cares needs to write to their governments and newspapers putting pressure on them to act."

"But I thought in many countries that the trade in animal parts was illegal?"

"So it is, but governments are doing nothing to enforce it. Public opinion must be made to force their hand," Matt replied emphatically.

The discussion went on for fully an hour – Carla, immensely impressed by Matt's fervour and dedication to the conservation cause.

Finally, looking at his watch, he declared it was time to try and contact Rachana again. The result was the same. All he got was the ringing tone. By 10 p.m. he had made five attempts, all to no avail.

"I think I'll drive over. Maybe she's trying to play hard to get."

"Perhaps you should. After all, she did come over to apologise, and obviously figures the next move is yours, Matt."

"Will you be all right here by yourself? I'll leave Jana here with you," he said.

"I'll be fine, don't you worry about me." Then, as he reached the door, she called softly, "Matt?"

"Yes," he exclaimed, turning.

"Look, I love being here, but as things are between you and Rachana, I really think I should move into an hotel tomorrow. Don't you?"

Barlow halted, his hand on the door catch. He turned and walked slowly back towards her. Stopping, he placed both hands on her shoulders and looked her straight in the eyes.

"No, I don't think you should do that at all. I still believe you to be in considerable danger in India. Therefore, you are safer here with me."

"Is that the only reason?" said Carla, looking up at him from under her long lashes.

Their eyes met and locked, Barlow's hands sliding down to Carla's waist. Firmly, but gently, he pulled her into him. Somehow – Carla never knew how – their lips met in a long sensual lingering kiss. She could feel the tingle right down to her toes, like a surge of electricity. Carla had never meant to respond, but found herself a lot more than just a recipient of a kiss.

With an abandonment she had never known, she threw all caution to the wind. Locking her hands round the back of Matt's neck, she almost ate him. For fully a minute they remained locked together before Barlow was the first to break.

"Why did I do that?" exclaimed Barlow.

"If you don't know, I can't tell you, Matt," said a confused Carla. A moment later she turned and ran off towards her room. Over her shoulder, she called, "I'll see you when you return. I'm going to pack. There's no way I can stay now."

Barlow, puzzled by his own confused emotions, asked a question of Jana, who was watching him, her head on one side.

"What the hell am I doing, Jana?"

The tigress just nuzzled his hip bone in response.

*

An hour later found Barlow knocking on Rachana's apartment door. When he received no reply, he used his key and let himself in. The place was in darkness. Turning on the light, he saw that the clock was already reading 11.30. Of Rachana there was no sign. Nothing seemed to be out of place anywhere. Maybe she had just decided to go out for the evening. Odd though. If she had wanted to prove a point, why would she have come over to the plantation to apologise?

Some dried mud on the carpet took his eye.   Strange this. Rachana was always so fastidious about anything like that.   Barlow couldn't imagine her going out without first having removed the offending stain.   It was possible, of course, that she was waiting for it to dry first, but somehow he didn't think so.

Oh well, she would probably be in soon.   He settled himself down in an armchair with a magazine.   He would just have to wait for her.

The minutes and the hours ticked by.   By 2 a.m. Barlow decided to give up the vigil and return home, thinking that Rachana had chosen to teach him some sort of lesson and stay out.   Quite probably, she had booked into an hotel for the night.   He knew how wilful she could be on occasion.

He would just have to call round at her office in the morning.

*

Rachana, however, was far from a luxurious hotel.   Her two captors had taken her across town by car and out into the country. The fact that they hadn't bothered to blindfold her was ominous. Rachana's sharp mind deduced that they must be aware she knew Bangalore and the surrounding area like the back of her hand. Therefore, she could come to only one conclusion.   Wherever they were taking her was going to be a one-way trip!

For one brief moment of hope, she realised that they were heading out towards Matt's plantation.   Could it be that he was kidnapping her for a joke?   Almost as soon as the idea dawned, she dismissed it. Matt would never do such a thing, and, even if he did, he certainly wouldn't be employing thugs like these two.

Therefore, it came as no surprise when they turned off on the road for Silas Craig's plantation.   Somewhere, at the back of her mind, Rachana had half sensed that he was probably behind her kidnapping. Hope surged anew.   Surely he would be the first person Matt would suspect?   Yes, Matt would come looking for her.   Then, with horror, she remembered their estranged state of play at the moment.

"My God!" She thought. "What if he just thinks I've run out on him?"   A cold feeling hit at the pit of her stomach.   After all he had the Wayne girl to console him now.

When they arrived at Craig's plantation, there was no sign of him. The two men had simply bundled her from the car into a dark outhouse. There, they securely tied her to a wooden support beam and, leaving her still gagged, left without a word.

Once the door was shut and the vehicle had noisily pulled away, Rachana was left to her thoughts. A shaft of moonlight penetrated between some broken slats near the roof, giving minimal illumination. The place seemed to be some sort of grain store. Several full sacks were stacked on a raised platform in front of her and an array of tools were hung on the walls, held there by makeshift nails. To her left was an old ox plough, long since fallen into disuse. A few ropes and some folded empty sacks in a pile were about all the other contents.

Rachana wriggled and squirmed in an effort to free herself. All to no avail – these men had done their job only too well. All she succeeded in doing was chafing her wrists and making them sore.

Suddenly, she recalled one of the men's words when they had surprised her in her apartment. Something about 'being the star of the show'. What could he have possibly meant by that? Whatever it was, she was in no doubt that it wouldn't be pleasant as far as she was concerned.

Time ticked by slowly. No one came near and she had no way of knowing how long she had been there. Every now and then she heard a scuffling sound from somewhere within the sacks in front of her. Obviously a rat! 'I hope it stays there,' she thought.

The night passed in slow torture, both in mind and body. She ached in every limb, and couldn't even stretch her legs to alleviate the cramp.

Finally, the moonlight paled into the false dawn, which gave her some idea of the time. Then it was darker than ever within the outhouse. The only sounds from outside were the call of the nightjars and owls. Eventually, the cry of a jungle cock told her that the real dawn was approaching and a little later the gloom within became lighter.

With it, her spirits rose a little, and she looked round desperately for some inspiration of a means for escape. The optimism was short-lived. There was none!

It must have been light for some three hours when she heard someone approaching. The shuffling noise of feet grew ever nearer.

Rachana craned her head as best she could to watch the door. An elderly Indian, dressed in a shabby white dhoti, and carrying a tray, entered. He spoke to her in a rasping old voice, but in reasonable English.

"Your breakfast, memsahib. I take off your gag now. No good you scream. No one hear you, only Craig Sahib, and he know you here anyway. I untie your hands so you can eat and drink. Very good. Yes?"

The relief she felt when the gag and finally her hands were freed was immense. Maybe she could grab this old man and overpower him. Then she realised that her feet were to be left tied and also the rope round her middle, securing her to the post.

Her throat was as dry as tinder so she quickly gulped down the sweet mint tea. The food she pushed away. It looked like some sort of cereal biscuits, probably made from maize.

The old Indian simply picked up the tray and balanced it on top of the folded sacks whilst he retied her. If she had hoped that he wouldn't do such an efficient job as her original captors, she was to be mistaken. Her bonds and then finally the gag were as tight as ever.

She made protesting sounds, as best she could, through the muffled cloth.

"Me bring you lunch later, memsahib. Better you should eat, then I think Craig Sahib he come see you later."

With that, he shuffled out and was gone. Once more Rachana was left to her thoughts and all alone. And so it must have gone on, for another two or three agonising hours. Rachana had no way of gauging the passing of time, other than from the brightness of the sun, filtering through the missing and cracked boards of the outhouse. It became stifling hot and sticky and the numerous flies began to bother her. She was powerless to stop them settling on face, legs and arms. They were even more bothersome than the mosquitoes of the night had been.

Just when she judged that the sun had reached its zenith, the door burst open, to reveal the loathsome Silas Craig leering at her, his belly projecting over the thick leather belt holding up his khaki drill shorts.

He ambled over to her, and, placing a podgy hand under her chin, forced her head back against the beam to which she was tied. Grinning from ear to ear, he exclaimed, "Not so sure of yourself now, are you bitch, with no tigress to save you?"

Rachana tried to utter an obscenity, but with the gag over her mouth it sounded more like a moan. Craig laughed and pushed his face down, uncomfortably close to hers.

"We have real good plans for you, lady."

A moment later the old native, still dressed in the same dirty dhoti, shuffled in with her lunch on a tray. Craig turned to him.

"Take off her gag and untie her hands. We want her to keep up her strength for what's planned for her."

Once the gag was removed, Rachana lambasted Craig with verbal abuse. Stepping forward, he struck a back-handed blow across her face.

"Silence! Bitch!" he screamed.

As soon as her hands were released, Rachana clutched at her stinging face.

"That's just a sample of what you will get if you don't do as you're told," he grunted, roughly pulling her hand away from her reddened face.

"Why have you brought me here?" Rachana fired at him.

Craig grinned.

"You will find out in time, woman. For the moment eat and drink whilst you have the chance."

Rachana gulped the drink down. She was feeling quite light-headed and dehydrated.

"Can I have another drink please?"

Craig indicated for the servant to pour her a refill of the passion fruit cordial.

Craig exclaimed, "That's better. I'm glad you have decided to be polite. After you have finished your lunch, I might just decide to have you untied and moved into the house."

*

That morning, at breakfast, Barlow related to Carla how he had failed to find Rachana the previous evening.

"Oh, I thought when you didn't return until the early hours that you must have found her," retorted Carla.

"Unfortunately not. I'll go into town and call in at her office this morning." Then Barlow suddenly noticed that Carla was packed and ready to go. "You don't have to, you know," he said softly.

"I think it's better this way, Matt."

Barlow looked uncomfortable and didn't quite know what to say.

"Look, if it's about what happened yesterday evening, I'm sorry," he blurted out self consciously.

"I don't think it's fair to Rachana for me to stay on here."

"You can trust me, Carla, it won't happen again." Barlow looked thoroughly miserable.

"But can I trust myself, Matt? That's my main worry," said Carla softly.

Barlow recovered and played his trump card.

"It's too dangerous for you to leave here. Don't forget that they have already tried to kill you once."

"But that was in Jaipur."

"These people are highly organised and have eyes everywhere. I don't think you realise how ruthless they can be and to what lengths they will go."

Carla began to waver.

"I can't argue with that. Two conservationists have already been killed, just because they were ready to talk to me."

Barlow supported his argument.

"And now they will know you have already sent two adverse reports back to your magazine in New York. They won't want you to continue making their business as difficult, so—"

"So," agreed Carla, "they will want to put me out of the way permanently."

"Exactly! So you'll stay here?" said Barlow hopefully.

Carla looked uncertain. There was a long pause before she replied.

"I shouldn't let you talk me into it, but now that you put it that way, I do feel a lot safer here with you and Jana."

"Good! That's settled then," said Barlow, picking up her things and taking them back into her bedroom.

Carla stood and watched him, feeling mixed emotions of confusion and relief. She told herself that she wanted to see the organisers of the poachers brought to justice. That was her main reason for staying on.

Chapter Twenty
Srinath Enlists Help

Matt Barlow left Carla with Jana at the plantation after breakfast and drove down to Bangalore. He went straight on to Rachana's travel agency and spoke to the two young women assistants there, Gargy and Jacqui. Neither had seen hide nor hair of Rachana since she had left the office yesterday evening. Gargy, a small petite, but well-made girl, said that she was very surprised as Rachana always arrived at the office before either of them. Jacqui, a heavily made-up Indonesian girl, with a flirty disposition, after provocatively fluttering her eyelashes at Barlow, agreed that it was all very odd.

Leaving a message with the more reliable Gargy for Rachana if she came in, he said, "I'll go back to her apartment."

As the office door closed behind him, Jacqui did an imitation swoon.

"I wouldn't run if he was looking for me, unless it was backwards," she said.

Gargy laughed and said, "Hands off, Jacqui. The boss saw him first."

"Some people have all the luck," retorted the former.

Twenty minutes later, Barlow was experiencing the same sort of luck at Rachana's flat. A quick look round told him that she hadn't returned since his departure last evening.

Now Barlow was extremely worried. This wasn't Rachana being difficult. Something had definitely happened to her. But what? Who could possibly have anything against her? She had always been popular about town, and as far as he knew, had no enemies. Unless someone had done something to get at him, Matt Barlow. Could that be it? Who would want to do that? The only one he could think of was Silas Craig. But then that fat oaf wouldn't dare, after the beating he had given him the last time! Unless, of course, he had someone to back him up! Was it possible that...? Suddenly, his thoughts were interrupted as he set foot outside in the act of leaving Rachana's apartment. A familiar face was approaching. For a moment Barlow couldn't place it. Then he remembered – Inspector Ramon Srinath.

"Ah, I was told I might find you here, Mr Barlow."

"You were?" retorted a surprised Barlow.

"I rang your house this morning, and Miss Wayne informed me I might find you here."

Barlow wore a puzzled expression.

"What can I do for you, Inspector?"

"Is there anywhere we can talk, sir?"

"Yes, we can go back into Rachana's apartment, if you like," agreed Barlow.

When both were inside, Barlow said, "Can I get you a drink, Inspector?"

"A coffee would be nice, sir."

"Okay. Follow me into the kitchen and we can talk while I make it." Barlow ferreted out the requirements and put the kettle on to boil. "Afraid it's only instant. Takes too long to make the other sort."

"That will do nicely."

Once seated with their drinks, the small chat and pleasantries came to an abrupt end.

"I'll be perfectly candid, Mr Barlow. I need your help."

"Okay. Shoot," replied Barlow.

"I'm told you probably know more about tigers than any man living. Some even go so far as to say you are half tiger."

Barlow laughed.

"Now don't tell me, Inspector, that you believe that nonsense?"

Srinath ignored the reply and pressed on.

"I shouldn't really be telling you this, sir, but I've had quite an altercation with the DC here, over the affair we were discussing at your place recently. The tiger poaching gangs, and the people who employ them."

"I see," said Barlow, immediately interested.

"In short, he won't give me the men to search your neighbour Craig's plantation. As you remember, he is one of our chief suspects. Rao says he hasn't the manpower and that tiger poaching and the rotten medicines trade are not really his concern."

"And I take it, Inspector Srinath, that you are keen to bust the organisers of such gangs," said Barlow, probing Srinath's sentiments.

"I don't have to tell you, sir, that if we can't stop these devils, there won't be a Bengal tiger left by the turn of the century."

Barlow looked Srinath straight in the eye.

"I'm delighted to hear that somebody in India agrees with me, anyway," was all he said.

"I'm prepared to act, Mr Barlow, but officially I can't do anything without the DC's permission."

"And unofficially?"

"I'm going to do all I can, off the record. The DC has put one man on watch on the road leading to Craig's plantation. That's as far as he will go. I expect the lorries to arrive with the tiger carcasses some time today, if my assumption is right."

Barlow looked thoughtful.

"Kepel Rao's not a bad chap. A trifle indolent of nature and hanging on for retirement, so I'm not surprised really. Like a lot of Indians – no disrespect to yourself – conservation is not high on his list of priorities."

It was Srinath's turn to ignore the last remark.

"What I want to say, sir, is if the man reports the lorries have arrived, will you go in with me, unofficially, under the cover of darkness?"

Barlow gave a wry smile. "You sound like a man after my own heart, Inspector. I'm your man!" The inspector beamed, but Barlow cut him short. "Now perhaps you can help me, Inspector?"

"I will if I can, Mr Barlow."

Slowly relating Rachana's disappearance and his suspicions, Barlow went on at length. On completion of his narrative, Srinath's face took on a grave and troubled look. He then proceeded to relate the happenings at Ranthambhore National Park and the human sacrifice that had taken place there.

Barlow, not fully comprehending Srinath's train of thought, cut in, "Oh no, Inspector. Rachana only disappeared yesterday."

Then realisation dawned. With horror, he exclaimed, "You mean these same people have kidnapped Rachana to sacrifice her!"

"It could be, sir. These people call themselves the Sons of Kali. They stage demonstrations to impress the natives. This way they can make them totally subservient and afraid. Obedient to every order given."

"The same people who murdered Swarmy and Patel, you mean?"

"The same," confirmed Srinath.

"My God!" was all a numb Barlow could utter, then, recovering, he exclaimed, "What can we do?"

"Well sir, I think they are going to stage another show, like the one in Ranthambhore, down here. If I'm right, and we can get wind of where it's going to happen, we can move in, bag the organisers, and save your girlfriend, Miss Dev, if she's there."

Draining his coffee cup, Barlow rose determinedly.

"Let's go and raid Craig's place now!"

Srinath jumped up and placed a restraining hand on Barlow's arm.

"Not so fast, sir. I can understand your concern for Miss Dev, but if we go in too soon, without any evidence, other than my suspicion, it's you and I who are going to be for the high jump!"

Noting Barlow's disappointment, Srinath continued. "I assure you, sir, just as soon as my man reports that the lorries have arrived, I'll contact you and we can go in that night."

"But supposing they have already done something with Rachana?"

Srinath shook his head. "No sir. No chance of that. These festivals – as they term them – always happen at night."

Barlow exclaimed, "I hope you are sure of that."

"I am very sure. These people trade on illusions to impress the natives, and that can better be achieved under the cover of darkness. And we don't know for sure that they have Miss Dev, sir. She may still turn up."

"No, she won't, Inspector. I know her too well. If Rachana was around, she would have been back at work this morning."

"For the time being, Mr Barlow, might I suggest you return to your place. I'll contact you the moment I hear from the man watching Craig's plantation. We can then make plans."

"If you are sure there's nothing we can do before?"

"Believe me, sir, I'd like to, but if we go in too early and find nothing..." Srinath's words tailed off.

"All right, Inspector, we have no option but to leave it like that."

"I'm glad you see it my way, sir."

*

When Matt Barlow arrived back at his house, he was surprised to find Steve Berkeman there with Carla.

"Steve's come to apologise, Matt," exclaimed Carla, before Barlow had a chance to speak.

Berkeman moved from one foot to the other and back again, fiddling with the thick gold chain around his neck.

"I guess I've been a damn' fool, Mr Barlow. Don't know what to say really, except I'm sorry for any trouble I might have caused. If there's anything I can do to make amends, just let me know."

Barlow, a wry grin on his face, let Berkeman squirm for a moment before replying.

"Apology accepted. I was never one to bear malice," he said, offering his hand.

Berkeman took it warmly, while Carla watched, her expression one of relief.

"There may be a way you can help, Steve. Carla tells me you are an ex-marine," said Barlow.

"True. I came out about five years ago and started my private detective agency."

Barlow then proceeded to inform them of his talk with Inspector Srinath and of their concern for Rachana's safety. Carla's face expressed horror and Berkeman's anger."

"What can I do, man?" he asked.

Barlow thought for a moment or two before replying.

"I guess Srinath and I could use some help, but it's only fair to warn you that these people are killers. If, and when, we go in, and any of us get caught, it's not likely we would be left alive to tell the tale."

Berkeman, with a rueful expression, agreed. "The very least I could do to make amends."

Chapter Twenty-one

Craig Strikes

Silas Craig was just finishing his lunch when a servant brought him a message that his new foreman Panjit wanted to see him urgently.

"Show him in then, girl." The maid hurried away, to return with a swarthy Indian in a grey turban. Craig dismissed the girl before addressing Panjit.

"What's the problem? I hope it's worth disturbing my lunch for."

"When you say lorries arrive, sahib?"

Craig looked at his watch before replying.

"The last telephone call I received would place their arrival in about one hour's time from now, give or take a few minutes. Why?"

"It may be of no matter, Craig Sahib, but one of our men tells me that a man has been watching the entrance to this plantation for the last twenty-four hours."

Craig sat bolt upright in his chair, and his fork fell from his fingers.

"What! Why did you not tell me of this before, Panjit?"

"I have only just of the news received, sahib."

Craig, leaving his lunch, leapt up from the table.

"Go and find the man who gave you this information, and then bring the four-track round to the front. We will go and see what this man is doing there."

Panjit hurried away to comply, while Craig went to check on Rachana before leaving. He hurried upstairs. Damn the interruption! It had quite spoilt his plans for the afternoon. It had been his intention to have some fun with the bitch before her role as a sacrifice was brought to fruition.

Turning the key, he let himself into the room where she was being held. Although no longer gagged, Rachana was still tightly bound on a large double bed. Craig tested that the ropes were still as tight as ever. They were.

Rachana said nothing but her eyes expressed their loathing and hatred.

"I'll be back to see you tonight, bitch. You would do well to be more friendly towards me."

Rachana spat venomously at him. Craig wiped his face with his handkerchief and gave her another backhander across the face. Rachana, not wanting to give him the satisfaction of knowing that he had inflicted pain, bit her lip.

Craig hurried out, locking the door behind him. She heard his ponderous steps descending the stairs and breathed a long sigh of relief – even if it was only temporary.

Outside, Craig joined Panjit, who, together with one of the plantation workmen, had driven up with the four-track. Getting in the front seat, he commanded, "Right! Let's have a look at this character. Drive somewhere where we can see him and he can't observe us."

"Yes, Craig Sahib." Letting the clutch out jerkily, Panjit drove away.

Ten minutes later Craig, through his field-glasses, was studying the man on the road below him. Concealed in thick vegetation, he was confident that they couldn't be spotted from the road. There was no doubt about it. The man, also with binoculars, was watching both the plantation and the road leading to it. Craig deduced that he could only be a plain-clothes policeman. He was leaning against the bonnet of a small Datsun car and in his other hand held a mobile phone.

"We've got to get rid of him and quickly. The lorries will be arriving soon, and we can't afford him seeing them."

Panjit reached in the back of the four-track for a rifle.

"No! You fool! Put that away," snapped Craig. "We must make it look like an accident."

Panjit looked bemused.

"How can we do that, sahib?"

"You and the man here," grunted Craig, "will approach him from the front and get his attention. Leave the rest to me."

The foreman and the native plantation worker moved out silently. Circling the thick undergrowth, they began to descend through a wooded area that led down into a small nullah. Once there, it was a simple matter to gain the narrow dirt road and approach the watching man. He had his back to them and therefore didn't notice their silent approach until they were nearly up to him. Panjit engaged the fellow in conversation, addressing him in a pleasant manner.

Out of the corner of his eye, he could see Craig creeping up from the other end of the nullah on to the road. On tiptoe, he approached the observer's back. Too late, the man sensed something was wrong and half turned, just in time to see Craig's rifle butt sweeping down in a great arc towards his head.

Throwing up a protective arm, he succeeded only in half-stopping the blow. His arm cracked with a sickening thud, before the butt cannoned into his temple. Tottering round in a circle, he slumped to the ground before a second blow from Craig's rifle cracked his skull. Face down, he lay inert on the dirt road.

Panjit and the native looked on, speechless and aghast. Craig glowered at them before reaching into the fallen man's pockets for his car keys. Triumphantly, he produced them, walked over to the Datsun and started the engine. Above the noise of the engine, he shouted to Panjit.

"Pick him up between you and get him over here, behind the wheel."

The foreman and the native, after a moment's hesitation, reluctantly complied, half carrying and half dragging the lifeless and bloodied form to the vehicle. The diesel engine continued to chug noisily.

"Give me a hand pointing the vehicle towards the watercourse, there," demanded Craig, pointing to the nullah running adjacent to the road. Reaching through the open driving window, he gripped the steering wheel, whilst the other two men pushed the Datsun from the rear. When he was sure of the direction in which it would go, he ordered Panjit into the front passenger seat.

Once there, Craig yelled, "Put her into gear, let out the clutch. Then, as soon as you get her rolling, jump clear."

Craig stood back and observed the procedure. Panjit leapt out at the last moment before the vehicle toppled over the edge into the dried-up nullah, crashing into rocks and boulders on the shallow bed. They heard the engine cut out abruptly. Craig rushed to the roadside and the rim of the watercourse and looked down, thoroughly satisfied.

Although the nullah was no more than twelve feet at its deepest point, it would do nicely. He turned to the still numb Panjit, who had joined him to witness the scene, and exclaimed, "When the police come looking for him, it will simply look like the poor sod has accidentally run off the road. Now let's get the hell back to the plantation, before somebody else arrives."

*

Half an hour later the lorries, with Anil Dehra the Indian fakir seated in the passenger seat of the leading one, arrived and swung off the road on to Craig's plantation.

Dehra, his wild hair blowing madly in the draught from the open window, took in everything with his piercing eyes. These men would make good partners, it would seem. There were rich pickings to be had here. The long four day drive from Jaipur had been arduous in the extreme, but now it all looked like being worth it to Dehra. After all, what could these men do without him? True, they had the money but he, Anil Dehra, had the craft and skill. The lorries wound their way round the plantation roads until they drew up on the drive at the house.

Dehra saw Craig coming out to meet them, and climbed down. It was good to feel his bare feet on the warm earth once more.

Chapter Twenty-two

The Plot Thickens

It was late afternoon when Inspector Ramon Srinath received the call from the DC.

"The man posted to watch Craig's plantation has had an accident," said Kepel Rao matter-of-factly.

"What do you mean, an accident?" fired back Srinath impatiently.

"Went off the road in his car, finished up in the nullah. Hit some boulders and was killed outright." He waited for Srinath's reaction. He didn't have long to wait.

"Who reported it?"

"Apparently, someone rang him on his mobile, from the station here. When they received no reply, a car was sent down to investigate. That's when they found him."

"Have they moved the body?"

"No. I said I'd contact you first, as it's your case, so to speak. I gave orders for a man to be left there at the scene until I spoke to you."

"Thank you, sir. I'll get down there now. With any luck I'll make it before dark."

Kepel Rao exclaimed, "I don't know what you expect to find, Inspector. Sounds like a straightforward accident to me."

"Well, until I arrive I won't know, but it's beginning to sound highly suspicious to me, sir. Can you give me the location?"

Rao obliged.

"Oh yes. I know. It's the other side of the road from Matthew Barlow's plantation." With that Srinath said goodbye and hung up. Losing no time, he hurried to his hired car and set off.

The site of the accident was easy enough to find. On his approach, he saw the police car with the constable standing guard at the roadside, long before he got there. A little crowd of natives had gathered and the young constable was endeavouring to keep them back and out of the nullah.

Srinath pulled up and got out. The constable saluted and the huddle of natives moved a few paces backwards to allow his entry. Returning the constable's salute, he peered down into the nullah.

"The man appears to have a fractured skull and a broken arm, sir."

"Did you know him, Constable?"

"Only slightly, sir. His name was Anil Kittur, not been with the Bangalore force long."

"Keep these men here, Constable, whilst I climb down and have a look," said Srinath, indicating with his eyes the huddle of excited natives.

"Very good, sir."

Srinath clambered down the side of the watercourse to reach the vehicle. The body was slumped over the wheel. The safety belt was unfastened. He made a fairly thorough examination of the body, which showed a massive cut on the back of the head and a smaller one over the right temple. The right arm was at an odd angle, and obviously broken. There was quite a lot of blood both on the man's skin and clothes and on the upholstery of the car. Next, Srinath walked round the vehicle, making some notes in a little red book. The natives on the roadside peered down on him, wide-eyed, held there as if with invisible string, by their curiosity.

Finally, Srinath scrambled up the dried-up and rocky sides of the watercourse. Without speaking, he began to walk the road from which the car had appeared to come, studying its surface meticulously. Abruptly, he stopped and crouched down.

"Come and look at this, Constable," he called back. The young constable came at the double, the native watchers following at a slower pace in his wake. Srinath pointed at a red sticky patch on the dust road, and another a yard and a half further on.

"Did you see these, Constable?" he enquired.

"Why, no, sir. I didn't," said the young man honestly. "Perhaps an animal was knocked down here," he put forward by way of explanation.

"Perhaps not, Constable. Do you see any skid marks anywhere?"

"Why? No sir, I don't."

"Doesn't it strike you as strange that a car goes off the road with no attempt at braking?"

"Now that you come to mention it, sir... Could it be the driver fell asleep though?" said the young constable, suddenly inspired.

"Come now, Constable. We are not talking about any driver. This was a plain clothes policeman, stationed here to watch both the road and the plantation. Why would he even be driving? No. He would have been here until he was relieved at 6 p.m. Half an hour from now. Do you see what I'm getting at?"

The youngster looked rather sheepish.

"Are you saying this wasn't an accident, sir?"

"Yes, Constable, that is exactly what I'm saying. This was cold-blooded murder, by persons unknown. The man's injuries should have told you that, without any of this. Not even the car's windscreen was broken. In fact, the damage to the vehicle was fairly minimal. That car never went into that nullah at any appreciable speed. The main damage to the driver was on the back of his head. I'm no doctor, but I'd say it was a skull fracture that killed him. So what did he do? Somersault into the windscreen and then sit back in the driving seat after he was dead?"

The young policeman squirmed uncomfortably at Srinath's scathing sarcasm. Srinath reached forward and patted the lad on the shoulder in a conciliatory manner.

"Just remember, Constable. Never accept the obvious, if you want to get on in the force."

"Yes sir, I'll do that next time."

"Right, now ring through for a wagon to remove the body, and wait for a replacement before you leave. I want this place watched at all times. Is that clear? Keep me posted if anything moves in or out of there," exclaimed Srinath, indicating Craig's plantation.

It was now approaching dusk, with the shadows lengthening appreciably. Srinath returned to his car, waved goodbye to the young officer and swung back off the road on to Barlow's plantation. 'Might as well keep him up to date on developments as I'm in the vicinity,' he thought.

*

Ramon Srinath was greeted by an impatient Matt Barlow on his arrival at the latter's house.

"Are we ready to go in, Inspector? I've been champing at the bit all day!"

"Hold your horses a little longer sir, if you please," replied Srinath.

Barlow showed him through to the lounge and introduced him to Steve Berkeman.

"Miss Wayne you already know, of course."

Srinath shook hands with both.

"Take a seat," invited Barlow, pulling up a chair for him. "You can talk in front of Berkeman, Inspector, he's offered to help," prompted Barlow.

"That's very good of you sir. We can use all the help we can get with these people, but I feel I must warn you first of the dangers," said Srinath to the American.

"Take it as read, Inspector. Mr Barlow here has already filled me in. I am fully aware of what I'm in for."

"Very well then," went on Srinath. "The problem at the moment is, we don't know if the lorries have arrived or not." He went on to outline what had befallen the constable on observation duty.

"My God, that's terrible!" exclaimed a shocked Carla.

To endorse his earlier point concerning the dangers involved, Srinath continued, "Now you can see that these people will stop at nothing. If they will do this to someone they suspect is watching them, think what your fate will be if anything goes wrong."

Barlow cut in. "Yes, Inspector, I think we are more than aware of what to expect."

Berkeman nodded his assent.

"A new man has been positioned to keep watch on Craig's plantation, so we must wait for confirmation that the convoy has arrived," stated Srinath.

"Can't the police just go in and arrest this Craig man for murder?" suggested Carla.

"No, ma'am, we have no proof that Craig was involved in the murder. We must be able to make it stick, you understand," replied Srinath.

"It's a pound to a penny he was!" snapped Barlow, then, turning his attention to Srinath, he exclaimed, "surely it's possible that the lorries have already arrived, and that's why your constable was killed – to stop him talking."

"It's possible, sir."

"That being the case then, they might have plans for Rachana tonight!" exclaimed an anguished Barlow.

"I don't think so, Mr Barlow. Almost certainly they won't want to lose any time, but I can't see them being able to set up a ceremony before tomorrow night at the earliest."

"You don't *think*!" snapped Barlow, sarcastically. "That's not good enough, Inspector Srinath. It's Rachana's life we are talking about."

Carla laid a calming hand on Barlow's arm.

"We must wait for something definite, sir," said Srinath sympathetically.

"No Inspector! *You* must wait! I'm going over there tonight, because if you are wrong in your conclusions Rachana could be dead by the morning."

"I would remind you sir, that we don't know for sure Miss Dev is being held there."

"I'd put a bet on it, anyway," snapped Barlow.

"Go in tonight, and you could rock the boat, Mr Barlow."

"Then that's a risk I'll have to take."

"And I'll be going with him," added Steve Berkeman.

"If you do," replied Srinath, "it will be off the record. You will be entirely on your own. I understand your concern gentlemen, but I beg of you, wait!"

Carla forced her way into the conversation.

"I'll be going in with them too, Inspector."

Barlow and Berkeman's expressions showed their amazement and Srinath threw his hands up to the heavens in shock.

"This is getting completely out of hand. At times I simply do not understand you Westerners! You are a woman!" exclaimed Srinath incredulously.

"And somewhat different from your subservient Eastern variety of female," put in Carla, hotly.

In spite of himself, Ramon Srinath began to chuckle. "Well, I must say the whole lot of you are a hot-headed bunch as ever I saw. All right, reluctantly, and against my better judgement, we'll look the Craig place over tonight – will that appease you, Mr Barlow?"

"Now you are talking my language, Inspector," Barlow replied. Turning to Carla, he said, "I suppose it's no good me trying to talk you out of coming?"

"No way, Matt. In for a cent – in for a dollar!"

*

Late that afternoon, Ravi Tata and Venkat Singh had received the call from Craig that the lorries had arrived at Bangalore. They had left immediately in Tata's Lear jet from Delhi and three hours later arrived in Bangalore. Craig's foreman, Panjit, was at the airport to meet them and convey them to Craig's plantation home. By 9 p.m. they were all being entertained by Craig at his table. A fine banquet of roast wild boar had been prepared in their honour.

Over dinner, Craig informed them how he had disposed of the young constable, expecting praise for his initiative.

Ravi Tata looked far from pleased, and showed it by fiercely scowling before speaking. Ignoring Craig, he turned to Anil Dehra, the fakir.

"Can you bring everything forward for the ceremony in the Nilgiri Hills for tomorrow night, Dehra?"

Dehra smiled, an all-knowing look on his face.

"I have already attended to it. When Mr Craig told me what he had done with the policeman, I knew there was no time to lose, so I got busy. We can expect a large crowd of impressionable natives to witness my magic." Ignoring Craig, he continued to address Ravi Tata. "I have also hired a helicopter in your name to take us down later tonight."

Craig looked fit to explode.

"Why, you! You two-faced devil, you never said a word to me about any of this."

Ravi Tata cut in abruptly, ignoring Craig completely.

"You did well, Dehra. Very well indeed. Very resourceful if I might say so. What of the carcasses?"

"All in excellent condition, unloaded and in the refrigerator unit here."

Ravi Tata beamed. "At least someone is efficient!"

"Might I say, though, Mr Tata, it would be wise to move them out as soon as possible, because if Mr Craig's accident ploy doesn't work, we are going to have the police sniffing around here pretty soon," said Dehra.

Craig butted in.

"Nonsense! The police are fools and anyway they eat out of my hand here. They dare not touch me."

Venkat Singh joined the conversation, menace written all over his swarthy scarred face, which he pushed almost into Craig's.

"It seems to me, Craig, you have been overconfident and put us all at some risk."

Craig looked to Ravi Tata for support, but none came. Turning to Venkat, the latter snapped out an order.

"Dehra is right, we cannot now risk keeping the carcasses here. They must be shipped out at once."

"B, but—" stammered Craig.

"But nothing!" snapped Tata. "Either arrange for them to be sent down the Cauvery river to Chidamraram, or by rail to Madras. We can ship them out to China, Laos and Vietnam from either."

"Very good, Mr Tata," exclaimed Venkat, rising and leaving his dinner. "Do you have any preference?"

"The Cauvery will be safer, I think. Try that avenue first, man."

Anil Dehra responded immediately.

"Pardon me, but I think there is some urgency needed. One of Mr Craig's workers who was at the scene of the er, accident said that the senior policeman who attended later didn't seem to believe it was an accident."

Craig cried hotly, "Why didn't he tell me that? I'm his employer!"

"Maybe you didn't ask," said Dehra, wearing a cunning expression.

Ravi Tata's response was instant.

"Go down at once, Venkat, and supervise the loading of the lorries. Under the circumstances, the sooner we are out of here the more I shall like it. What time is the chopper coming, Dehra?" he enquired, turning once again to the fakir.

"Eleven p.m. Was that in order?"

"Perfectly." He swung back on Silas Craig. "What of the girl? Is she ready?"

"Would you like to see her, Mr Tata?" enquired Craig, hopefully.

"Perhaps I had better see her. You seem to have messed up everything else, Craig."

"Can I also have the pleasure? As it is I who will have to deal with the girl," asked Dehra.

"Certainly, Dehra," agreed Tata. "Let us go and inspect the maid."

Venkat Singh having already departed, the two of them fell in step behind Silas Craig, as he led them upstairs.

Throwing the door open, Craig waited for both men to enter the room before meekly following. Tata and Dehra walked over to the bed and looked down on the helpless and bound Rachana.

"Is she not a beauty, Mr Tata?" said Craig, hoping for some sort of praise.

"Indeed she is," agreed Tata, running a hand up the shapely leg nearest to him. She squirmed at his touch and swore vehemently at him. Tata did a mock recoil, and exclaimed, "Such words from a lady!"

Then, turning to Dehra, he enquired, "Will she do for your purpose, fakir?"

"Indeed she will, Mr Tata, admirably."

Craig forced his way between the two men.

"Have her if you want, Mr Tata. I saved her for you. Seems a pity to waste such beauty. I mean, after tomorrow night, there won't be another chance. I mean..."

"I know full well what you mean, Craig. Unfortunately, we have work to do. Because of your foolish and headstrong action disposing of that policeman, we must get out of here in a hurry. Therefore, I need your telephone, as we need to arrange deliveries quickly of the tigers we already have."

"I will show you where it is," said Craig, subserviently leading the trio out of the room.

As they departed down the stairs, Rachana heard the man called Tata say to Craig, "Oh, and Craig, don't think you are going to slip back to that girl. I want you standing next to me, by the phone, when I'm talking, just in case I need any local information from you. Is that clear?"

Rachana heard Craig's almost inaudible reply – with relief. The swine had tried earlier to force himself upon her, but she had bitten his bulbous nose savagely and he had run off bellowing, to her intense satisfaction.

She shook with terror now though, when she recalled his words to Tata: 'After tomorrow night there won't be another chance.'

Obviously, she had only twenty-four hours left before they killed her, but why? Her mind in turmoil, she made another frenzied attempt to get loose, all to no avail.

*

Hidden in a grove of tamarind trees, some two hundred metres from Craig's house, George Brook – the erstwhile foreman of Craig – crouched low, a pair of binoculars raised up to his eyes.

They were loading something from that new refrigeration unit into three lorries. Brook couldn't believe his eyes. Could it be? Yes! It was! No doubt about it! Tiger carcasses! So that was it. That was what that treacherous swine Craig was into.' Ever since the plantation owner had sacked him, Brook had looked for a chance to get even. Now he wouldn't have to do a thing, just go and tell Barlow. After all, he was into tigers and would come down on Craig like a ton of bricks. Brook rubbed his hands with glee. If he could only find out where the lorries were going, that would really stitch Craig up. Better to tell Barlow than the police. Craig had always boasted that the police were in his pocket, as long as he paid his dues to certain people.

The first lorry was loaded, the men were just shutting the tailgate. An idea came to Brook. The driver wouldn't know him from Adam. Putting his binoculars back in their case, he sprinted off through the tamarind grove, away from the house, and cut through a little wadi to re-emerge back on the drive well out of sight of the house. The lorry would have to pass this point on its way out. He heard the droning sound of the engine, wending its way round the copse to pass his hidden position.

Just before the lorry came abreast, he ran out, raising his hands above his head.

"Stop!" he shouted.

The ancient lorry ground to a stop. There were two Indians in the cab. The driver poked his head out indignantly.

"What for you stop me?" he shouted.

Brook stepped forward confidently, and addressed the driver.

"Mr Craig asked me to get you to repeat the orders you were given."

"Why?"

"He wants to make sure there are no mistakes and you know where you are going."

"Me know very well. Venkat Singh he tell where to go. Not know Craig. Or you."

Brook manoeuvred quickly. He hadn't counted on this turn of events.

"That's right. Venkat Singh, he works for Mr Craig. He wants to know."

"Why you not say in first place?"

"Come on, man. Repeat your orders or it will go badly for you with Mr Singh," commanded Brook.

"I must take this load through night, to Erode, on the Cauvery river. There I must unload on to boat."

"What's the name of the boat?"

"You already know this."

"Yes, but I must make sure you know."

"Do they think I am mad? It is the Kathmandu, bound for Chidamraram."

"Away with you then. I'm only carrying out orders. Sorry to delay you," lied Brook.

The driver snorted contemptuously, let in the clutch and bumped away through the gears.

A hasty look to left and right, convinced Brook that he hadn't been spotted by anyone from the house. Silently, he set off to where he had left his car, concealed behind an overgrown thicket. He had come here often with one of the maids when he had been working for Craig.

Just as he reached the car, he heard an unaccustomed throbbing noise. Listening intently, he soon realised it was an approaching helicopter. There was no need to hide, the moon having not yet come up, so there was little chance that he or his car could be seen from the air. The chopper flew right overhead, and proceeded on towards the house. Brook noted the change in engine noise, and realised that the aircraft was landing right outside Craig's house.

"Just what the hell is going on here?" Brook said, half aloud. "I think Barlow will be glad of this news." Unlocking his car, he got in and started the engine, gradually easing the little Beetle out over the lumps and bumps of the terrain, onto the driveway.

*

It was just on midnight, the time designated for Barlow's party to go into action. Reluctantly, Barlow had agreed that Carla could drive the four-track. Srinath, against his better judgement, had decided to go along with Barlow's plan of attack. Zabu, the little tracker, had also been enlisted. Barlow, Berkeman and Carla all had their faces blackened, but only the first two named carried guns – Barlow his trusty Winchester 405, and Berkeman the automatic he had appropriated in Jaipur. The policeman, Srinath, was unarmed and refused the loan of a rifle from Barlow.

All five of them were just about to venture out and board the four-track when they heard Jana give a low growl and saw her move towards the door.

"We have a visitor," remarked Barlow dryly.

"What! At this time of the night?" exclaimed an incredulous Carla.

Barlow picked up the 405 and tiptoed towards the door. As he silently opened it, he interrupted Brook, who was reaching for the bell. It would be hard to say who was the more surprised. Barlow, however, was the first to recover, and, grabbing Brook by his shirt front, pulled the startled man into the room.

Brook looked in amazement at the blackened faces surrounding him. The only one he recognised, of course, was Barlow.

"What the hell are you doing snooping around here at this time of night, Brook?" Barlow fired at him.

"Got some information for you. Something I thought you might be glad of, Mr Barlow," exclaimed a nervous Brook, his eyes shifting from one blackened face to another.

"Why would you want to do anything for me Brook?" said Barlow.

"I don't particularly. I just want to get even with Silas Craig for the way he treated me."

"Okay. Out with it, man. We haven't got much time," snapped Barlow impatiently.

George Brook related all that he had seen and heard, including the arrival of the helicopter.

When he had completed his narrative, Berkeman said, "Do you think we can trust this guy?"

Barlow replied, "I wouldn't trust Brook further than I could throw him, but on this matter I think we can believe him."

"It certainly all adds up," remarked Srinath. "Looks as if the birds have flown the coop."

"Come on, everybody, we have to get there before that helicopter takes off," exclaimed Barlow, "Or they're going to take Rachana off to God knows where." Even before he had finished speaking, everyone became aware of a chugging noise growing ever closer. Barlow, followed by Jana, rushed outside in time to see the lights of a helicopter in the night sky. It passed almost overhead and a forlorn Barlow watched its passage on a south-westerly course until it disappeared from sight.

By now everyone, including Brook, was outside, gathered round him. He turned to Srinath.

"What now?" was all he said.

Chapter Twenty-three
Terror in the Air

Aboard the hired chopper wending its way south-westerly on a warm Indian night the pilot was wondering just what kind of deal he had landed himself in.

He had been amazed – to say the least – when, just before take-off, a girl with her hands bound behind her had been forced aboard at gunpoint by a scar-faced, heavily built individual. The other three occupants were a motley assortment. A wild-eyed Indian with flowing long hair, dressed in a white robe. An expensively dressed and elegant looking executive type, who was obviously the one giving orders, and a fat middle-aged, frightened looking colonial type in long khaki drill shorts.

"What's going on here? I don't want to do anything illegal," he had told the one in the finely cut linen suit.

"Mind your own business and fly south-west," the man had replied and given him a paper with the co-ordinates written on it. The girl had looked at him, an appealing helpless look about her. Now, as he sat in his seat, flying the chopper, silence reigned behind him.

He thought about radioing for assistance, but how did he know that one of these men wasn't a pilot? Supposing they simply pushed him out and took over. He decided to do nothing and wait. Maybe, after all, they were just kidnapping the girl, who was a runaway bride. These things happened in India. Yes, that was it. Nothing to worry about. Just mind your own business.

Then it all began to happen behind him, and he realised how wrong he was.

A bitter argument had started. He could hear the men shouting above the noise of the engine. The girl at the back remained silent. The pilot turned and looked over his shoulder. The big swarthy fellow with the angry scar down his face had the fat fellow in the khaki shorts up against the hull of the chopper, one arm forced up behind his back.

"No! No! You need me," screamed the red-faced colonial type.

"I think not. It would seem he is expendable, Venkat," said the elegant city type, who had remained coolly seated throughout the rumpus.

Forcing the fat one's arm farther up his back, until he screamed with pain, the man addressed as Venkat enquired, "What do you want done with him, Mr Tata?"

"Toss him out. We are flying over dense jungle. He will probably never be found," said the elegantly dressed one matter-of-factly.

The pilot, Bishen Tendulkar, almost froze with terror. Who were these men? Never had he encountered anything like this. What should he do? They were going to throw this man out in mid-air. He tried to protest. The one with the flying mane of grey-white hair was struggling to open the door for scarface.

"Please, gentlemen. The pressurisation. Remember the pressurisation. Open the door and you will kill us all!"

"Be quiet, liar, and mind your own business. This is no concern of yours. Just fly the aircraft and no harm will come to you."

Bishen, the pilot, had tried to lie about the aircraft being pressurised. Obviously, the ploy hadn't worked. The city type knew differently. His immediately confident response had borne witness to this. The pilot could feel the draught on the back of his neck now, so they had obviously succeeded in sliding the door open. The fat one's screams could be heard above the roar of the engines and the howl of the wind.

Bishen risked another terrified glance over his shoulder. All three men were now engaged in manhandling the terrified and screaming individual towards the open doorway – the poor girl looked horrified. 'How could they do this?' he asked himself. 'What could he do to stop them?' Bishen began to bank the chopper over, thus giving them an uphill struggle to reach the door.

Scarface, realising what he was up to, roared at him, above the engine and the wind.

"Level off! Or it will be the worse for you, pilot!"

The terrified Bishen complied. The fat one had both feet planted either side of the door frame now, and was panting and yelling in his futile efforts to prevent the other three from pitching him out.

With his bare feet, the wild-looking fellow, his white mane of hair flowing in the wind, kicked savagely at the outer side of the victim's right knee.

Bishen took the aircraft slowly down; maybe they wouldn't notice. It might just give the portly fellow an outside chance of survival, but he doubted it. What more could he do?

As low as he dared now, and not far above the height of the tallest jungle trees, he levelled off.

He glanced behind him again, and was just in time to see the rotund figure being prised loose from the door frame. An instant later, a final kick from Scarface and a push from the city type sent him spinning out into space. Even above the internal noise of the aircraft, he could hear the girl scream, and Bishen would never forget the terrified cry of the man as he found himself in space, before plummeting downwards to his death.

He heard one of the men slide the door shut, and felt the final click and knew it would probably seal his own doom. Silence reigned in the aircraft – no one spoke for a long time. Bishen flew on to the co-ordinates he had been given, a thousand thoughts in his mind and none of them good!

There was no way that these people were going to leave him alive. Bishen had enough sense to know that. Even if he promised not to talk, he couldn't imagine – from what he had just witnessed them prove themselves capable of – that they would take the risk. He wondered whether any of them could pilot the chopper. If not, he would be safe until he flew them out of the Nilgiri Hills and back to wherever they wanted to go. They would need him until then. He decided then and there that it would be a foolhardy risk to wait. Better try and make a run for it, just as soon as they touched down in the hills. Maybe, if he could set her down near some cover, he would be able to make a dash for freedom. That seemed his best hope.

Bishen could feel his shoulder muscles going into spasm, and was conscious of his hands tensing on the controls. His mouth felt dry and there was a cold feeling at the pit of his stomach. He couldn't even trust himself to speak to the passengers, feeling that, if he did, they would sense his thoughts and fears.

*

Barlow, experiencing both frustration and hopelessness, listened to the receding noise of the helicopter. Almost certainly, they had Rachana on board and were taking her to her death, to God knows where. Never had he felt so impotent to do anything effective.

The little group gathered on the veranda saw the chopper's lights recede into the night sky. When the final sounds of its engine had died, Srinath, sensing Barlow's depression, put a hand on his shoulder.

"It's not all bad, sir."

"Oh really, Inspector! They are going to murder Rachana, and you tell me it's not all bad. I fail to see how it could be much worse," exclaimed a sarcastic Barlow.

Srinath smiled sympathetically before adding, "You see, sir, it will be relatively easy to find out where they are taking Miss Dev."

"It will?" exclaimed an incredulous Barlow.

"Yes, if I might use your telephone, Mr Barlow?"

"Certainly! Come this way!" Barlow led him back inside, and pointed out the telephone. Standing close enough to hear when Srinath dialled, he waited expectantly.

When the ringing tone was answered, Srinath began to issue instructions to the person on the other end of the line.

"Give this immediate priority. This is Inspector Ramon Srinath, Delhi police, speaking. Who am I speaking to?" Barlow couldn't hear the response but he heard Srinath continue.

"Check with every firm operating helicopters within a hundred kilometres of Bangalore." Srinath placed a hand over the mouthpiece and enquired of Barlow, "What's Craig's actual address?"

Barlow told him.

Srinath relayed it down the line and then continued with his instructions.

"I want to know of all helicopters hired out this evening and their flight plans: who hired them, and where from. Check everyone thoroughly – this is a matter of life or death. Do you understand me? Good. Just as soon as the information is to hand, ring me at this number." He relayed Barlow's number off the telephone label, then went on. "I am particularly interested in any aircraft rented out to the first address I gave you. Exact times, flight plans, estimated time of arrival, et cetera. Get on to it immediately, and remember I am waiting here for the information. Goodbye." With that, he hung up and turned to Barlow.

"It shouldn't be long, sir, before we have the information we need."

Barlow looked a lot happier.

"I see I have underestimated you, Inspector."

"Each to his own job, sir."

By this time, the others had come in from the veranda, George Brook trailing in behind them.

"Now, whilst we wait for the information, I'd better arrange for a reception committee for those lorries when they get to Erode, on the Cauvery river. We can jump on them there before they are off-loaded," Srinath said, again reaching for the telephone. Barlow put out a hand to stop him.

"Look, can you guarantee that those carcasses will be destroyed and not passed on? I hate to say this, but there's every chance of corrup—"

"You were going to say corruption in the police, Mr Barlow, and of course, there are some crooked policemen, just as there are tea planters."

"*Touché*," agreed Barlow. "Craig seems to be a shining example."

"Don't worry, sir. I am going to order the carcasses destroyed as soon as the lorries can be apprehended. Remember, I'm just as concerned as you are that the consignment could be passed on to the wrong people. Now, if you will permit me to use the telephone once more, I can make the necessary arrangements."

"I'm very sorry to question you, Inspector. I now see there was no need. Please accept my apologies," Barlow exclaimed. Handing the phone to Srinath, he crossed the room to talk to the others.

"It looks as if I owe you my thanks, Brook, for bringing us this information, even if you did have an ulterior motive of vengeance against Craig."

"I hope it in some ways makes amends, sir," said Brook, looking uneasily from one to the other of the party for their reactions.

Barlow, ignoring the appeal, shot a question at him. "Are you sure you didn't see Rachana at Craig's place, or hear anything about her, whilst you were watching?"

"No sir, I didn't."

"One thing interests me, Brook. Why were you there anyway? What were you going to do?"

"I guess I was just looking for a way to get even with Craig, and was watching for an opportunity."

"Have you got a job now, Brook?"

"No sir, nothing since Craig chucked me out."

"Well, you and I will never be friends, so I'm not going to offer you a job, but you were good at your work, and I do know of a foreman's job going up near Madras. I could put in a word for you, if you promise to keep your nose clean."

"Oh I will, sir. That's real generous of you, that is," Brook almost grovelled.

"Okay. Off with you now. Give me a ring in a few days' time."

After Brook had left, Carla whispered to Barlow.

"That was extremely generous of you, Matt, after what you told me, the other day."

"Wasn't it, though. Call me a fool, but I never could bear malice," responded Barlow, in a low voice.

"Well, I suppose the fellow gave us the only chance we've got. Now we've just got to twiddle our fingers and thumbs waiting for the information to come through," said Carla.

Srinath had finished on the phone and came over to join the others.

"Well, that's all taken care of. The lorry drivers will find a hot reception, when they reach the Cauvery."

"So there should be," remarked Berkeman.

Barlow remarked that it wasn't any good throwing the book at them. They had simply been hired to drive a cargo. Any cargo, as far as they were concerned.

"True," agreed Srinath, "but some example will have to be made or people like them will just keep on doing it."

Half an hour later, which seemed to Barlow more like hours, the phone rang shrilly, penetrating the conversation of the little group.

"You get it, Inspector. At this time of the night it's sure to be your call," exclaimed Barlow.

Ramon Srinath picked up the hand-piece and gave his name. The others watched him expectantly, with bated breath.

"You did? Good... Very good... When? How long? Tomorrow night... he... you don't say? Two birds with one stone. We've been after him for a long time... You have done well... Thank you very much... Goodbye." He replaced the receiver and turned towards Barlow.

"Well sir, it appears that the helicopter was chartered from a small firm run by a chap named Tendulkar. Flies the thing himself – small charters, you understand. He was told to report with the aircraft to Craig's place, not later than 11 p.m. tonight, to convey a party to the Nilgiri Hills for some sort of special occasion. Apparently, they needed to be there to set it up for tomorrow night. The strange thing is, he was told to take five passengers out, but that there would be only three returning to Bangalore."

Berkeman cut in.

"Does that mean two people are going to be sacrificed, Inspector?"

Srinath looked thoughtful.

"It's possible, although I wouldn't have thought so. The problem is – how are we going to reach the Nilgiri Hills in time? The police force won't stand the cost of a helicopter, and by road it will be like looking for a needle in a haystack." The latter remark was addressed to Barlow.

"Don't worry about the cost, Inspector. I'll stand that. Just get on the blower and order one here post haste."

Once more, Srinath headed off for the telephone. Barlow turned to Carla and Berkeman.

"The Nilgiri Hills are as Godforsaken a place as you ever saw. Some of its area is covered by thick dense jungle, full of swamps, mosquitoes and leeches. Few tigers have ever stayed there, as they hate the ticks and leeches, although I did have to go in once after a man-eater. There are even a few old long-disused Buddhist temples in the area, if you can find them. Our only chance of finding hide or hair of the rascals will be from the air."

Zabu, who had remained seated and overawed by the gathering, spoke up.

"Barlow Sahib is right. Place no good for man or beast."

Srinath returned to the group a few moments later.

"The only one I could get is not going to be available until the morning, I'm sorry to say. In any case, we could never hope to spot them in the dark from the air."

"Nothing for us to do but wait. I suggest everyone grabs some sleep. It's going to be a long, tough, arduous day tomorrow. What time did you say the chopper would arrive?" enquired Barlow, of Srinath.

"I didn't. But they promised it for 8 a.m."

Berkeman looked at his watch. It was 2 a.m.

"Gives us six hours to get some shut-eye," he commented.

*

Bishen Tendulkar was now flying over the designated area and could feel his hands still trembling on the controls. He felt a tap on his left shoulder and glanced round. It was the scar-faced one.

"Any moment now, you will see a flashing fluorescent green light somewhere down there. That is where you will land. Keep your eyes peeled, pilot."

Bishen switched on his landing lights. All he could see was dense jungle below him. The tops of the tallest trees were only a hundred metres beneath the chopper. How on earth was he going to land here, he asked himself. Just when he was thinking the task impossible, something attracted his attention about a kilometre to his right.

Yes. This was it. The flashing green light. All the more conspicuous because of the dark forest below. Bishen banked the aircraft and headed for it. His landing lights suddenly illuminated a clearing. Now he could see a man dressed all in white, with a signal lamp, flashing it on and off.

A new spasm of fear gripped Bishen. Whatever these men wanted to come here for could only be something evil. Looking down, he could see an old Buddhist temple at the back of the clearing, looking somewhat eerie with the combination of fluorescent and landing lights throwing strange shadows.

"Keep your belts fastened, gentlemen," mumbled Bishen nervously, as he prepared to go through his landing procedure.

A few moments later, the chopper descended the last few metres and settled on a stone paved area. Once, it must have served as a road to the old temple, but little of it now remained. Bishen switched to whisper mode and then finally systematically shut down everything.

The silence was stunning and ominous; so swift was the transformation, that Bishen's mind began to race. Dare he risk staying around looking for a better chance to escape, or make a dash for it now? There were no doubts in his mind that these people couldn't afford to let him live, but would they need him for the return flight? It all depended on whether any of them could fly, and, for all he knew, they might have another pilot on the ground.

He couldn't take that risk, and decided then and there to go for it now. Hopefully, they would be concerned with getting the girl out and overlook him.

Reaching into the glove compartment, he pocketed a small compass, knowing that his only chance of escaping on foot from this desolate area lay with it.

"Excuse me, gentlemen. I've got to make a slight adjustment at the tail section," he said, trying to sound as natural as possible. Bishen rose from his seat and made for the door. The native with the fluorescent light, now switched off, was approaching it from outside.

"Stay right where you are, pilot."

Bishen turned to face the speaker and found an automatic levelled at his head by the scar-faced one.

"There is nothing wrong with the tail section, pilot. You'll move when I tell you – is that clear?"

"Er, yes sir."

"Now hand me your keys, pilot. We don't want you running out on us before we are ready to leave, do we?"

Obediently, and with no real choice, Bishen complied. The elegant city type and the Indian with the flowing white hair were already descending from the aircraft. The native with the light gave a polite bow and held out a hand by way of assistance.

"We are very pleased to see you, Mr Tata," he exclaimed.

The man addressed as Tata brushed his hand aside, and brusquely enquired, "Is everything ready? I trust our sleeping accommodation is satisfactory?"

"It is so. Allow me to convey you there."

Tata turned to Scarface through the sliding door of the chopper.

"I will go on with Dehra here. We have matters to discuss. You, Venkat, will wait here until this fellow returns to escort you and the prisoners. After they have been safely ensconced you may join us."

Bishen shot a look at the girl. She returned it, with equal apprehension. He wondered what was in store for them both.

*

Carla couldn't seem to sleep. The night was hot and sultry, and her mind raced wildly. Try as she might, it proved impossible to dispel thoughts of all that had transpired, and even more so on that about to happen. Only a cotton sheet covered her naked body, but even that felt restricting. Tossing it off, she slipped into a light sundress and, stepping over Jana, who was peacefully sleeping outside her bedroom door, crept out quietly to the veranda. 'No sense in waking anybody else,' she reasoned.

Closing the front door as silently as she could, she was startled to see someone already out there. It was Matt, idly swaying to and fro in a basketwork rocking chair.

"Hi, you obviously couldn't sleep either?" Carla greeted him.

"Didn't try. I had some packing to do, and when that was finished, came out here for some fresh air – I often do."

Carla swept her gaze over the moonlit plantation and took in the twinkling myriad of stars above.

"I'm not surprised – it's beautiful, and so much cooler out here." Turning, she leant back against the balcony rail to face him, arching her neck backwards, hands behind her head, revelling in the peace and freedom of the moment.

Barlow was only too aware of the nearness and appeal of Carla, but with the moonlight behind her, silhouetting a firm lithe figure through the flimsy cotton dress, the effect was quite breathtaking. He was unable to take his eyes off her.

"You said you were doing some packing, Matt?" Carla enquired.

"Oh, just a few things we shall need tomorrow – or rather, today," he said, looking at his watch, becoming conscious of the passing hours.

Carla moved over towards him and he was immediately aware of the lingering aroma of an Yves Saint Laurent perfume. She laid a warm hand on his shoulder and looked into his eyes.

"What do you think will happen tomorrow, Matt?"

"I'll tell you one thing, Carla. I wish you weren't going with us."

Carla looked hurt.

"Why?" she shot at him.

"These people are killers who will stop at nothing. The evil trade in tiger parts and the money that it brings in is all that interests them."

Carla reasoned, "Yes, but you will be in just as much danger as I will – and, anyway," she added, "it can't be half as dangerous as going after man-eating tigers single-handed."

"You think not? I'm telling you, this is going to be much worse," Barlow argued. "We may not even be able to locate them in the Nilgiri Hills, but if we do, some of us may not be coming back."

Carla shuddered. Even on such a hot night a cold shiver ran down her spine. She moved even closer to Barlow and whispered, "Thank you for being so concerned on my behalf, but I'm still coming with you. Don't forget I've a story to cover, and I want to be there for the finale."

Barlow leant forward in his recliner, and placed a large hand either side of her slender waist. Without being aware of it, Carla ran her fingers through his hair, lingering at the temples. He buried his head against her and Carla's fingers transferred to round the back of his neck.

"It's so beautiful out here, Matt. Strange to think it could be our last night on earth," she murmured.

Barlow's mind was in turmoil. With Rachana in such deadly peril, he knew that he shouldn't become involved with Carla, but was only too aware of the effect she was having upon him.

Attempting to give himself some mental fortitude, turning his face upwards to look at Carla, he whispered, "If we don't get there in time tomorrow night, Rachana may never see another sunset."

"Poor Matt. You miss her terribly, don't you?" Carla stroked his face gently with the back of her fingers.

Barlow could feel his resolve weakening. Why did she have to look so damn' desirable in the moonlight? True, he did miss Rachana, but he was becoming aware that he would miss Carla too, when she went back to America. Could it be true, what the natives said about him being half tiger? From his own experience, he knew that the animal moved on to new partners, frequently leaving the tigress with cubs to look after and bring up.

Barlow tried to justify his motives. Once before he had asked Rachana to marry him? She had refused, in spite of the fact that she said she loved him. Carla was watching him intently. He could almost believe by her expression that she could read his thoughts.

Gently, he pulled her down on to his lap. The basketwork rocking chair creaked and settled again. Their lips met in a powerful and passionate exchange. Both could feel the hunger in the other.

Finally, as they came up for air, Carla murmured, "I'm sorry, Matt. I know you are feeling vulnerable. I shouldn't have led you on."

"So you are saying you wish that kiss had never happened?" whispered Barlow.

Carla could feel her heart beating wildly, and her legs trembling.

"No, I wish I could say that for Rachana's sake, but I can't," she said, looking deeply into Matt's eyes. "I don't want to be alone tonight of all nights."

With Carla in his arms, Barlow rose from the chair and carried her back into the house, and through to his bedroom. Gently pulling her flimsy dress over her head, he laid her naked on the bed. Barlow then slowly disrobed himself, never at any time taking his eyes off her.

Looking at her, blonde hair strewn over the pillow, in the moonlight streaming through the window, he muttered in a husky voice, "God! You're beautiful, Carla!"

Carla, gazing up at him from the bed, saw his hard muscular frame, not an ounce of extra flesh anywhere. 'So are you,' she thought. How would he take her? Would it be rough, like the tiger? She wasn't sure if she could stand that.

Gently, Barlow lowered himself on to the bed beside her, slowly caressing her on the lips and then covering every aspect of her slender body with kisses. Just when she thought that she would burst with longing and ecstasy, he entered her, smoothly, like silk on satin.

Never, in her whole life, had she experienced such a magical sensation. So deep inside her, that they seemed as one, then deeper still, until she crashed over the edge of orgasm and, with joy, felt him climax with her.

Why did the morning ever have to come? If only the night would go on for ever!

Chapter Twenty-four
Nilgiri Hills Landing

The helicopter arrived on time. Barlow's foreman, the ever-gracious and smiling Surendra Naqshband, was there to see them off. After going through final instructions, Barlow said, "Don't forget to look after Jana, and give her the meat on time." This was said whilst fondly hugging the tigress.

"It would be more than my life's worth not to, sahib," exclaimed Surendra with a great smile. Everyone, after the pilot Subhra Girota had introduced himself, climbed aboard. Surendra had to forcibly restrain the eager Jana from following the others.

"Not this time, girlie," he said, pulling on her collar. It was all he could do to stop her.

This time, even Inspector Ramon Srinath had agreed to carry a gun, and he was equipped with a twelve bore, lent by Barlow, who carried his favourite Winchester. Berkeman had given his automatic to Carla, as it was felt that she would be able to cope with it better than a rifle. Berkeman, therefore, had borrowed Barlow's Holland & Holland, whilst little Zabu had been entrusted with a 2.2 air rifle, of which he was justly proud.

The pilot commented on this show of armaments with amazement. Barlow felt that it was only fair to put him in the picture, and gave him a quick explanation of their mission. He concluded by saying, "Of course, we don't expect you to do anything other than get us there and bring us back, afterwards."

The pilot Girota replied by saying that he was prepared to do anything that would help, but even to find the site in the Nilgiri Hills would be like looking for a needle in a haystack.

Barlow reassured him.

"I know the area quite well, so should be able to direct us to the most likely places. It's just whether we are going to spot any activity from the air that's worrying me."

"What happens when and if we do spot them, sir? Do you want me to land?"

"Good heavens, no!" exclaimed Barlow, "behave as if you are just passing over on some route or other, and fly on. We will have to get down somewhere else and work our way back on foot. You will stay with the helicopter and wait for our return."

The pilot looked anxious.

"How long do you want me to wait?"

"One hour after dawn tomorrow morning. If we haven't returned by then, take off without us, and inform the police of our failure to return," instructed Barlow.

Hearing this, Carla shuddered inwardly. She had already thought about the consequences, but hearing it out loud somehow made it more final. Seated at the rear, she looked down through the perspex as they took off, climbing steeply. The plantation grew smaller. Shortly after their departure, the Cauvery could be seen, the early morning sun reflecting off its surface.

For a while, the pilot followed the river's course before pulling away to the south-west. Soon only jungle appeared below, occasionally broken up by small villages. Finally, even they seemed to peter out, and only undulating tides of green jungle stretched before them – a mass, broken only by the differing heights of the green canopy making up the forest.

The chopper seemed to be on an endless flight to nowhere. The time ticked by slowly. Conversation was difficult. To make oneself heard above the noise of the aircraft was an effort, so everyone soon lapsed into silence.

Carla watched Barlow's broad shoulders seated up front, next to the pilot. He was anxiously scanning the terrain both ahead and below. Both he and the pilot wore earphones and were keeping in constant touch.

She wished that she could communicate with him, for she was feeling very mixed-up and alone. Last night had been marvellous, but she couldn't rid herself of the feeling of guilt. She had conveyed the impression to Rachana that, as far as Matt was concerned, she could be trusted. Why had she allowed herself to become involved? Surely now one of them would get hurt and most probably her, she reasoned. How could any girl compete with a vision like Rachana?

Much as Carla hated herself, she knew that if the chance came again she would do the same thing. After a while, with the hot sun on the perspex and the continuous drone of the rotors, she fell into a fitful sleep.

Barlow too was having trouble keeping his mind on the job in hand. Guilt also assailed him. How could he have made love to Carla with Rachana in such a predicament? Yet, in his heart he knew that he didn't regret it. The American girl had reached him spiritually as well as physically in a way that Rachana never had. She accepted him for what he was and didn't try to change him.

Forcing his mind back to the job in hand, he addressed the pilot over the earphones.

"Nilgiri Hills region coming up. Can you take us down lower, Subhra?"

The pilot looked across and nodded, without speaking. The chopper began to lose height, descending towards the green blanket of foliage below them.

For Zabu, whose first ever ride in a helicopter it was, the whole thing was wildly exciting. The little tracker continually switched his gaze from ground to occupants and back again, seemingly amazed that they weren't as excited as he was.

Berkeman and Srinath, seated together, scrutinised the ground, not really knowing what they expected to see below them.

Subhra, the pilot's voice, came over the intercom to Barlow.

"One problem – fuel. If we haven't spotted them within the next two hours, I'll only have enough left to make the return trip."

"That's bad news," retorted Barlow.

For the next hour everyone continued to scrutinise the terrain below and ahead of them, until they felt as if their eyes were on cornstalks. Apart from a few scattered and sparsely populated native villages, nothing remarkable emerged.

Time and fuel were running out fast. Another half hour passed with the fruitless search continuing. Barlow, of necessity, came to a sudden decision. Over the earphones he addressed the pilot after studying the terrain below.

"Turn and head due south, Subhra."

As the pilot complied, Barlow turned in his seat to face the others. He tried to explain the position regarding the fuel, and then went on to say, "So I'm going to play a hunch. As I told you earlier, I know this area. If I was organising this festival – or whatever these devilish Sons of Kali call it – there's an ideal place about fifteen minutes flying time from here. It's not going to serve any purpose to continue flying on aimlessly, so I'm going to have the pilot set us down – as near as he can – to the site I think they will use. There's a huge risk involved, so I won't think badly of anybody who prefers to return with the chopper to Bangalore."

He looked at each in turn. Everyone nodded in agreement.

"Right, that's settled then," yelled Barlow, above the engine noise, turning back to study the terrain ahead. The chopper continued on its relentless whining course. Below, the first real signs of civilisation appeared in the shape of railway lines and a dirt road.

"Rail track to Trichuro on the coast," called out Barlow, jerking a thumb downwards. "Joins up with the coastline which goes on right up to Mangalore or south to Cape Comorin."

Everyone craned their necks to observe this phenomenon of civilisation. A moment later, and they were over dense jungle again. Barlow studied the ground meticulously, like a hawk searching for its prey. Five more minutes ticked by.

Berkeman yelled out, "Looks like swampland beneath us."

Barlow nodded. "Swing in east a little, Subhra. If I remember rightly, there's a mossy clearing we should come across where you can set her down."

Another three minutes ticked by before he excitedly yelled, "There it is!"

Subhra Girota prepared to cut his speed and lose height, before finally descending.

"Don't land completely. Take her within a metre or so off the ground, and I'll jump down to make sure it's firm enough for you to come in."

"What if it's not?" shouted Srinath above the noise of the rotor.

"I'll try to find you a spot that is," yelled Barlow, who already had the sliding door open in readiness. "Listen, Subhra. After I jump out, go back up to about twenty metres and watch me. I'll guide you in."

They were still about a metre off the ground when Barlow jumped out to land on all fours. Quickly to his feet, he waved the chopper back up. Carla, peering down through the perspex, could see Barlow testing the mossy ground in several different places. At one point, she saw water ooze up over his boots.

Further on, he was stamping his foot to find solidity in the terrain. Obviously satisfied, he removed a white handkerchief from his pocket and laid it on the ground.

Then, standing back, he indicated to the pilot to come in slowly on the marker. With utmost caution, Subhra effected the manoeuvre before bringing the helicopter to rest and shutting down.

Everyone climbed out, the soil at this point proving reasonably firm. All around the marshy clearing was dense jungle, with no sign of life.

Zabu, last to clamber out before the pilot, carried Barlow's rifle as well as his own. A moment later the pilot, carrying Barlow's heavy backpack, joined them.

"Do you think you will be able to find this spot just after dawn tomorrow, Subhra?" enquired Barlow.

The pilot looked somewhat doubtful.

"I hope so, sir."

"Don't worry," replied Barlow. "After you've taken off again, I'll mark the spot with a white cross on the moss, a large one."

"Oh, and what with?" said a sarcastic Berkeman.

Barlow just smiled and opened his enormous backpack, producing a spray can of white paint.

"This guy never fails to amaze me," exclaimed Berkeman.

Ignoring the remark, Barlow turned his attention to the pilot once more.

"Get down as soon as you can after dawn tomorrow and wait no more than one hour. After that – pull out!"

"Very good, sir, but I don't like leaving you all in this wilderness."

"We'll be okay. Now off you go."

Five minutes later, the little party of five watched the chopper receding into the distance. Gradually the noise of the rotors diminished and it looked no bigger than a bird in the sky, before disappearing altogether from sight on the horizon. Barlow got to work with the spray can, creating a large letter X on the green moss.

"There! That should stand out from the air," he said, standing back in satisfaction.

Srinath addressed Barlow.

"Well sir, you seem to know where we are. Might I ask what happens now?"

Barlow struggled into his backpack, having first replaced the spray can within its confines.

"First off, has everyone got their water bottles?" he enquired.

Each in turn nodded their affirmation.

"Good. I suggest you all take a small drink now, then take little sips regularly throughout the day. The last thing we want is someone going down with dehydration out here."

"Yes Mummy," said Berkeman sarcastically.

Carla gave him a scathing look, but it was Ramon Srinath who spoke.

"I suggest, Mr Berkeman, you do as Mr Barlow requests. He knows this climate and its pitfalls. You don't!"

Berkeman looked somewhat subdued by the remark, but quickly recovered.

"What about food? Is there anywhere we can get any?"

"Oh yes," said Carla contemptuously. "There's a McDonald's round every corner!"

Everyone laughed, even Berkeman, which seemed to ease the tension a little.

"No problem, sahib," said little Zabu. "I carry food in my bag for all."

"So what the hell has he got in that great pack, then?" exclaimed Berkeman, pointing at Barlow's large backpack.

"You will have to wait until the time comes to find that out, Steve," said Barlow with a smile. "Now, if you are all set I suggest we make a move. If I'm right, we have a lot of ground to cover."

"And if you're wrong, sir?" asked Srinath pointedly.

"For Rachana's sake let's pray I'm not!"

He set off, the others following in single file behind him, with the exception of Zabu, who ambled along beside Barlow.

"Keep tight round the edge of this mossy clearing, it's pretty swampy in the middle," called Barlow.

At the edge of the dense jungle Barlow withdrew a small compass from his tunic pocket and studied it, before also checking the sun's position.

Finally, he nodded to Zabu and pointed into the bamboo. The little tracker withdrew a wicked looking, long, straight-edged knife from his belt, resembling the Malaysian parang.

Commencing a furious onslaught on the bamboo, he proceeded to cut them a way into the interior.

'If it's all going to be like this,' thought Carla, 'we aren't going to get very far.' It wasn't. After the first thirty metres of thick bamboo, huge areas of lantana interspersed the trees. Usually, it was possible to skirt round most, but one or two areas forced the group to crawl through on their stomachs. Carla felt the back of her shirt rip badly on the thorns. On emerging on the other side of this section, it was good to stand vertical again.

Then came more swamp. A large disgusting area stretched for some two hundred metres before adjoining a stream wending its way through curves and spirals through the jungle. Vines and creepers hung down from the high trees to the water's edge, some of the roots of the massive trees actually sticking out of the water.

Carla could feel the perspiration running down between her breasts and down her back. It was so hot and humid. Berkeman, in front of her, was continually slapping at mosquitoes. The place was a paradise for the vicious little insects. She was thankful that she had remembered to take her paludrine and avloclor regularly. What was that black thing on Berkeman's arm she could see as they waded through the brackish water? Oh and yes, there was another one, just above the waterline, an inch below where the bottom of his shorts reached.

"My God! They're leeches!" she gasped aloud, and then, looking down, saw that there were two on her, both on the same arm.

Barlow heard her and called back, "Don't anyone attempt to pull them off! They won't harm you. Leave them until we are clear of this swampy area, and I'll show you how we get rid of them."

Carla screwed up her nose at the sight of the disgusting sluglike things clinging to her arms. Her first impulse was to tear them off her skin, but she steadfastly heeded Matt's words.

By the time they were on firmer terrain she had collected another two, one on each arm. Berkeman, however, in front of her, was sporting at least seven that she could see from behind.

She turned round to look at Inspector Srinath. He pulled a wry face, indicating that he had his own share of the filthy things. Carla remembered Barlow's words – tigers rarely come here. They don't like the leeches and ticks. 'The tigers are good judges,' she reflected.

Another fright occurred when a snake fell from an overhanging tree and into the water, right in front of her. As she recoiled in horror, the snake swam away across her path, in that strange twisting motion peculiar to the species, and disappeared.

Now, once more on dry land, she heaved a sigh of relief, although the vegetation still pressed in upon them.

Again, Barlow called back.

"Hang on, everybody. There's a waterhole up ahead if my memory serves me correctly. I'll sort you all out once we get there."

In fact, so thick was the vegetation that it took at least another forty-five minutes before they reached it. A couple of waterbuck, disturbed in their drinking, scampered away from its edge. In one area, round the perimeter of the waterhole, the mud had dried to a hard firm paste.

"I'll sort these leeches out for everyone, then I guess it's time to stop for some lunch," he added. "Ladies first," he called.

Carla could hardly wait.

"Ugh! Get these horrid things off me, Matt. Please."

Smiling, he produced a packet of salt and dusted the back of each leech liberally. All but one fell off, leaving a small red mark.

"Why isn't that one going, Matt?" enquired a worried Carla.

"It will. Head is too deeply embedded for the salt treatment." So saying, he extracted a box of matches from his trouser pocket, struck one, then instantly blew it out. He placed the match's hot end on the dorsal aspect of the leech's head. Carla watched, revulsion on her face as it literally reversed itself and fell off.

Barlow then withdrew a spray from the first aid kit and aimed it at each red mark on Carla's arms. The medicament, which went on as a fluid, rapidly dried to a powder.

"Next please," laughed Barlow.

Berkeman stepped up to receive the same treatment, followed by Srinath. Barlow and Zabu attended to themselves.

"Thank God those loathsome things have gone," exclaimed Carla, greatly relieved. "What would happen if we just pulled them out, Matt?" she asked.

"One of two things. A nasty sore – and jungle sores can be very difficult to heal – or the head is left inside to erupt later and cause trouble."

"Ugh!" exclaimed Carla.

"Right, Zabu. Flush out the lunch, will you."

The little tracker, offering his best toothy grin, produced a small tin foil pack for everyone, then sat down on the baked earth to unwrap his own.

Biting into a sandwich, Srinath said to Barlow, "You've done well, sir. Very tasty."

Each member had a round of sandwiches, a hard boiled egg and a banana, plus a packet of saltine crackers. Barlow handed out a couple of salt tablets to each.

"Get these down. In this heat you will all need them!" He then proceeded to wash two down his own throat, with a swig of water from his flask.

While they all sat quietly consuming their packed lunches, Berkeman fired a question at Barlow.

"How much further before we get to this site of yours."

"With any luck we will make it before sunset," replied Barlow.

"Christ, man! You mean we have to go through an afternoon like this morning?"

"That's about it," replied Barlow.

"You don't even know for sure it's the right place when we get there?"

"No, that's right, I don't. But have you got a better idea, Steve?"

Berkeman looked indignant and mumbled something under his breath.

Barlow began to feel his usual placid manner deserting him. Looking hard at Berkeman, he snapped, "I thought you said you were an ex-marine. Seems to me you've gone soft, if a little thing like this throws you."

Berkeman jumped to his feet and moved menacingly towards Barlow, who backed away not one inch. The two stood eyeball to eyeball. Srinath, like lightning, pushed his way between them.

"Now, gentlemen, we can do without this. I think you will both agree that we have enough trouble on our hands without fighting between ourselves." He turned his attention on the glowering Berkeman. "I am sure, Mr Berkeman, if you don't want to go on, we can arrange to pick you up here on our way back."

"I didn't say that I didn't want to go on," put in Berkeman hotly.

"For heaven's sake then, calm down, Steve, and shut up. None of us like what we are doing, but we don't have a lot of choice," said Carla, butting in.

"That's the most common-sense thing I've heard all day," exclaimed Barlow.

The lunch break continued in silence.

Zabu, mystified, looked from one to the other.

Chapter Twenty-five

Swamp Misery

Rachana and Bishen Tendulkar had spent a miserable night, and most of the next day tied back to back. At least they had been able to converse, as their captors had not seen any need to gag them. Food had been brought to them at regular intervals when, under guard, they had been untied and allowed to visit a makeshift toilet.

Their prison was an old cellar arrangement underneath the ruins of the old Buddhist temple. Rachana calculated that it must be quite late in the afternoon, and as the day had progressed so had her fear of the coming night.

Bishen too, sensed that he would never leave here alive, and, even if he did, would never survive the return trip. If they still needed him to fly them back, perhaps he might be able to make a forced landing in the wilds and escape. This, he felt, would be his only chance, a slim one at that.

Rachana could see no ray of hope or light at the end of the tunnel for her. She had been brought here for a purpose, that was the only thing she knew for sure. Trying to wonder for what reason, only increased her panic level. 'Stay calm,' she told herself, 'it's your only chance,' but that was easier said than achieved. Talking to the pilot, Bishen, failed to throw any light on her captors' plans for her. He was as much in the dark, and just as afraid for his own safety, as she was.

A light meal was brought to them by a young native girl, accompanied by the usual guard with the gun, who untied their hands to enable them to eat. Not expecting to be told, Rachana asked the girl the time, and was surprised when the guard answered, "Four thirty p.m."

After consuming the Goan bread and maize cake and drinking the home-made Indian beer, the usual visit to the toilet was allowed before they were securely retied.

After the girl and the guard vacated the scene, Rachana and Bishen, back to back, conversed for a while, once more speculating on the reason for their capture. Neither had anything positive to add and they soon lapsed into silence.

It was growing dark when the next visit occurred. This time the heavily built scar-faced Indian accompanied the guard instead of the native girl. It was he who addressed her brusquely.

"The time has now come for your preparation, woman. Untie her, and retie the pilot. We have no need of him yet." The latter remarks were addressed to the guard.

"W, what are you going to do with me?" stammered a frightened Rachana.

"First you will be prepared to serve the Sons of Kali. A little later you will feel nothing."

"What is going to h, happen to me?"

"Silence, woman! That is our concern, not yours!"

Rachana attempted to protest, but was given a back-handed slap across her face, to remind her that obedience and silence would serve her better. She was half dragged by Scarface, and shoved from behind by the guard, as they exited from the makeshift prison. With a gun at her back, she was forced up a crumbling stone staircase to cross, what she assumed, had once been a courtyard. Their progress took them out of the temple, through a huge columned doorway, the top of which had long since disappeared with age, and fallen into ruin. Rachana was surprised to see that several tents had been erected on a grassy area to the rear of the old building. It was to one of these she was directed. Striped in black and white, it reminded her of those used by the Arabs in the Sahara. All the other tents were of a dirty khaki colour, blending in with the jungle behind.

The flap was pushed aside by the guard, and she was forced to enter.

Already in residence were the two other occupants of the helicopter. The wild-looking individual with the flowing grey hair, in his white robes, studied her from head to toe with his dark piercing eyes.

The other man, the one she had heard addressed as Mr Tata, who was obviously the overall leader of these devils, studied her with equal interest.   Also in the canvas interior were two young Indian native girls dressed in pale blue saris.

Fearful of another painful slap, Rachana resisted the impulse to speak. Tata turned, picked up a case from the floor and set it on top of a collapsible card table. Opening it, he removed a hypodermic syringe to which he fitted a needle.

To Rachana's increasing horror, he then produced a vial of colourless solution and meticulously transferred some of its contents into the syringe.

When he saw Rachana's wide eyes of terror, he laughed and said, quite matter-of-factly, "Now, girl, we are going to give you a little injection. It will not kill you so you have no need to worry. It will simply make you more compliant, for Dehra to handle." He indicated the fakir, with a flamboyant wave of his other hand.

"No, no! You can't do this!" screamed Rachana, almost hysterical with fear.

"Oh, but we can and will. Hold out her arm, Venkat."

Scarface, whom she had quite forgotten forced his powerful body behind her, and, with one arm encircling her waist, used the other to stretch her right arm, palm upwards, out in front of her.

Struggle as she might, she was but a toy in his powerful grasp. Tata advanced on her, needle at the ready, a cunning grin on his face. Rachana's mind raced.

Trying desperately to play for time, she forced herself to say, "Shouldn't you sterilise the skin first?" All three men laughed derisively.

It was Venkat who answered.

"Where you are going, woman, you won't have to worry about little things like that."

She gasped as Tata stabbed her arm with the needle. Squirm as she might, Rachana couldn't prevent the syringe's contents from being slowly emptied into her vein.

Almost immediately, she felt a pleasant, drowsy sensation beginning to assail her whole being. The sense of fear began to leave her. She experienced a form of weightlessness, as if she were floating in space, and yet she was still on her feet.

She was dimly conscious of the needle being withdrawn from her arm, but nothing hurt any more. She could hear voices going on in the room, but seemed unable to locate the speakers.

One voice was saying, "I trust a goodly crowd is beginning to build up?"

Another responded with, "Hundreds of natives already and more coming. By the time we are ready to start the ceremony, there should be close on a thousand in front of the temple, waiting for Dehra to perform his magic."

A third voice entered the conversation through the swirling mists of Rachana's mind.

"How can so many be found in such a remote area?"

"Our agents' little bribes to get them here have worked well. Most have trekked from far and wide."

"When Dehra has finished with the natives, we can transport any of them just about anywhere in India to hunt down tigers."

Tigers... tigers... tigers... The words echoed somewhere in the back recesses of Rachana's mind, but meant nothing. She was conscious of people moving around her and of voices, but nothing registered any more.

Anil Dehra moved the flat of his hand back and forth over her eyes, before saying to Ravi Tata, "It is good. Mentally she will respond now to my wishes, when we are ready to use her." Turning to the two Indian native girls in saris, he commanded, "It is for you girls to physically prepare her, just as I have instructed you. We shall leave now, as we have other matters to attend to. See that she is in complete readiness when Venkat here returns for her. Is that clear?"

Both girls gave a little bow and nodded without speaking. Dehra, together with Ravi Tata and Venkat, strode out of the tent.

The two girls led Rachana towards a makeshift camp bed. Almost in a trance, quite passively she allowed them to totally undress her before assisting her to lie down on the bed. One of the girls produced a bag, from which she extracted several pots and jars with an assortment of bottles.

After a few moments' discussion between them, the two girls began methodically, and without emotion, to massage a delicately scented oil into Rachana's naked almond coloured skin. The recipient, by this time, was far away, in a pleasant island of dreams.

*

To the front of the temple, great expectation and excitement was building up. Ravi Tata's agents had done their work well. Hundreds of natives were being marshalled and assembled into a roped-off area to the anterior of the old temple. Some of the agents were mingling amongst them, whipping up fervour and issuing everyone with a cheap hessian masked hood, which they were instructed to pull on immediately, lest the Lord Shiva be offended.

Ravi Tata reflected that the whole operation had been organised in haste, and had proved very costly, although the individual bribes to each man to get them there had been a mere pittance.

'What matter,' he concluded, 'when one dead tiger – in the right market, using every part of the carcass – could fetch as much as £35,000!' Looking out at the rapidly increasing and gathering throng, it was quite mind-boggling. By the time these natives had been effectively brainwashed, he would be able to transport hunting gangs all over India, and to all the national parks.

Why – in a year's time, he could probably have moved all the remaining Bengal tigers in India!

His financial mind began to work on the possible gains. Already a very wealthy man, he would become like an emperor.

He watched the fakir going through his meticulous preparations and reasoned – quite cold-bloodedly – that after Dehra had performed for them today, he would have little further use for the man. In fact, another partner would only minimise the profits and he already had Venkat Singh to carry out all the unpleasant and unsavoury tasks!

Taking stock of the situation, his eyes swept up towards the tall towers of the old temple. Floodlights in various colours had been installed there, as was the case in the tall trees surrounding the ruin. All in readiness to go on at a flick of a switch, to be controlled by a console hidden inside the building.

Ravi Tata could hardly wait for the ceremony to begin, as he gazed out into the darkness beyond the throng in the cordoned-off area.

*

Barlow's party had found their passage restricted by dense lantana, thick undergrowth, bamboo and an assortment of rotting fallen trees all afternoon. Progress had been deadly slow and even more unpleasant than Barlow remembered.

Since his last visit to this part of the Nilgiri Hills, the vegetation seemed to have run wild. The recent monsoon season had left the swampy areas even more so, and the mosquitoes abundantly plentiful.

Everyone soldiered on nobly, uncomplaining, with the exception of Steve Berkeman, who kept up a continuous and irksome barrage of objections about everything from the terrain to the hopelessness of the quest. Barlow wished that he had never consented to the American's help, but now he was stuck with the man.

Just before sunset, a further much-needed rest was taken, to have a drink and refreshing snack of fruit. Carla sat next to Matt on the root of a huge banyan tree, overlooking a muddy shelf, leading down to a stream covered with water lilies.

She whispered, "Are we going to make it before dark, Matt?"

"I'm afraid not, Carla. The damned place has become considerably more overgrown since my last visit here."

A noisy flock of birds preparing to roost flew in, silhouetted against the crimson sky of the setting sun, and circled the trees above them.

Further along the bank of the twisting stream, a leopard appeared from out of the bamboo and, crouching down, watched them from some hundred metres away.

Steve Berkeman saw what Barlow was watching and reached for the Holland & Holland. Picking it up, he carefully took aim, but before he could squeeze the trigger Barlow's voice, cold as ice, hissed, "Put that rifle down! If you pull that trigger, I'll pull this one." Berkeman turned to see Barlow's Winchester levelled right at him.

"Gee, man, you would too," mumbled Berkeman, lowering the rifle.

"That leopard is no threat to you or us. He's just having a look to see what we are up to. You see, he's going back into the bamboo now."

Everyone saw the animal force its way back into the undergrowth. For a moment, its head re-emerged for one last look, before making off into the interior.

"Besides," went on Barlow, "the last thing I want is anyone firing a shot now and alerting our enemies."

"Are we that near?" enquired Srinath.

"About an hour's trek in this jungle, but that's no distance at all for the sound of gunfire to carry."

"Baloney, man!" put in Berkeman.

"You don't even know where we are going, or if there's going to be anyone there when we eventually arrive."

Carla seethed. Everyone knew that Matt was doing everything possible. What was it with Steve Berkeman? He had saved her life and she owed him a lot, but he had changed beyond recognition since their arrival in Bangalore.

"Shut up, Steve, and give it a rest, will you. For a start, *you* offered to help. No one asked you to accompany us. So start helping, instead of hindering," Carla said with feeling.

Berkeman bit into his banana savagely, and didn't retaliate, but no further complaint issued from him that day.

The party prepared to move on; the sun was even lower now and sinking rapidly beneath the trees. Berkeman made as if to wade into the stream, in the process of crossing it, but little Zabu hauled him back roughly.

Before he could speak, Zabu pointed to the water lilies.

"Mugger," was all he said.

Barlow was forced to smile at Berkeman's puzzled expression.

"What does he mean, mugger?" asked Berkeman.

"Crocs is what he means," replied Barlow. "That's not a floating log under those lilies. We call these crocodiles muggers."

"My God, Zabu. You probably saved my life," said an amazed Berkeman.

"Not probably, but certainly," put in Barlow.

"So, how do we cross?" asked Srinath.

"I was about to tell you, when Berkeman here pre-empted me," replied Barlow. He pulled on some of the vines and creepers hanging from the giant banyan tree, until he found one to his liking.

"The stream is only narrow. We can swing across quite easily. Zabu will go first and show you how. I'll bring up the rear and collect anything you can't carry yourselves," Barlow stated.

The little tracker demonstrated how easy it was.

Carla was the next to make the attempt.

"The secret is to let go the moment you are level with the other bank," said Barlow.

Carla smiled.

"Me Jane, you Tarzan," but although she joked, she was very aware of the crocodile lying in wait under the pad of lilies in the murky water. After dragging one foot in the stream, she made it, the relief flooding through her. Next to go was Ramon Srinath, who, to Barlow's surprise, effected the manoeuvre quite easily for a city type.

Berkeman next, crashed through the latter stage, clumsily ploughing through the water, but his impetus luckily carried him clear.

Barlow, like Zabu, used to such problems, accomplished the swing in the manner born, and joined the party on the far bank. Getting themselves together, the party hastily moved off. Above them, in a large vee formation, a flock of wild geese, calling noisily, headed west towards the setting sun.

Another hour passed. The going became even worse with the coming of darkness. A nightjar called from a thicket to their right, and there were frequent rustling noises from the jungle on both sides.

Suddenly Zabu clutched Barlow's arm, with a finger to his lips.

"Do you hear it, Barlow Sahib?"

Barlow listened, his ears attuned to the sounds of the wilderness and jungle.

The thin strains of music, penetrating the bamboo surrounding them reached his ears.

"*Sarangi* and *mridang*," he whispered to the others, who looked expectantly at him. He went on to elaborate. "Indian musical instruments played by many of the natives. We are nearly there, and thank God it looks as if I have guessed right. The so-called festival is going to take place here at the old Buddhist temple."

Silently, with Zabu in the lead, the little group crept forward, mindful of the need for absolute caution. Their one hope lay in surprise. Any unnecessary noise could not only ruin their slim chances of success, but would endanger their lives in the process.

Another ten minutes brought them up to the sound of the music and the sound of many voices. Flares and candlelight could be observed through the undergrowth and through the branches of the trees.

Barlow whispered, "Stay here, everyone. I'm going to get nearer and take stock of the place. Come on, Zabu." He unbuckled his pack and laid it down.

The two of them crept off and after a few metres dropped on to their stomachs, before twisting and wriggling forward under the lantana to reappear a few moments later in tall, reedy grass to the right of the temple ruins.

Barlow suppressed a gasp when he saw the size of the crowd.

"There must be at least five or six hundred men out there, Zabu," he muttered.

"Yes, Barlow Sahib, and all hooded. This is very bad place."

The flares and candles stationed round the ruins threw some parts into deep shadow, and exposed others to a flickering eerie light. Barlow could see an arrangement covered with a black and gold embroidered cloth right in front of the main entry steps.

"Is that what I think it is, Zabu?" said Barlow nodding, indicating towards the object.

"Yes, Barlow Sahib. It is for the sacrifice of animals."

"Umm. That's what I thought, only this time I fear it's not for animals that it's going to be used."

Zabu responded with a puzzled expression, and Barlow didn't elaborate, as he was already too pre-occupied in studying the situation. To say that he didn't like what he saw would have been a colossal understatement.

Armed guards had been stationed at each corner of the temple, whilst another two were positioned at either side of the area in which the native watchers were cordoned off.

Barlow whispered to Zabu, "Go back to the others, and tell them to hold where they are for the time being. I'm going to work my way round the back and see what the situation looks like there."

Not waiting for an answer, Barlow crawled away and disappeared into the long, reedy grass. Zabu slowly made his way back to the waiting trio.

Ten minutes later found Barlow ensconced in dense bracken to the rear of the temple. As he had expected, the area was guarded, but, as far as he could make out, only by one man armed with what looked like a sten. Very little light illuminated the rear of the temple, so Barlow carefully waited to make sure there were no others. Obviously, these Sons of Kali, as they called themselves, considered that they had little cause for concern from the back quarter.

The guards at the front were merely a back-up in case the natives got out of hand and something should go wrong.

After waiting some five minutes or so to see if anything else presented itself – the only other thing he saw were several tents, some illuminated inside. Barlow retraced his passage, widely skirting the area to rejoin the others.

Everyone was eagerly awaiting his return, and he reported on his observations. Berkeman, at once, suggested a full-scale frontal attack taking out the guards.

Srinath looked at him in horror.

"No, sir. That would be madness. Too many people will get hurt. If that multitude panics and stampedes, think of the carnage."

Berkeman looked sheepish, and remarked, "You are quite right, Inspector. I hadn't thought of that aspect."

Before anyone could comment further, they realised that the Indian music had ceased and the floodlights were turned on to full power, only to be slowly turned down to nothing. A loud fanfare of music echoed from the temple, pervading the jungle's interior, masking the sound of the muffled generator.

A spotlight situated in the trees on the other side of the clearing centred on the temple steps. Into its beam strode an Indian, dressed in a long white robe, his white hair flowing in the night breeze. He raised both arms, palms outstretched to the multitude.

A great roar rose to greet him from the watching throng of natives. Then all fell quiet.

"This is beginning to look like Ranthambhore all over again," whispered Srinath.

Barlow placed a finger to his lips. It was so quiet now. All that could be heard was the low hum of the generator. An air of expectancy hung over the audience.

The Indian fakir moved slowly to his left, towards a huge mound of brushwood. He made as if to extract something from out of the very air, then hurled an imaginary object at the stacked pile.

Immediately, as if by magic, it burst into flames with a great swooshing roar, the pinnacles of which licked up towards the sky.

"Pre-planted petrol," hissed Barlow. "The man is an Indian fakir."

Noting Carla's and Berkeman's puzzled expressions, Srinath translated.

"Magician or illusionist," he explained.

Dehra extracted something else from the very air and threw it into the flames, which immediately turned blue. He repeated the act twice more, the colours changing from green to silver and back again.

He turned to address the crowd of amazed natives, producing a red silk handkerchief. After showing both sides to the audience, he threw it into the air and it became two doves, which immediately flew up and disappeared into the night sky.

The watchers gasped – the accumulated sound swelling the clearing and echoing off the old stone ruins.

There was only the one spotlight on Dehra now. Incredibly, the man himself seemed to change colour several times before their very gaze. His robes became blue, red, yellow, green, then back to white.

"How the hell does he do that?" hissed the watching Berkeman.

Barlow wasn't even watching. He had the large pack open and was extracting certain objects, which he laid out on the floor. The others were too busy watching the fakir to notice him. 'No wonder the natives are so easily taken in,' thought Barlow.

Now Dehra produced a rabbit from out of thin air, and set it on the ground. The frightened animal immediately ran for cover. Another gasp came from the huge assembly.

Suddenly, Dehra raised his hands again, palms outwards and in a powerful voice addressed the multitude for the first time.

"Do ye believe in Kali, second only to the Lord Shiva? It is she who has summoned you here. Kali, the Goddess of Destruction. I am but her mouthpiece."

With this, he produced a coil of rope and immediately it stiffened into a pole, reaching some ten metres into the night sky. In his bare feet, the fakir began to ascend it and disappeared into a cloud of smoke at its apex. A long drawn-out murmur of astonishment ran round the cordoned off zone.

"That's incredible," whispered Carla to Barlow.

"But it's still an illusion," he replied softly.

Dehra slid back down the rope, apparently from nowhere, with remarkable agility for one of his years. He threw some white powder on to the ground, the rope crumpled into a heap and a moment later was replaced by a hissing cobra. The fakir scooped up the snake and appeared to eat it. To all intents and purposes, it disappeared.

Stepping forward, again he addressed the throng.

"The Goddess Kali knows each and every one of you. She has commanded me to be her mouthpiece. Should you not do as I say, she wishes me to consume you in a fiery furnace or eat you as you have seen me devour this cobra..."

The dialogue continued in the same flowery hypnotic style. Barlow was no longer listening. He sensed that the grim finale would soon commence. He addressed Berkeman in a half whisper.

"Do you think you could take out the fellow in the trees over there, operating the spotlight, without anyone knowing?"

"I reckon," replied Berkeman. "Why?"

"No time to explain fully now," said Barlow. "Once you've got possession of the spotlight continue to work it on whatever's going on in front of the temple there." Berkeman nodded.

Barlow continued, "Until you hear this thunderflash explode up on the temple roof." He withdrew the firework from his pocket and showed it to Berkeman, who looked really puzzled now. "As soon as the thunderflash goes off, move the light, swinging it upwards to the left-hand domed terrace. The light will pick up the Goddess Kali standing there in all her magnificence. Count to exactly five seconds, not a moment longer, and swing the light on to the right hand dome. Right on the top, for the terrace has crumbled away there. Keep the light on the dome whatever happens, and be prepared for a surprise."

"Yes, but I don't under—"

Berkeman's intended remark was cut short by Barlow.

"No time for explanations. Go now and just do as I ask."

Berkeman took one last, long, puzzled look and crawled away. Barlow turned to Carla.

"I need you with me. Can you carry some of these objects on the ground? I'll carry the heavy stuff." He indicated the objects he had unpacked. An astonished Carla began to pick up a variety of strange articles. Barlow turned his attention to Srinath.

"What are you like with a rifle, Inspector?"

Srinath replied, "Well, I gained a marksman certificate at the police academy."

"Good man. Go with Zabu and keep out of sight. Your cue will be when you hear me say lights out. Take my rifle as well as your own."

"What do I do then?"

"Shoot out each of the floodlights. Zabu can pepper them with his 2.2 as well, not that he'll hit anything," he added with a smile. "Great tracker, but no marksman." As Srinath and the little tracker turned to leave, Barlow hissed, "For God's sake, don't miss, Inspector. Our lives will depend on your accuracy."

Carla, her arms full of articles, watched mesmerised, as Barlow picked up the rest.

"Come on," he whispered. "Follow me."

Crawling through the undergrowth towards the rear of the temple, they could hear Dehra still continuing with his mass hypnotism act.

"Behold her high priest."

Barlow risked a quick peep. Another figure in a purple robe, with a hood of black and gold, swept regally down the steps to join Dehra.

"Come on, Carla. Time's running out," urged Barlow, speeding up his crawling motion, though impeded by the articles he carried. Everyone's attention was riveted on the events taking place in the lit arena, so in the shadows there was little chance of detection now.

Barlow, with Carla following, quickened his pace still further.

Chapter Twenty-six
The Goddess Kali

To the rear of the temple all seemed quiet, and even the lights further back in the tents had been extinguished.

"Hurry, Carla. Strip to the waist, you are going to impersonate the Goddess Kali."

Carla looked at Barlow in amazement.

"I'm going to do what?" she murmured incredulously.

"Come on, I'll explain as we go."

Whilst Carla removed her torn blouse and bra, Barlow busied himself unwrapping something which was concealed in a sari of gold tapestry-like material.

She saw, to her amazement, that it was a skin-coloured plastic torso, or rather the front of it. From it, projected the front aspects of many arms.

"Hold your arms out," said Barlow. Carla, feeling rather stupidly self-conscious standing there stripped to the waist, dutifully obliged.

"I suppose you know what you are doing, Matt."

There were recesses in the plastic torso for her breasts and two of the arms fitted over Carla's own. Barlow then produced a second section, identical to the first, only it was a corresponding back plate with rear arms. Fitting it on to Carla he buckled the two together.

"See if you can move your own arms. Don't worry about all the artificial ones, they will take care of themselves," he invited.

A quick test showed that she could, the hinged joints at the shoulders moving easily.

"Squashing my breasts a bit, though."

Barlow smiled. "Obviously Kali wasn't as well-endowed as you. Perhaps that's why she wanted to destroy everything – jealousy. Goddess of destruction and all that. Don't worry, you won't have to wear it very long."

He stooped and picked up the golden sari, carefully wrapping it round her waist and tucking it into her belt. He then rolled up the legs of her jeans and rearranged the sari so that it came down to just below her ankles. Standing back to admire his work, he exclaimed, "There! That ought to fool everybody at a distance! After all, you are only going to be seen for five seconds."

Before Carla could reply, another fanfare of music could be heard from the front of the building.

"Come on, there's not a moment to lose," he said. "Follow me. This sounds like the finale beginning."

With everything in darkness, they easily gained the rear gateway and stealthily crept through it. Of the guard Matt had seen earlier, there was now no sign.

Crossing what had once been the courtyard, with tufts of grass forcing their passage up and between the flagstones, they heard a low moaning sound.

"It's coming from down those stairs over there," hissed Barlow. "Stay up close against this wall. I'll have to investigate before we move on up."

A moment later he disappeared like a wraith in the mist, and Carla found herself alone and trembling. Three minutes later, although it seemed like hours to her, he re-emerged, another man with him, walking very stiffly as if all his joints ached.

"This is Bishen, the pilot who brought them here. They had him tied up in the cellar."

The pilot stared at the vision of Carla in Kali attire, and gulped.

"Do you know where they have hidden your helicopter, Bishen?" Barlow fired at him, shaking him out of his mystified staring at Carla.

"They said something about camouflaging it with netting, after taking my keys away from me," said Bishen.

"Do you think you can have a shot at finding it and putting it out of commission, temporarily?"

"I can try," replied a recovering Bishen, relieved at a new lease of life.

"Good man. Off you go. Then after you have done it, hide nearby."

Silently, the pilot crept away. Barlow peeled off his shirt and withdrew the tiger mask from his pack, together with the tape recorder and a tape. The latter two objects he handed to Carla.

"I think you know what to do with these," he said, smiling.

"When do you want me to do it, Matt?"

"Just as soon as the last light is extinguished. You and I will have to take care of the ones on each dome, and hope to God Ramon Srinath can cope with the ones on the front of the building and on the sides of the roped area. Come on, let's get up there. Yours first," exclaimed Barlow, indicating the crumbling stairway to their right.

To Carla, dressed as she was with her upper torso encased in plastic, it proved no mean feat to navigate the stairway. They made their way along the wall buttress and rounded the curve of the domed tower, picking their passage carefully where stones were either crumbling or missing.

An amazing sight met their eyes.

Below them, in the glare of the spotlight, in front of the temple steps and alongside the makeshift altar, two hooded men had Rachana standing between them. Each had a vice-like grip on her arms.

She appeared as if in a trance, staring straight ahead of her, not appearing to see the fakir in front of her. Dressed in a long white toga and with her black hair braided, she looked incredibly beautiful.

Carla, high up on the edge of the tower, felt mesmerised, her eyes fixed on the scene below. She felt a tug on her arm and Matt pulling her further round on to the balcony in front of the dome. A floodlight set on the dome shone on the arena.

Barlow whispered, "We have to put that out of action at the right moment."

He crawled on his hands and knees under the lighted area.

"Ah! Here it is. An extension lead. Come and look."

Carla edged forward to get a better glimpse.

"When you hear my thunderflash go off, pull this plug out – not before. Okay? As soon as you have done that, stand up on this rail and lean back against the dome." He tested the stone rail. "Yup! It's solid ... Have you got all that, Carla?"

"I think so," she said nervously.

"Good girl. You will be illuminated for five seconds only. No time for anyone to draw a bead on you and get a shot off, so you've no need to worry. Just try and look disdainfully regal."

"Where will you be?" Carla clutched nervously at his arm.

"On that other dome over there. Unfortunately, illuminated for a great deal longer than five seconds," he replied, pulling a wry face.

*

Meanwhile, Steve Berkeman had worked his way round to the rear of the man operating the spotlight, who was sitting in the fork of a muthee tree. A rope ladder hung down to the ground. To where the man sat, with his back to him, was about seven metres from the ground.

Berkeman silently moved up to the trunk of the tree and flattened himself against it. He laid the rifle on the ground, and took a firm grip on the automatic he had borrowed back from Carla.

One step at a time, pausing to listen in case he had been detected, he edged up the rope ladder. It proved a precarious ascent, but he reassured himself that everyone's attention was on the floodlit area in front of the temple. When nearly to the fork of the giant tree, he softly called out, just loud enough for the light operator to hear him.

The man said something, but nothing happened. After a few seconds, Berkeman called again, in a loud whisper. This time the man poked his head out to investigate.

It was his ultimate undoing, and just what Berkeman wanted and was waiting for. His hand shot up, the heavy automatic barrel crashing on to the man's temple. A moment later, the luckless operator lurched and tumbled out of the tree, to hit the ground with a sickening thud below, narrowly missing Berkeman on his way down. Without a downward glance, Berkeman hauled himself into the fork of the tree and, getting himself comfortable, studied the beam of the light. What he witnessed nearly made him lose his balance behind the spotlight.

Two men, in long purple gowns, both hooded, had pushed Rachana, all in white, towards the wild-looking Indian fakir with the flowing hair. She appeared to be in some sort of trance, and unable to help herself. Nothing to do now but wait for Barlow's thunderflash.

"I hope to hell he knows what he's doing," he half muttered to himself.

The fakir turned towards his spotlight and raised his arms to the audience.

Once more he addressed the assembled throng.

"As you have seen me demonstrate the power bestowed on me by the Lord Shiva through his consort, Kali, you will now know you are all subject to my will completely. As I instruct you to do, so will you do. This power is also bestowed on the two high priests of Kali."

He pointed a bony index finger at the two purple hooded figures behind Rachana and continued with his address.

"Remove your hoods, high priests of Kali, so that everyone can recognise you and obey your orders." Ravi Tata and Venkat Singh swept off their hoods and stepped into the light for all to see.

"Behold the high priests. Fall on the earth and worship them."

Berkeman saw that the hooded mass of humanity in the roped area was sinking obediently to their knees.

"Say after me, we salute and obey," commanded Dehra.

The united response sounded like a roll of thunder as some six or seven hundred natives repeated the words, "We salute and obey."

Berkeman watched, almost spellbound, as Dehra placed two stakes vertically in the ground. The fakir then scooped up Rachana in his arms and laid her horizontally between and on the two poles, one under her feet, the other supporting her head.

First, he removed the pole at her feet. The crowd gasped as she remained horizontal. An even louder murmur rose from them when he removed the support from underneath her head. She appeared to float in space. One of the high priests produced a wooden hoop, which he handed to Dehra. The fakir then proceeded to pass it along the whole length of Rachana's body.

A great roar of approval rose from the assembly. Then he commanded her to stand. Obediently, she complied. Dehra raised his hand for silence, and turned his back on the multitude to face Rachana, who still stared sightlessly ahead of her, as if in some sort of trance.

"Maidservant of Kali, remove your gown," Dehra commanded in a loud booming tone.

Berkeman watched with an involuntary intake of breath as Rachana bent mechanically forward, to grasp the hem of the long white gown with both hands.

Slowly, in one fluid movement, she swept it upwards and over her head, leaving herself totally naked.

Berkeman, in the tree, could hardly believe his eyes. Her beautifully formed body glistened in the spotlight. The nipples of her full breasts had been painted so that they represented large circular red flowers. Her pubic hair had been completely removed, and an array of orange and red flames decorated her abdomen in an arc rising from her mound of Venus to her navel.

Berkeman thought that he had never seen anything so beautiful in his whole life.

The fakir's next words turned his blood to ice-water.

"We offer this woman to you, our Mistress Kali. As a sign of our obedience we give you her blood, that you may drink well this night and satiate your everlasting thirst."

The other high priest handed Dehra a wicked-looking knife with an ornamental handle, then, together with the first priest, they carried the naked Rachana and laid her on the altar of black and gold.

"For Christ's sake, Barlow! What are you waiting for!" muttered Berkeman, raising his automatic and lining it up on the fakir, although he knew in his heart he hadn't a hope in hell of hitting the man at this distance with a hand gun. If only he had the rifle, but it lay under the fallen man at the foot of the tree.

Knife raised, Dehra advanced on the altar and Rachana's prone form. Berkeman's knuckles began to whiten on the trigger of the automatic.

Suddenly, there was a blinding flash and an explosion on top of the temple. At the same instant, both floodlights on the domes blacked out. The very building and surrounding jungle seemed to shake and echo with the explosion.

Berkeman suddenly remembered in his shock. Switch the spotlight to the left-hand dome. God, he had quite forgotten.

Instantly recovering, he grasped the controlling handle and swept the beam upwards. There, caught in its rays, was the Goddess Kali, with all her many arms. She stood regally looking down, an arrogant expression on her face. Fully three seconds elapsed before the realisation dawned on him that it was Carla Wayne, her blonde hair flowing in the breeze.

Two more seconds and he recalled – switch the light to the other tower. Cutting the switch, he transferred to the red filter, and aimed at the other dome – switched on again to an even greater shock. A powerfully built man, stripped to the waist, with the face of a tiger, was standing on the very dome itself. With one leg either side of the apex of the dome, hands on his hips, he surveyed the scene below.

Consternation was breaking out in the roped-in multitude. Berkeman could see that the scene in the central area was just as confused. Dehra looked at the two pseudo-high priests, who themselves were gazing upward in amazement.

On the dome the tiger apparition began to address the assembly in a deep, booming, threatening voice.

"Be still, you sons of vermin. You have been privileged to witness the Goddess Kali in all her wrath. I am the instrument of both her and the Lord Shiva."

A further murmur followed by cries of fear rose to greet the statement, which continued in the same vein.

"These men before you are not those whom they would have you believe. They are treacherous fakes who would destroy a true sister of Kali."

Dehra let the hand holding the knife sink to his side, totally thrown by the strange turn of events. The two high priests looked from one another to the figure on the temple dome. It was impossible to read their minds or observe their expressions.

Berkeman, in his shock, suddenly realised that it was Barlow up there. How could the man possibly disguise his voice like that? Barlow continued in that menacing tone, causing the natives to cringe in terror.

"I, the tiger god of all India, will exterminate all who trap tigers falsely using the name of Kali, whom you have seen here this night, and this is what these men before you would have you do."

Barlow could see nothing of the effect his dramatic monologue was having, because he was temporarily blinded by the spotlight picking him out.

Venkat Singh could sense the changing mood of the multitude and reached inside his gown for the pistol he carried there. Ravi Tata put a restraining hand on his arm. Maybe they could still control the mob.

Above them, Barlow, glowering down at them through his tiger mask, continued, "Touch a hair of the woman's head at your peril, and I shall call on all the tigers of the forest to come and destroy you."

Carla, lying flat on the terrace, now unseen from below, had her finger poised on the tape recorder switch, nervously awaiting her cue. Berkeman crouched in the tree fork. The moment Barlow finished, he knew he must kill the light. The wonder was that as yet none of the mercenaries guarding the area had taken a pot-shot at the tiger apparition, high above them and silhouetted for all to see. Srinath and Zabu awaited their cue; both had rifles already lined up on two of the floodlights.

"Evil impersonators will surely die. Even now, my tigers are approaching to destroy them, just as I shall put these lights out."

Srinath squeezed the trigger and the first lamp shattered to a thousand pieces. Zabu missed completely, but Srinath swung the rifle on the second in quick time and extinguished that also. Whilst Zabu tried to reload the 2.2 Berkeman realised, after killing his spotlight, what was afoot, and took a pot-shot at the nearest lamp with the automatic.

Damn! If he only had the rifle up here with him. Another crashing retort from Srinath's nearby position took care of the last floodlight. Apart from the candles and flares, the place was now in semi-shadow, creating a truly eerie atmosphere.

Carla pushed the play button and turned the volume slowly up. From the now blacked-out dome, Barlow did his tiger imitation. Zabu lost no time in answering it from the bush.

Pandemonium broke out. The mob, in their haste to escape, trod down the ropes that had been used to cordon them off.

Screaming and yelling in mortal terror, they dispersed in all directions, some rushing into the temple, but most into the surrounding jungle.

Venkat Singh fired his automatic into the air and shouted at the top of his voice.

"It's a trick that has been played upon you! Stay where you are! Nothing will happen to you!"

He might as well have tried to turn back the waves. Nothing now could halt the terror-stricken mob from dispersing. He levelled the automatic at the girl. Everything had gone wrong! She was obviously precious to these invaders – whoever they were. To kill her would, at the very least, spite them.

He never succeeded in squeezing the trigger. A bullet from Srinath's rifle found its mark in his throat. With a gurgling sound, followed by a fountain of blood, Singh was knocked backwards off his feet, to lie in an ever increasing pool of crimson.

The horror-stricken Ravi Tata grabbed the still naked Rachana round the neck, screening himself from the direction of the shot.

Dehra, the fakir, thrown into panic, looked for an avenue of escape and ran first in one direction then another. He collided with one of the stampeding natives and was knocked to the ground. A moment later, his screams were drowned as some hundred or so terror-stricken Indians ran over him on their way into the forest. His crushed and crumpled lifeless form lay still in their wake.

Ravi Tata still had one ace left – the girl! He would use her as a hostage. Perhaps he might yet escape. Using her as a shield, he knew the risk of being shot was minimal.

Slowly edging his way backwards, dragging the sedated Rachana after him, he made it to the jungle's edge and disappeared into the bamboo.

Berkeman watched their exit, making a fix on the position in his mind's eye. Swinging precariously on the rope ladder, he climbed down the tree. Picking up the rifle, at the foot of the tree, he cautiously set off in pursuit, unseen by anyone else in the dimly lit area.

Following them was easier said than done. The escaping mob were everywhere. Screams and yells, besides the continuous crackling of branches and undergrowth under their panic-stricken feet.

Neither Barlow nor Carla had seen the disappearance of Ravi Tata and Rachana into the interior. Barlow's first thought now was to check that Carla was all right, and get down from the ruins to find the others.

Carla, shaking like a leaf, flung her arms round his bare torso, as they stood, precariously embracing, on the crumbling surround at the base of the dome.

"That light was on you so long I thought someone must shoot at any minute! I know how frightened I was, for just five seconds, standing there in that beam, seeing nothing beyond," whispered Carla.

"You were magnificent, Carla. Just what was wanted. Now, let's get down, find our clothes and locate the others."

By the time these two things had been accomplished, only faintly receding noises could be heard from the surrounding jungle. Even the mercenary guards had departed with the mob, whether in an effort to prevent them or to join in the stampede, the group had no means of knowing.

Barlow, Carla, Srinath and Zabu found only the bodies of Venkat Singh and Dehra in front of the temple. Srinath turned Venkat's head and, after studying the face said, "I've been after this fellow for a long time."

"Where's Berkeman?" questioned Barlow. "Has anyone seen him? Where's Rachana?"

No one could answer any of the three questions fired at them by Barlow. Blank faces greeted him. Zabu, throwing back his head, sniffed the air and began moving round in slow circles.

Carla whispered to Barlow. "What's he doing that for?"

Matt answered in the same low tone.

"I think it's perfume. I can smell traces of it too."

Uncomprehending, Carla replied, "But I'm not wearing any."

"Not yours, Carla. At a festival of this type and the way they had painted and oiled Rachana, it's a certainty they would have used perfume."

By now the little tracker had moved over to the very edge of the forest and was urgently beckoning them over.

Carla exclaimed, "You mean, he can actually detect Rachana's perfume, even when she's not here?"

"It isn't difficult for a man who can tell you which way a tiger has passed, simply by the smell of urine left behind on a rock or bush, even if it was the day before."

The three of them moved smartly over to join an agitated Zabu, who was inspecting a trail of broken-down vegetation leading into the jungle.

"This way, Barlow Sahib. Miss Dev, she taken this way – half drag, half carry. Another man, he follows."

Just as they were about to go into the interior, the pilot, Bishen Tendulkar, appeared from a nearby section of bamboo and hurried up to confront Barlow.

"I have found the chopper where they had hidden it, sir. It's been covered with netting, but there are no keys."

"One of them possibly has it." Barlow nodded towards the two corpses, still staring sightlessly skyward in the middle of the clearing.

"Search them, and wait here. We are going after the other one, and the girl he has taken as a hostage," put in Inspector Srinath before turning to follow the other three, who were already going into the undergrowth.

Chapter Twenty-seven

Pursuit

The effects of the drug were slowly wearing off Rachana. At first she thought that she was dreaming. Who was this figure, dressed in a purple robe, dragging her through she knew not where? Why was she as naked as the day she was born? And why ever was she painted up in such an absurd fashion?

Slowly, reality began to flood back. Her head ached and her throat was dry. Bracken and thorn scratch marks on her skin irritated as the man dragged her through the bush. With her return to consciousness, she punched and pummelled at the robed figure – this devil who had given her the injection, the man the others had addressed as Mr Tata.

She remembered everything up until then, but nothing since. What had they been doing with her and why was the man so agitated now? Obviously someone was in pursuit of them, and Rachana's quick mind deduced that whoever it was must be on her side.

She began to scream, "Help! Help!" at the top of her voice. The man silenced her with a backhanded slap across the face. It hurt, but at least confirmed her suspicions. She began to struggle violently, scratching his face and kicking at his shins with all the fury she could summon up.

"Damn you woman!" cursed Ravi Tata, striking out and knocking Rachana to the mossy earth.

Peering all around in the darkness, Tata snarled.

"Well, woman, you have served your purpose. I have escaped our pursuers now and have no need of you any more. In fact, you are an encumbrance." With this, he foraged around in the purple robe and withdrew a small automatic.

Rachana, seeing the end was near, thought quickly.

"If you shoot me, the shot will be heard for miles. Whoever is chasing us will certainly hear the sound." An evil smile spread over Tata's face.

"You speak sensibly, woman. I shall kill you myself, much more subtly." He advanced on her supine form hands stretched out.

Rachana scrambled hurriedly to her feet and tried to run, or, more aptly, blunder through dense undergrowth. Branches and thorns tore at her flesh, but she was oblivious in her headlong flight. To her distress, she could virtually feel Tata's hot breath on her naked neck and back. Rachana knew that she had only seconds to live now.

With bare feet in this spiteful terrain, she had no chance of outrunning him. Any minute she would feel his hand upon her, choking out her life for ever.

Suddenly, she felt water round her ankles and realised that in the dark she had run straight into a stream. Going forward, Rachana sensed the water level creeping up her legs until she was forced to wade.

Risking a glance over her shoulder, she ascertained that the man, Tata, had stopped at the edge, uncertain whether to follow, and was staring out to where she was noisily splashing around. The water was now up to her waist and she could dimly see the other bank outlined against the water's edge.

Without a second thought, she dived in, swimming in a powerful overarm action towards it and possible sanctuary. Suddenly a new terror assailed her thoughts. What if there were crocodiles in this stream? A vision of herself being torn apart by these relics of prehistoric times forced her to strike out even harder for the other bank.

Her hand hit something hard in the water. She shrieked with terror, then realised it was nothing more than a piece of rotting driftwood floating on the murky surface. A moment later and she had reached the other bank. She tried to scramble to her feet, but it was too deep and she couldn't touch bottom.

Almost hysterical now, she felt her toes brushing against the reeds. The bank was vertical at this point and too slimy to pull herself out. She launched herself sideways and struck out along the bank, looking for somewhere lower to scramble out.

A loud explosion was followed by a spout of water, only a metre away from her head. Tata had abandoned all caution and was going to shoot her after all. Desperately, she ploughed on through the dark lily-covered waters. Another shot followed. This time she was terrified by its closeness as water showered over her back.

Then, mercifully, her right hand hit something big, solid and static. She realised at once that it was the submerged root of a huge banyan tree, reaching out into the water. A second later her knee scraped against another.

Hurriedly, she dragged herself forward, pulling herself up the length of the tentacle-like root until she was just above the waterline. She slumped exhausted against the huge base of the banyan, dragging air into her lungs in huge gulps.

A third shot crashed into the massive voluminous trunk just above her head and sent a sliver of wood bark down on her. Instantly motivated anew, she worked her way round the trunk. Now at least she had the giant tree to screen her from Tata.

The desire to peep round the trunk was almost overwhelming. Was he now swimming across too? Was he unable to swim? Had he run out of ammunition?

Rachana forced herself to stay where she was, listening for the sounds of splashing or some evidence of pursuit. All she could hear were the night noises of the forest. In the dark she could see numerous fireflies dancing amongst the trees.

The mosquitoes were making her acutely aware of her nakedness, with innumerable bites on her flesh, but of Tata there was no sound. The suspense was nearly killing her. Had he given up and moved off or had he crossed somewhere further up or downstream? Was he even now edging towards her position at the base of the banyan tree? She forced herself to tiptoe away from the shelter of the tree into the surrounding bamboo and waited with bated breath.

Ten minutes later, she could hear something or someone blundering through the bush on her side of the stream coming her way.

A few moments later, from her place of concealment, she could actually make out the figure of Tata approaching the banyan tree. His long flowing cloak made him easy to identify.

Rachana crouched down, fearful of detection. Luck was against her. The moon emerged from behind a bank of cloud, illuminating the forest.

He had his back to her and was studying the ground intently. Suddenly he turned round and slowly advanced towards her position, screened in the bamboo. He must have crossed further upstream and worked his way back. Now, of course, he could see her naked footprints in the soft mud, and was following them right to her position.

Then, for a moment, he halted. He was so close now that she could make out his face in the moonlight. Rachana realised he was perplexed. The wet footprints had run out when she hit the drier firmer ground. Inexplicably, he moved off to her right and travelled slowly for about another twenty metres trying to pick up her trail. He peered into the bamboo. Then the incredible happened with a suddenness almost beyond Rachana's comprehension.

As Tata stooped to inspect the source of a sound from the thick bamboo, a huge black shape hurtled out, launching itself through the air with a ferocious roar to knock him backwards.

Tata screamed in terror. Rachana watched, rooted to the spot with fear, as the two combatants rolled about on the soft earth. The snarls of the panther and the screams of Tata intermingled in a bloodcurdling symphony of horror. The panther, holding on with his forepaws, raked Tata with his hind claws almost down the length of his body, tearing his cloak to purple shreds.

Try as he might, Tata's efforts to dislodge the animal he had inadvertently disturbed were futile in the extreme. Rachana would never forget his screams of pain and sheer terror as long as she lived.

The panther fastened his teeth on Tata's throat and the screams were suddenly quenched, turning into a death rattle or gurgle. The panther stood off, surveyed his quarry, snarled and made off.

A split second later, from downstream, Steve Berkeman arrived, and from upstream four more people. Rachana realised that they were Matt, Carla, Srinath and Zabu.

Berkeman raised his rifle, aiming it at where the panther had disappeared a moment before. Barlow called out.

"Hold it Steve! I think justice may have been served here. Anyone seen Rachana?"

"No. I was following them, but lost the trail," exclaimed Berkeman.

Everyone advanced on the fallen figure of Tata, laid out in a pool of blood already soaking into the moss.

Rachana watched from her place of concealment, so shocked that she could hardly make her presence known. Everything had happened so suddenly.

She could see the little group huddled round Tata's body but couldn't seem to get a word out. Their words came floating through the bamboo to reach her.

"The swine got exactly what he deserved. Live by the knife, die by the knife. He was responsible for scores of tigers being killed and he has been avenged by a panther."

Srinath was kneeling down examining the body carefully.

"It certainly made a mess of him, Mr Barlow. Would you say this panther was a man-eater?"

"No way, Inspector. He just happened to virtually walk in on the animal, who was more likely to have thought he was under attack from the guy. I'm more worried about where Rachana is and what has happened to her. If this devil Tata has killed her..." The sentence petered out.

There was a faint cry from the bamboo, further along from there.

"It's me! I'm here."

Rachana had finally found her voice. Everyone hurried to the position whence the voice had come.

From the thick area of bamboo, a voice filtered out to them.

"Do you think you could pass a shirt, or something in here, Matt. I could sure use some clothes."

Barlow, relief flooding his face, tore off his shirt and hurried into the bamboo with it.

*

Some thirty minutes later found the little group reunited with Bishen Tendulkar, the helicopter pilot, back at the temple clearing.

Barlow deposited the mutilated body of Ravi Tata heavily and unceremoniously on to the earth from the fireman's lift position in which he had been carrying it on his powerful shoulders.

Rachana, dishevelled and dressed in Matt's shirt, which reached nearly to her knees, was still ignorant of developments from when Tata had injected her with the drug up until the last hour in the interior.

"Can someone tell me what is going on and what this is all about?" she cried, almost hysterically, seeing the prostrate bodies of Venkat and Dehra stretched out on the earth some twenty metres away.

Steve Berkeman, who had been supporting her with a protective arm round her waist on the return trip, took her aside to explain. Meanwhile, the rest of the group discussed their next move.

Bishen happily waved his keys at them.

"I found my keys on one of the bodies. The one with the scar on his face," he exclaimed, pointing at the bodies. "The chopper is over there covered in netting. If some of you can help, we can uncover it and drag the machine into the clearing." He produced a small metallic object from his pocket. "Once I put this back, we can take off and return to Bangalore."

Inspector Srinath cut in.

"Good man, pilot. We can load the bodies and get the hell out, as you Americans say," he said, grinning at Carla.

"I'm afraid it's not that easy, Inspector," replied Bishen. "The machine will just about carry all of us, but not the extra weight of three bodies."

"No matter," said Srinath. "We'll haul the bodies into the temple for safe keeping, and I'll organise a patrol to be sent out by the Kepala authorities in the morning."

Barlow, ignoring the comment, asked a question of his own.

"Is your radio still intact in the aircraft, Bishen?"

"I would think so, sir. Why?"

"Because if we are going to fly back directly from here, we will need to get a message through to stop our own pilot returning on a fruitless errand to pick us up."

"No problem, sir. If you can give me the details, I can relay a message once we are in the air to stop him coming."

"Champion," said Barlow and walked off, over to where Rachana was standing with Berkeman. Putting an arm round her slender waist, he gave her a gentle reassuring squeeze.

"We'll soon have you out of this, Rachana, and safely back home," he said. "Are you feeling stronger now?" Rachana shook herself free of his protective arm.

"Oh, so you have finally got round to me, have you Matt? Isn't your little blonde American friend enough for you?"

Barlow looked as if he had been cut with a knife. Berkeman couldn't resist a look of triumph showing on his face at Barlow's discomfiture.

Recovering quickly, Barlow exclaimed, "You are obviously shocked and overwrought, Rachana, so I shall forget that you ever said that."

"Don't bother, Matt. I can see how it is," snapped Rachana, with a toss of her luxuriant black hair.

"Perhaps you should know that Carla played a very brave part in your rescue from these villains," Barlow went on.

"From what Steve tells me, it was because of your tiger conservation ideas that I was taken in the first place," she retorted hotly.

Matt looked somewhat crestfallen. "I guess I can't argue with that, and I'm truly sorry, Rachana."

"But you would still do the same thing again, Matt," she said. With that she turned indignantly and flounced off towards the helicopter.

Berkeman, a satisfied grin on his face, looked at Barlow.

"I think you've blown it this time, Barlow."

Matt Barlow turned square on to face him, big hands on hips, his jaw clamped tight. He counted to ten then spoke softly.

"You don't like me much, Berkeman, and I can tell you, I like you even less. Nevertheless, I formally thank you for your help in rescuing Rachana and bringing these villains to a timely end. That said, I'd like to give you a long-deserved present."

With that, his right hand flashed up to connect with Steve Berkeman's jaw in a bunched fist. Rachana, walking towards the concealed helicopter, turned in time to see Berkeman crumple in a heap on the dusty terrain. With an indignant dismissive gesture, she turned again and continued towards the aircraft.

The rest of the group turned, nonplussed at the sight before their eyes. Both Carla and Ramon Srinath had a ghost of a smile hovering round their eyes.

Carla exclaimed to the inspector, "Well, you can't say he hasn't been asking for it."

She was surprised at the enigmatic Srinath's reply. "Full marks to Mr Barlow, miss. I thought he would crack earlier. I hope I could have shown such patience, in the light of such continual provocation."

Carla nodded towards the retreating form of Rachana.

"I don't think Miss Dev shares your view, Inspector."

"It would appear not, miss," replied the puzzled Srinath.

"Come on, everybody," called Barlow. "Let's get this chopper out in the clear. The sooner we are out of here the better, just in case any of these mercenaries take it into their heads to return for another look."

Shaken out of their conjectures, everyone but Berkeman, who was still sitting on the ground rubbing his jaw and working it gingerly up and down and sideways, joined in. Even he, after satisfying himself that his jaw was not broken, finally and reluctantly ambled over and joined in.

Once in the clear, Bishen Tendulkar replaced the part he had appropriated from the aircraft, and tested the engine. The rotors moved slowly at first, then burst into life.

Barlow shouted above the noise of the whirring blades. "Okay girls, get in. Whilst Bishen goes through the necessary pre-flight checks we'll get these bodies inside the temple."

Zabu assisted him with the body of Venkat Singh, whilst Berkeman and Srinath carried the fakir Dehra's corpse between them. By the time that they re-emerged from the temple for the last remaining cadaver – that of Ravi Tata – Barlow was amazed to see Carla Wayne trying, single-handedly, to drag it towards the temple, Rachana sulkily watching her efforts from the plane's glassed interior.

"Here, let me, Carla," said Barlow, heaving the body over his shoulder. "At least it's a lot lighter than Scarface."

Carla gave an involuntary shudder.

*

Ten minutes later they were in the air, heading back for Bangalore. Carla, looking down, could see the dying embers of the once huge bonfire in the clearing still glowing. The ruined temple was bathed in moonlight, throwing ghostly shadows across the cordoned-off area, now deserted. Was it possible that this had all happened, or was it a dream? She pinched herself to prove the reality – it hurt.

Could so much have happened in so short a time? What a story she would have to write for *Liberty* magazine and Edwin Strobe. On landing at Bangalore, Srinath hurried off to make his report and arrange for collection of the bodies, leaving the others to make their own arrangements. Bishen Tendulkar offered gallantly, though visibly shaken by the ordeal, to fly them back to Barlow's plantation. Barlow, however, wouldn't hear of it.

"No, you have done a great job. Go home and get some sleep. We can get a taxi."

"Well, if you are sure, sir," said the obviously relieved pilot.

By now it was 4 a.m., and signs of the false dawn were just appearing as they approached the rank of ancient Ambassador cars serving as taxis.

"Is everyone coming back to the plantation with me?" enquired Barlow, looking at Berkeman, expectantly.

"No, you can drop me off at my hotel," snapped Berkeman. "I'm leaving for New York first thing tomorrow – I've had India."

Rachana's dark eyes flashed at Barlow, as she shot a question at him.

"Is she going back to your place, Matt? If so, you can drop me off at my apartment."

Carla, trying to pour oil on troubled waters, interjected, "No, that's not necessary, Rachana. I can easily book into an hotel."

"No you won't. You are staying at the plantation as my guest. All your things are there anyway, and you have a report to write for your magazine."

"That's true, but I could easily—"

Barlow cut her off in mid-sentence.

"Rachana knows she can come back with us, she is just choosing to be difficult," Barlow said, softly.

"That does it!" snapped Rachana. "Drop me off at my apartment, Matt."

"So be it then, but understand it's of your making, not mine."

They all clambered into the taxi, Zabu in the front with the driver.

During the taxi ride everyone lapsed into silence. First Berkeman, then Rachana were dropped off at their respective destinations. As the car rumbled on through the retreating night towards Barlow's plantation, Carla broke the ominous silence.

"Look Matt, you mustn't let me cause problems by staying on with you at the plantation. Rachana is obviously deeply distressed by me being with you. I could just as easily move into an hotel and fax my final article to New York from there."

"Nonsense," cut in Barlow. "Wouldn't hear of it. You're my guest, and anyway, you seem to forget, it was Rachana who invited you in the first place."

"But things were different then," reasoned Carla.

"I don't see that. Rachana just wants her own way."

"I would feel the same if the position were reversed, Matt."

"No, you wouldn't. You would see the sense of it."

"Are you sure of that?"

Barlow patted her hand on the seat beside him.

"I'm tired, so don't let's argue. Let's talk about it in the morning."

Carla, with an engaging smile, said, "How about lunchtime? It's morning now!"

"Suits me," agreed Barlow, with a chuckle.

Chapter Twenty-eight

Uncertainty

It was, in fact, well after lunchtime when Carla and Barlow surfaced. Neither had realised just how exhausted they were or how much the last twenty-four hours or so had taken out of them.

However, by the time each had taken a shower and eaten, normal service was ready to resume. Barlow remarked that he ought to go over and see Rachana to pour oil on troubled waters. Carla intimated that she thought that would be an excellent idea, and whilst he was away she would prepare her final report to *Liberty* magazine.

"I'd like you to read it through first though, Matt, before I fax it to New York."

"Love to," replied Barlow. "It should make interesting reading."

Carla laughed. "You want to bet! Don't forget I'm supposed to lack heart and feeling. That's why Strobe sent me out to India."

"I'm willing to guarantee that the piece will be just great, Carla. I don't think you lack anything."

Their eyes met and held a moment too long. Carla coughed and said, "Weren't you going to see Rachana?"

"I guess so," he agreed and, blowing her a theatrical kiss over his shoulder, called out as he turned to leave, "don't make me sound too bad in your article, will you."

Jana stretched and rose to her feet, intent on following him out. Barlow crouched down and gave the tigress a hug and a playful pat on the shoulder.

"No Jana, you stay here with Carla – she's going to write all about you."

The big cat looked from one to the other and almost as if she understood, flopped down to rest by the settee once more.

*

An hour later Barlow was given a frosty reception by Rachana at her apartment.

"I wondered when you would show up, Matt."

"I figured everybody would need some sleep to calm down somewhat – you most of all, after the ordeal you have been through."

"You can say that again! I suppose you do realise that all this was your fault, don't you, Matt?"

"What brings you to that conclusion, Rachana?"

"It's this preoccupation with interfering with tiger poaching and the gang-busting you have taken on yourself. They have tried to get back at you through me! Don't you even realise that?" Rachana's dark eyes flashed in temper, her breasts stretching the thin silk sari, the blue material looking as if it would burst with her rapid breathing.

"Well, if that is the case, then I guess I'm sorry," said Matt, moving towards her.

"You guess!" Rachana shot at him. "You love danger so much you're not even aware of what you are doing to the people around you."

Barlow shrugged.

"Somebody has to do it. I would have thought that you, an Indian would have understood, Rachana."

"*Half* Indian," she retorted hotly. "If it's a choice between the tiger's welfare and mine – I choose mine every time."

Barlow tried to reason with her, slipping an arm round her slender waist. She twisted nimbly out of his encircling arm.

"No, it won't wash, Matt. The time has come for you to make a choice." Rachana sat on the settee turning her head away. Sunlight coming through the window shone on her lustrous black hair and reflected back off the gold clip retaining it.

Barlow sat down next to her and said softly, "Of course I'm terribly upset about what happened to you, and on this occasion maybe it was to get at me. That doesn't mean it will ever happen again."

"You're damn right it won't!' she exclaimed, turning back to face him, venom in her tone. "If you loved me you wouldn't have spent so much time with that American blonde, over at your place."

This time it was Barlow's hackles that rose.

"I would remind you, Rachana, that it was you who invited Carla to stay, then, when I returned, walked out on me."

"Only to make you apologise to Steve Berkeman for being so rude," she said, defensively.

Barlow's mouth tightened before he opened it to speak.

"I didn't consider he deserved an apology and nothing has changed my mind since."

"Well, how about apologising to me, Matt, for all I went through?"

"I've already said my piece concerning that," retorted Barlow.

The argument swung back and forth rising from mildly heated to boiling point. The phone's staccato ringing tone broke the momentum.

Rachana reached for it and stated her number into the mouthpiece. She listened intently until a smile appeared on her attractive face.

"Hold the line a moment please," she said to the caller, and placed a hand over the mouthpiece. A strange superior look appeared on her countenance as she turned back to Barlow.

"It's Steve Berkeman. Wants me to have dinner with him tonight at his hotel."

"Up to you, isn't it?" replied Barlow, abruptly.

Rachana peered coyly at him under her long dark lashes.

"I won't if you don't want me to Matt."

Barlow's reply was instant in coming.

"I don't want you to see the guy at all... I've had him up to here." He drew a line across his throat.

"Very well, Matt. If you promise me you will have nothing further to do with tiger conservation and the gangs that are poaching them, not to mention going after man-eaters, I'll tell him no. And that's the end of it."

Barlow's eyes widened and met hers, in a steady gaze, before he opened his mouth to speak.

"That is something I'll never do, and you haven't the right to demand it of me."

Rachana screwed the handpiece savagely in her free hand and bit into her lip.

"Last chance, Matt. Yes or no?" she demanded.

"The answer is and always will be no, Rachana. You knew what I did before we became lovers. Nothing has changed."

She removed her hand from the mouthpiece and continued her conversation with the caller.

"Yes, Steve. That would be lovely. Pick me up here at eight."

Barlow rose to his feet, turned on his heel and left, slamming the door behind him. Even as Rachana replaced the receiver, the smile left her face and was replaced by tears. Sadly, Barlow was no longer there to see them.

By the time he arrived back at the plantation, Carla was just adding the finishing touches to her article. Barlow sank into an armchair and watched her typing.

"Won't be a minute, Matt, then I'll let you read it," she said, intent on her labours. Finally, she pulled the last sheet out of the machine, bunched everything together and, sitting on the arm of Barlow's chair, handed it to him.

Slowly and carefully he read the article then, saying nothing, he turned back to the beginning and worked his way through it all over again. Carla looked by this time quite dismayed and could stand the suspense no longer.

"Don't you like it, Matt? Isn't it any good? I can change it if you like?"

Smiling, he swept his arm round her waist and pulled her on to his lap, giving her an affectionate hug.

"Like it, Carla? I should say I do! It's great! Absolutely great! How can this Strobe guy say you don't have heart in your writing? You almost had me in tears reading it. If this doesn't do some good for the tiger nothing will."

"Then I can fax it through to New York?" Carla said excitedly.

"Just as soon as you like."

She jumped up and headed for Matt's office.

"One thing though," said Barlow, softly.

Carla stopped and turned, looking puzzled. "Did you have to make me out to be such a hero?" exclaimed Barlow.

She walked back over to him and sank onto her knees at his feet, placing her blonde head on his lap.

"You are a hero – I haven't exaggerated anything." Carla murmured, sincerity all over her face.

Barlow ruffled her golden hair playfully and Jana, thinking she was missing out on the affection, came trotting over to join in.

After some mutual adoration between Carla and the tigress, Barlow rose from the armchair.

"I'd better have a walk round the plantation before dusk. I've been neglecting it horribly lately, and you need to fax off that article to New York. Afterwards, I'll come back and take you into town for dinner. That's if you would like to?"

"Oh" said Carla, surprised. "I thought you would be going out with Rachana tonight! I—"

"No – that's all over. She's having dinner with your American colleague, Berkeman."

Carla looked stunned. "But you and her – I mean, Rachana. I thought..."

Barlow shrugged and made for the door.

"Is it yes for dinner, or no?" he called back, over his shoulder.

"Why, I guess it's yes."

"Great! See you later." He was gone, Jana at his side.

Walking to the window, she watched the broad shouldered plantation owner, accompanied by the ever-faithful tigress, striding off down the drive. Whatever had happened between Matt and Rachana to break them up? Could it be her fault? She had never seen herself as a home-wrecker. Surely Rachana couldn't prefer the brash Steve Berkeman? No, that wasn't it. Maybe there was something else? Perhaps Matt would tell her tonight at dinner.

*

Dinner, in fact, proved an embarrassing affair.

By some remote chance, both couples had inadvertently chosen the same restaurant in downtown Bangalore.

Although seated on opposite sides of the dining room, both were very aware of the others' presence. It was only after they had been seated that Barlow saw the others, but pride made him pretend not to notice. Berkeman, however, called over a noisy greeting. Carla looked awkward and Barlow simply nodded in return.

During the meal, Carla noted Rachana's pointed and blatant flirting with Berkeman and guessed that she was trying to make Matt jealous. He, however, appeared not to respond, and continued to talk about Carla's article.

"If this Edwin Strobe doesn't like it, he needs kicking."

"Perhaps you will tell him for me," laughed Carla. "I don't think I'd better, or I could be out of a job."

It was a relief to Carla when, the meal finished, Barlow suggested they leave for the plantation because, by this time, she was beginning to feel very guilty, blaming herself for the break-up of Barlow's romance. She tried telling herself that it wasn't as if she was in love with Matt herself, and, after all, she had a career ahead of her as a top journalist. Nothing must get in the way of that, and, even if Matt hadn't said he liked the article, she sensed that it was good.

She looked over at Matt driving the car. Why did he have to be so damned attractive! God! She was going to miss him when she returned to America. In spite of all the unexpected excitement and drama since arriving in India, she had to admit that she loved the place. So different from New York.

She'd be all right, she told herself, when she got back to America. In no time at all she would forget Barlow, Jana and India.

Carla felt a tear tickling the skin on the left-hand side of her face. Fiercely, she brushed it off. There would be equally challenging assignments to stretch her journalistic talents against!

Why, then, tonight, did she want to feel Matt's arms around her?

Suddenly an awful thought struck her. Perhaps he was just using her as a substitute in Rachana's absence. Perhaps the other night hadn't meant anything to him other than sexual pleasure. After all, what was it they said about tigers? They could never be monogamous and the natives said Barlow was half tiger! God! Last night on the temple dome she had almost found herself believing it to be true, with those realistic roars ushering from his throat.

By the time they arrived back at the plantation, she found herself to be emotionally falling apart, and, blaming it on a headache, excused herself to her room. Maybe it was all the stress of the last few days catching up with her. She slept fitfully and badly, and only fell into a deep slumber just before dawn.

Consequently, it was 10 a.m. the next morning when she awoke. After a shower, she slipped on a robe and went through for breakfast. Of Matt or Jana there was no sign. A note on the table said, *See you at lunchtime*. Obviously, he was attending to business on the plantation. The shrill ringing of the telephone interrupted her thoughts.

She picked it up. To her surprise it was Steve Berkeman.

"Great!" he exclaimed. "It was you I wanted."

"What for?" she found herself saying, somewhat abruptly.

"Don't sound so pleased to hear from me,' he retorted sarcastically. "Look, I'm going back to New York tomorrow. Strobe wants you to return with me."

Carla felt her skin go cold all over.

"But he gave me a month and that's not up yet."

"Well, apparently he's delighted with your progress and wants you to fly off and cover the Bosnian crisis in Europe." There was a stunned silence at Carla's end.

"Well?" he prompted.

"I couldn't possibly go yet," stammered Carla.

"Strobe said at once."

Carla played for time.

"How about you and Rachana? I thought..."

A mirthless laugh came back down the receiver.

"You've got to be joking. That dame's so hooked on Barlow she just used me, and I – poor sap – fell for it hook, line and sinker. I just want to get out of India and back to Uncle Sam and you're coming with me."

"No!" snapped Carla. "I'll follow on later in a day or two perhaps. I'm not very well at the moment."

"Touch of the Barlowitis," sneered Berkeman. "Strobe won't like it one little bit. He's used to people doing as they're told in his outfit."

"Have a good trip, Steve," said Carla, replacing the receiver. Now why on earth had she done that? Her work here was finished. She could have gone. 'I don't like being told what to do,' she thought. 'That's the only reason I'm staying on in India.' She didn't believe it for one minute!

Half an hour later the telephone rang again. This time it was Inspector Ramon Srinath, calling from Delhi.

"Ah! Miss Wayne. I thought I recognised your voice. How nice to speak to you." The pleasantries over between them, Srinath came to the point. "Is Mr Barlow there?"

"No, I'm afraid you have missed him. Out on the plantation somewhere. I can give him a message when he comes in though."

"Well, it's a little embarrassing for me to ask his assistance again, after what he has just accomplished for us."

"Suppose you tell me, and let him be the judge of that Inspector, when I acquaint him with it."

"So be it then, miss. I have evidence of a gang of tiger poachers operating in the Sunderbans region and I wondered—"

"Whether he would come and help you out," Carla put in.

"Err, yes. Aptly put and to the point, too. Perhaps he would give me a call, at his earliest convenience."

"I'm sure he will, Inspector. Give me the number." She wrote it down, said goodbye and hung up.

'I wonder whether Edwin Strobe would let me go with Matt to look into this one,' mused Carla. She tossed several ideas round in her mind, all revolving round staying on in India.

Before Matt's return she received one more call. It was from Rachana, who was very abrupt with her and demanded that Matt telephone her the moment he returned. She promised to relay the message.

It was not until about 4 p.m. that Barlow returned, Jana bounding in through the door ahead of him, flopping down on her usual rug by the settee. After greeting one another, Carla gave him the message. True to the nature of the man, his first concern was for Carla.

"So what will happen? Will this Strobe guy fire you, if you don't return with Berkeman tomorrow?"

Carla looked at her watch.

"It's only 7 a.m. in New York. Too early to ring *Liberty*. He never comes in until 10 in the mornings."

"So if you ring from here just after 8 this evening, you should catch him," put in Barlow, eagerly.

"And be told what? To return at once," exclaimed Carla dismally. Then her mood swung to one of enthusiasm. "Will you go and help Srinath in the Sunderbans, Matt?"

Barlow smiled.

"Yes, if I can do anything to save the tiger, I will."

"Could I go with you, if Strobe allows me to stay on?"

"It will be dangerous. These people play for high stakes."

"I seem to remember you telling me that once before."

Both laughed.

"Oh, by the way," exclaimed Carla, "you never did tell me where you got that Kali costume from, that you made me wear."

"Oh, that. It was left over last October, from one of the Durga Puja festivals. I thought I'd use it on one of my walls – but it sure looked better on you."

"God! I was scared stiff, Matt!"

"But you still did it, Carla," he said, taking her into his arms.

"No, Matt," said Carla firmly. "You belong with Rachana."

Rubbing her eyes, she dashed off to her room. Throwing herself face down on the bed, she sobbed bitterly.

Barlow shook his head uncomprehending, and studied the closed door. He tickled Jana affectionately behind the ear. The huge tigress nuzzled him in response.

"Animals are a lot easier to understand than women," he said aloud.

Chapter Twenty-nine
Decision of the Heart

Some time later Carla re-emerged, having regained her composure and reapplied her make-up. Barlow was engrossed in preparing dinner.

"Here, let me help," said Carla, busily entering into the preparations. Slicing up some potatoes, she enquired, "Did you ring Rachana?"

"Yup!" replied Matt casually.

"And?"

"And nothing. She's still laying down conditions which, I would add, I will never agree to."

"Are you sure, Matt? You love her – you know you do!"

"I used to think so, now I'm not sure any more. Can we drop the subject?"

"Okay. How about Inspector Srinath? Did you call him?"

"Yes. I've arranged to fly up at the end of the week and meet him in the Sunderbans. He makes this lot of poachers out to be a particularly nasty bunch."

The two of them continued preparing the meal in companionable silence.

*

Dinner finished, they were enjoying liqueurs with their coffee when Barlow reminded Carla of the time.

"Ten a.m. in New York."

Carla pulled a face and rose from the table without much enthusiasm for the task in hand.

"I guess I know what he's going to say," she said, dispiritedly. She walked across to the phone and dialled. It took ages to get through before finally she was put through to Edwin Strobe. Barlow, of course, could only hear one end of the conversation.

"Oh, I'm so glad you liked my piece, Mr Strobe. Well, it's nice of you to say so, sir." Carla went into a long explanation of why she should be allowed to stay on in India. It was obvious from her expression that Edwin Strobe was not of the same mind. "Well, you see, I'm not sure I could be ready to travel tomorrow. Couldn't you send someone else to Bosnia? I do appreciate the difficulties, sir, but there is still some valuable work left for me to do here before returning to New York. Can't you give me a few days' extension? After all, you did say a month originally."

Barlow watched Carla's expression turn to one of dismay. Now he could hear Strobe's voice, obviously raised in annoyance.

"Stop pussy-footing around and get back here at once young lady, if you still want a job!" The line went dead as the New York end was cut.

Barlow looked at her sympathetically.

"No need to relay anything. I caught the gist. Obviously he won't budge?"

"In short, I either return tomorrow with Steve Berkeman to New York or I needn't bother to return ever."

"My God!" snapped Barlow, rising in anger. "There's gratitude for you! Everything the man wanted you have given him, and quicker than he asked for too. Will it help if I talk to him?"

"No, Matt. That's the magazine world for you. News today, another assignment tomorrow. I guess there's nothing for it but to return if I want to keep my job, and I am supposed to be a journalist. Can I prevail on you to have Zabu or the foreman drive me to Bangalore Airport tomorrow morning?"

"I'll drive you myself if you really must go, Carla."

"No, Matt. I'm going to miss you terribly as it is, and I hate goodbyes. I'd rather say goodbye to you here, just the way I'll always want to remember you, on your plantation."

Barlow, a lump in his throat, could only nod and add, "So be it then. I'll have Surendra drive you to the airport. He's a better driver than Zabu."

"You will write to me and let me know what happens in the Sunderbans? Oh! How I wish I was coming with you."

A long uncomfortable silence followed before Carla broke it by saying, "Well, I guess I'd better go and pack for the morning. If your foreman is going to drive me to the airport, will there be a chance to say goodbye to Zabu? I'd like to thank him for everything."

"Sure," said Barlow. "I'll have Surendra stop at his hut on the way to the airport for you."

"Thanks. I wouldn't want to leave without seeing him."

As she turned for her bedroom Matt said softly, "Thank you for everything."

"I didn't do much really," she replied, half turning.

"The words in your article were great. They will do more for the plight of the tiger than I could ever hope to do here. The article came straight from your heart."

"You gave me the heart, Matt."

Barlow reached for her, two teardrops were already on her cheek.

"No, Matt. Don't. Don't make it any harder than it is for me. I'll see you in the morning," she said, slowly departing for her bedroom with dignified grace.

*

Carla tossed and turned for a long time, her mind in turmoil. Had Matt actually said that he loved her, she would have told Edwin Strobe what to do with his job and stayed on in India and blown her whole journalistic career for him. The fact that he hadn't caused her to believe that he must still love Rachana, and why shouldn't he? What right had she to think anything had changed? Sure, the pair had experienced some differences of opinion, but nothing that couldn't be resolved if she, Carla, vacated the scene and left them a straight run. Maybe if things had been different – but the situation was just the same as it had always been.

Finally, just before dawn, Carla came to a decision. She would leave Matt a clear road. After all he had done for her, she owed him that much.

Rapidly, she dressed and wrote a hurried note. Getting all her things together, she tiptoed through to the lounge and telephoned for a taxi. Whispering into the mouthpiece, so as not to wake Matt in his room, she gave the address, replaced the receiver and sat down to wait.

She had told them to stop short of the house by two hundred metres so as not to wake the other occupants. She would watch for the taxi from the window.

Twenty minutes later she saw the lights approaching at a distance. She gave the sleeping Jana a kiss on the top of her head. The tigress did not move as Carla stepped over her and let herself silently out on to the veranda.

There were tears in Carla's eyes and a lump in her throat as she pulled the door shut behind her and stole off towards the waiting taxi. The early morning sky was a mixture of orange and red as another Indian dawn made its appearance – the sun had yet to rise above the horizon.

She looked back towards the house. There, with her large head pushed under the curtains, was Jana, watching her departure from the window. Involuntarily, she blew the tigress a kiss.

A few moments later the taxi, with her aboard, rumbled off. Carla couldn't bear to look back. Her eyes were so misted up that it was doubtful she would have seen anything anyway...

Some two hours later, Barlow emerged from his bedroom, sleepily rubbing his eyes. He had already put the kettle on before he noticed the note propped up against a vase on the table. Simply scrawled on the envelope was the word *Matt*. Hurriedly, he tore it open and read the letter inside.

A cold hand seemed to grip his stomach as he scanned the one page note.

> *Dear Matt,*
>
> *Forgive me for running away like this, without even saying goodbye. Somehow I couldn't find it in my heart to say farewell. You don't need me complicating your life, so I have decided to leave. I wish you and Rachana every happiness for the future and hope you will both work it out. Thank you for everything you have done for me. I will never forget you. Please leave a little place in your heart for me. I wish I was*

going to the Sunderbans, but I guess it just wasn't to
be.
  Please say you forgive me, Matt.
  My love always,
  Carla
  x

Barlow stared sightlessly into space. He didn't even notice Jana rubbing her head against his thigh. Out of habit his hand came down and rubbed her behind the ear in response to her greeting.

The crumpled paper dropped to the floor. The tigress retrieved it in her mouth and pushed it at Barlow's hand.

Suddenly, he came to a decision. Wearing only his dressing robe, he hurried through to dress. No time to wash or shave. He threw his clothes on and grabbed the keys to the jeep.

"Stay and guard, Jana," he instructed the disappointed tigress. She had expected to accompany him and had hurried to the door ahead. Five minutes later, he was knocking up Zabu, hammering on the hut door. The little man, bright as a button, emerged with his toothy grin.

"Greetings sahib," his face creased from ear to ear.

"Have you seen the Memsahib Wayne this morning, Zabu?"

"That I have, Barlow Sahib. Before the sun rises, she comes to say goodbye to old Zabu. She say cannot go without wishing goodbye to world's greatest tracker."

Normally Barlow would have smiled or even laughed at the little man's good humoured conceit, but not today."

"Where did she say she was going, Zabu? Hurry man!"

"She in taxi, not stay long. Make visit to airport, she say, sahib."

Barlow turned and ran for the jeep. He had left the engine running. Zabu watched the vehicle disappear in a cloud of red dust.

"Me theenk tiger now chase tigress. 'Bout bleedy time too." The ever-present grin on his gnarled countenance, the little man watched the departing jeep approvingly.

It was a good hour's drive from Barlow's plantation to Bangalore airport but Barlow made it in fifty minutes, and must have lost half an inch of rubber off the jeep's tyres.

He parked the vehicle and rushed into the departure lounge. Apart from the clerks behind the desks, the place was almost deserted.

Through the large plate glass windows he could see a twin-engine plane on the runway, just about to take off. All this he noticed in a matter of seconds. He rushed to the nearest desk and fired a question at the pretty Indian stewardess. "That plane – where is it going?"

"Bombay, sir," came the reply.

"Can you tell me whether an American girl is on it?"

"There were two Americans on the passenger list, sir. I remember because the plane was only a third booked."

"Their names, miss, quickly!"

"I'm very sorry, sir, but I'm unable to give out that information."

Barlow waited impatiently, watching with one eye the plane warming up its engines prior to take off.

"Stop the plane, for God's sake. Stop the plane!" yelled Barlow.

"I'm sorry, sir, but I cannot. I haven't the authority to give such an order."

"Who has?"

"The air traffic controller."

"Get him on the phone."

The girl looked dazed and bewildered. Barlow realised it was too late anyway. The plane was accelerating down the runway. He watched in horror as it soared into the air and swung away towards the west. The girl looked sympathetically at Barlow's crestfallen expression.

"Is there anything I can do to help?" Barlow recovered quickly.

"The lady – has she a connecting flight at Bombay for New York?" he asked.

The girl hesitated, then consulted the screen once more.

"Yes sir. I can tell you that much. She's booked on to the Bombay Air India flight to New York via London."

"What time does that leave?"

Another agonising long check on the screen resulted in the reply, "She will have three hours on the ground at Bombay to wait for her flight."

Barlow's expression turned to one of enthusiasm.

"What time is the next flight to Bombay from here and will it get there in time?"

"I'm sorry sir, the next flight from here to Bombay today won't be until 6 p.m."

"But that's no good. I've got to reach Bombay in time to stop her boarding that plane."

"I'm sorry sir, but we haven't a plane going before 6 p.m. I have already told you that."

By now the two women on the adjoining desk, being unoccupied, were taking an interest in proceedings. One, a petite young girl with lively, sparkling brown eyes, put forward a suggestion.

"Perhaps I could help the gentleman?" she ventured, smiling engagingly at Barlow.

"If you could, miss I've just got to get to Bombay, post-haste," exclaimed Barlow, switching his attention to her.

"Well," she continued, "there is a small charter company operating a Lear jet from here, but it would be very expensive to hire, even if it were available, sir."

"Bother the expense! Do you think you could put me in contact with them?" The girl, whose tunic badge named her as Rania Divecha, reached for the phone on her desk.

"I'll try sir, but I can't promise anyone will be there this early in the morning." She dialled. Barlow could hear it ringing. No one answered. After a while Rania replaced the hand-piece. "I'm sorry, sir. Perhaps I could try later for you."

"If you could, miss. You see, I'm fast running out of time. Unless I get to Bombay before the New York flight leaves, I'm done for." Barlow ran his fingers over the unshaven stubble on his chin. The girls, entering into a debate, looked sympathetically at him. There were no other passengers around and he had their undivided attention. Indian girls loved romance – most of them anyway. Barlow played his last card in sheer desperation.

"It's a matter of the heart. If I can't get to Bombay before that planes leaves, the woman I love will be gone from India for ever. My life will be destroyed for all time." Barlow hated himself for the moment of weakness, but saw immediately that it had worked. All three girls were now involved and avidly making suggestions. Barlow listened intently to their interchange of ideas.

It appeared one of them knew the pilot of the Lear jet. She had, it seemed, gone out with him a couple of times. She produced her handbag from under the desk.

"I'm sure I've got his home number somewhere." She rummaged through the large Danni bag whilst Barlow shuffled his feet, and fiddled with his hands, impatient but hopeful.

"Ah! Here it is! I knew it was somewhere," she said, triumphantly producing a small white business card. "Shall I telephone him for you?"

"Would you please?" urged Barlow.

She dialled a number, which was answered quite promptly. A conversation followed in Hindi, a language with which Barlow was quite familiar. From the response at the girl's end of the line, he quickly learnt that, yes, the pilot would take him in two hours' time.

Before she could relay this to him, Barlow interjected, "That's no good! Tell him if he gets over here at once, I'll double his fee."

She passed on the offer and after a few seconds replaced the receiver.

"He will be here in half an hour. It will take him all of that to reach the airport."

Barlow thanked the three women profusely and he was given instructions as to where to go in the airport to meet the pilot. After handing over a handsome tip, which, to their credit, none of the women expected, he was on his way. Exactly half an hour later the pilot, a stocky young Indian by the name of Anjit, arrived and introduced himself.

Barlow explained the problem.

"Will we make Bombay in time, Anjit?" he enquired.

"We won't if we stand here talking. Come with me," said the pilot, turning abruptly on his heel, and striding off across the concourse. Barlow strode purposefully after him.

*

Steve Berkeman was in a happier mood than he had been in for a very long time. He was about to depart for his idea of civilisation – New York. Waiting in the airport lounge at Bombay, he continued to crack jokes to a very subdued Carla. On the way from Bangalore, during the first flight here, she had said very little, not laughing or even smiling at any of his jokes. Little had changed since.

The second flight call came over the public address system.

"Will all those passengers travelling on flight Al 110 to London and New York please go to gate ten." Berkeman picked up his tote bag. Carla remained seated.

"Come on, what are you waiting for?" he quipped. "The monsoon season to come round again?"

"You go on. I'll follow," she said, without any enthusiasm.

Berkeman sat down beside her again.

"No way! I'm waiting until you go. I've promised Mr Strobe you'll be on that plane."

"You don't have to bother with me. I'm a big girl now, or hadn't you noticed, Steve?"

"Sure, sure you are." Berkeman, to Carla's relief, fell into a sullen silence. Ten minutes later came the third and last call.

"This is the final call for flight Al 110 to New York via London. Please proceed to gate ten immediately."

Carla looked round in desperation for some miracle to save her.

Berkeman noticed, and cruelly jibed at her.

"He's not coming, you know. Probably making it up with Rachana by now."

Carla glared coldly at him. Saying nothing, she rose and picked up her small holdall, and with the other hand produced her passport and tickets, together with boarding pass. They made their way towards emigration passport control.

The custom's clerk took longer than usual examining both passports.

"Cutting it fine, aren't you?" he enquired. "You're on third flight call you know. You should have come through here before this."

"I keep telling her that, officer," put in Berkeman, a smile on his face.

"Well, hurry along now, both of you. It's gate ten you need," prompted the customs man.

Carla turned to take one last backward glance before proceeding through the departure gate.

"Carla!"

She heard her name shouted above the general hubbub and mêlée from the middle of the concourse. It came again, only nearer this time. Even Steve Berkeman turned to look back.

To Carla's immense joy, she saw the tall frame of Matt Barlow pushing his way through the crowded concourse, leaping and stepping over piles of luggage impeding his progress.

Berkeman grabbed her arm roughly.

"Come on. We have a plane to catch," he urged, eyeing Barlow's frantic progress towards them. Carla tore herself loose from Berkeman's grasp and rushed back headlong into the crowded concourse.

The amazed customs man shouted above the din.

"You can't go back, memsahib. You will miss your flight."

"Come back, Carla," screamed a furious Berkeman. By this time Barlow and Carla had come face to face. For a moment in time they stood stock still, their eyes locked, aware only of each other.

A moment later saw them entwined in each other's arms, their lips hungrily devouring one another. Everyone around them stood watching the spectacle, an ethnic mêlée of several nationalities.

Suddenly a few American tourists clapped, some other Europeans cheered and even the Asians good-naturedly joined in.

As the couple came up for air, Berkeman yelled from the custom's gate.

"What do I tell Edwin Strobe?"

"Tell him I just resigned," replied Carla, at the top of her voice.

Barlow put an arm round Carla's shoulders and ushered her between the packing cases and through the teeming mass of cheering passengers.

Berkeman shrugged his shoulders and proceeded on through the gate.

As he passed the customs man, he uttered two words, "Goddamned women!" and was lost to sight from those in the concourse, hurrying on to catch his New York bound flight.

*

That night, back at Barlow's plantation house, with Jana on guard outside her master's bedroom door, neither Carla nor Matt got any sleep at all. When they weren't making wild, abandoned, passionate love to each other, they were talking and making plans for the future.

In three days' time they would depart for the Sunderbans in an effort to break up yet another tiger poaching gang. Ramon Srinath would meet them there. Carla watched the Indian night sky lighten slightly through the net curtains at the window.

"False dawn, Matt?" she enquired happily.

"False dawn indeed, but let us keep our fingers crossed that it's a new and true dawn for the tiger."